CLAMP

TRANSLATED AND ADAPTED BY
Anthony Gerard

LETTERED BY
Dana Hayward

BALLANTINE BOOKS · NEW YORK

Tsubasa Volume 1 crosses over with *xxxHOLiC* Volume 1. Although it isn't necessary to read *xxxHOLiC* to understand the events in *Tsubasa*, you'll get to see the same events from different perspectives if you read both!

A Del Rey® Book
Published by The Random House Publishing Group
Copyright © 2004 CLAMP. All rights reserved.
This publication — rights arranged through Kodansha Ltd.

All rights reserved under International and Pan-American
Copyright Conventions. Published in the United States by The Random
House Publishing Group, a division of Random House, Inc., New York, and
simultaneously in Canada by Random House of Canada Limited, Toronto.
First published in Japan in serialization and subsequently published in
book form by Kodansha Ltd., Tokyo, in 2003.

Del Rey is a registered trademark and the Del Rey colophon
is a trademark of Random House, Inc.

www.delreymanga.com

Library of Congress Control Number: 2004101711

ISBN 0-345-47057-5

Manufactured in the United States of America

First Edition: May 2004

10 9 8 7 6

Contents

Honorifics

Throughout the Del Rey Manga books, you will find Japanese honorifics left intact in the translations. For those not familiar with how the Japanese use honorifics, and more importantly, how they differ from American honorifics, we present this brief overview.

Politeness has always been a critical facet of Japanese culture. Ever since the feudal era, when Japan was a highly stratified society, use of honorifics—which can be defined as polite speech that indicates relationship or status—has played an essential role in the Japanese language. When addressing someone in Japanese, an honorific usually takes the form of a suffix attached to one's name (example: "Asuna-san"), or as a title at the end of one's name or in place of the name itself (example: "Negi-sensei," or simply "Sensei!").

Honorifics can be expressions of respect or endearment. In the context of manga and anime, honorifics give insight into the nature of the relationship between characters. Many translations into English leave out these important honorifics, and therefore distort the "feel" of the original Japanese. Because Japanese honorifics contain nuances that English honorifics lack, it is our policy at Del Rey not to translate them. Here, instead, is a guide to some of the honorifics you may encounter in Del Rey Manga.

-san: This is the most common honorific, and is equivalent to Mr., Miss, Ms., Mrs., etc. It is the all-purpose honorific and can be used in any situation where politeness is required.

-sama: This is one level higher than "-san." It is used to confer great respect.

-dono: This comes from the word "tono," which means "lord." It is even a higher level than "-sama," and confers utmost respect.

-kun: This suffix is used at the end of boys' names to express familiarity or endearment. It is also sometimes used by men among friends, or when addressing someone younger or of a lower station.

-chan: This is used to express endearment, mostly toward girl. It is also used for little boys, pets, and even among lovers. It gives a sense of childish cuteness.

Sempai: This title suggests that the addressee is one's "senior" in a group or organization. It is most often used in a school setting, where underclassmen refer to their upperclassmen as "sempai." It can also be used in the workplace, such as when a newer employee addresses an employee who has seniority in the company.

Kohai: This is the opposite of "-sempai," and is used toward underclassmen in school or newcomers in the workplace. It connotes that the addressee is of lower station.

Sensei: Literally meaning "one who has come before," this title is used for teachers, doctors, or masters of any profession or art.

[blank]: Usually forgotten in these lists, but perhaps the most significant difference between Japanese and English. The lack of honorific means that the speaker has permission to address the person in a very intimate way. Usually, only family, spouses, or very close friends have this kind of permission. Known as *yobisute*, it can be gratifying when someone who has earned the intimacy starts to call one by one's name without an honorific. But when that intimacy hasn't been earned, it can also be very insulting.

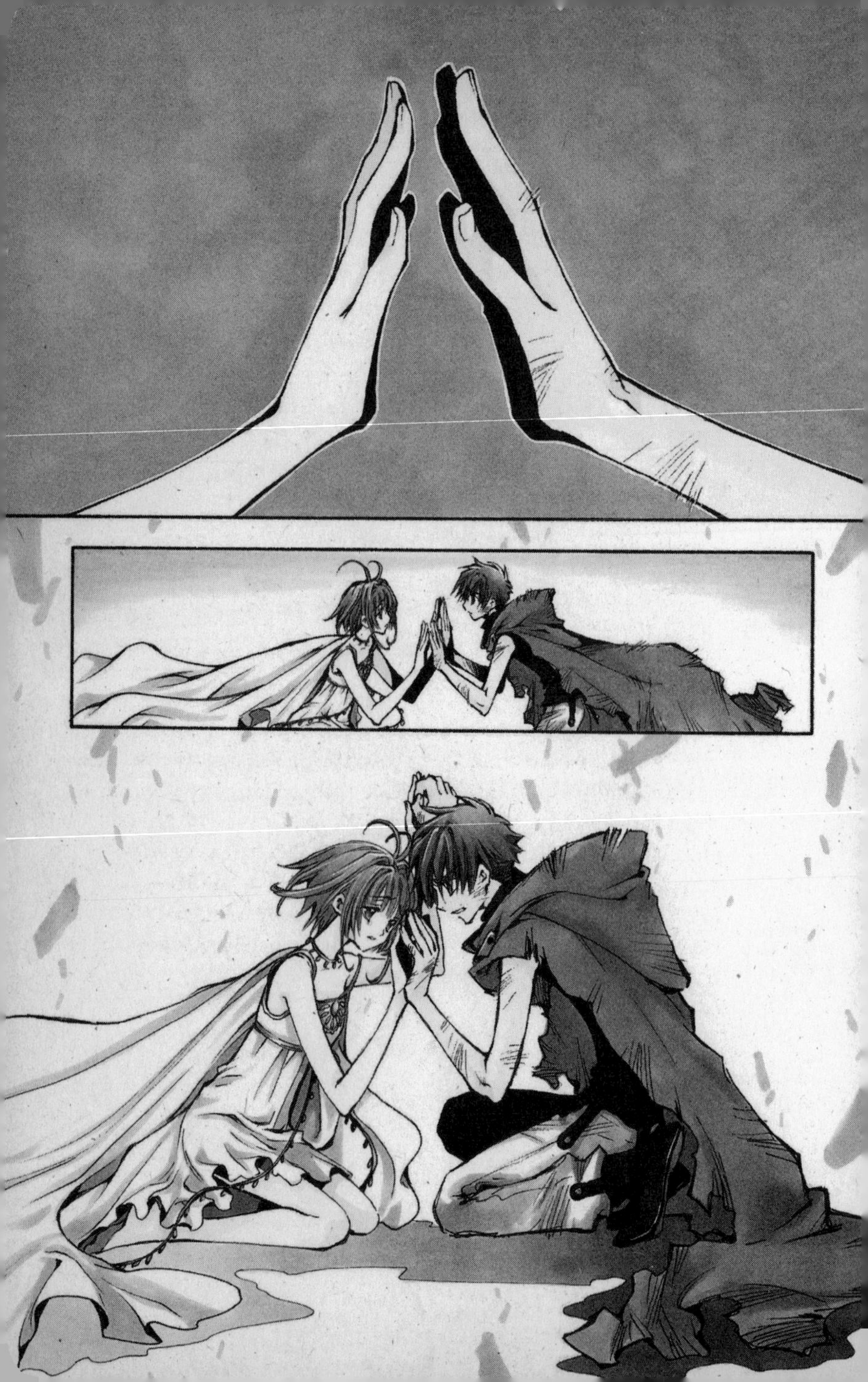

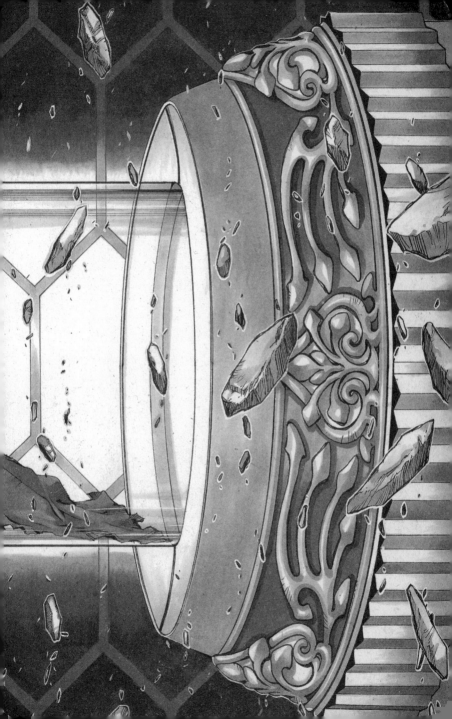

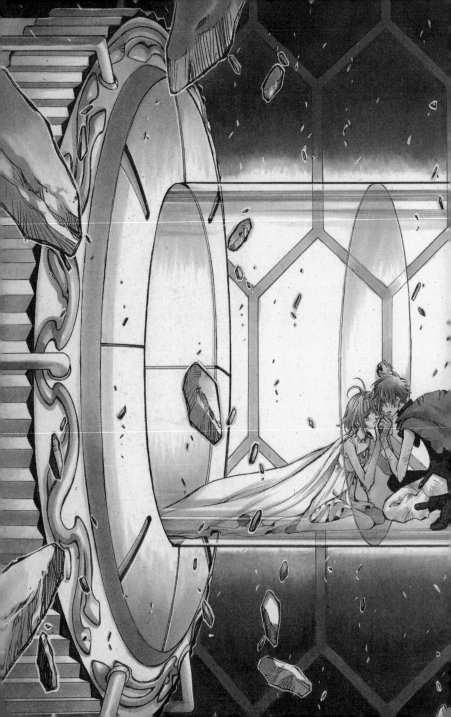

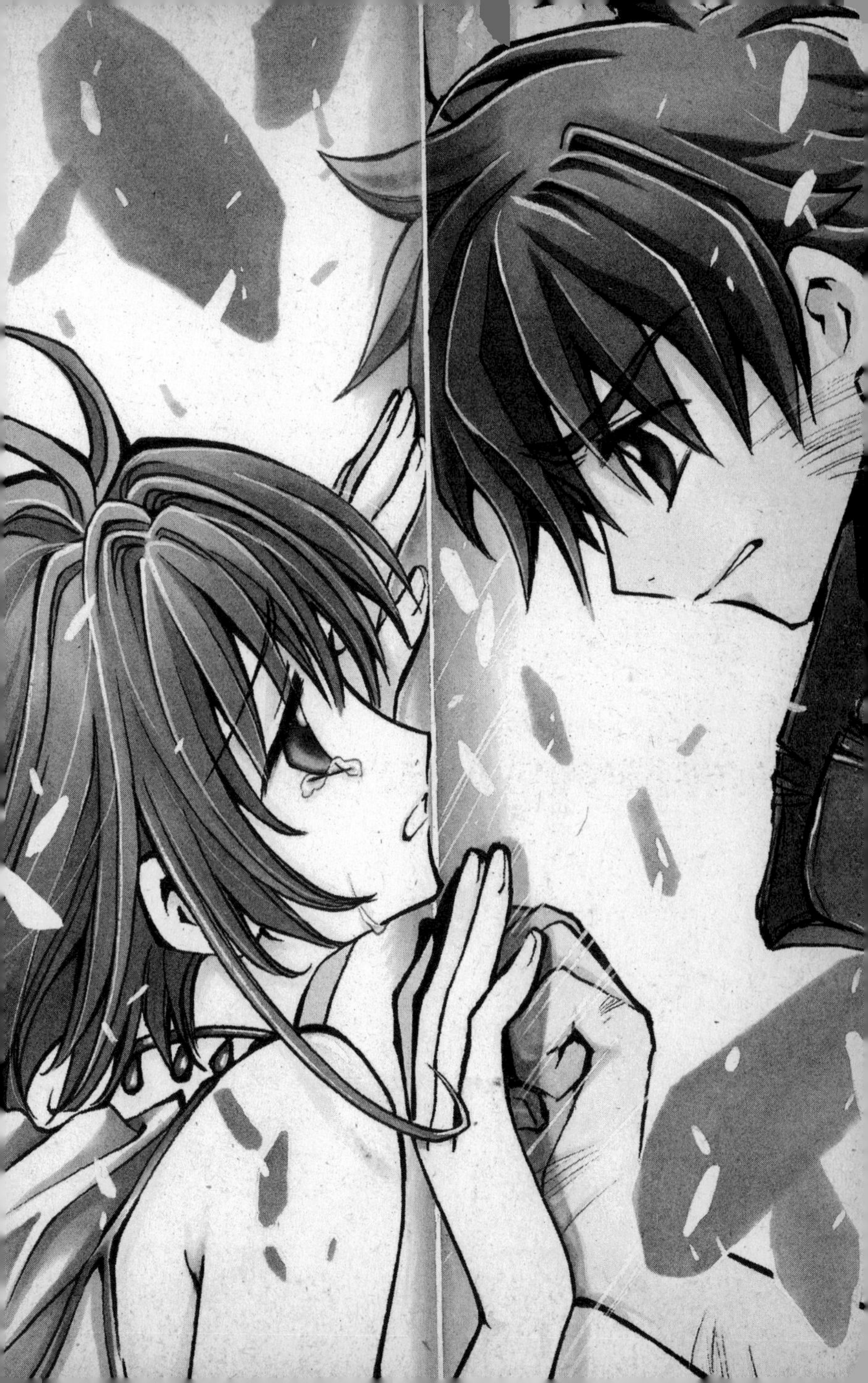

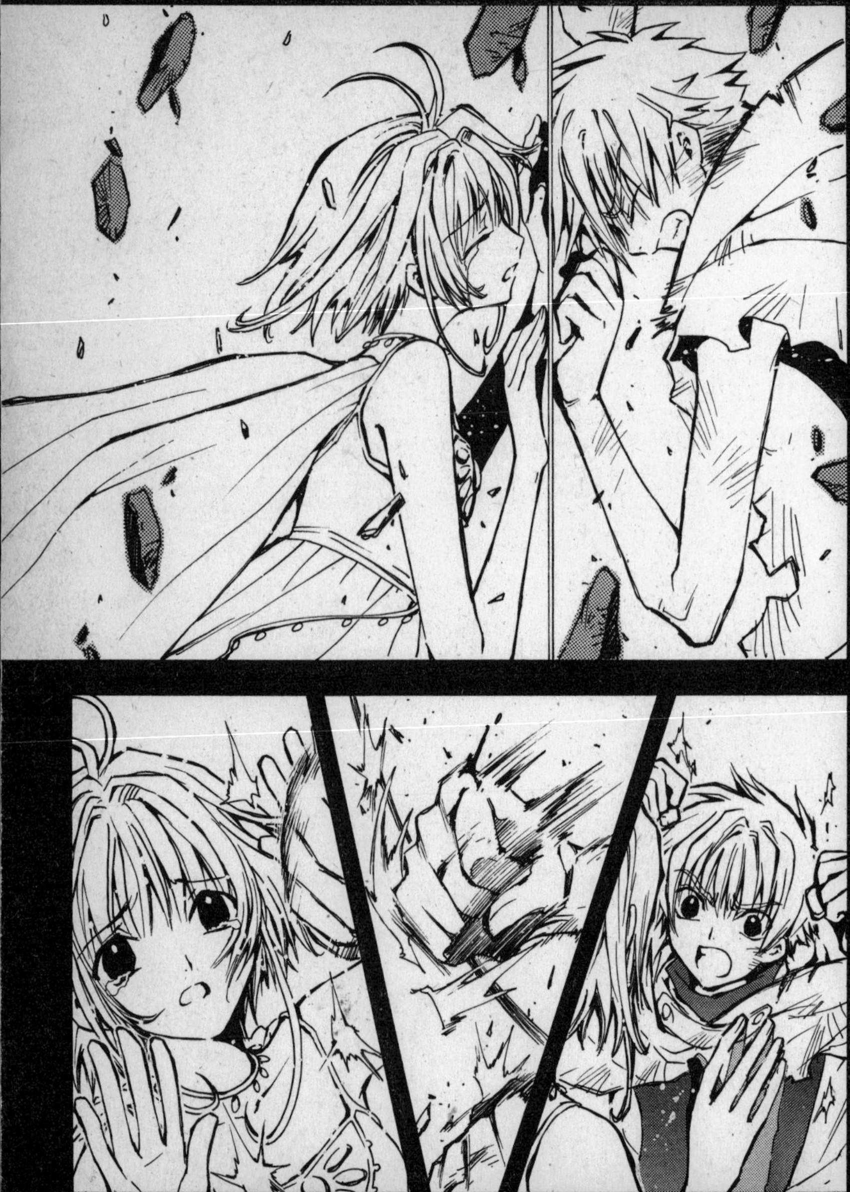

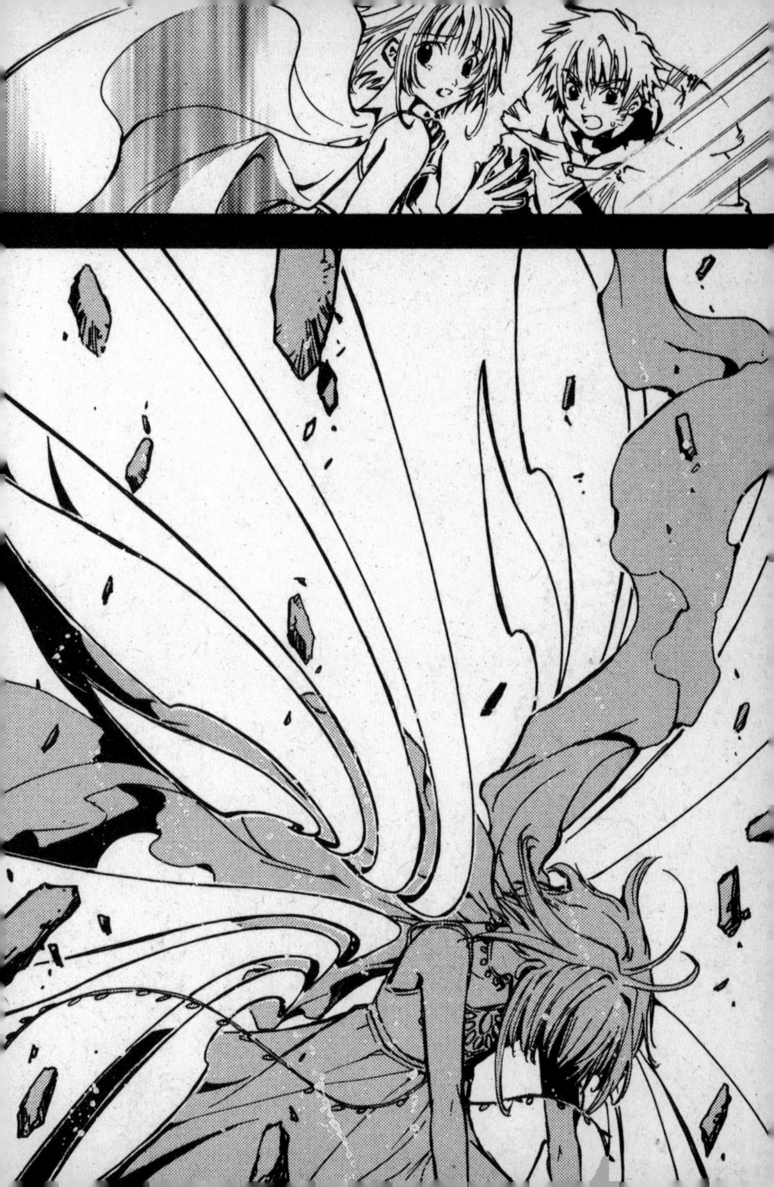

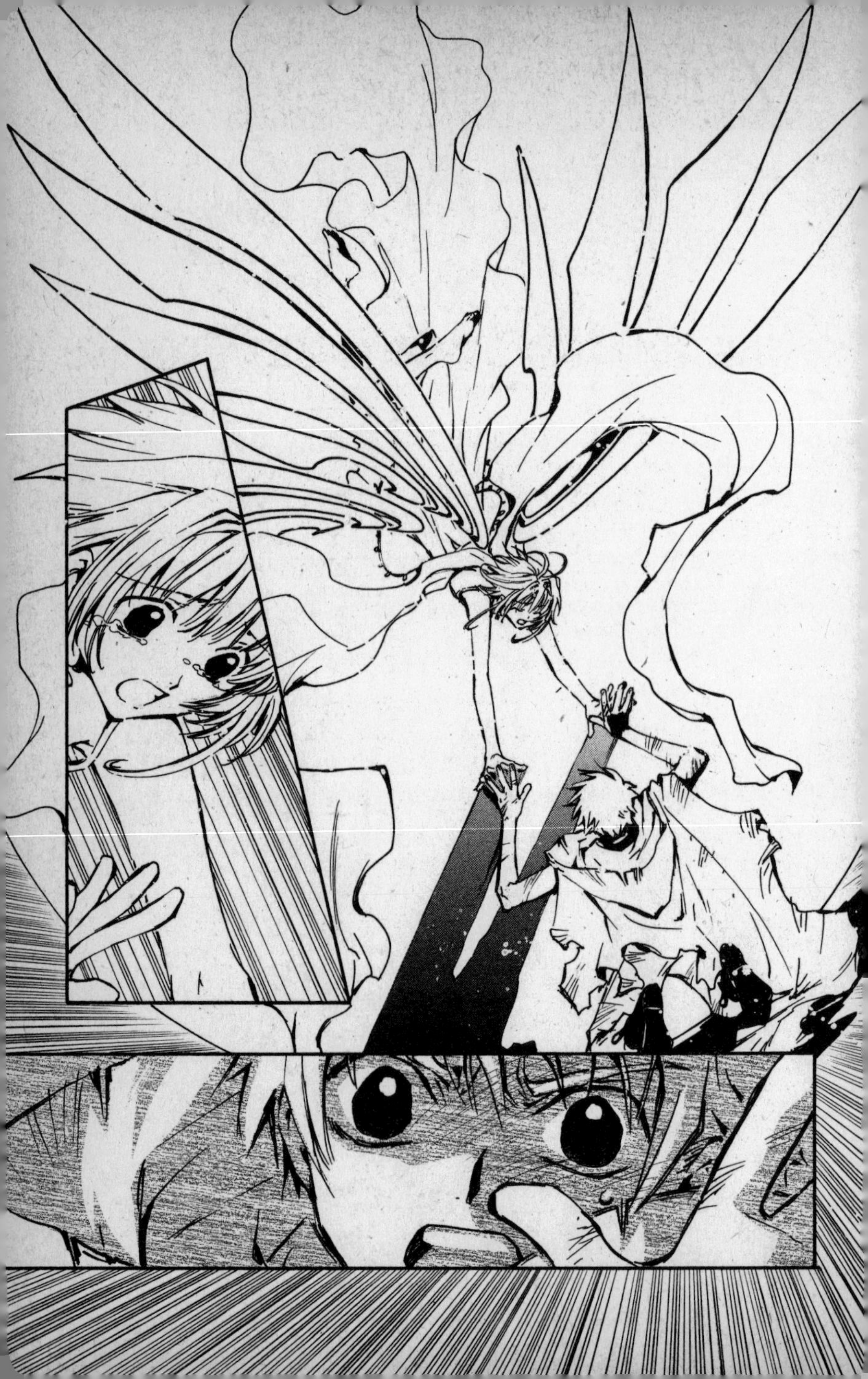

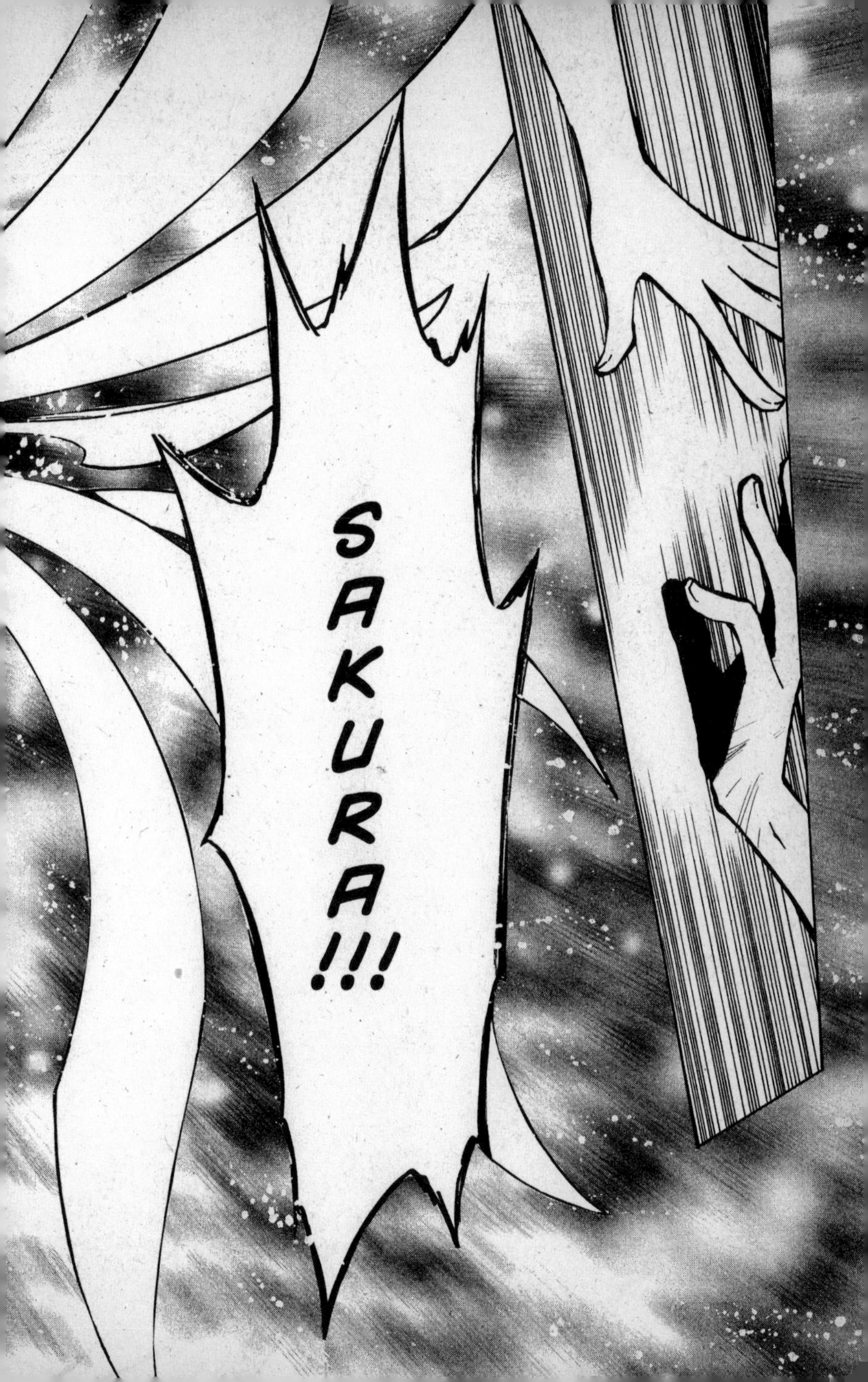
SAKURA!!!

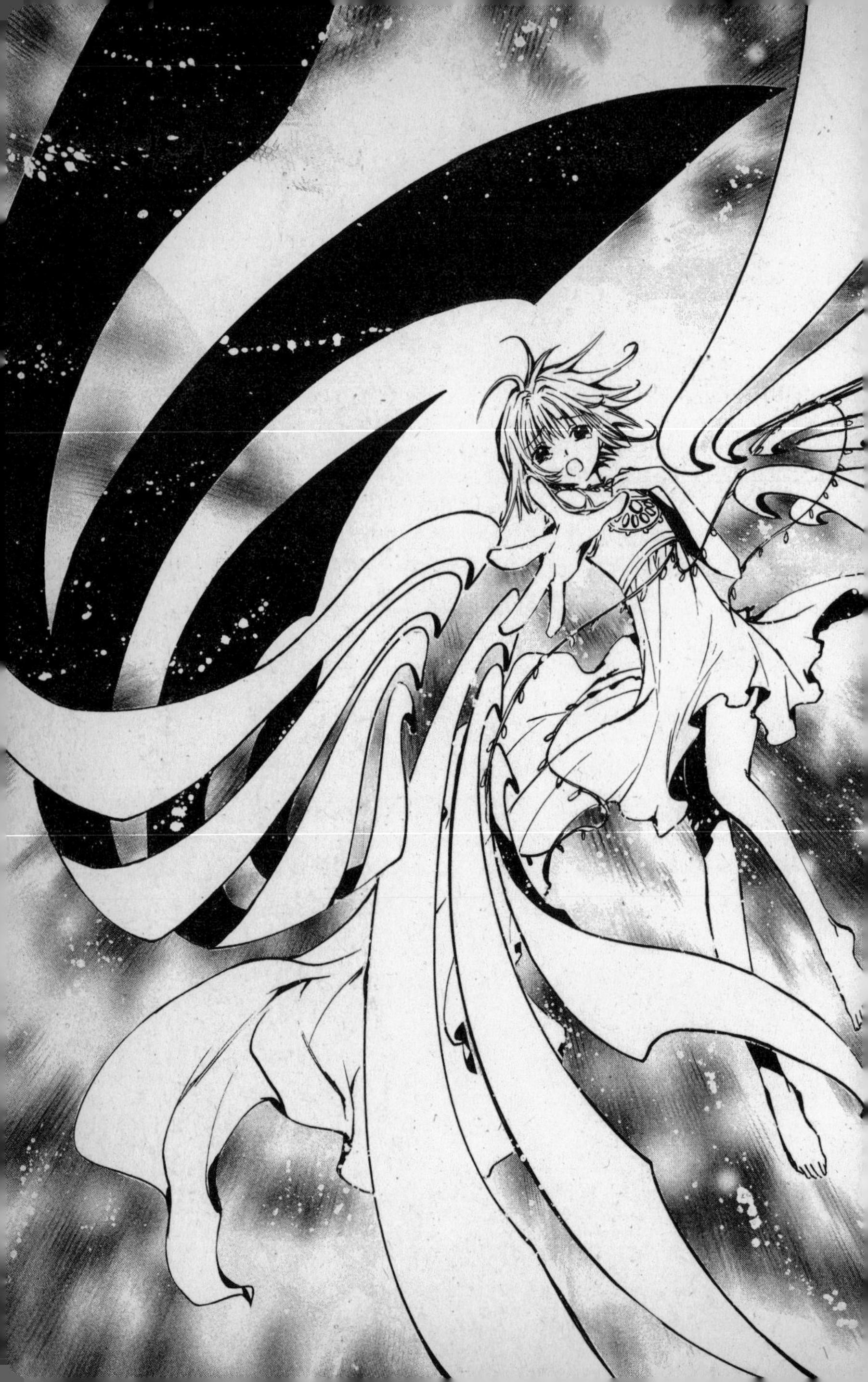

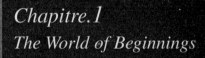

Chapitre.1
The World of Beginnings

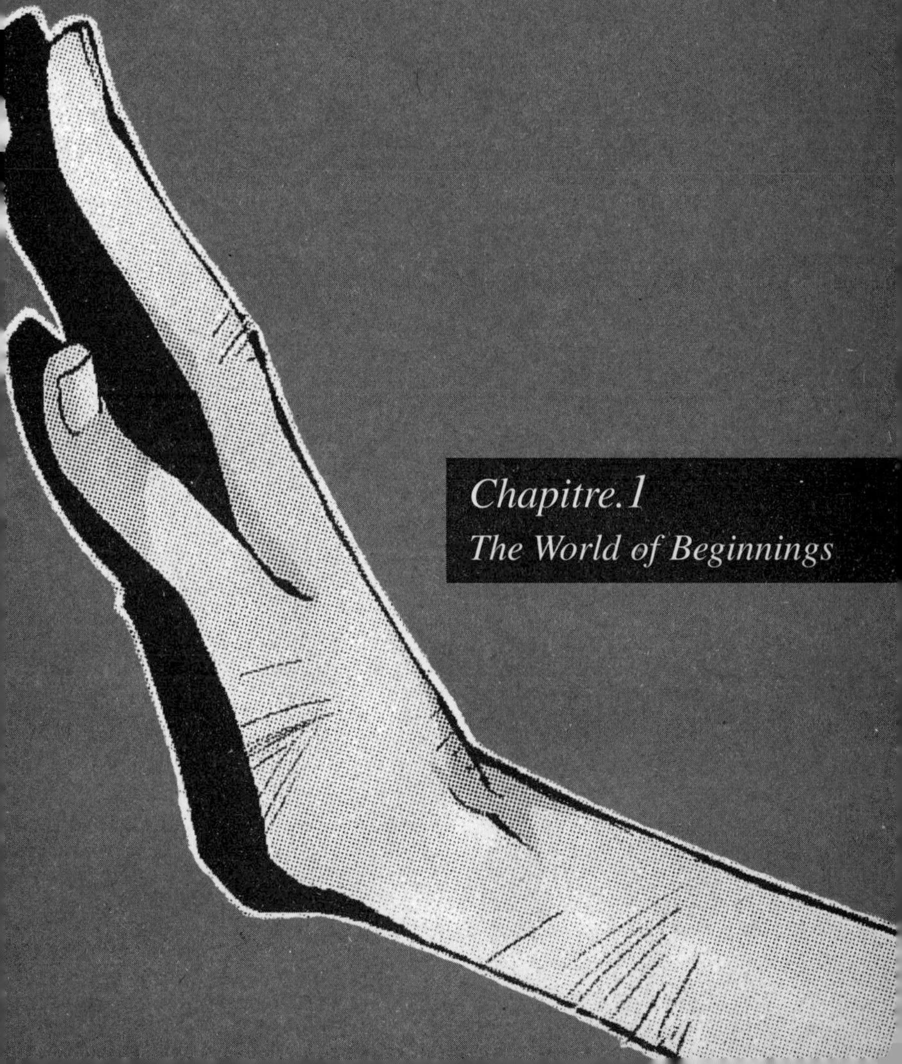

RESERVoir CHRoNiCLE
TSUBASA

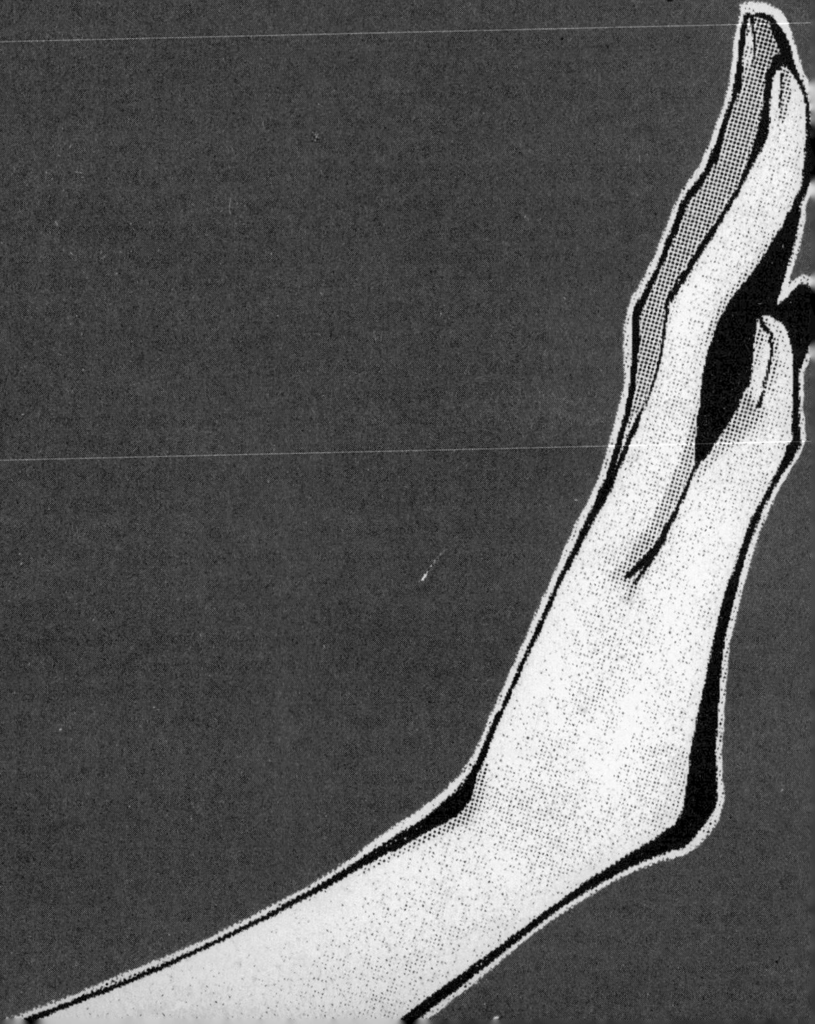

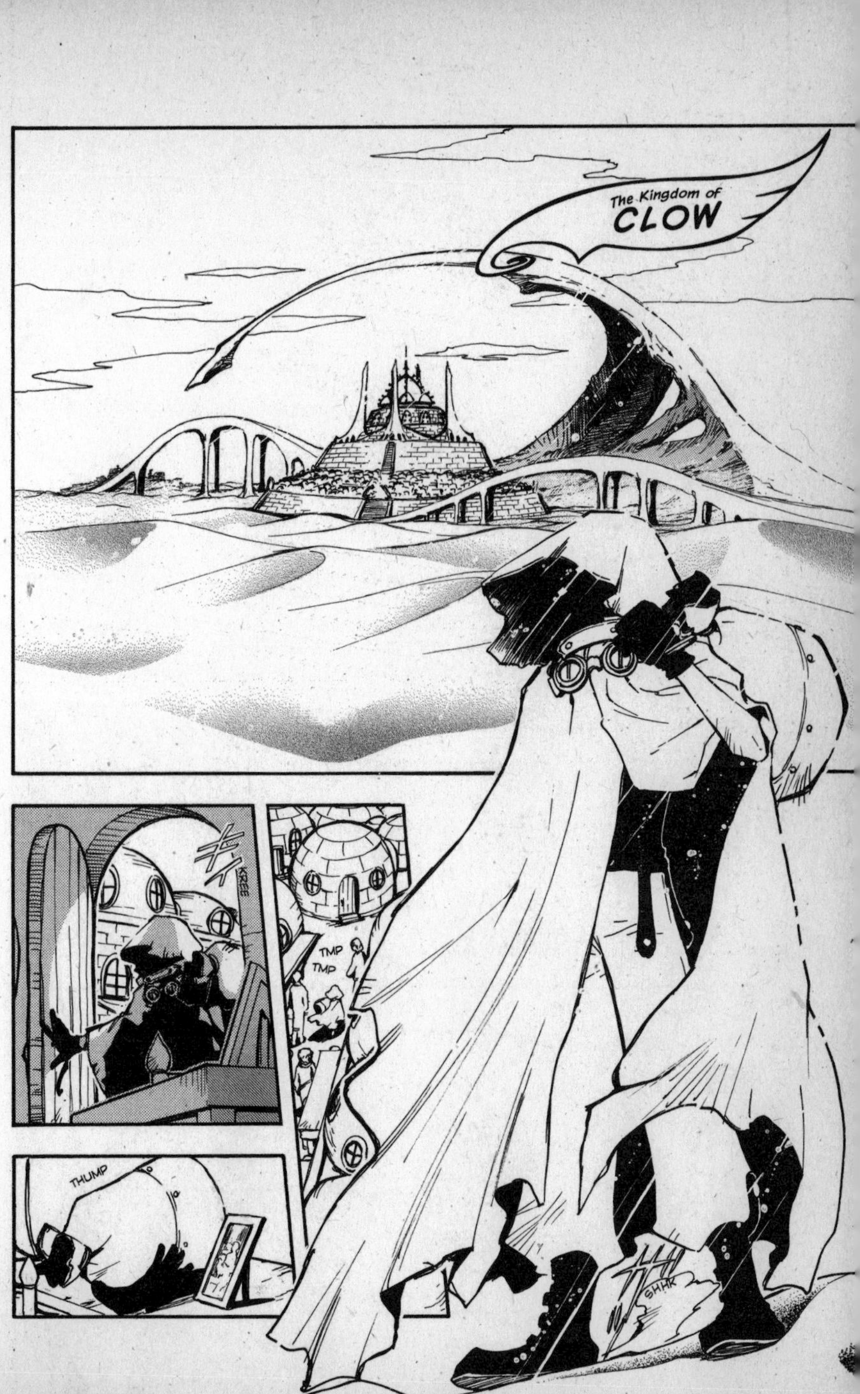
The Kingdom of
CLOW
SHHK
TMP
TMP
KREE
THUMP

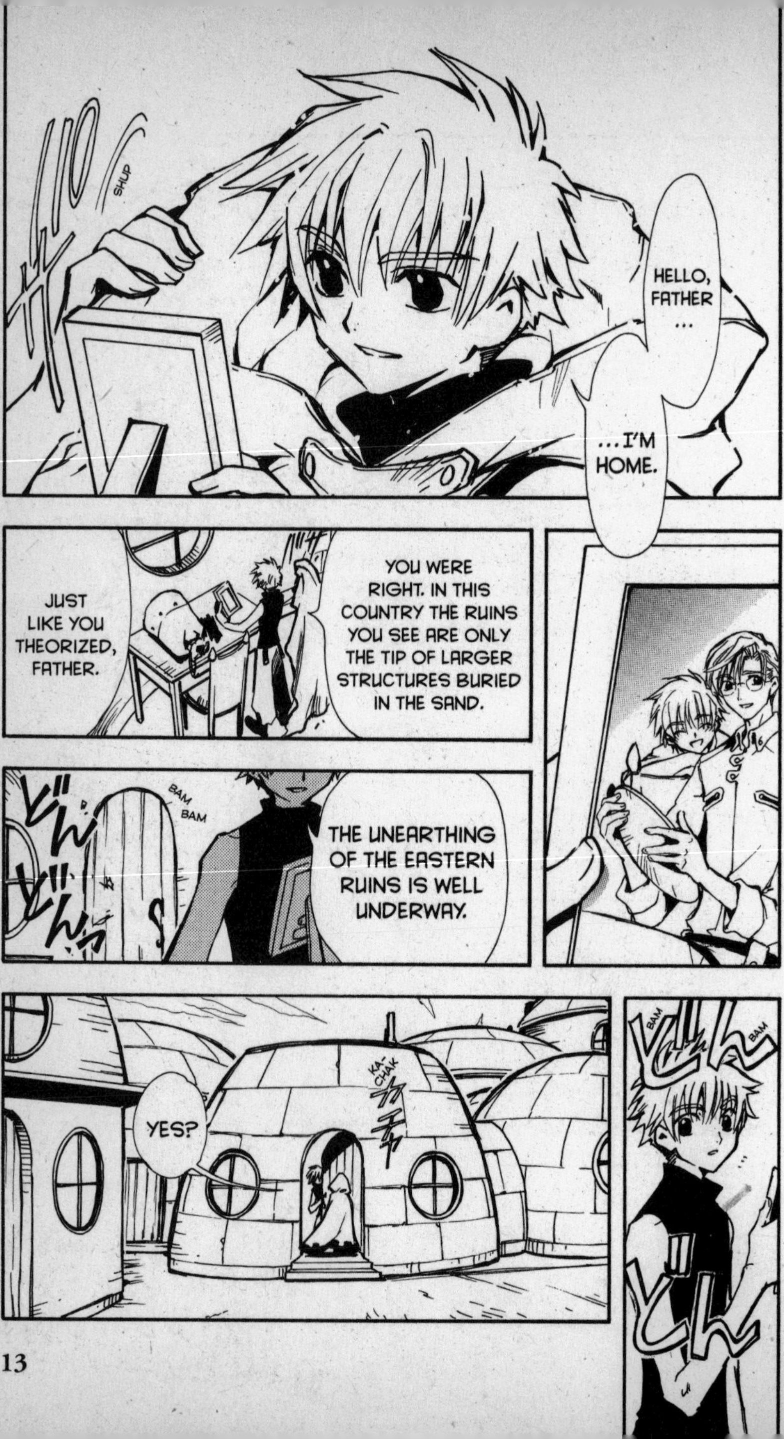

SHUP
HELLO, FATHER ...
...I'M HOME.
YOU WERE RIGHT. IN THIS COUNTRY THE RUINS YOU SEE ARE ONLY THE TIP OF LARGER STRUCTURES BURIED IN THE SAND.
JUST LIKE YOU THEORIZED, FATHER.
THE UNEARTHING OF THE EASTERN RUINS IS WELL UNDERWAY.
BAM BAM
BAM BAM
KA-CHAK
YES?

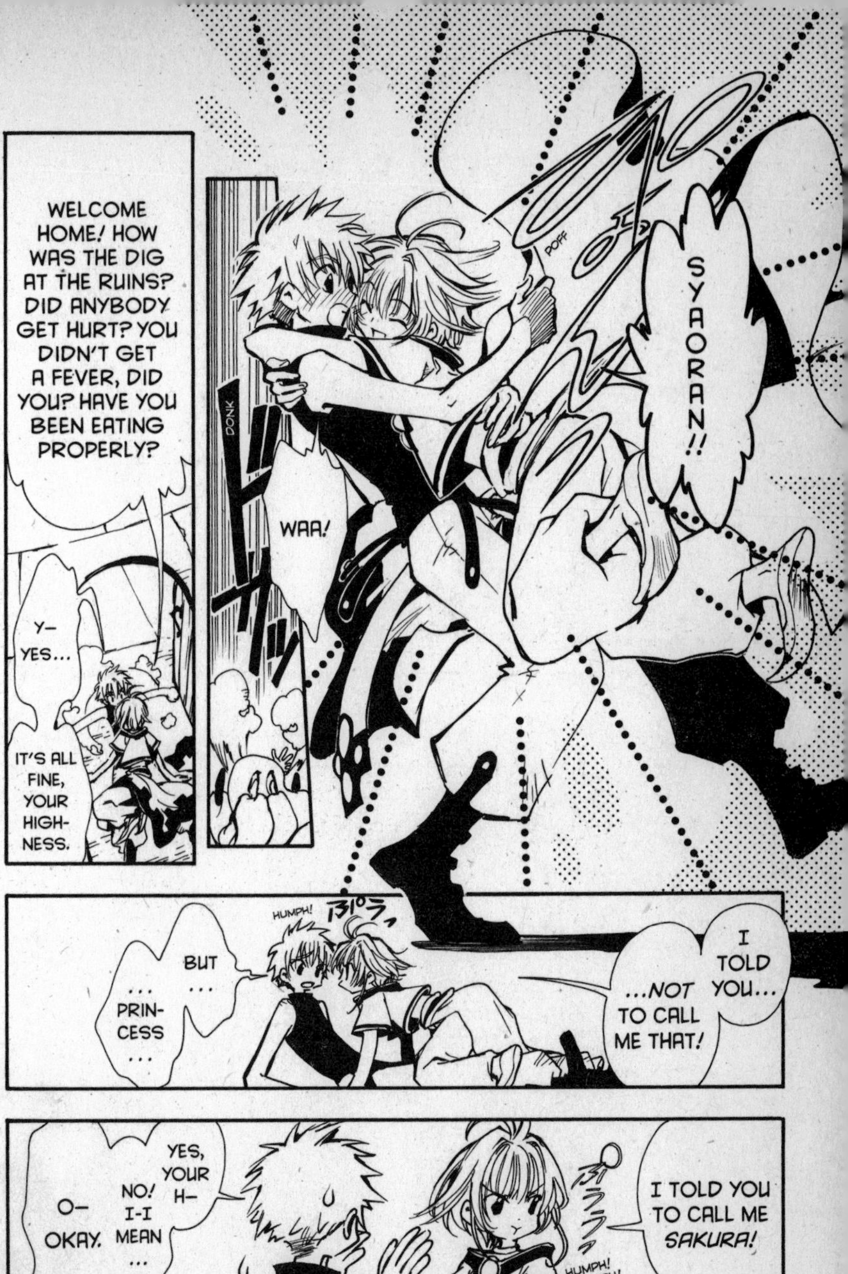
SYAORAN!!
POFF
WAA!
DONK
WELCOME HOME! HOW WAS THE DIG AT THE RUINS? DID ANYBODY GET HURT? YOU DIDN'T GET A FEVER, DID YOU? HAVE YOU BEEN EATING PROPERLY?
Y— YES...
IT'S ALL FINE, YOUR HIGHNESS.
I TOLD YOU... ...NOT TO CALL ME THAT!
HUMPH!
BUT ... ... PRINCESS ...
I TOLD YOU TO CALL ME SAKURA!
HUMPH! HUMPH!
YES, YOUR H—
NO! I-I MEAN ...
O— OKAY.

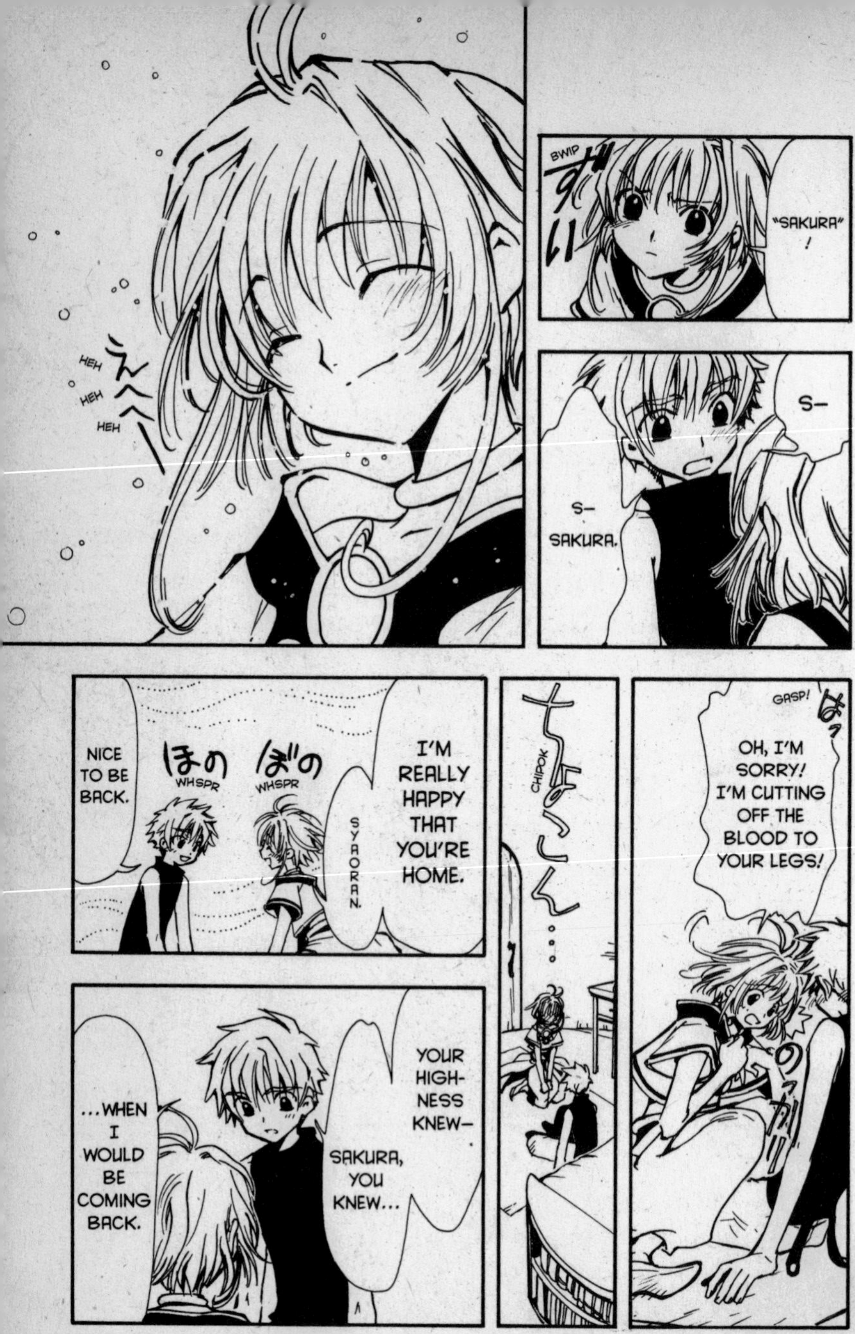
BWIP
"SAKURA"!
S—
S—SAKURA.
HEH HEH HEH
GASP!
OH, I'M SORRY! I'M CUTTING OFF THE BLOOD TO YOUR LEGS!
CHIPOK
I'M REALLY HAPPY THAT YOU'RE HOME.
SYAORAN.
WHSPR
WHSPR
NICE TO BE BACK.
YOUR HIGHNESS KNEW—
SAKURA, YOU KNEW...
...WHEN I WOULD BE COMING BACK.

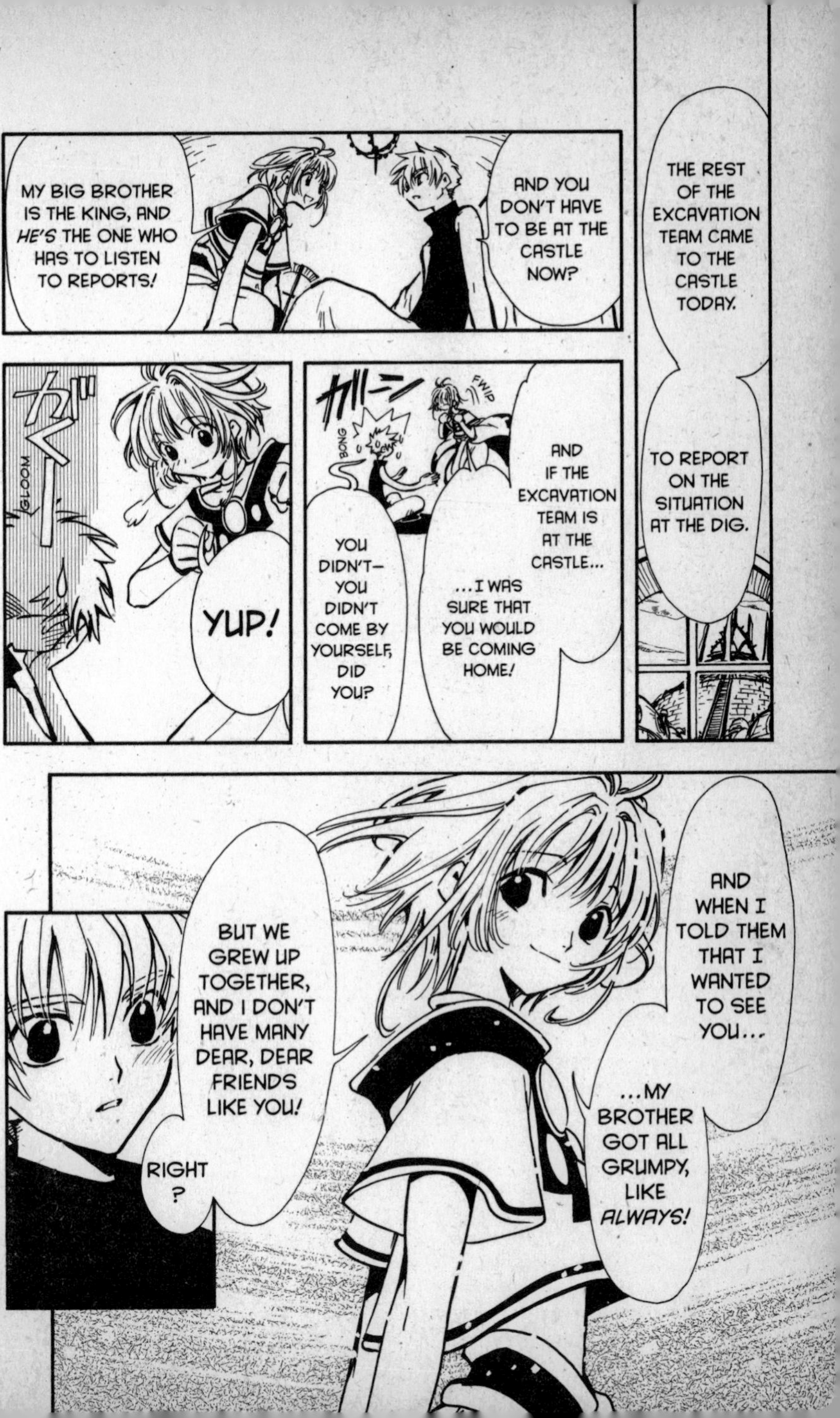
THE REST OF THE EXCAVATION TEAM CAME TO THE CASTLE TODAY.
TO REPORT ON THE SITUATION AT THE DIG.
AND YOU DON'T HAVE TO BE AT THE CASTLE NOW?
MY BIG BROTHER IS THE KING, AND *HE'S* THE ONE WHO HAS TO LISTEN TO REPORTS!
FWIP
AND IF THE EXCAVATION TEAM IS AT THE CASTLE...
...I WAS SURE THAT YOU WOULD BE COMING HOME!
ガーン
BONG
YOU DIDN'T— YOU DIDN'T COME BY YOURSELF, DID YOU?
YUP!
GLOOM
AND WHEN I TOLD THEM THAT I WANTED TO SEE YOU...
...MY BROTHER GOT ALL GRUMPY, LIKE *ALWAYS!*
BUT WE GREW UP TOGETHER, AND I DON'T HAVE MANY DEAR, DEAR FRIENDS LIKE YOU!
RIGHT?

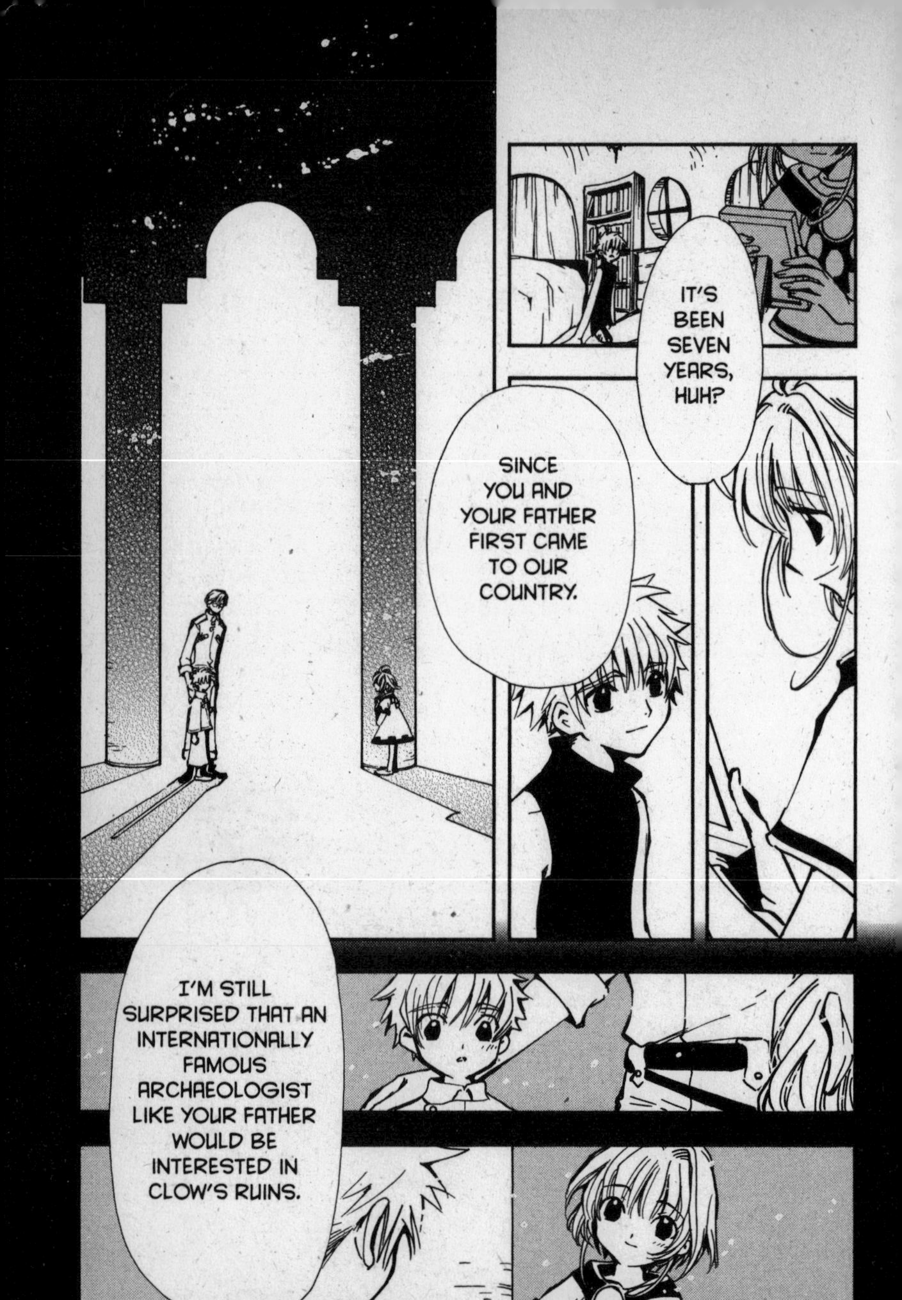
IT'S BEEN SEVEN YEARS, HUH?
SINCE YOU AND YOUR FATHER FIRST CAME TO OUR COUNTRY.
I'M STILL SURPRISED THAT AN INTERNATIONALLY FAMOUS ARCHAEOLOGIST LIKE YOUR FATHER WOULD BE INTERESTED IN CLOW'S RUINS.

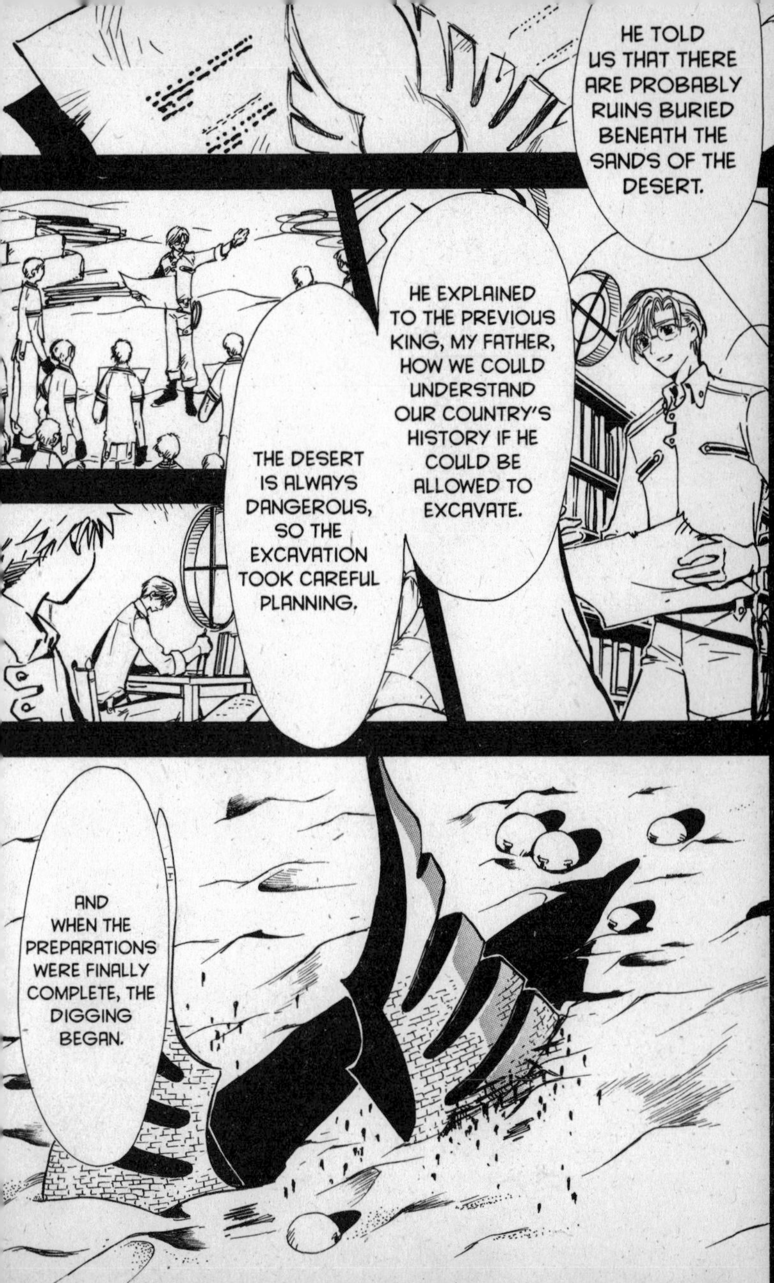
HE TOLD US THAT THERE ARE PROBABLY RUINS BURIED BENEATH THE SANDS OF THE DESERT.
HE EXPLAINED TO THE PREVIOUS KING, MY FATHER, HOW WE COULD UNDERSTAND OUR COUNTRY'S HISTORY IF HE COULD BE ALLOWED TO EXCAVATE.
THE DESERT IS ALWAYS DANGEROUS, SO THE EXCAVATION TOOK CAREFUL PLANNING.
AND WHEN THE PREPARATIONS WERE FINALLY COMPLETE, THE DIGGING BEGAN.

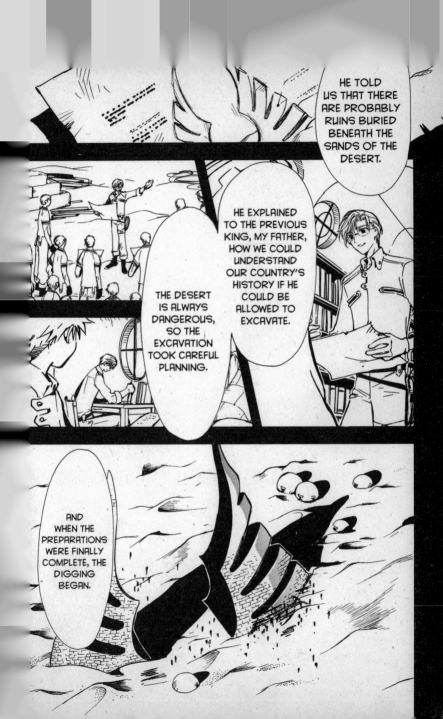

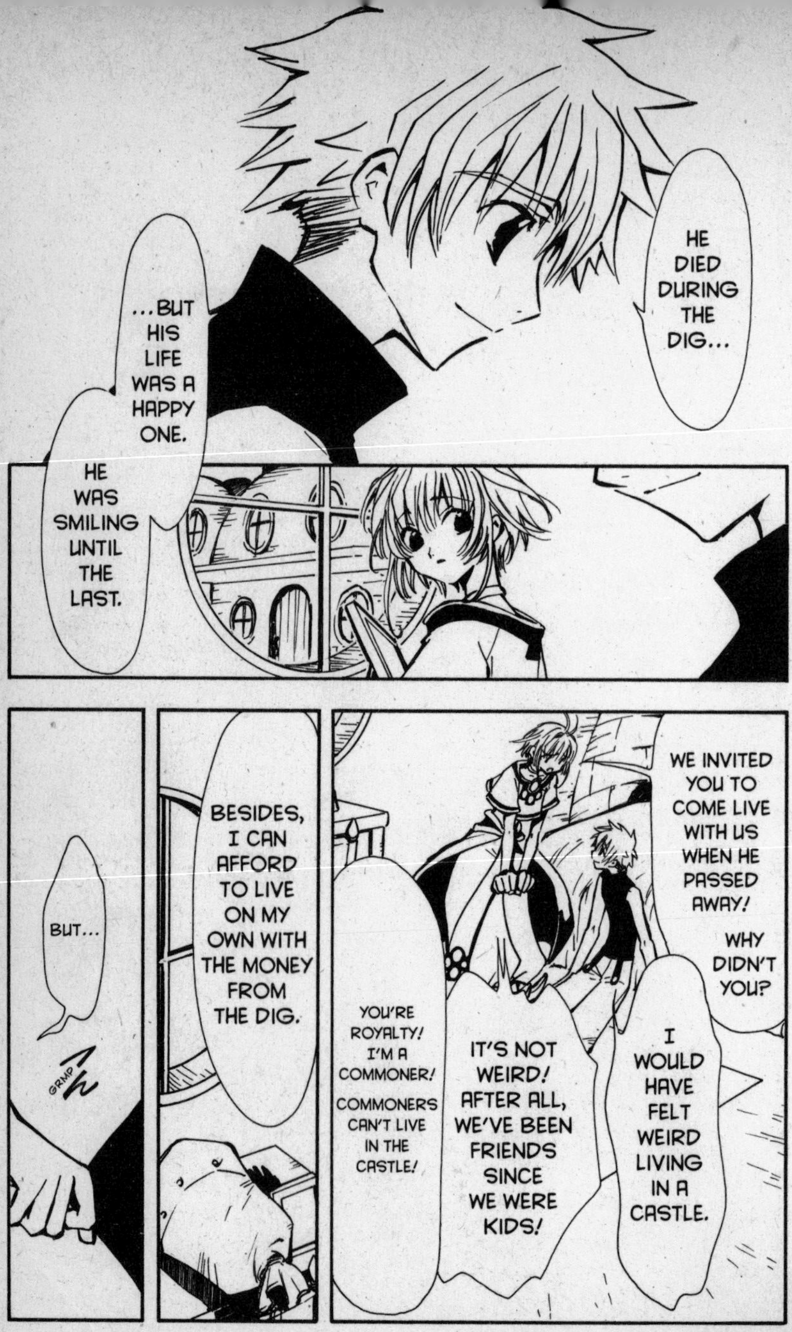
HE DIED DURING THE DIG...
...BUT HIS LIFE WAS A HAPPY ONE.
HE WAS SMILING UNTIL THE LAST.
WE INVITED YOU TO COME LIVE WITH US WHEN HE PASSED AWAY!
WHY DIDN'T YOU?
I WOULD HAVE FELT WEIRD LIVING IN A CASTLE.
IT'S NOT WEIRD! AFTER ALL, WE'VE BEEN FRIENDS SINCE WE WERE KIDS!
YOU'RE ROYALTY! I'M A COMMONER!
COMMONERS CAN'T LIVE IN THE CASTLE!
BESIDES, I CAN AFFORD TO LIVE ON MY OWN WITH THE MONEY FROM THE DIG.
BUT...
GRMP

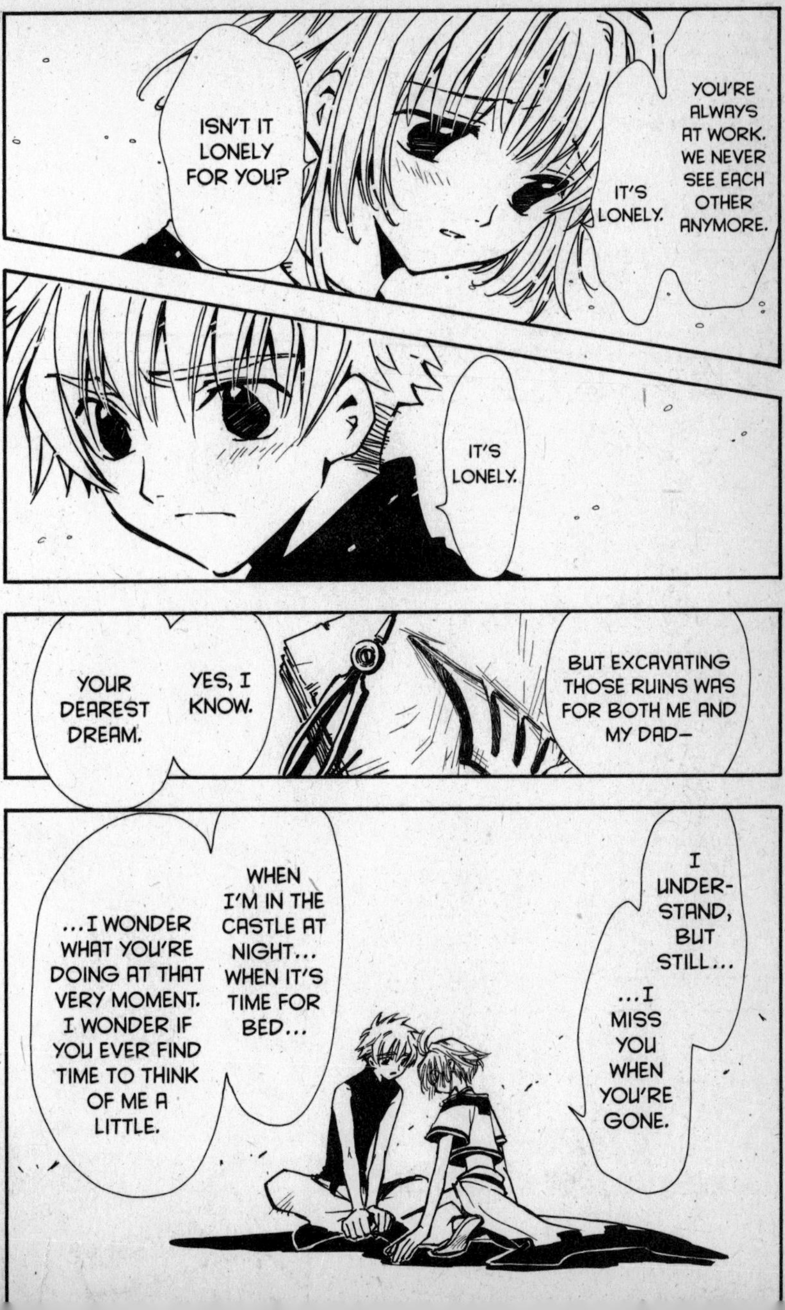
YOU'RE ALWAYS AT WORK. WE NEVER SEE EACH OTHER ANYMORE.
IT'S LONELY.
ISN'T IT LONELY FOR YOU?
IT'S LONELY.
BUT EXCAVATING THOSE RUINS WAS FOR BOTH ME AND MY DAD—
YES, I KNOW.
YOUR DEAREST DREAM.
I UNDER-STAND, BUT STILL...
...I MISS YOU WHEN YOU'RE GONE.
WHEN I'M IN THE CASTLE AT NIGHT... WHEN IT'S TIME FOR BED...
...I WONDER WHAT YOU'RE DOING AT THAT VERY MOMENT. I WONDER IF YOU EVER FIND TIME TO THINK OF ME A LITTLE.

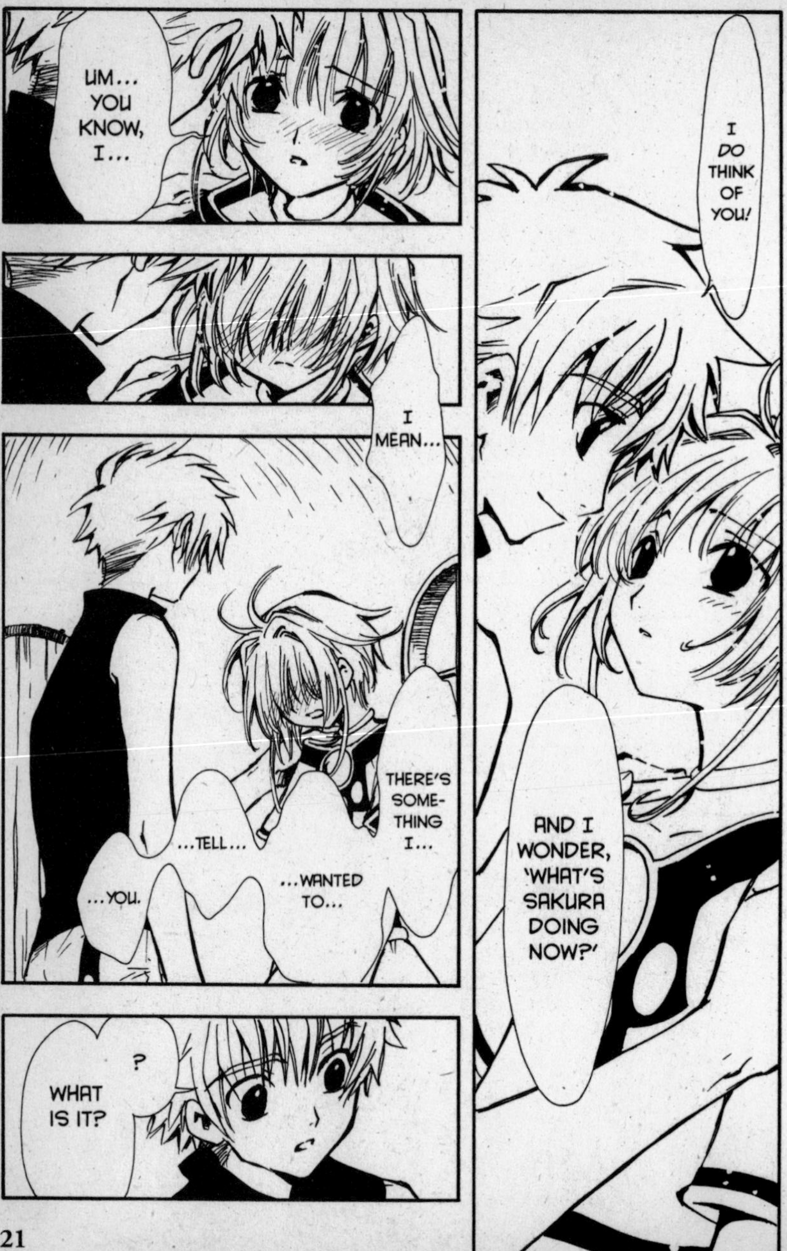
I *DO* THINK OF YOU!
AND I WONDER, 'WHAT'S SAKURA DOING NOW?'
UM... YOU KNOW, I...
I MEAN...
THERE'S SOME-THING I...
...WANTED TO...
...TELL...
...YOU.
?
WHAT IS IT?

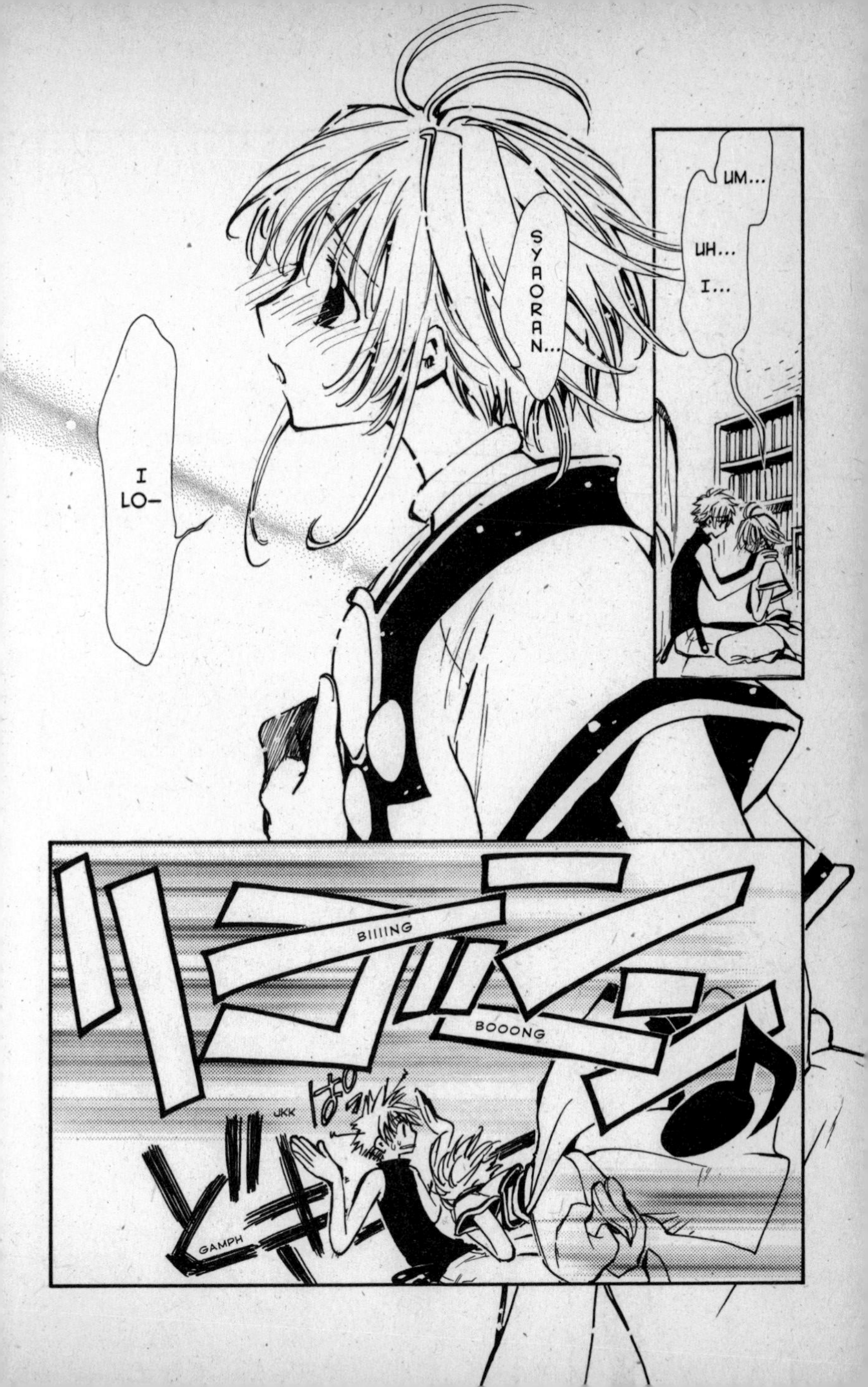
UM...
UH...
I...
SYAORAN...
I LO-
BIIIING
BOOONG
UKK
GAMPH

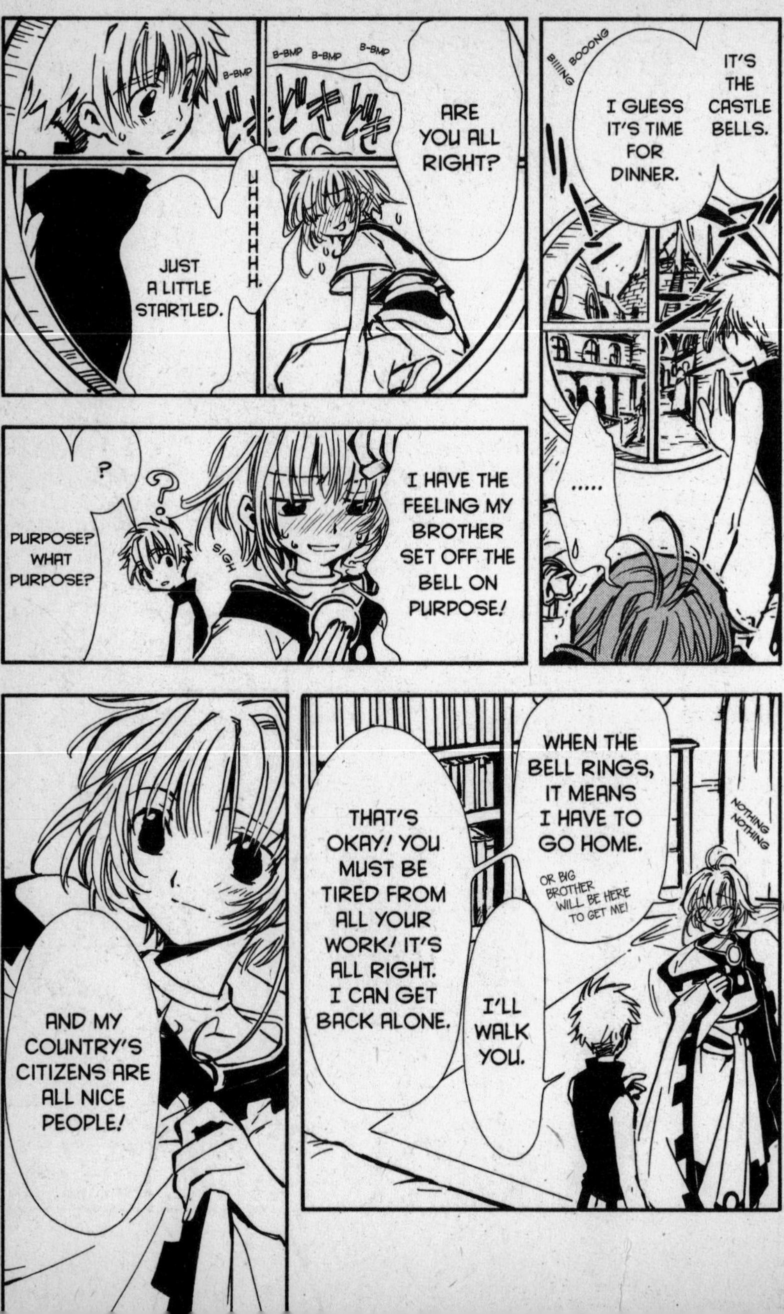
BIIING BOOONG
IT'S THE CASTLE BELLS.
I GUESS IT'S TIME FOR DINNER.
.....
B-BMP B-BMP B-BMP
ARE YOU ALL RIGHT?
B-BMP
UHHHHHHH.
JUST A LITTLE STARTLED.
I HAVE THE FEELING MY BROTHER SET OFF THE BELL ON PURPOSE!
SIGH
?
PURPOSE? WHAT PURPOSE?
NOTHING NOTHING
WHEN THE BELL RINGS, IT MEANS I HAVE TO GO HOME.
OR BIG BROTHER WILL BE HERE TO GET ME!
THAT'S OKAY! YOU MUST BE TIRED FROM ALL YOUR WORK! IT'S ALL RIGHT. I CAN GET BACK ALONE.
I'LL WALK YOU.
AND MY COUNTRY'S CITIZENS ARE ALL NICE PEOPLE!

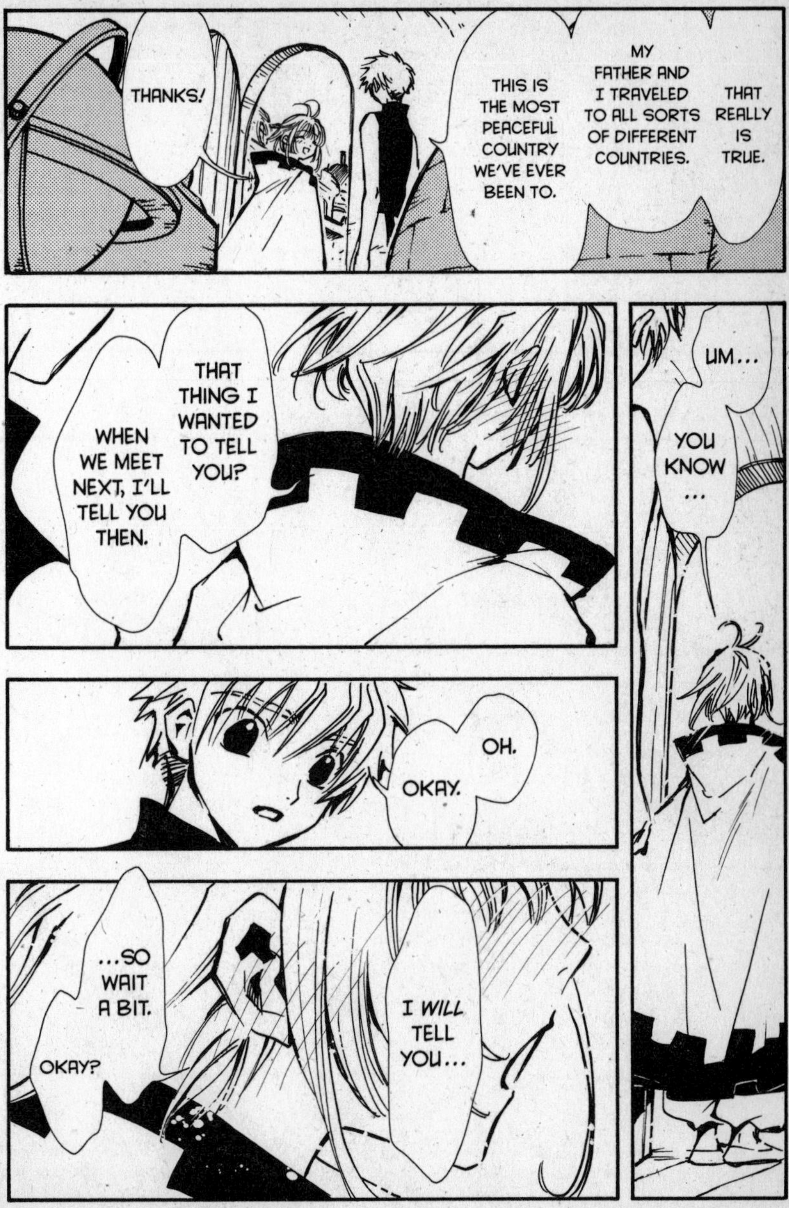
THAT REALLY IS TRUE.
MY FATHER AND I TRAVELED TO ALL SORTS OF DIFFERENT COUNTRIES.
THIS IS THE MOST PEACEFUL COUNTRY WE'VE EVER BEEN TO.
THANKS!
UM...
YOU KNOW ...
THAT THING I WANTED TO TELL YOU?
WHEN WE MEET NEXT, I'LL TELL YOU THEN.
OH.
OKAY.
I *WILL* TELL YOU...
...SO WAIT A BIT.
OKAY?

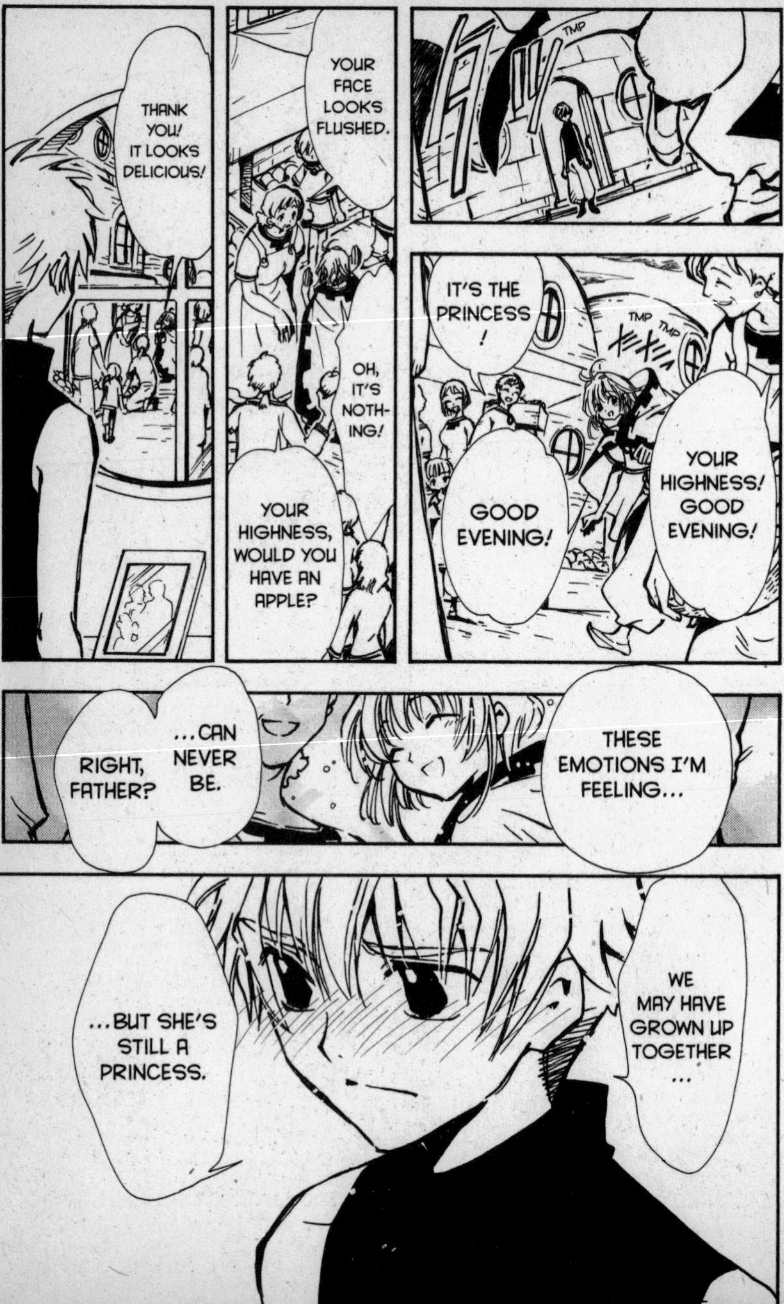
TMP
TMP TMP
IT'S THE PRINCESS!
YOUR HIGHNESS! GOOD EVENING!
GOOD EVENING!
YOUR FACE LOOKS FLUSHED.
OH, IT'S NOTHING!
YOUR HIGHNESS, WOULD YOU HAVE AN APPLE?
THANK YOU! IT LOOKS DELICIOUS!
THESE EMOTIONS I'M FEELING...
...CAN NEVER BE.
RIGHT, FATHER?
WE MAY HAVE GROWN UP TOGETHER...
...BUT SHE'S STILL A PRINCESS.

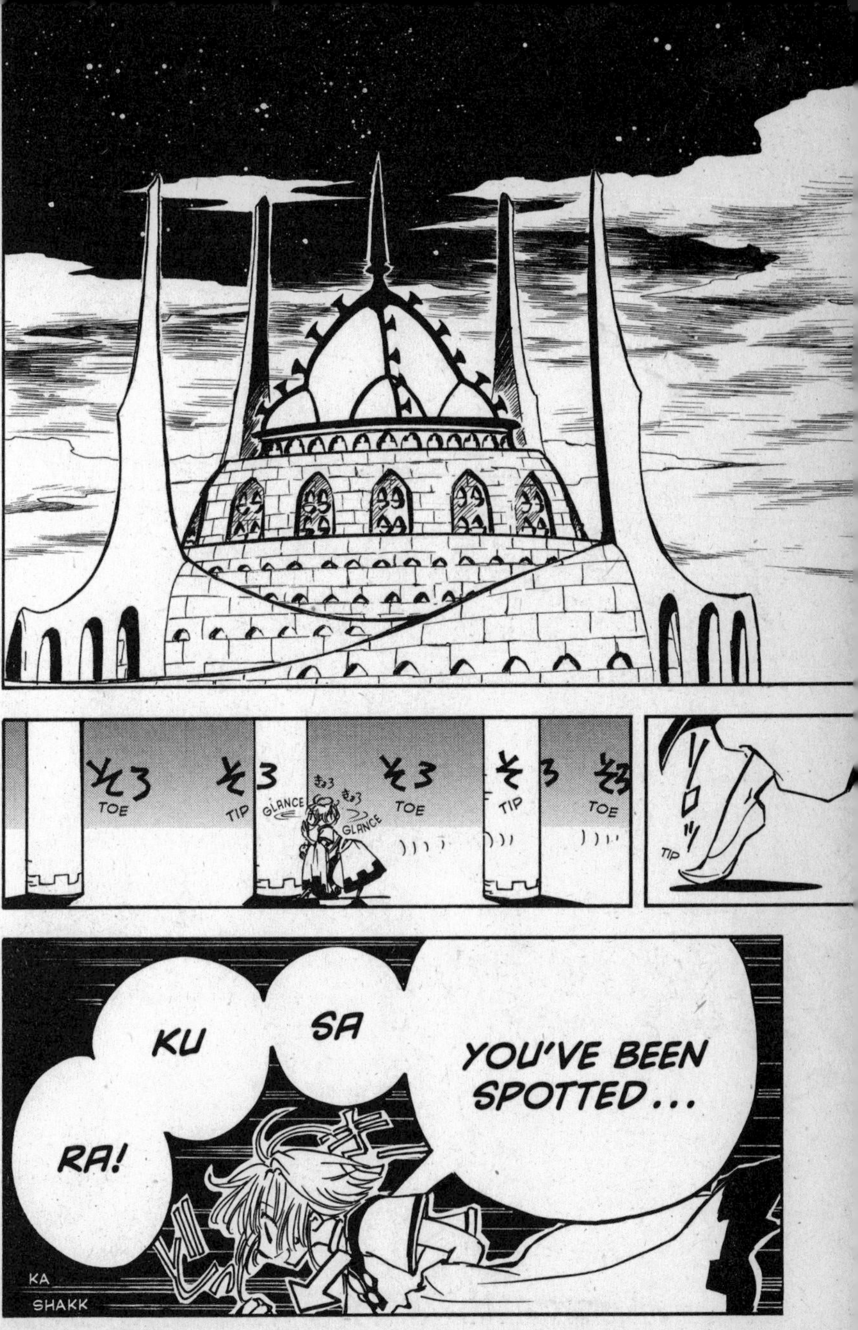
TIP
そろ
TOE
そろ
TIP
そろ
TOE
GLANCE
GLANCE
そろ
TIP
そろ
TOE
YOU'VE BEEN SPOTTED...
KU
SA
RA!
KA
SHAKK

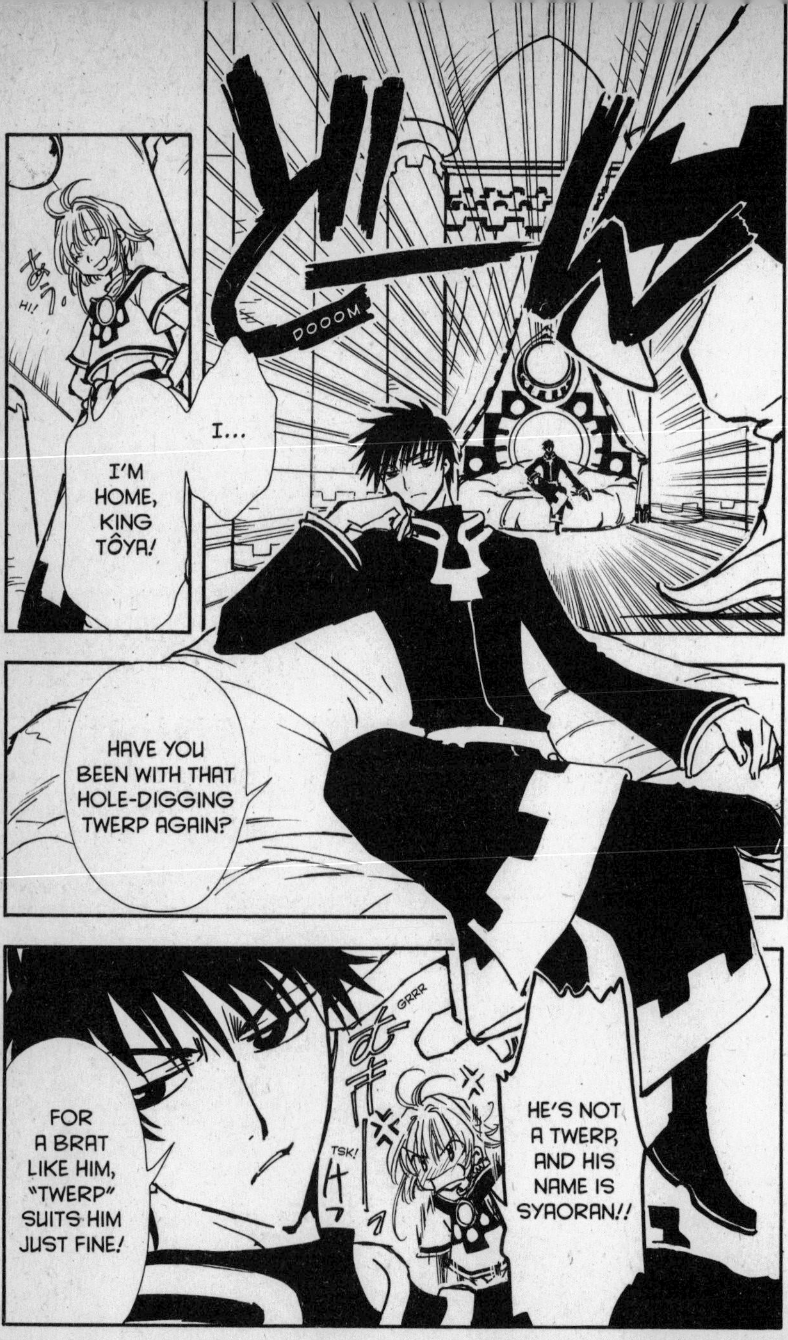
DOOOM
HI!
I...
I'M HOME, KING TÔYA!
HAVE YOU BEEN WITH THAT HOLE-DIGGING TWERP AGAIN?
GRRR
TSK!
HE'S NOT A TWERP, AND HIS NAME IS SYAORAN!!
FOR A BRAT LIKE HIM, "TWERP" SUITS HIM JUST FINE!

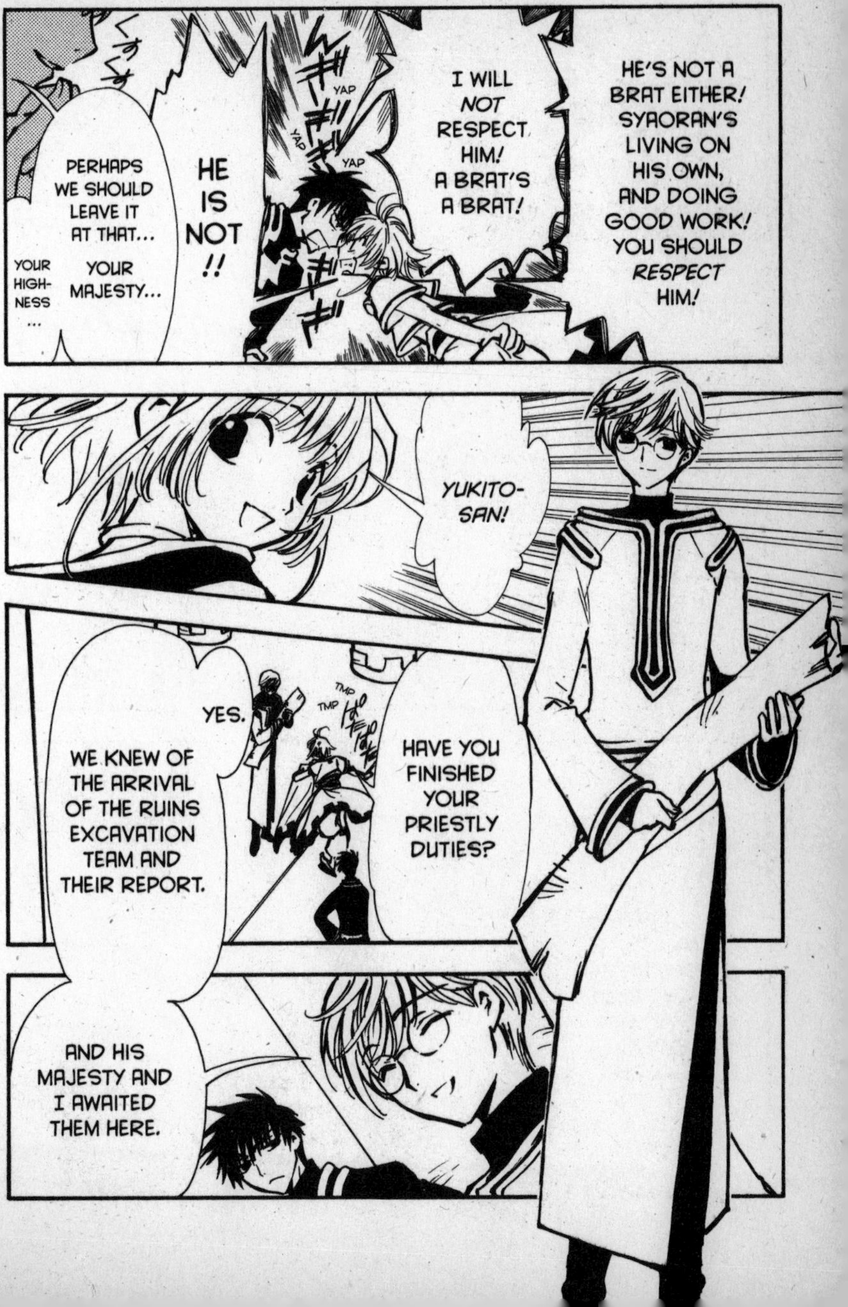
HE'S NOT A BRAT EITHER! SYAORAN'S LIVING ON HIS OWN, AND DOING GOOD WORK! YOU SHOULD *RESPECT* HIM!
I WILL *NOT* RESPECT HIM! A BRAT'S A BRAT!
YAP
YAP
YAP
HE IS NOT!!
PERHAPS WE SHOULD LEAVE IT AT THAT... YOUR MAJESTY...
YOUR HIGHNESS...
YUKITO-SAN!
HAVE YOU FINISHED YOUR PRIESTLY DUTIES?
TMP
TMP
YES.
WE KNEW OF THE ARRIVAL OF THE RUINS EXCAVATION TEAM AND THEIR REPORT.
AND HIS MAJESTY AND I AWAITED THEM HERE.

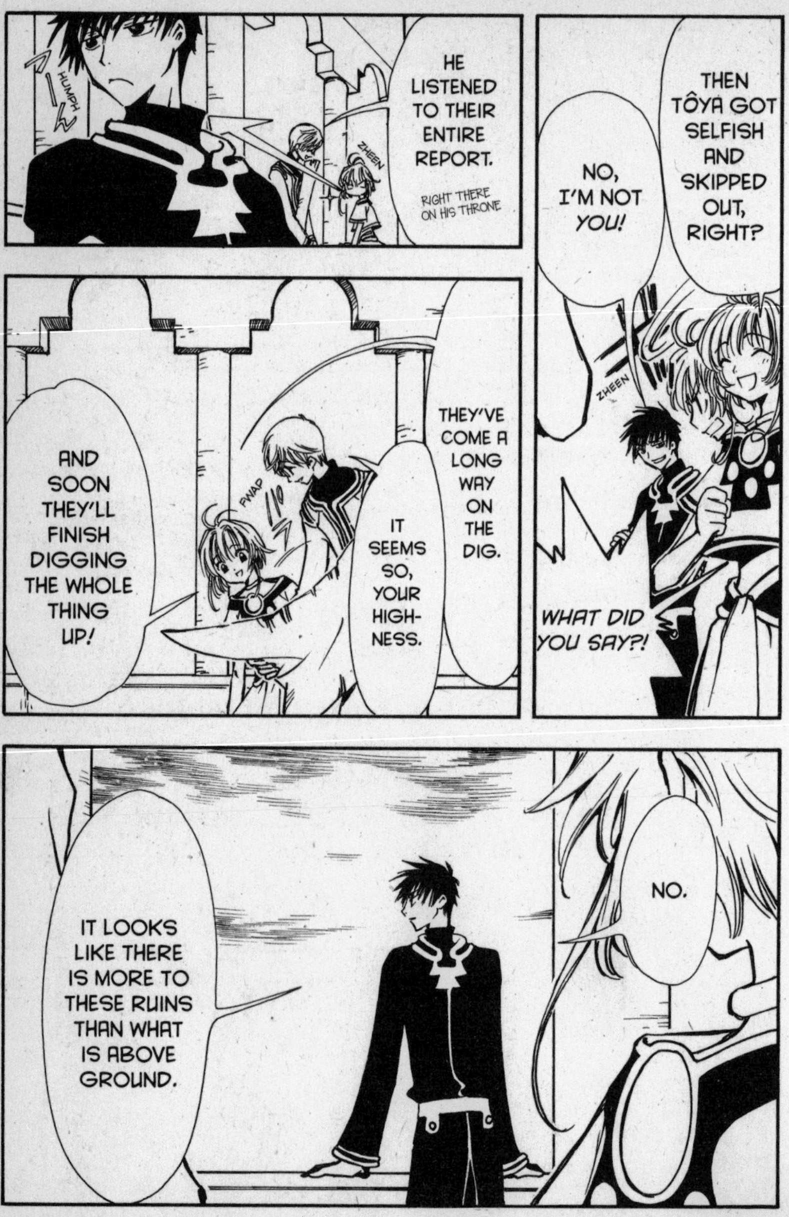
THEN TÔYA GOT SELFISH AND SKIPPED OUT, RIGHT?
NO, I'M NOT *YOU!*
ZHEEN
WHAT DID YOU SAY?!
HE LISTENED TO THEIR ENTIRE REPORT.
RIGHT THERE ON HIS THRONE
ZHEEN
HUMPH
THEY'VE COME A LONG WAY ON THE DIG.
IT SEEMS SO, YOUR HIGHNESS.
FWAP
AND SOON THEY'LL FINISH DIGGING THE WHOLE THING UP!
NO.
IT LOOKS LIKE THERE IS MORE TO THESE RUINS THAN WHAT IS ABOVE GROUND.

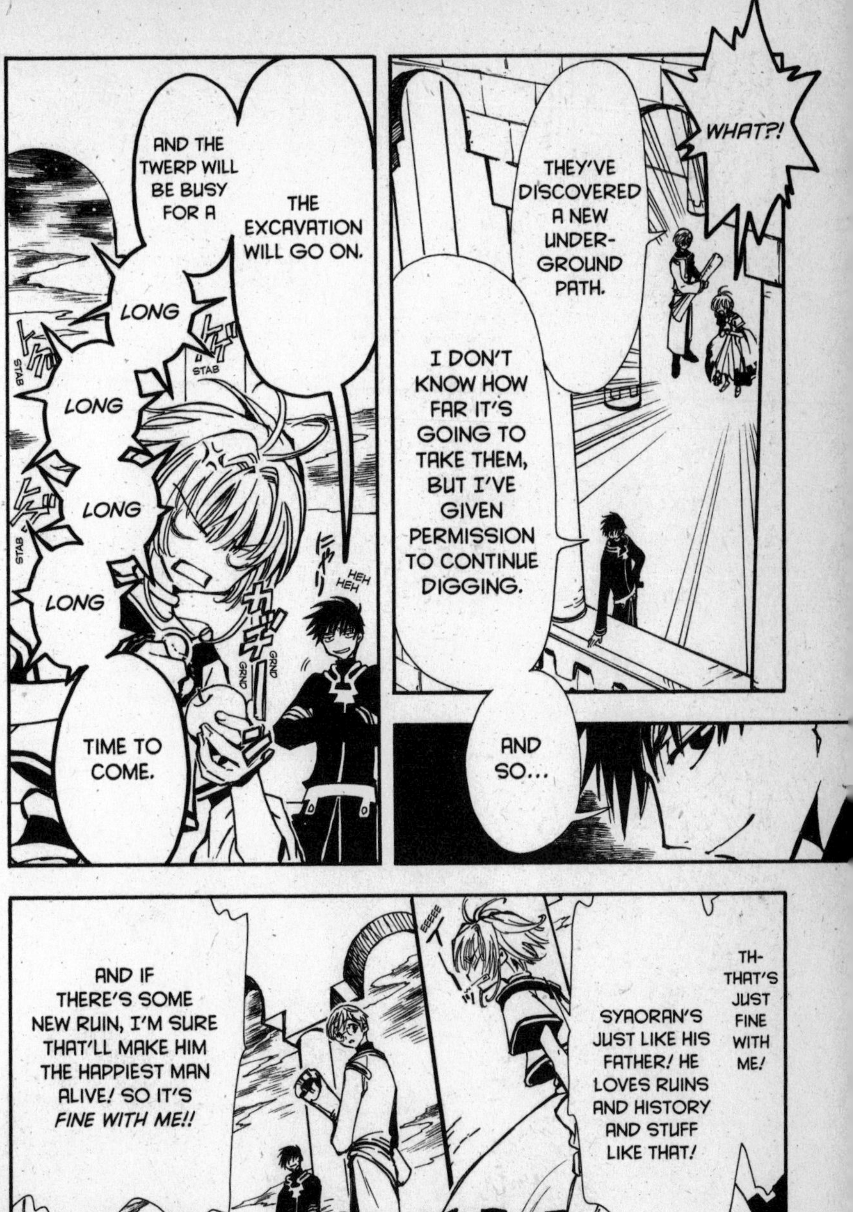
WHAT?!
THEY'VE DISCOVERED A NEW UNDER-GROUND PATH.
I DON'T KNOW HOW FAR IT'S GOING TO TAKE THEM, BUT I'VE GIVEN PERMISSION TO CONTINUE DIGGING.
AND SO...
THE EXCAVATION WILL GO ON.
AND THE TWERP WILL BE BUSY FOR A
STAB
LONG
STAB
LONG
HEH HEH
LONG
STAB
LONG
GRND GRND
TIME TO COME.
TH-THAT'S JUST FINE WITH ME!
SYAORAN'S JUST LIKE HIS FATHER! HE LOVES RUINS AND HISTORY AND STUFF LIKE THAT!
AND IF THERE'S SOME NEW RUIN, I'M SURE THAT'LL MAKE HIM THE HAPPIEST MAN ALIVE! SO IT'S *FINE WITH ME!!*

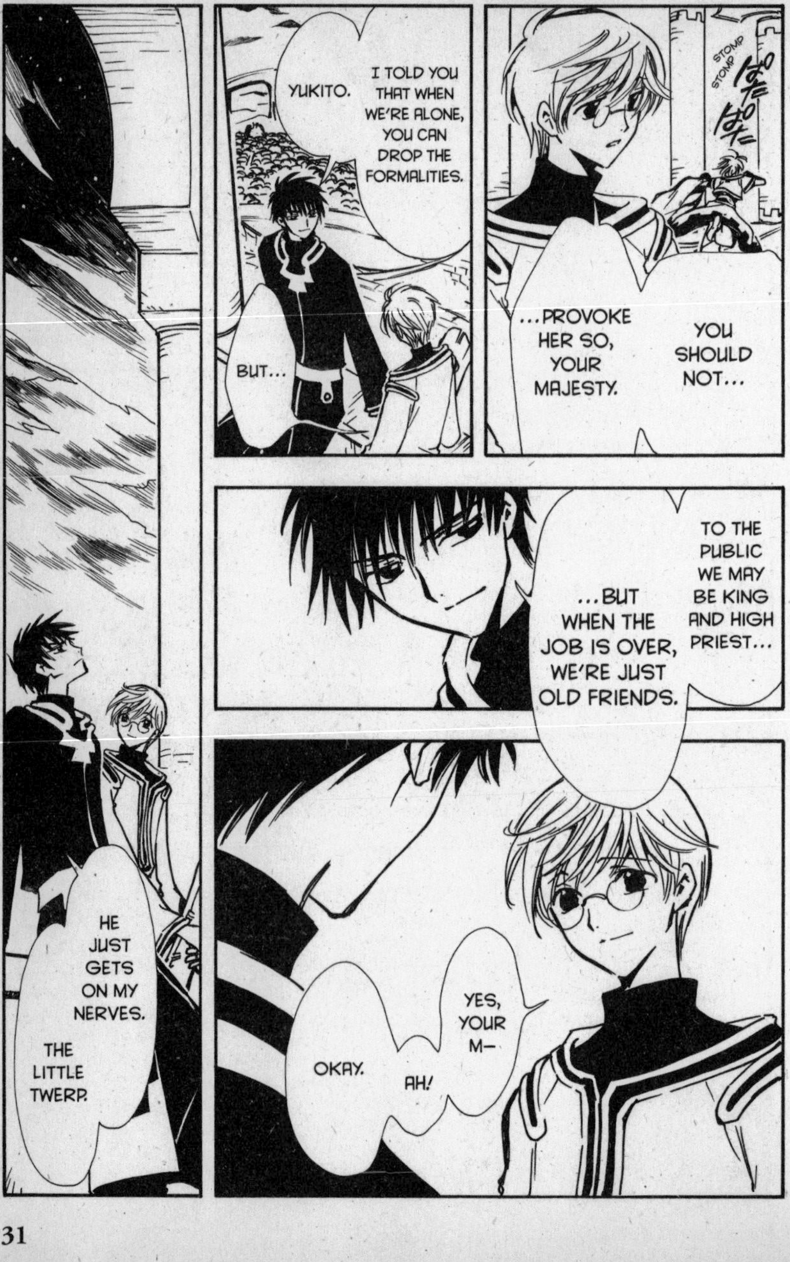
STOMP STOMP
ぱた ぱた
YOU SHOULD NOT...
...PROVOKE HER SO, YOUR MAJESTY.
YUKITO. I TOLD YOU THAT WHEN WE'RE ALONE, YOU CAN DROP THE FORMALITIES.
BUT...
TO THE PUBLIC WE MAY BE KING AND HIGH PRIEST...
...BUT WHEN THE JOB IS OVER, WE'RE JUST OLD FRIENDS.
YES, YOUR M—
AH!
OKAY.
HE JUST GETS ON MY NERVES.
THE LITTLE TWERP.

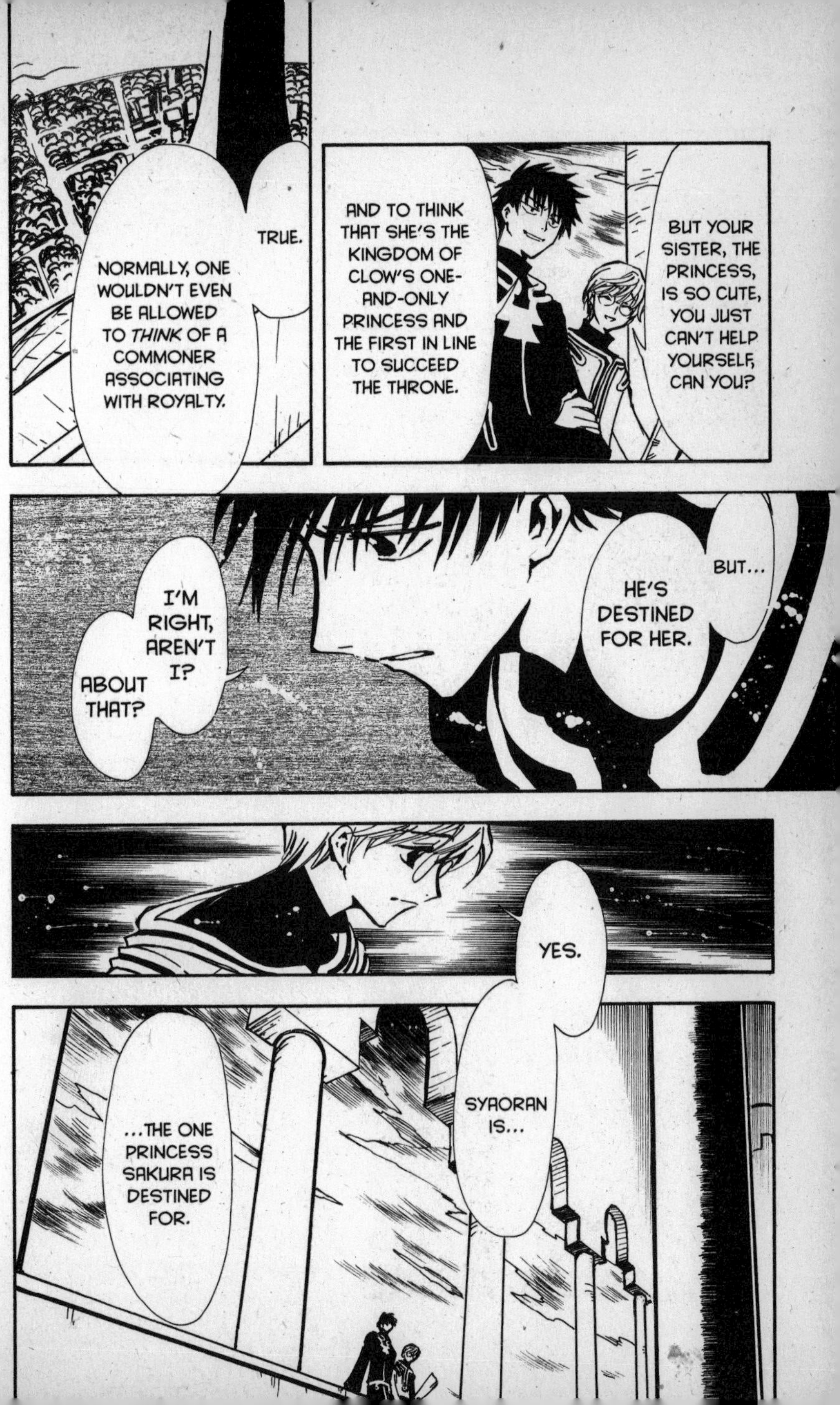
BUT YOUR SISTER, THE PRINCESS, IS SO CUTE, YOU JUST CAN'T HELP YOURSELF, CAN YOU?
AND TO THINK THAT SHE'S THE KINGDOM OF CLOW'S ONE-AND-ONLY PRINCESS AND THE FIRST IN LINE TO SUCCEED THE THRONE.
TRUE.
NORMALLY, ONE WOULDN'T EVEN BE ALLOWED TO *THINK* OF A COMMONER ASSOCIATING WITH ROYALTY.
BUT...
HE'S DESTINED FOR HER.
I'M RIGHT, AREN'T I?
ABOUT THAT?
YES.
SYAORAN IS...
...THE ONE PRINCESS SAKURA IS DESTINED FOR.

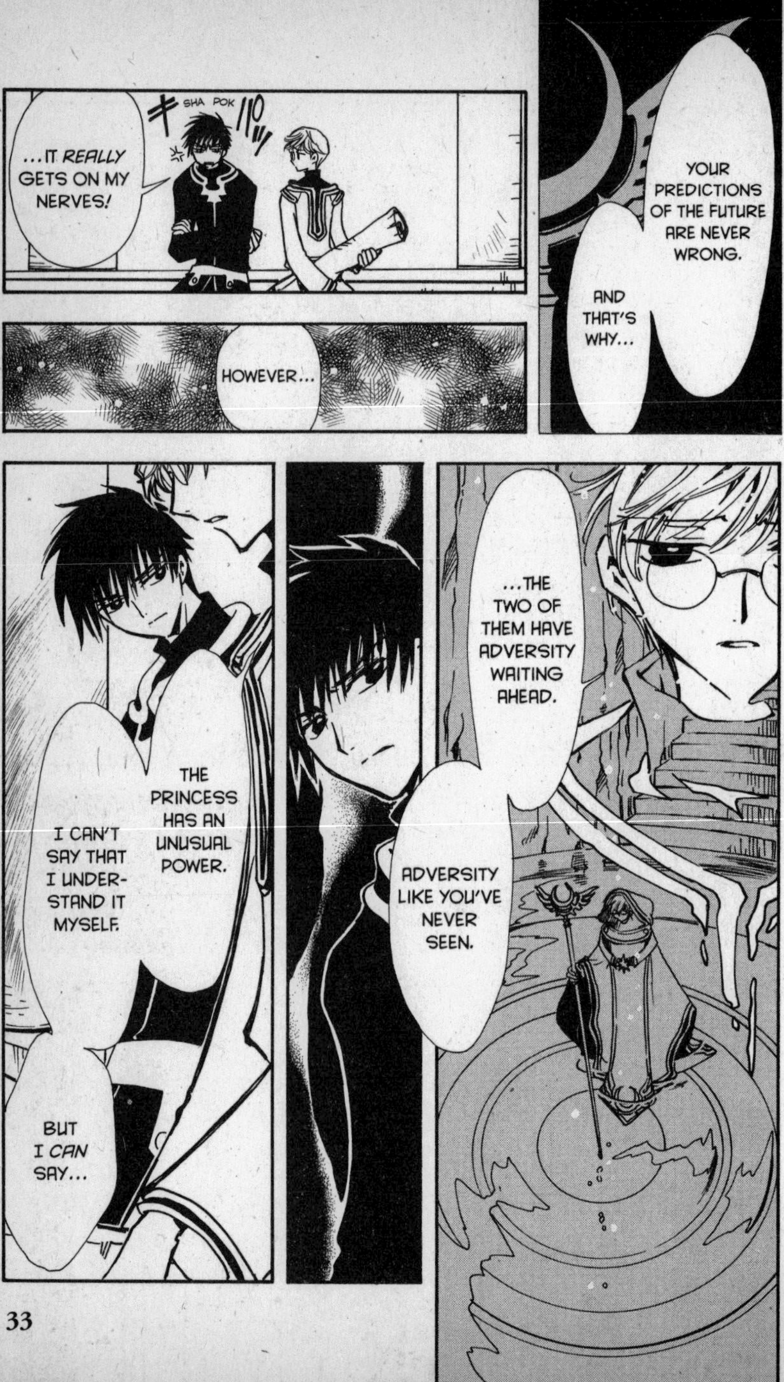
YOUR PREDICTIONS OF THE FUTURE ARE NEVER WRONG.
AND THAT'S WHY...
SHA POK
...IT *REALLY* GETS ON MY NERVES!
HOWEVER...
...THE TWO OF THEM HAVE ADVERSITY WAITING AHEAD.
ADVERSITY LIKE YOU'VE NEVER SEEN.
THE PRINCESS HAS AN UNUSUAL POWER.
I CAN'T SAY THAT I UNDER-STAND IT MYSELF.
BUT I *CAN* SAY...

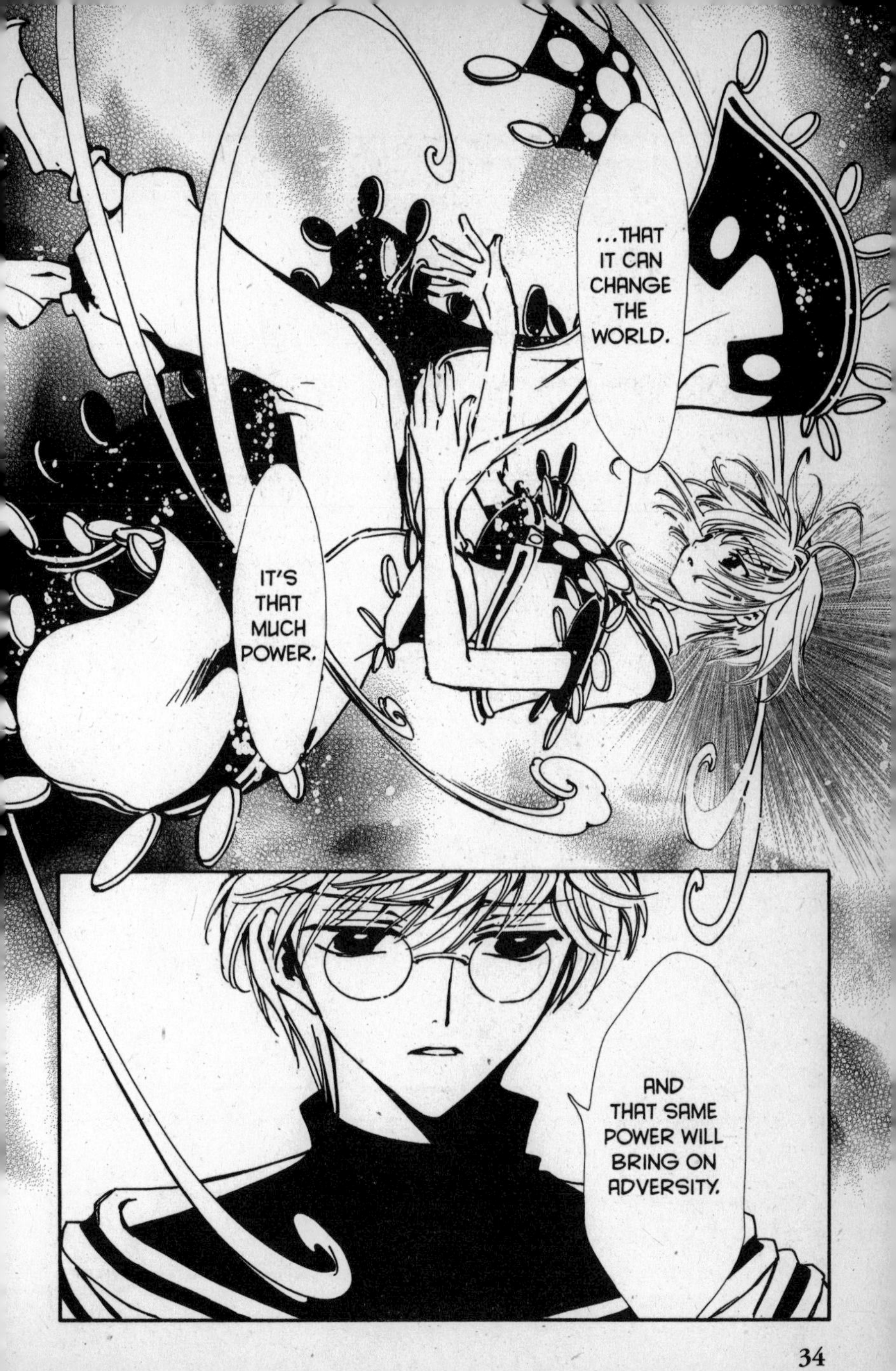
...THAT IT CAN CHANGE THE WORLD.
IT'S THAT MUCH POWER.
AND THAT SAME POWER WILL BRING ON ADVERSITY.

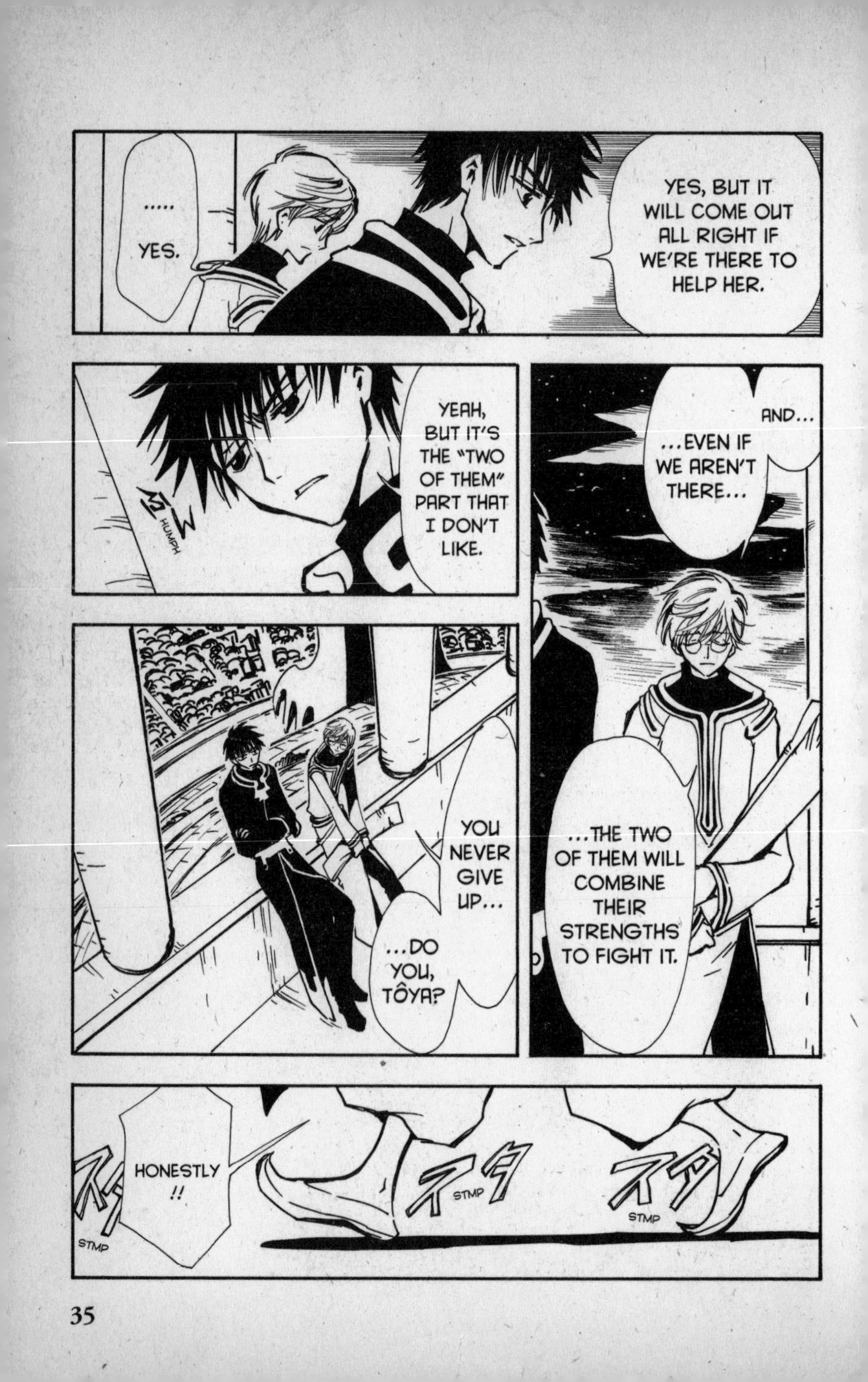
YES, BUT IT WILL COME OUT ALL RIGHT IF WE'RE THERE TO HELP HER.
..... YES.
AND...
...EVEN IF WE AREN'T THERE...
...THE TWO OF THEM WILL COMBINE THEIR STRENGTHS TO FIGHT IT.
YEAH, BUT IT'S THE "TWO OF THEM" PART THAT I DON'T LIKE.
HUMPH
YOU NEVER GIVE UP...
...DO YOU, TÔYA?
STMP
STMP
HONESTLY !!
STMP

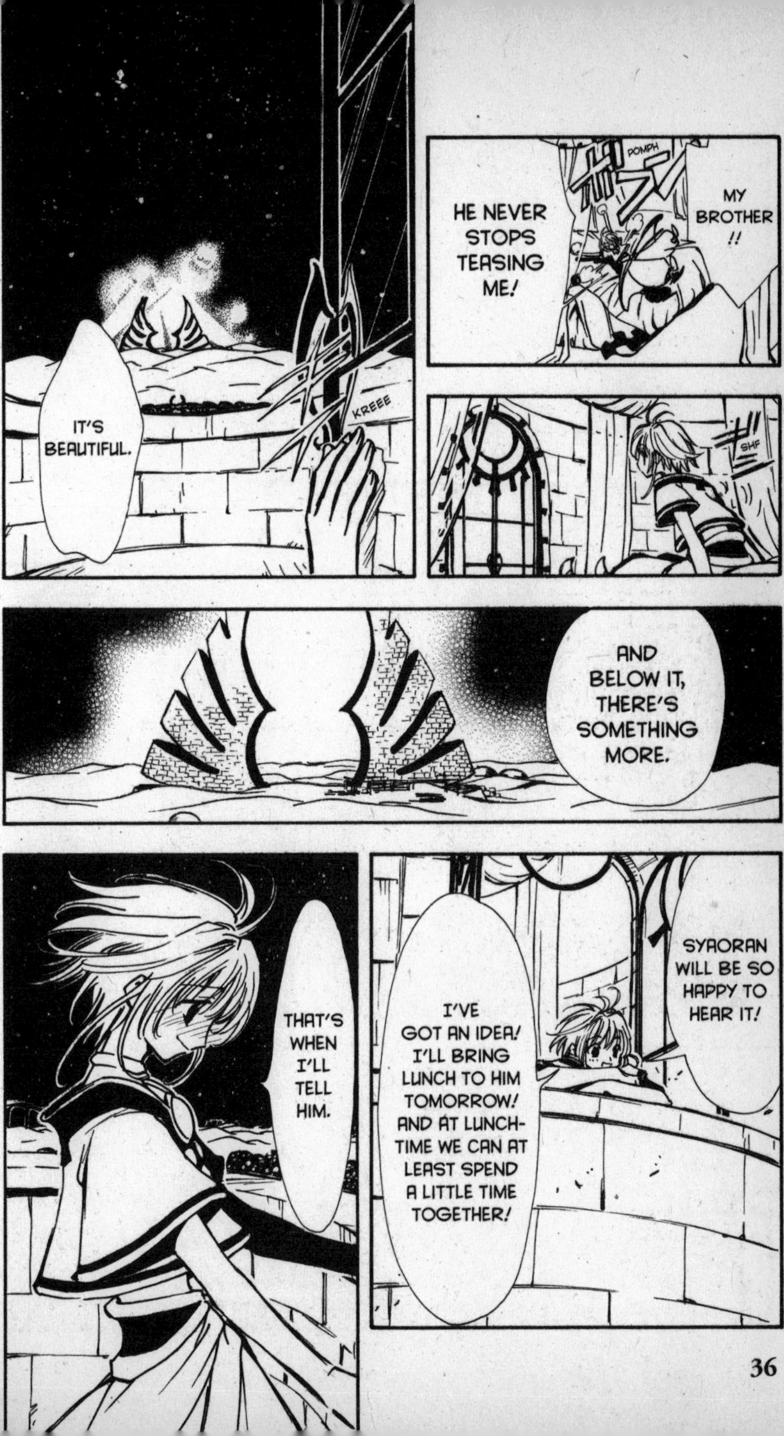
POMPH
MY BROTHER !!
HE NEVER STOPS TEASING ME!
SHF
KREEE
IT'S BEAUTIFUL.
AND BELOW IT, THERE'S SOMETHING MORE.
SYAORAN WILL BE SO HAPPY TO HEAR IT!
I'VE GOT AN IDEA! I'LL BRING LUNCH TO HIM TOMORROW! AND AT LUNCH-TIME WE CAN AT LEAST SPEND A LITTLE TIME TOGETHER!
THAT'S WHEN I'LL TELL HIM.

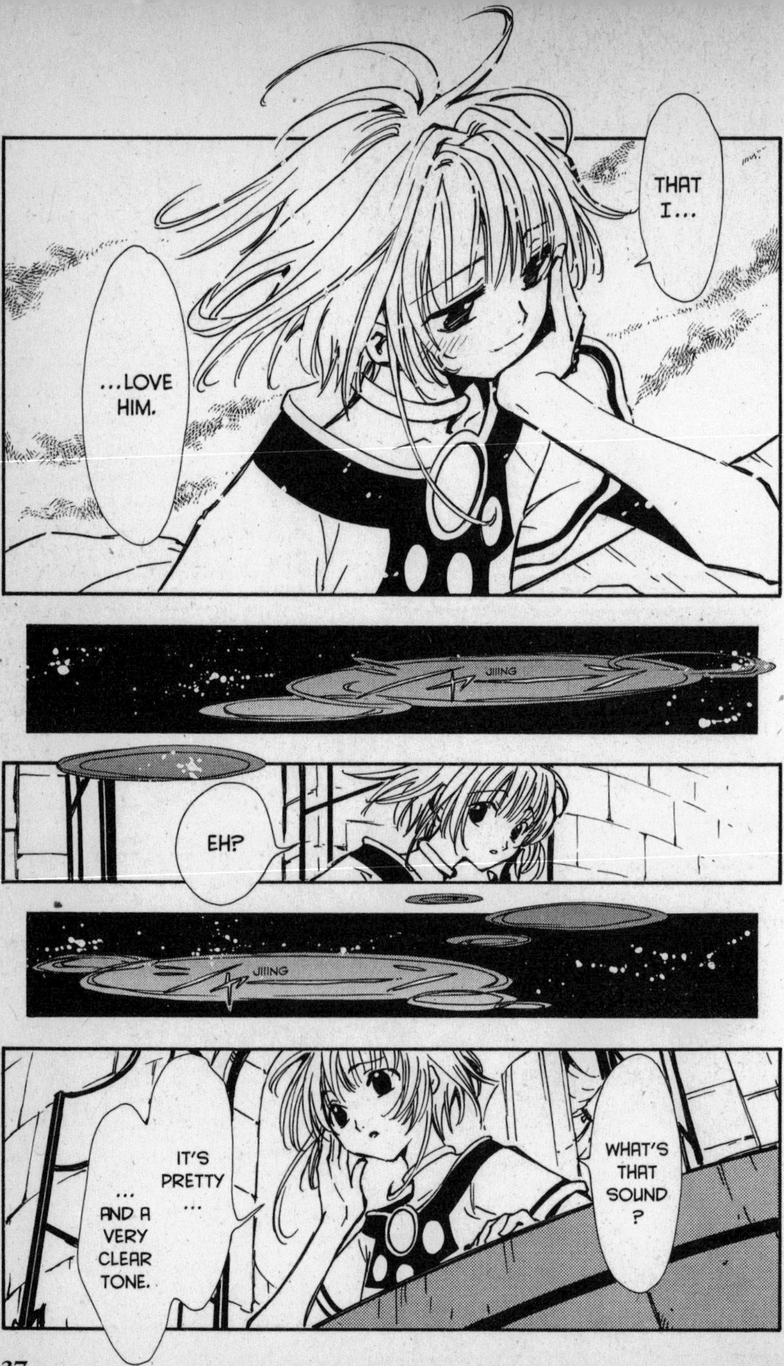
THAT I...
...LOVE HIM.
JIIING
EH?
JIIING
WHAT'S THAT SOUND?
IT'S PRETTY...
... AND A VERY CLEAR TONE.

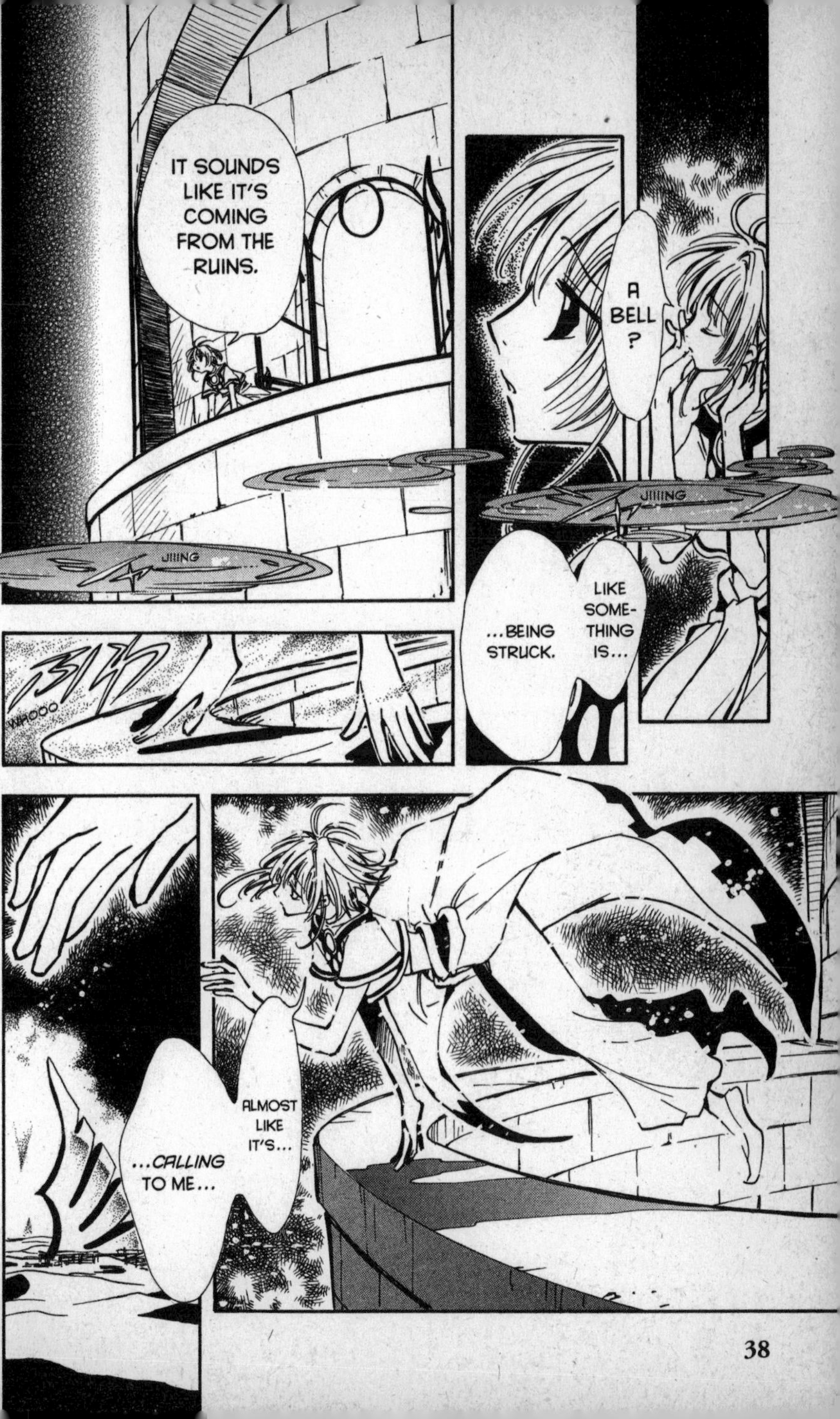
A BELL?
JIIING
LIKE SOMETHING IS...
...BEING STRUCK.
IT SOUNDS LIKE IT'S COMING FROM THE RUINS.
JIIING
WHOOO
ALMOST LIKE IT'S...
...CALLING TO ME...

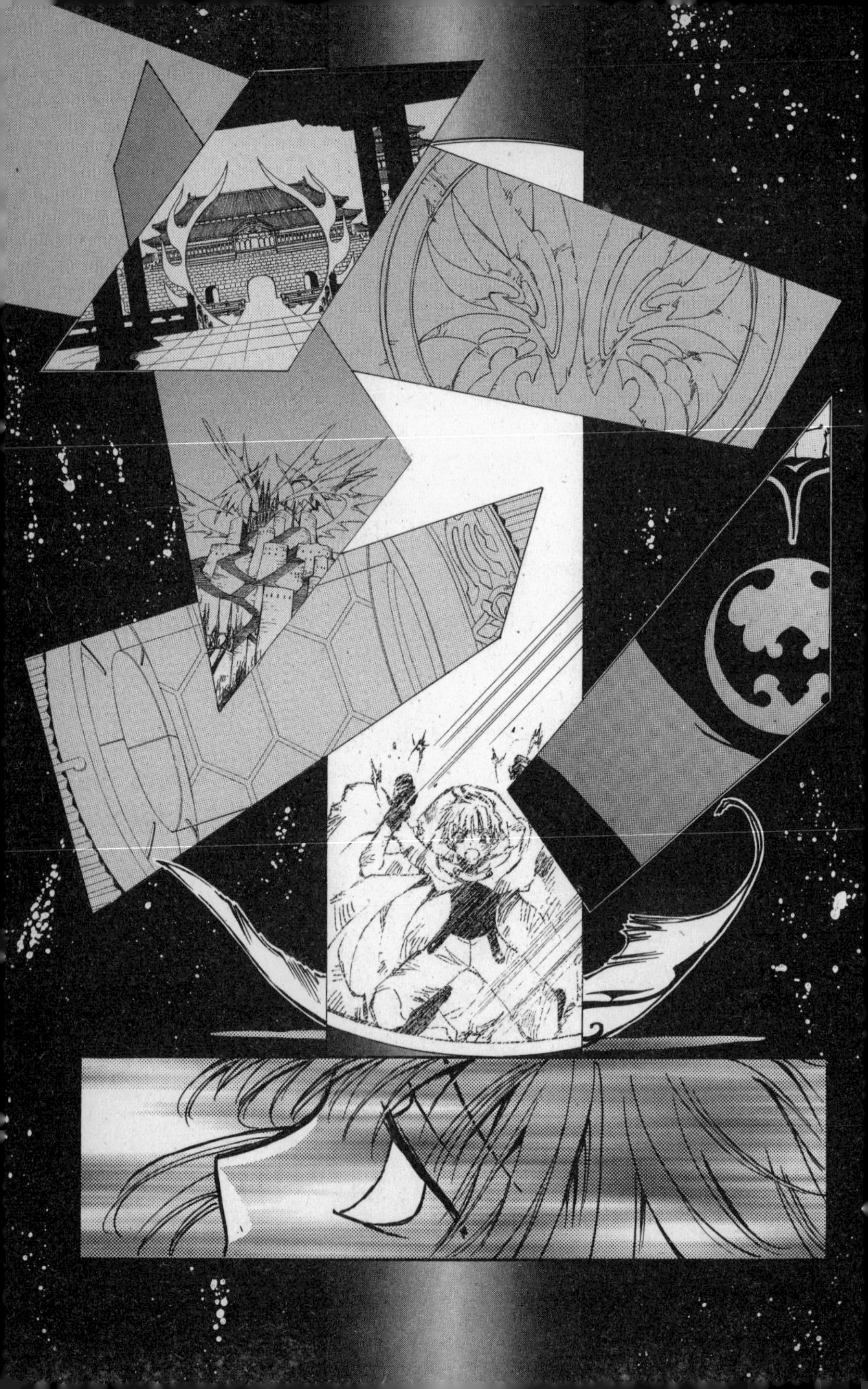

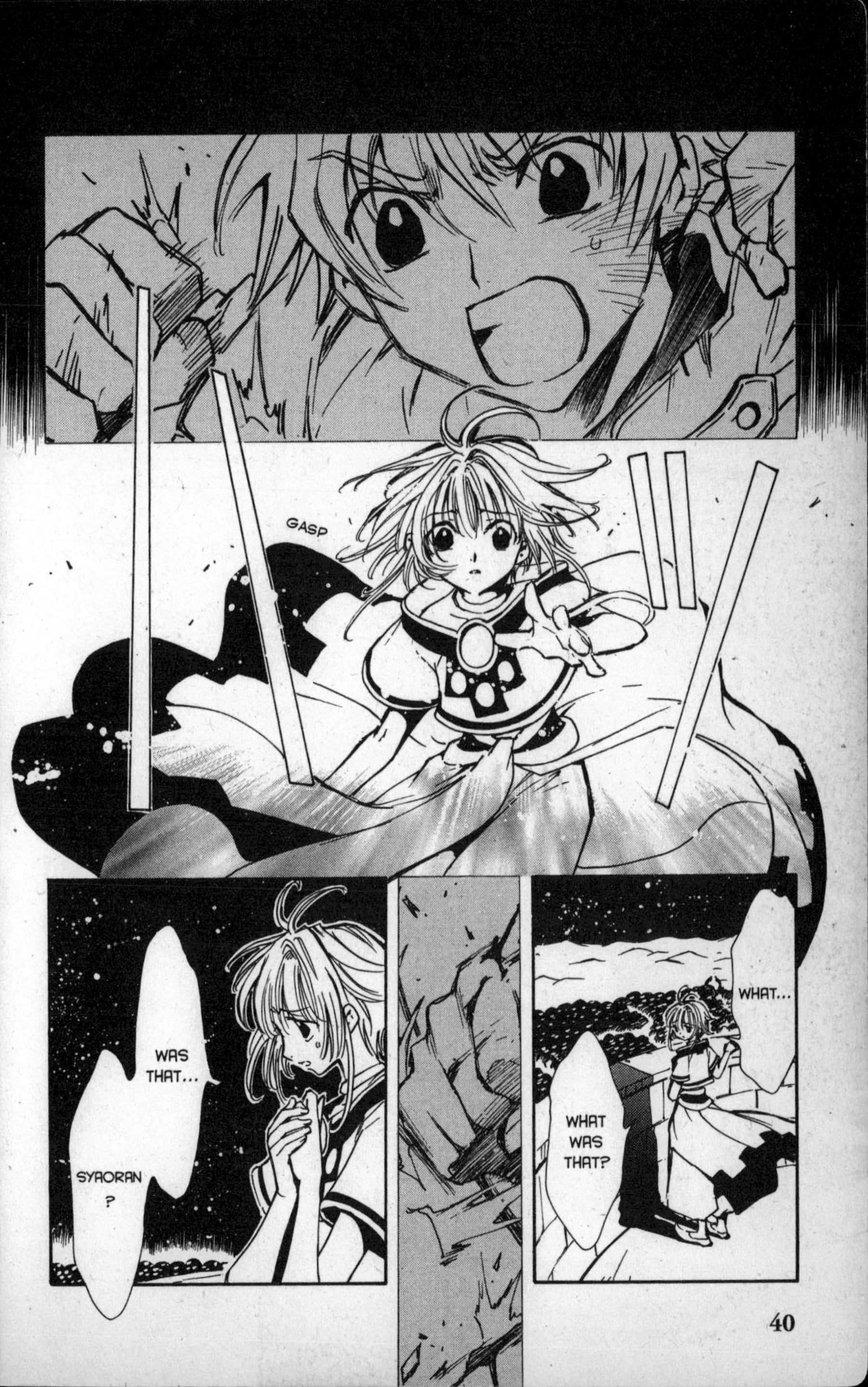
GASP
WHAT...
WHAT WAS THAT?
WAS THAT...
SYAORAN?

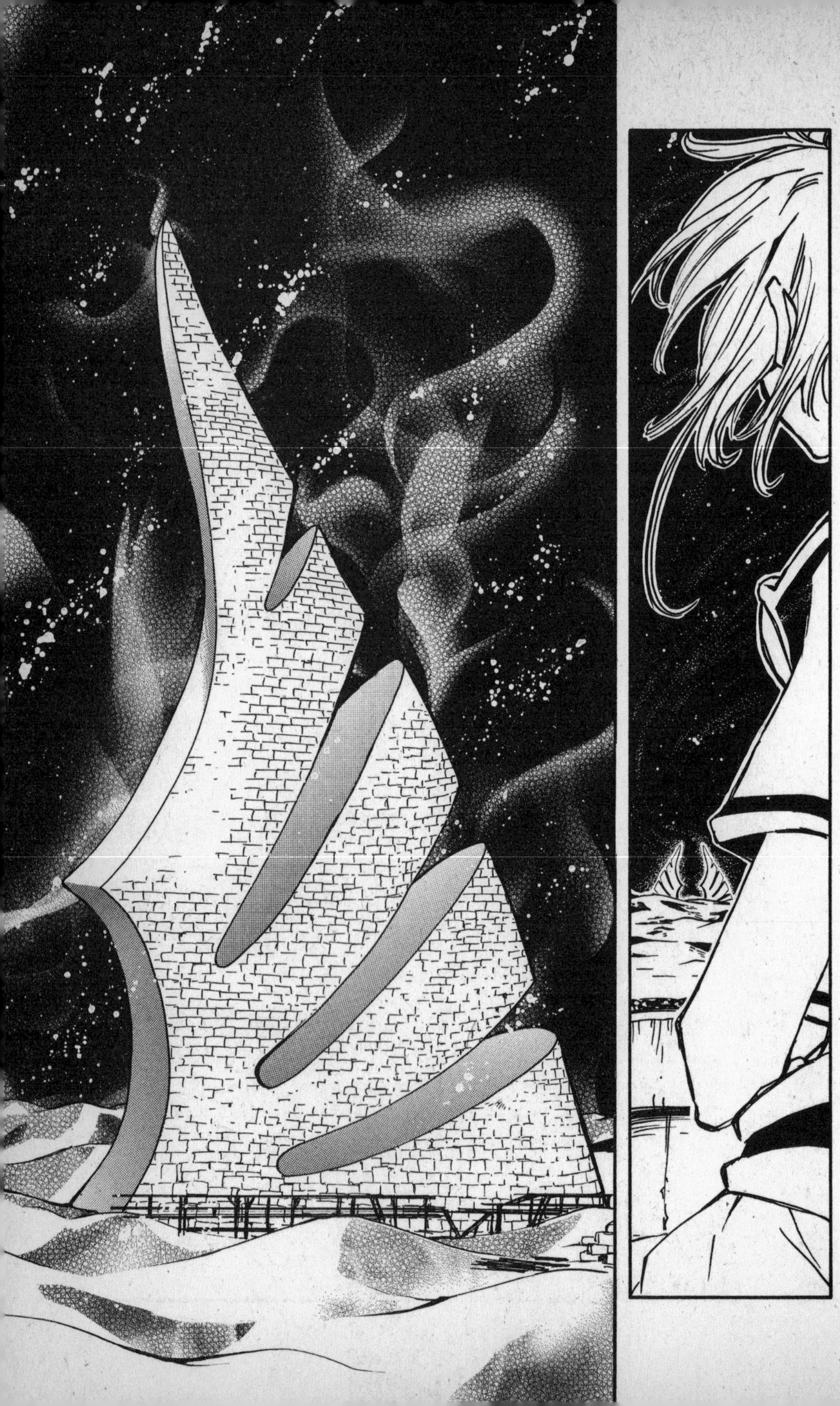

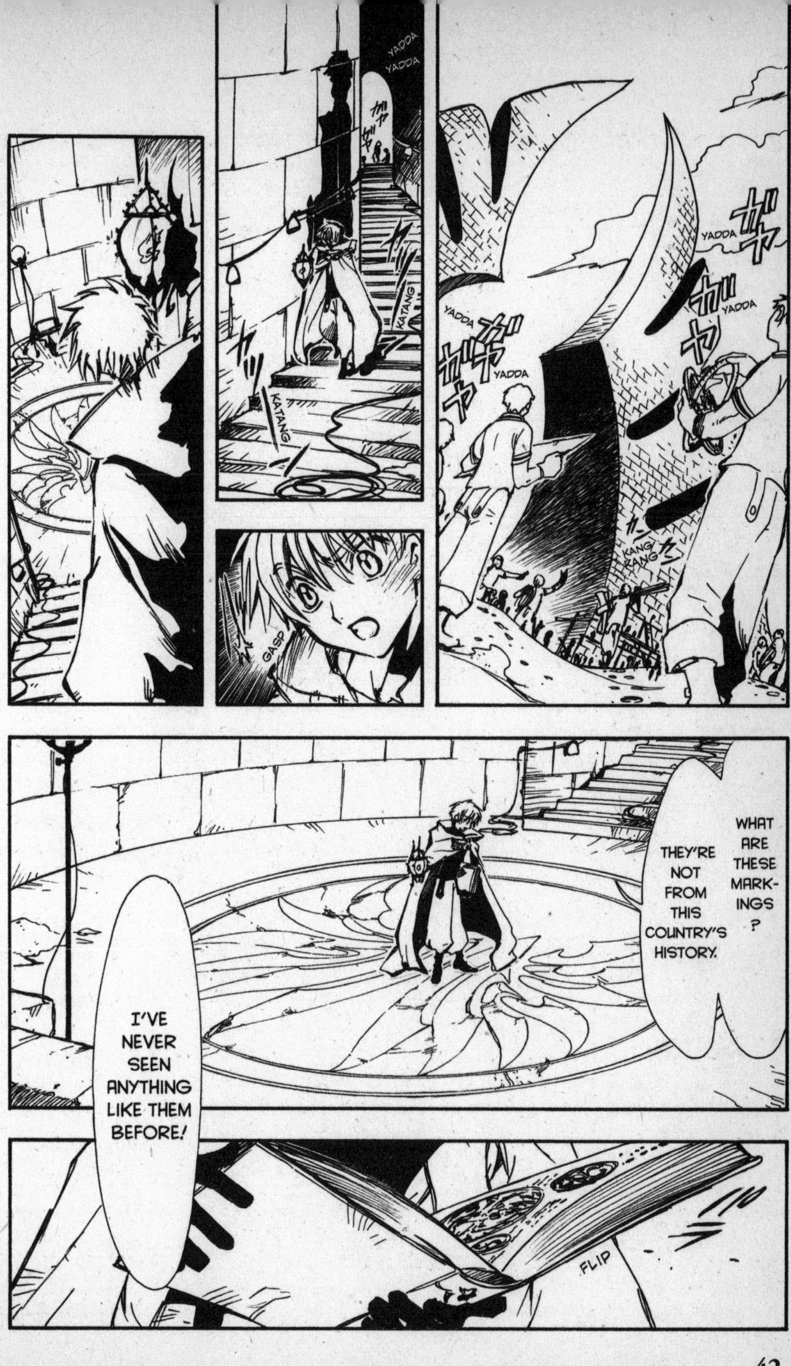
YADDA
YADDA
YADDA
YADDA
KANG KANG
YADDA YADDA
KATANG
KATANG
GASP
WHAT ARE THESE MARKINGS?
THEY'RE NOT FROM THIS COUNTRY'S HISTORY.
I'VE NEVER SEEN ANYTHING LIKE THEM BEFORE!
FLIP

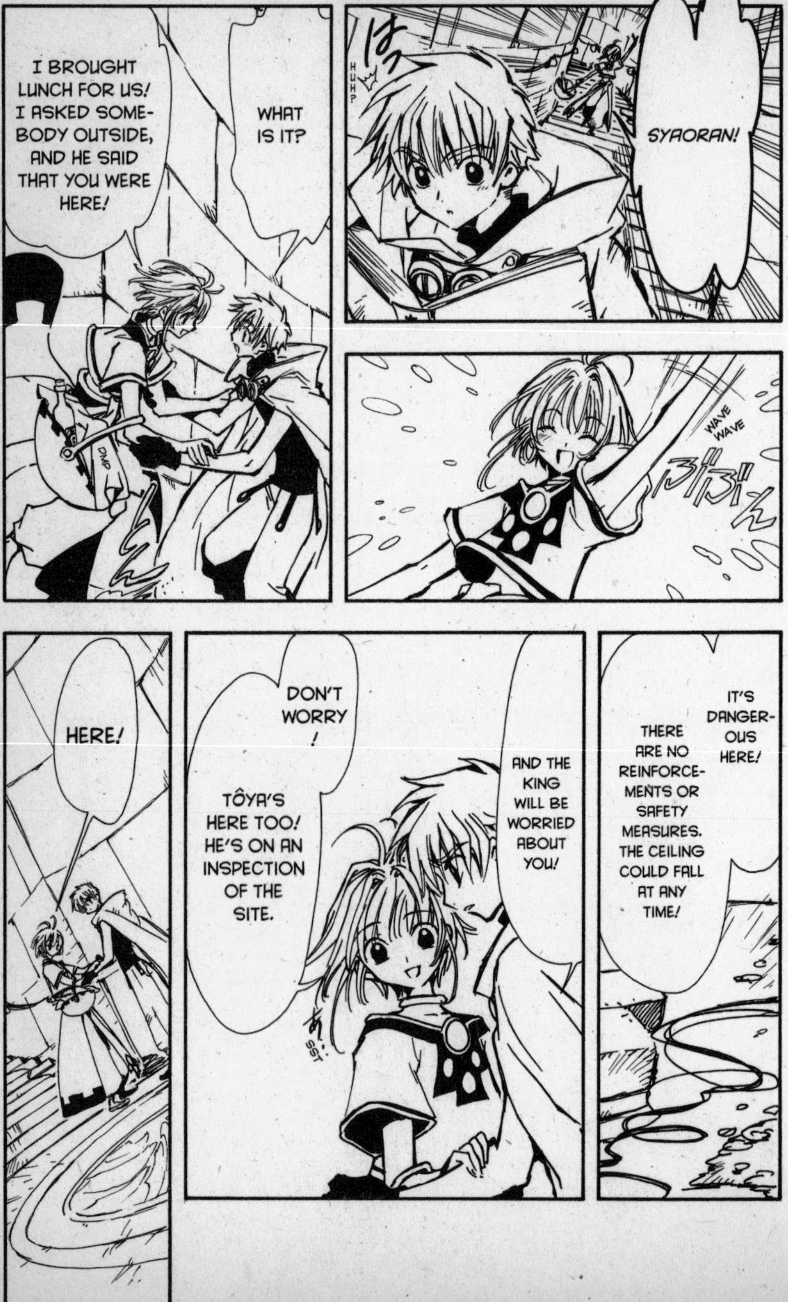
SYAORAN!
はっ
HUH?
WAVE WAVE
ぶんぶん
WHAT IS IT?
I BROUGHT LUNCH FOR US! I ASKED SOMEBODY OUTSIDE, AND HE SAID THAT YOU WERE HERE!
IT'S DANGEROUS HERE!
THERE ARE NO REINFORCEMENTS OR SAFETY MEASURES. THE CEILING COULD FALL AT ANY TIME!
AND THE KING WILL BE WORRIED ABOUT YOU!
DON'T WORRY!
TÔYA'S HERE TOO! HE'S ON AN INSPECTION OF THE SITE.
あ
SST
HERE!

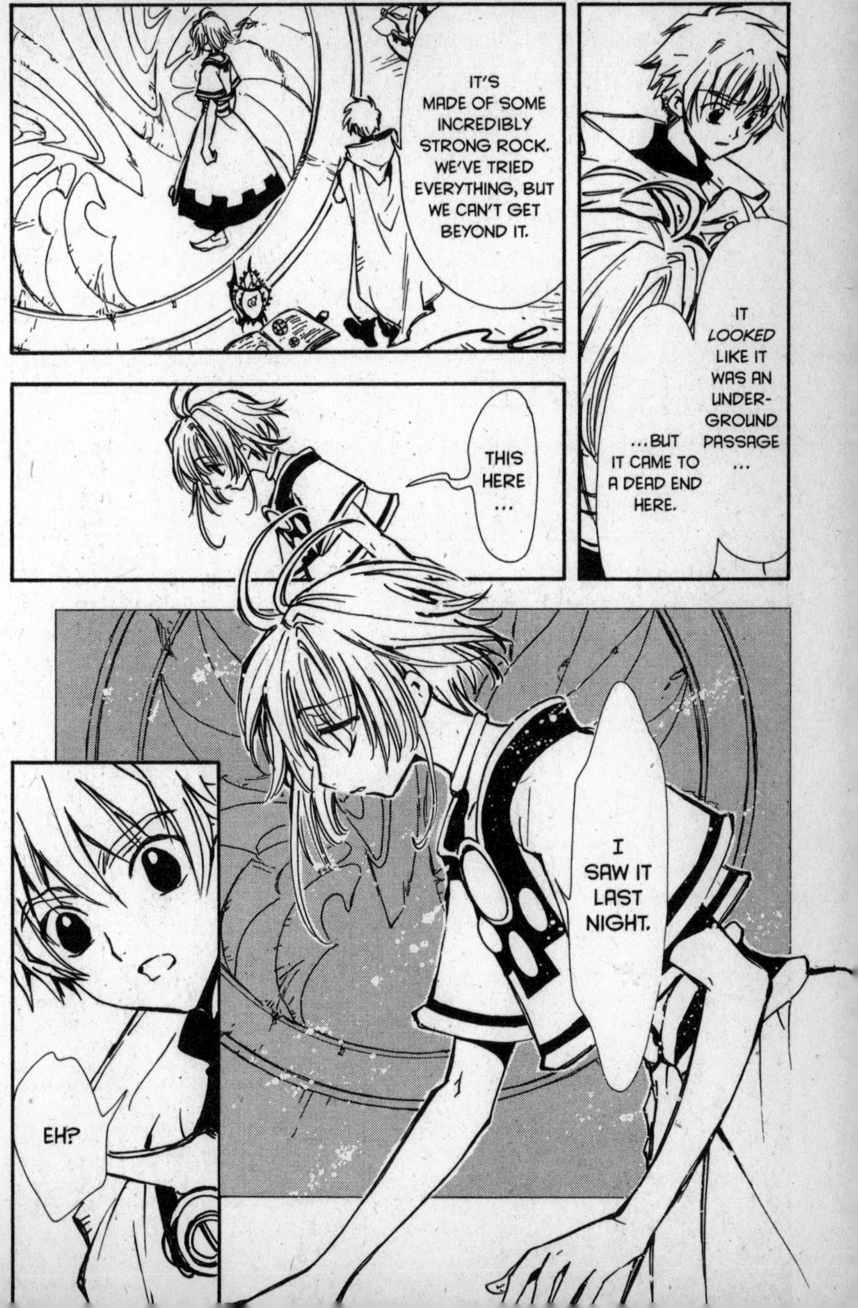
IT *LOOKED* LIKE IT WAS AN UNDER-GROUND PASSAGE...
...BUT IT CAME TO A DEAD END HERE.
IT'S MADE OF SOME INCREDIBLY STRONG ROCK. WE'VE TRIED EVERYTHING, BUT WE CAN'T GET BEYOND IT.
THIS HERE...
I SAW IT LAST NIGHT.
EH?

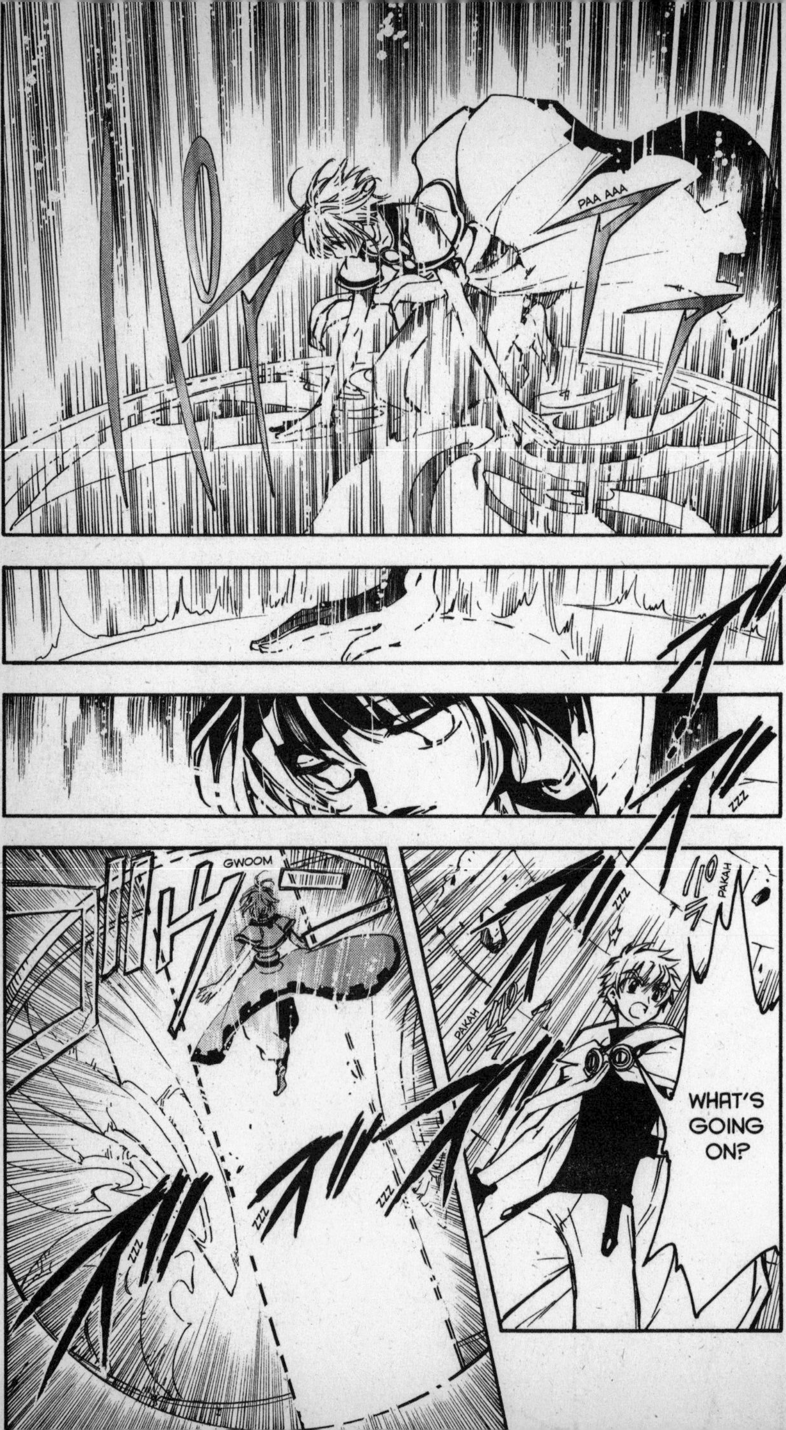
PAA AAA
ZZZ
ZZZ
PAKAH
ZZZ
PAKAH
WHAT'S GOING ON?
GWOOM
ZZZ
ZZZ
ZZZ

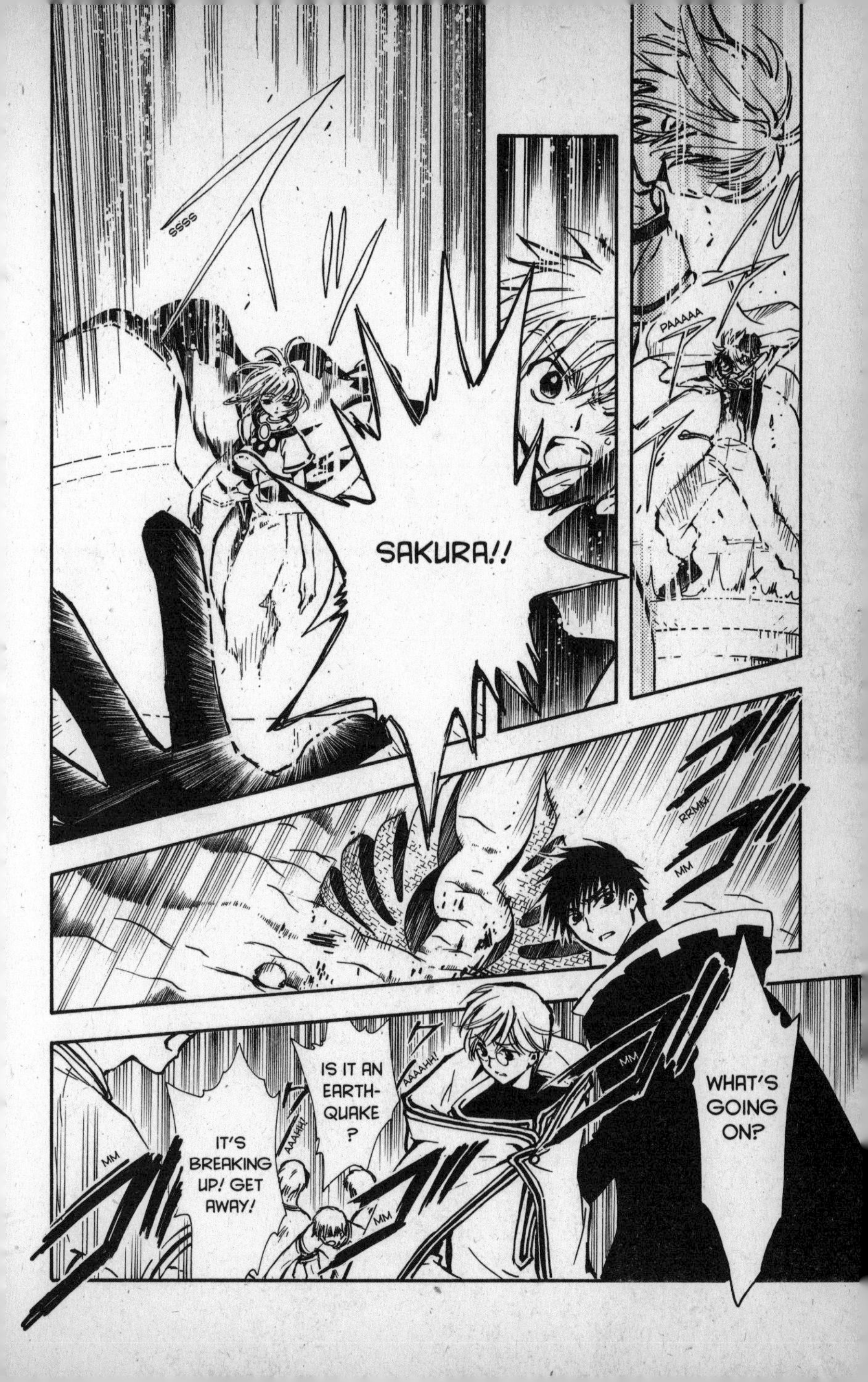
PAAAAA
SAKURA!!
SSSS
RRMMM
MM
WHAT'S GOING ON?
MM
IS IT AN EARTH-QUAKE?
AAAAHH!
AAAAHH!
IT'S BREAKING UP! GET AWAY!
MM
MM

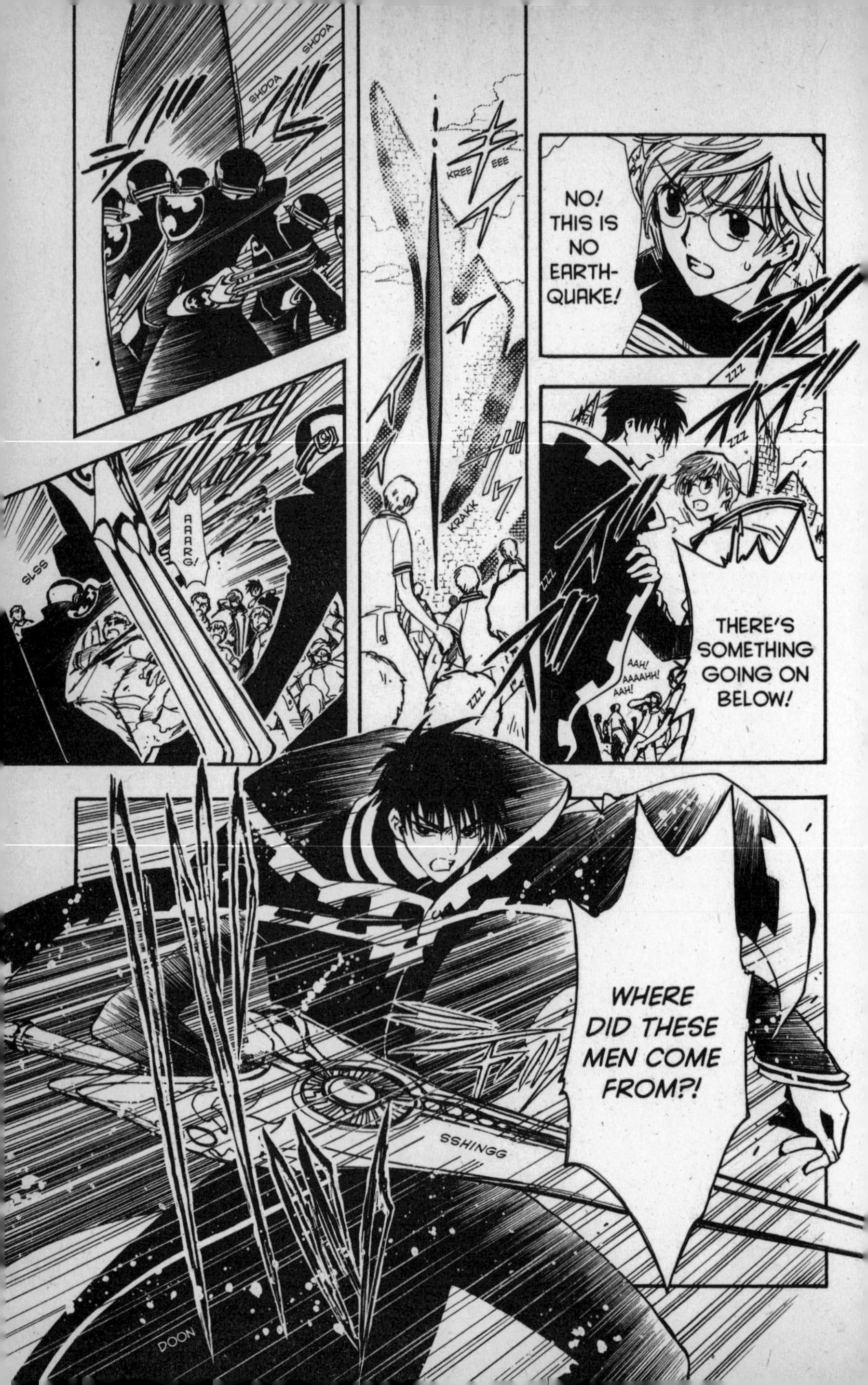
NO! THIS IS NO EARTH-QUAKE!
ZZZ
ZZZ
THERE'S SOMETHING GOING ON BELOW!
AAH! AAAAHH! AAH!
ZZZ
KREE EEE
KRAKK
ZZZ
SHODDA SHODDA
AAAARG!
SLSS
WHERE DID THESE MEN COME FROM?!
SSHINGG
DOON

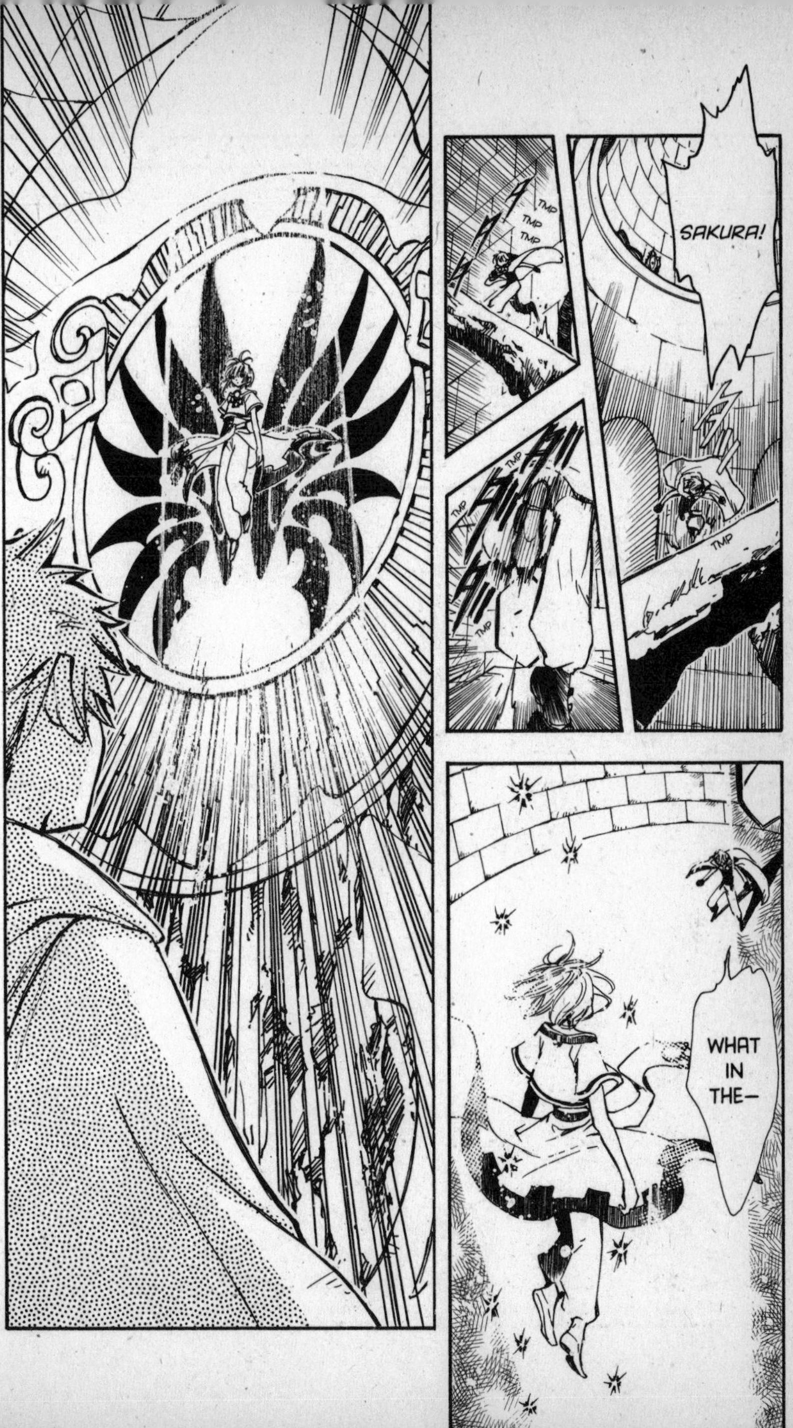
SAKURA!
TMP
TMP
TMP
TMP
TMP
TMP
TMP
TMP
WHAT IN THE—

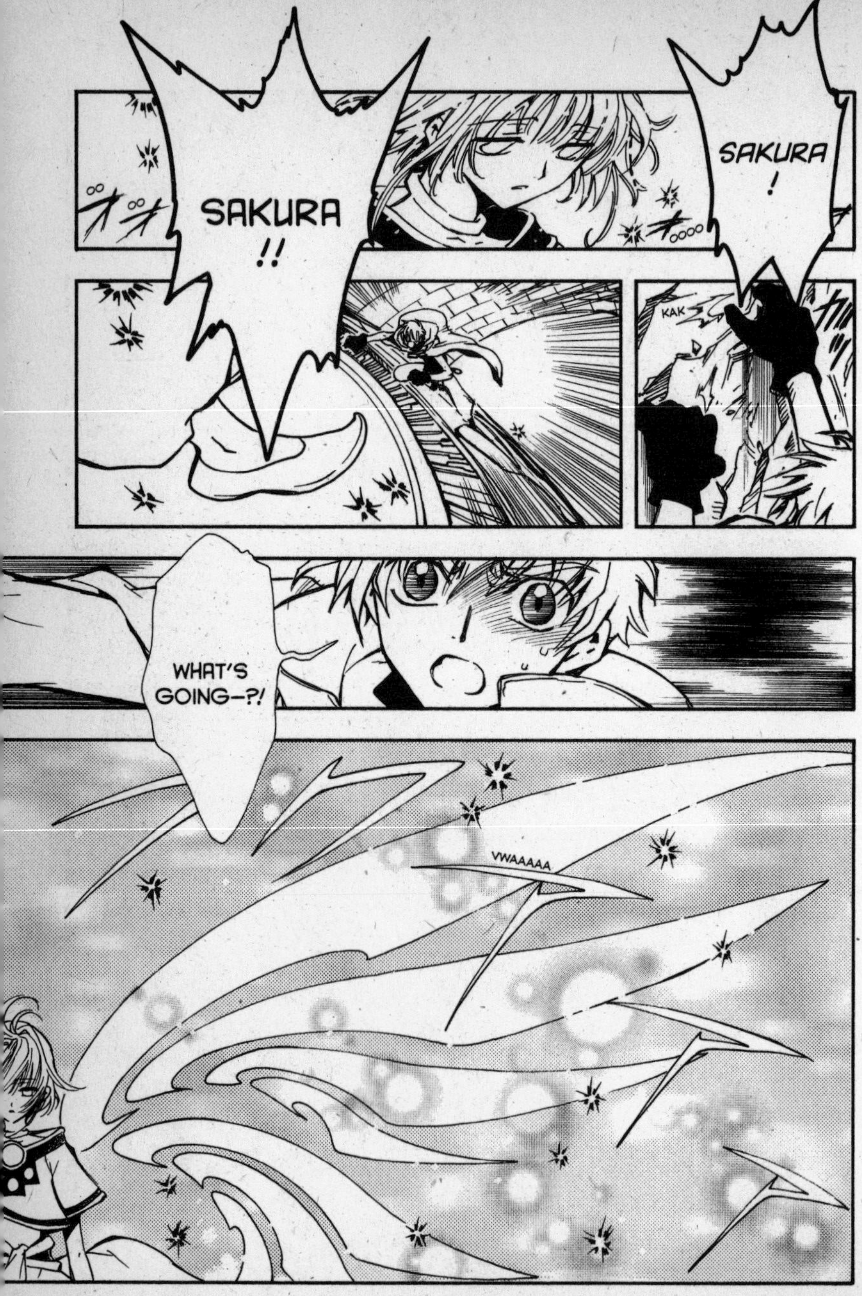
SAKURA !
SAKURA !!
KAK
WHAT'S GOING-?!
VWAAAAA

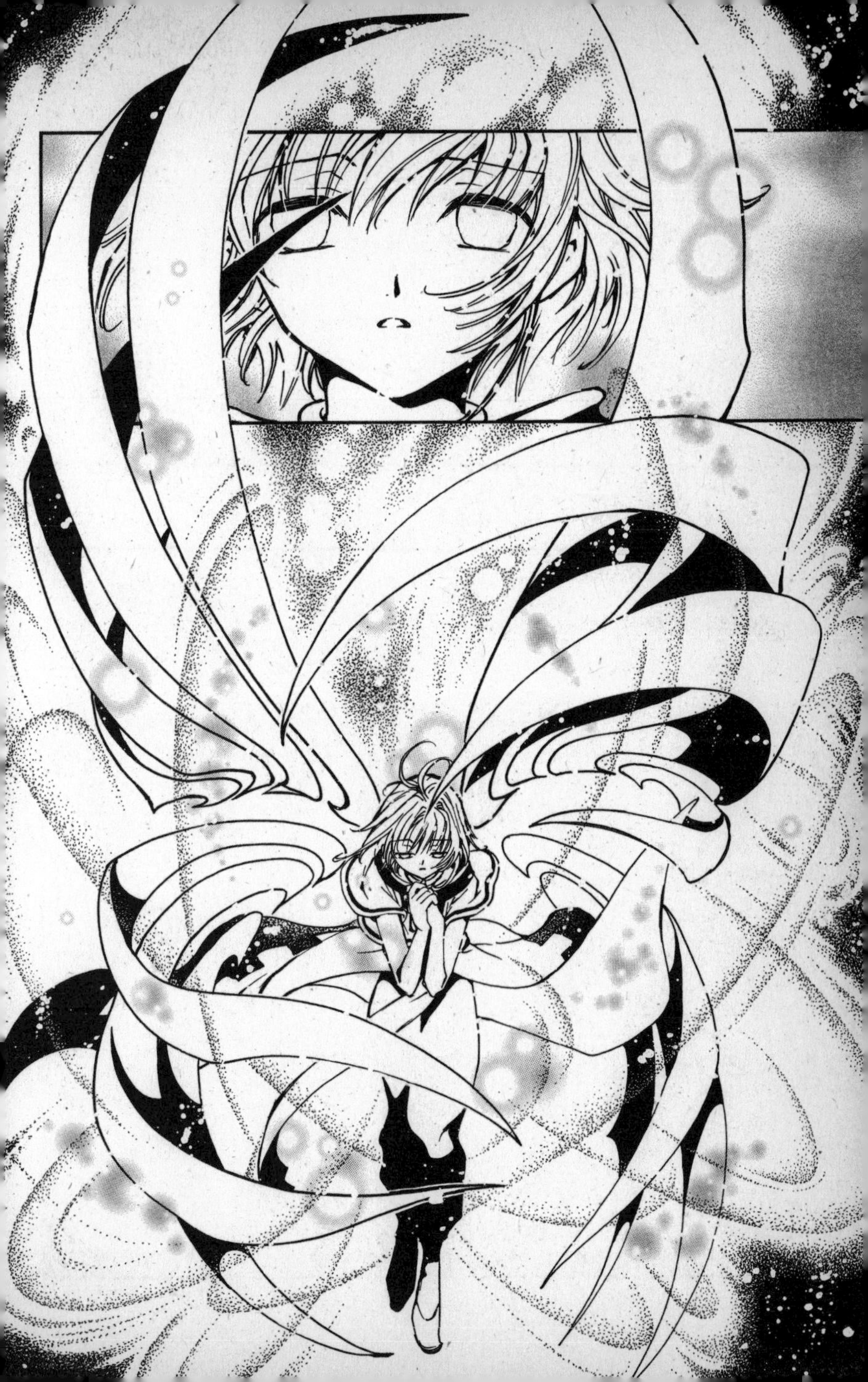

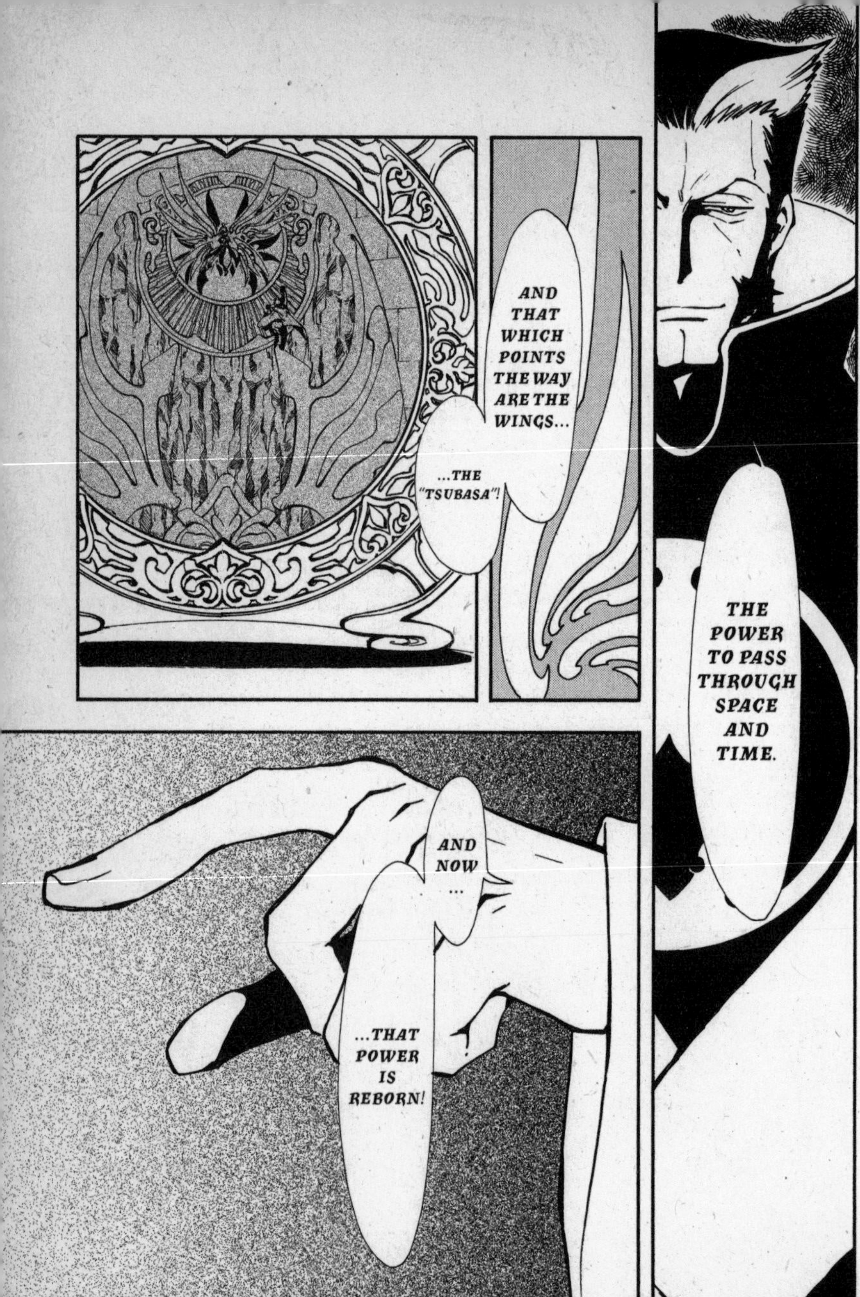
THE POWER TO PASS THROUGH SPACE AND TIME.
AND THAT WHICH POINTS THE WAY ARE THE WINGS...
...THE "TSUBASA"!
AND NOW...
...THAT POWER IS REBORN!

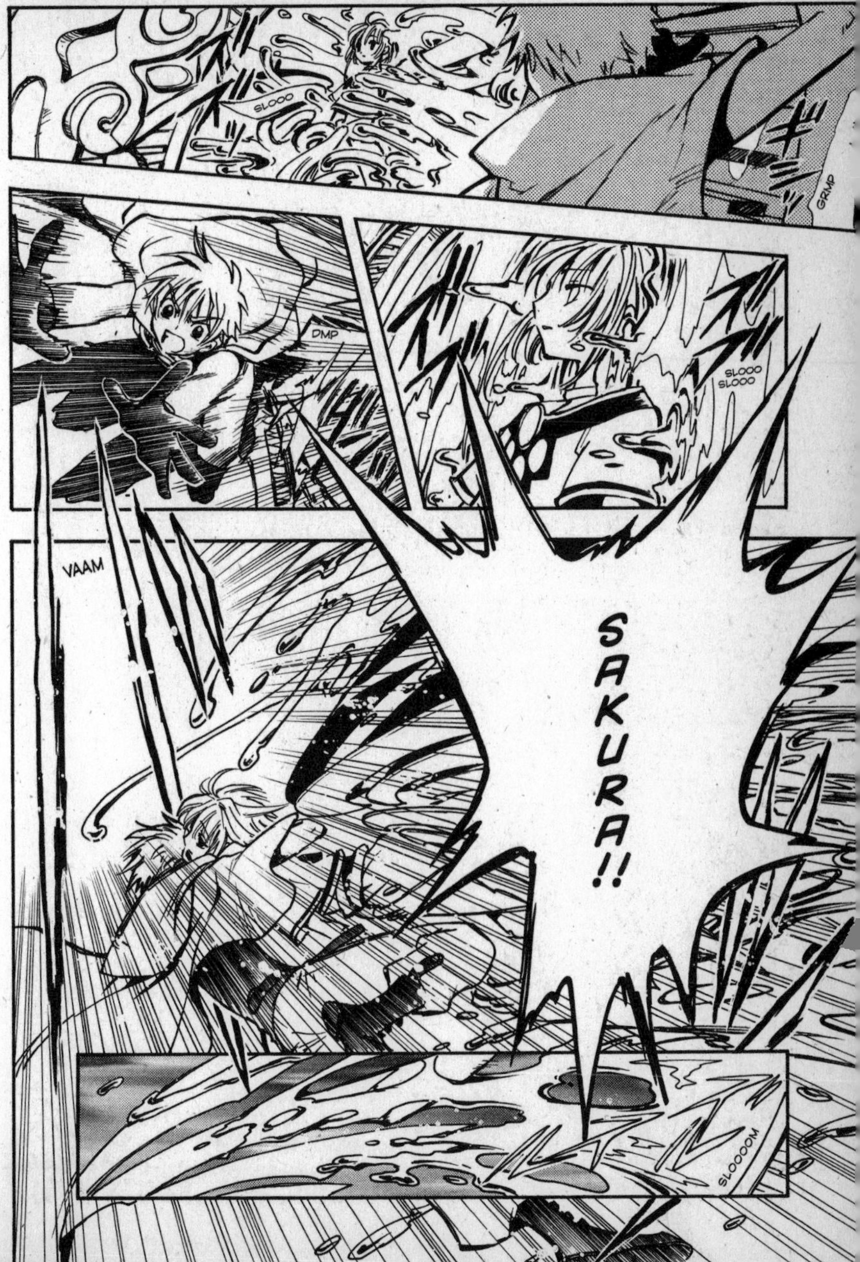
SLOOO
GRMP
SLOOO
SLOOO
DMP
SAKURA!!
VAAM
SLOOOOM

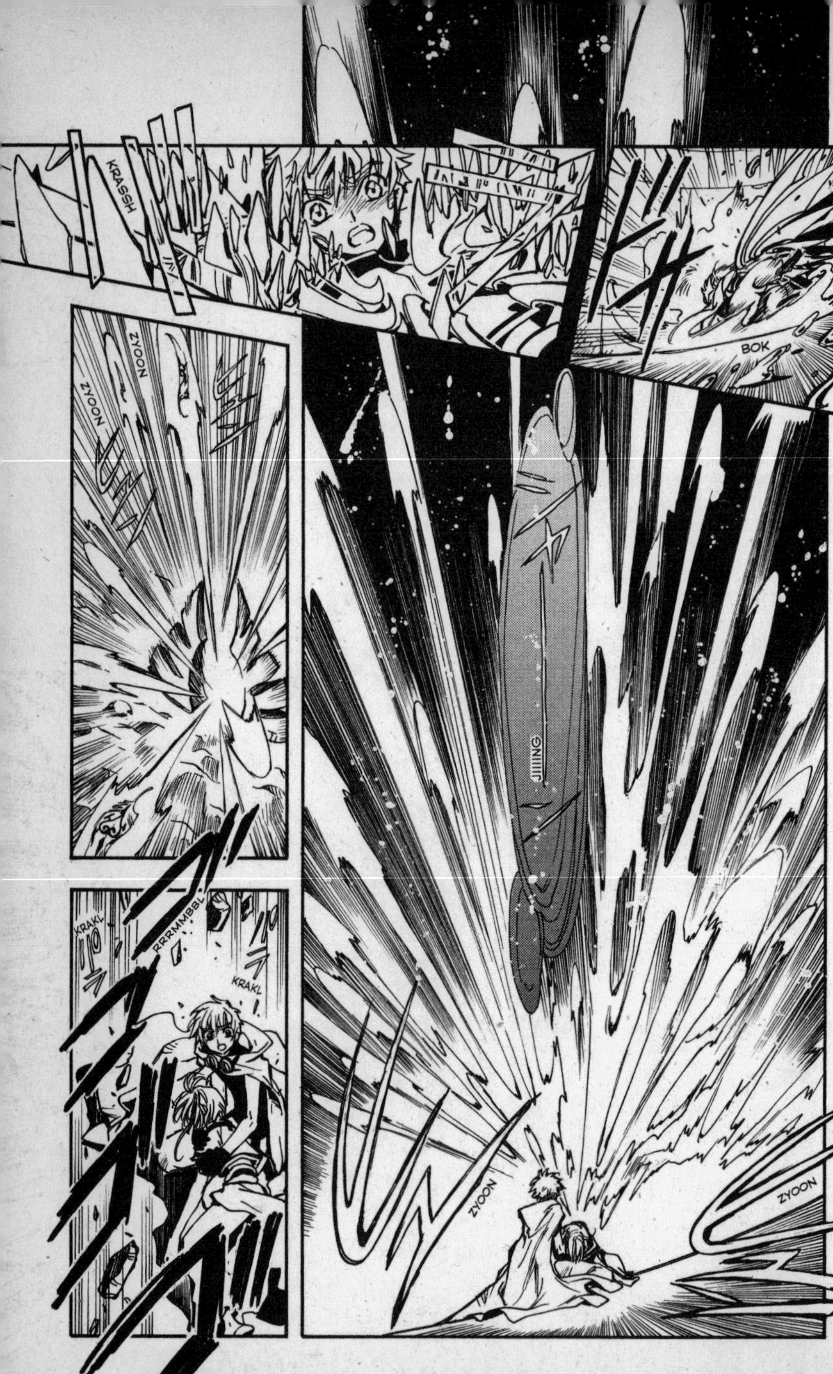
BOK
KRASSH
JIIIING
ZYOON
ZYOON
ZYOON
ZYOON
RRRMMBBL
KRAKL
KRAKL

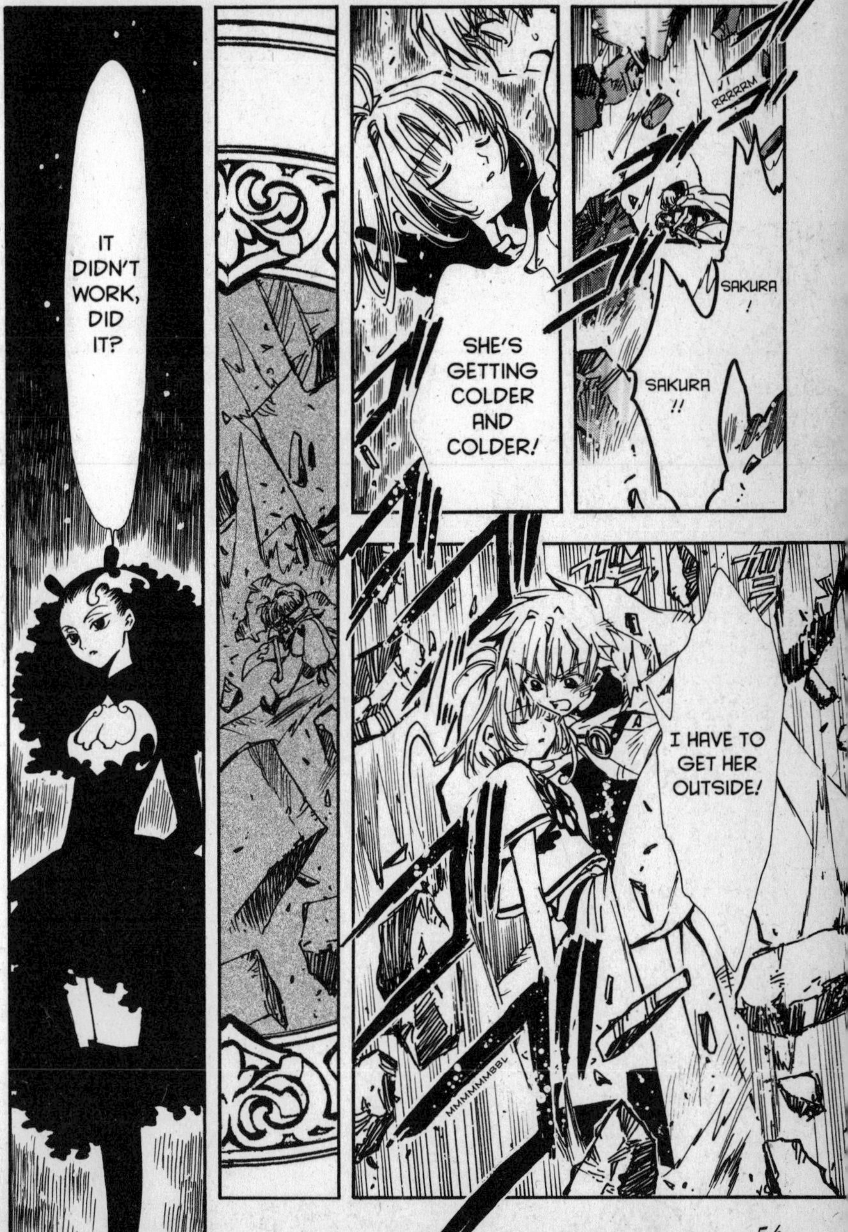
RRRRRM
SAKURA!
SAKURA!!
SHE'S GETTING COLDER AND COLDER!
I HAVE TO GET HER OUTSIDE!
MMMMMBBL
IT DIDN'T WORK, DID IT?

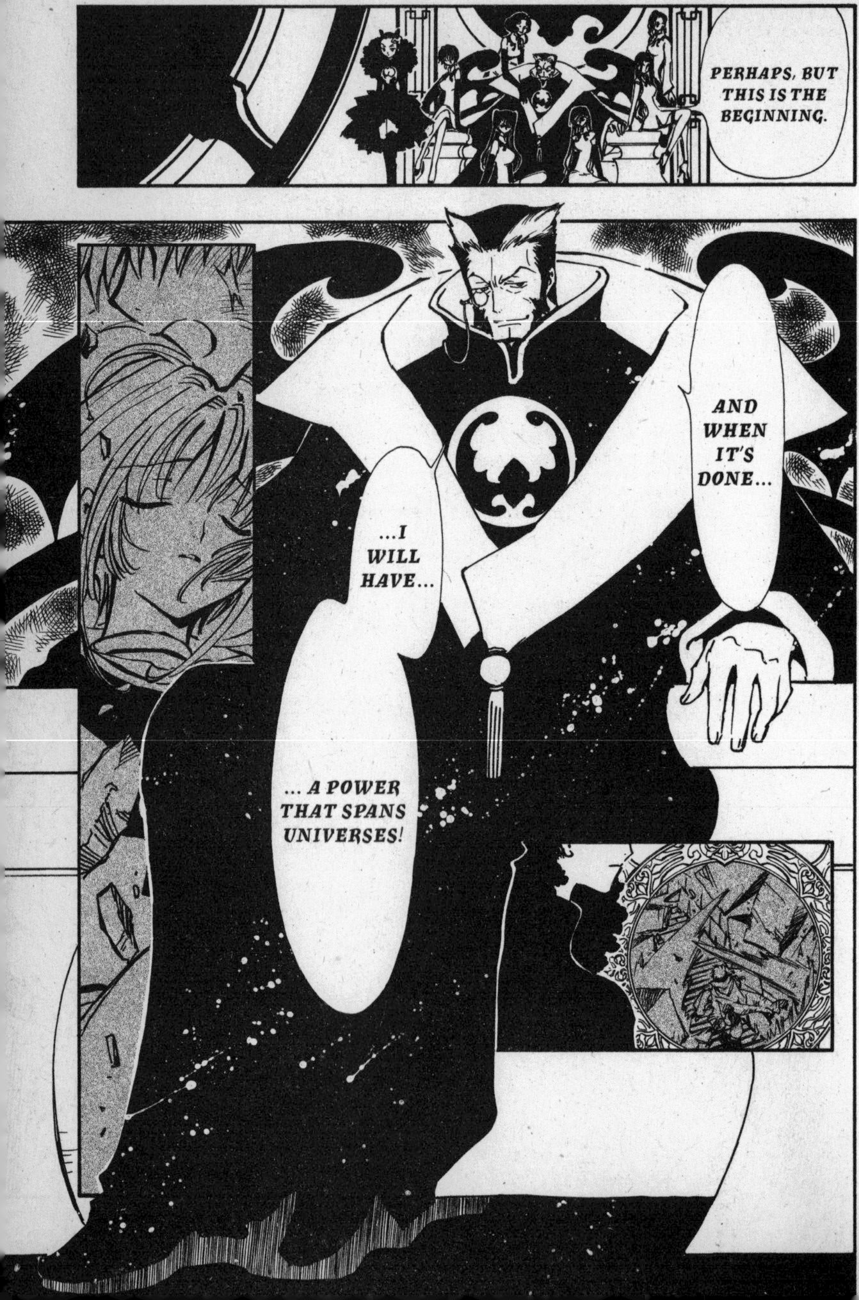
PERHAPS, BUT THIS IS THE BEGINNING.
AND WHEN IT'S DONE...
...I WILL HAVE...
... A POWER THAT SPANS UNIVERSES!

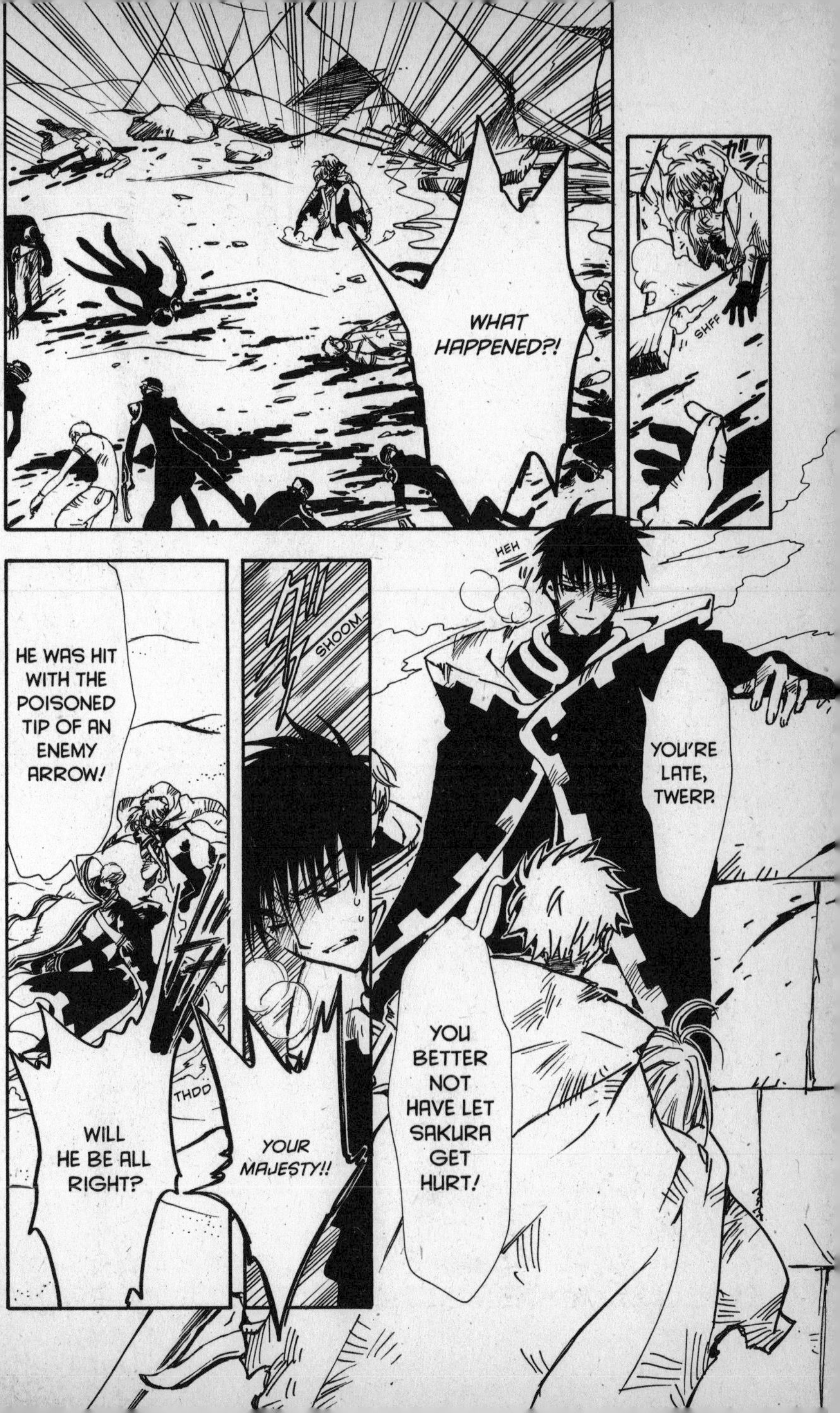
SHFF
WHAT HAPPENED?!
HEH
YOU'RE LATE, TWERP.
YOU BETTER NOT HAVE LET SAKURA GET HURT!
SHOOM
YOUR MAJESTY!!
HE WAS HIT WITH THE POISONED TIP OF AN ENEMY ARROW!
THDD
WILL HE BE ALL RIGHT?

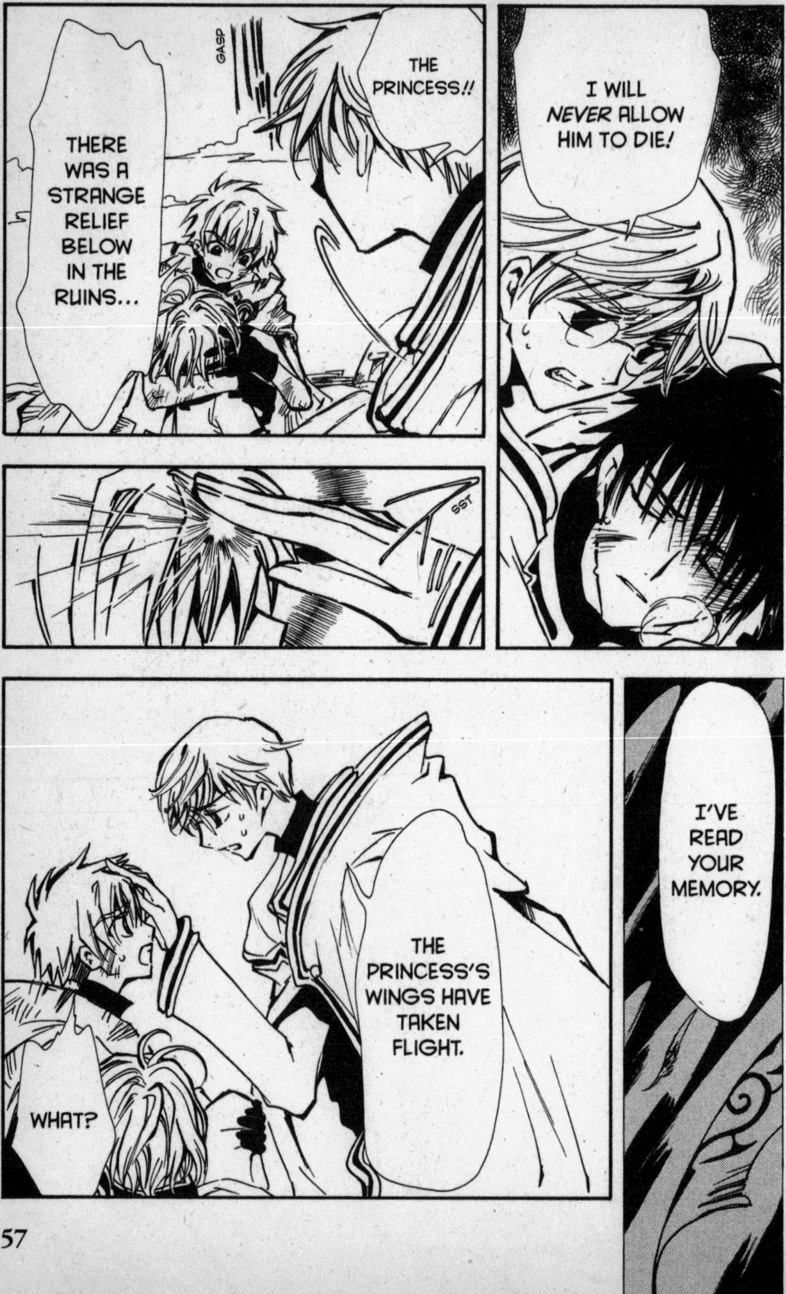
I WILL *NEVER* ALLOW HIM TO DIE!
THE PRINCESS!!
GASP
THERE WAS A STRANGE RELIEF BELOW IN THE RUINS...
SST
I'VE READ YOUR MEMORY.
THE PRINCESS'S WINGS HAVE TAKEN FLIGHT.
WHAT?

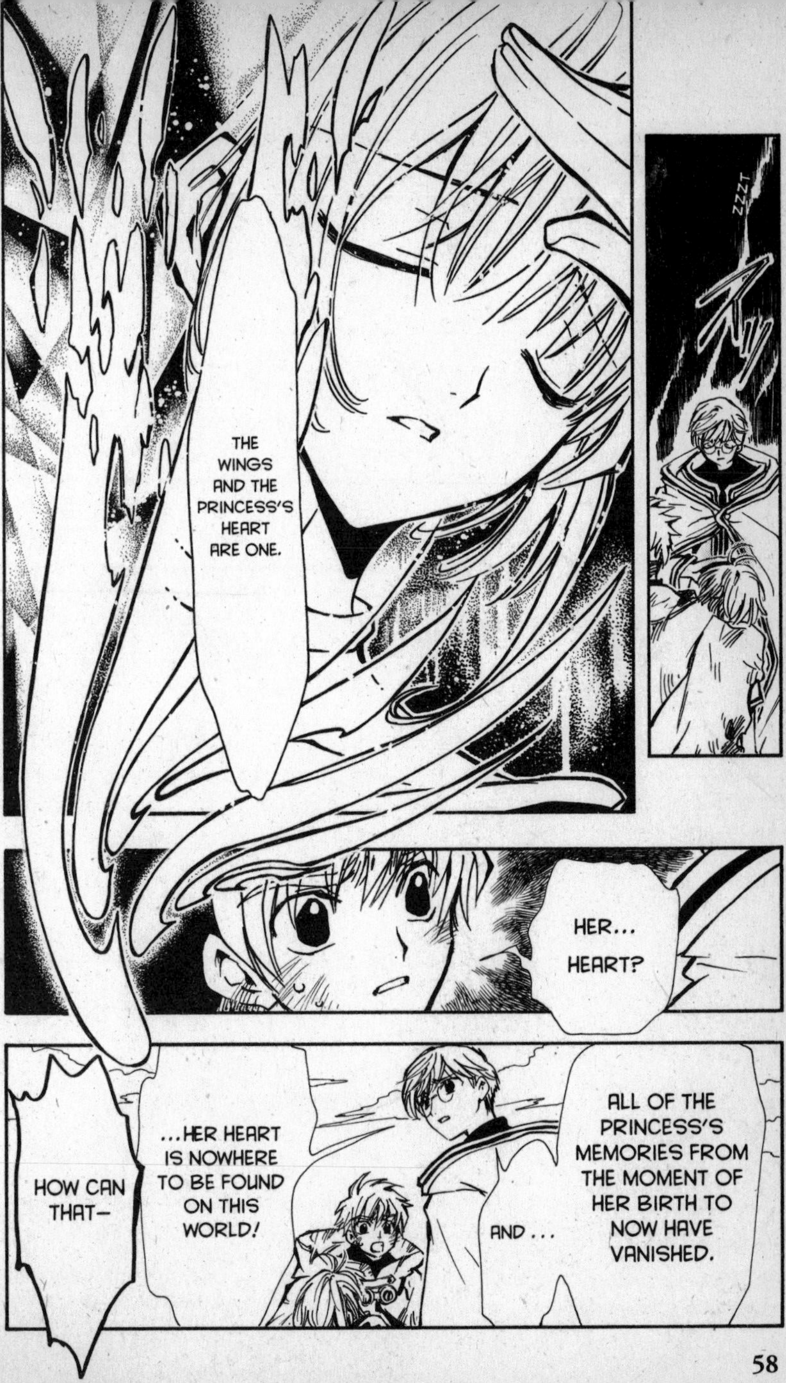
ZZZT
THE WINGS AND THE PRINCESS'S HEART ARE ONE.
HER... HEART?
ALL OF THE PRINCESS'S MEMORIES FROM THE MOMENT OF HER BIRTH TO NOW HAVE VANISHED.
AND...
...HER HEART IS NOWHERE TO BE FOUND ON THIS WORLD!
HOW CAN THAT—

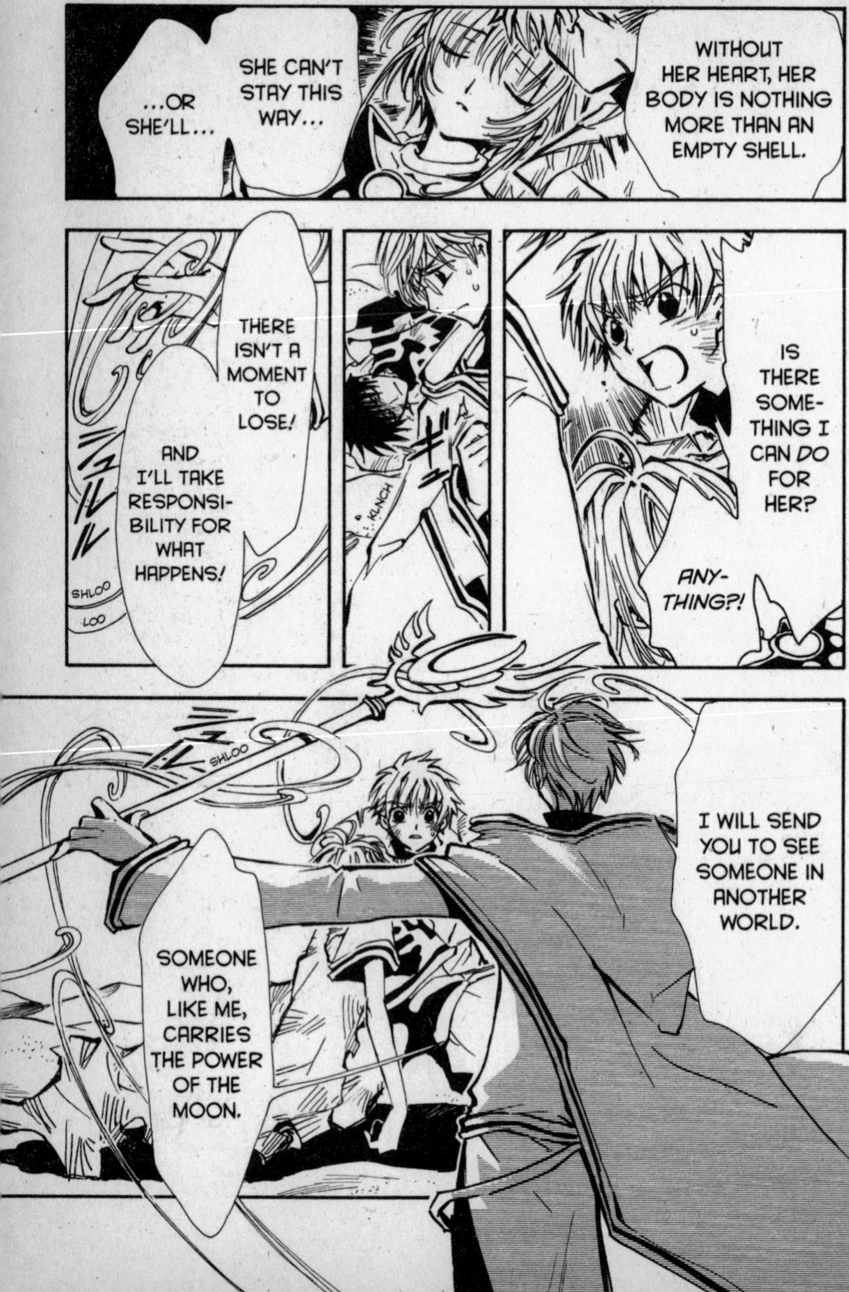
WITHOUT HER HEART, HER BODY IS NOTHING MORE THAN AN EMPTY SHELL.
SHE CAN'T STAY THIS WAY...
...OR SHE'LL...
IS THERE SOME-THING I CAN *DO* FOR HER?
ANY-THING?!
KLNCH
THERE ISN'T A MOMENT TO LOSE!
AND I'LL TAKE RESPONSI-BILITY FOR WHAT HAPPENS!
SHLOO
LOO
I WILL SEND YOU TO SEE SOMEONE IN ANOTHER WORLD.
SHLOO
SOMEONE WHO, LIKE ME, CARRIES THE POWER OF THE MOON.

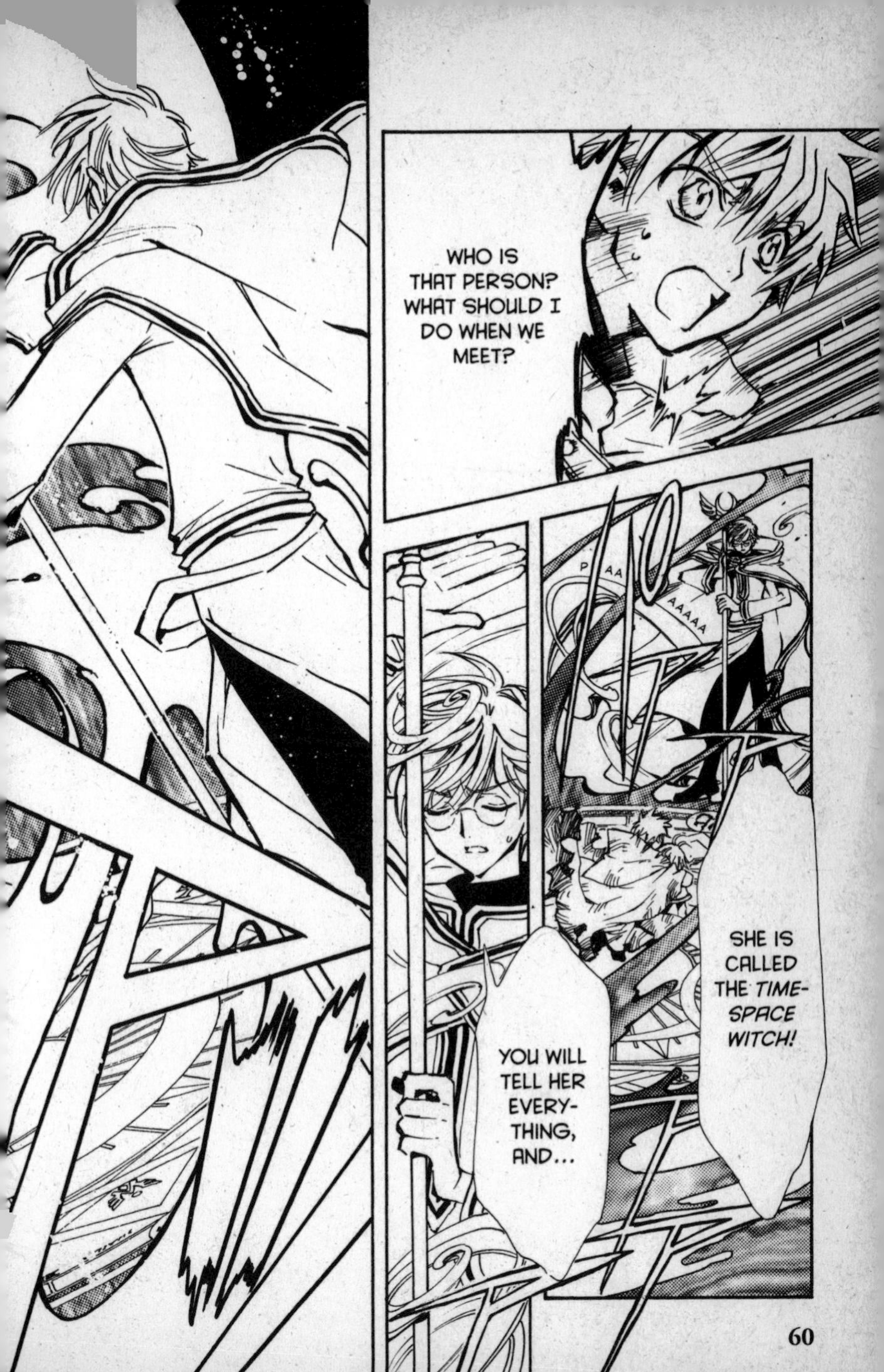
WHO IS THAT PERSON? WHAT SHOULD I DO WHEN WE MEET?
PAAAAAAA
SHE IS CALLED THE *TIME-SPACE WITCH!*
YOU WILL TELL HER EVERY-THING, AND...

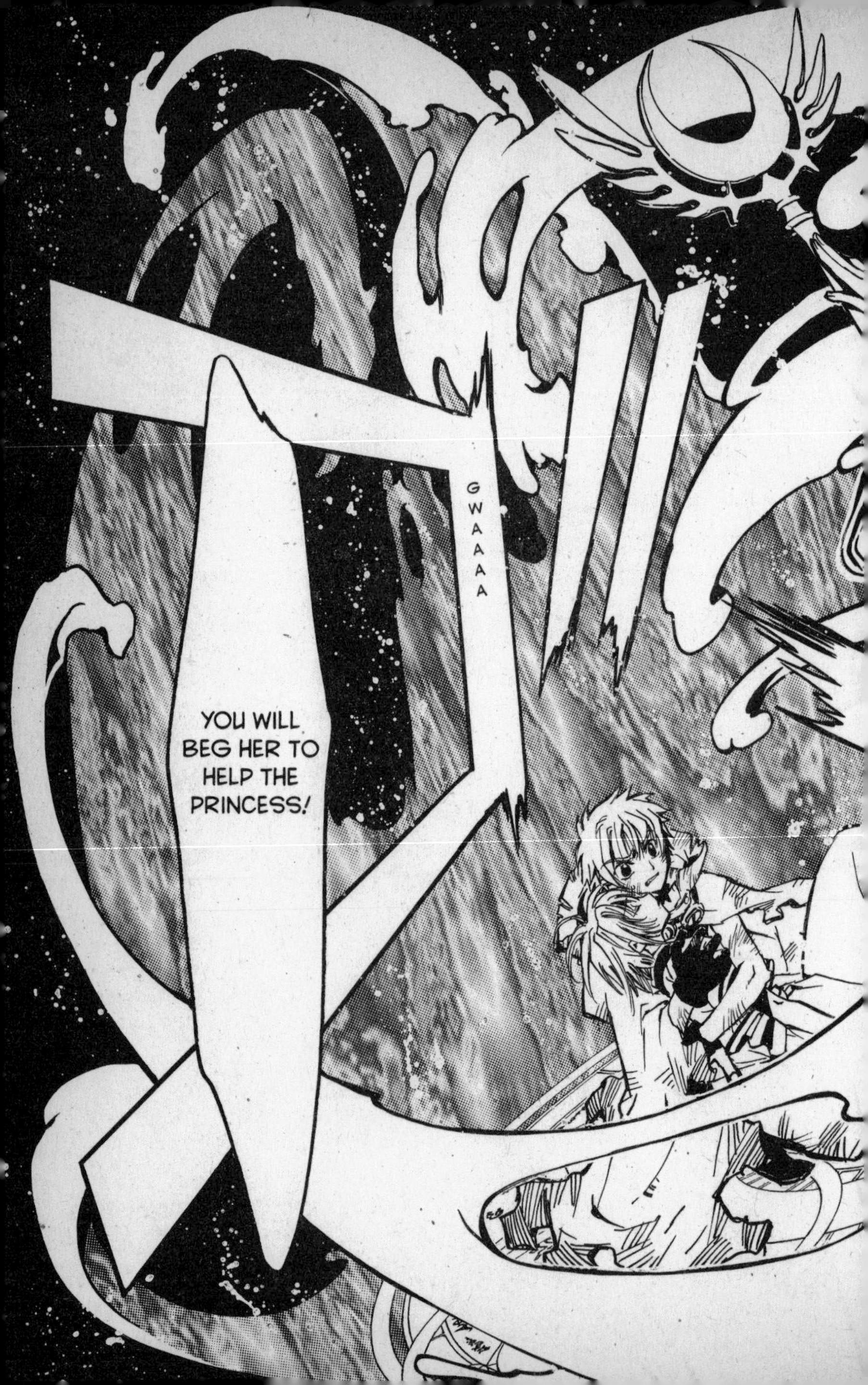
GWAAAA
YOU WILL BEG HER TO HELP THE PRINCESS!

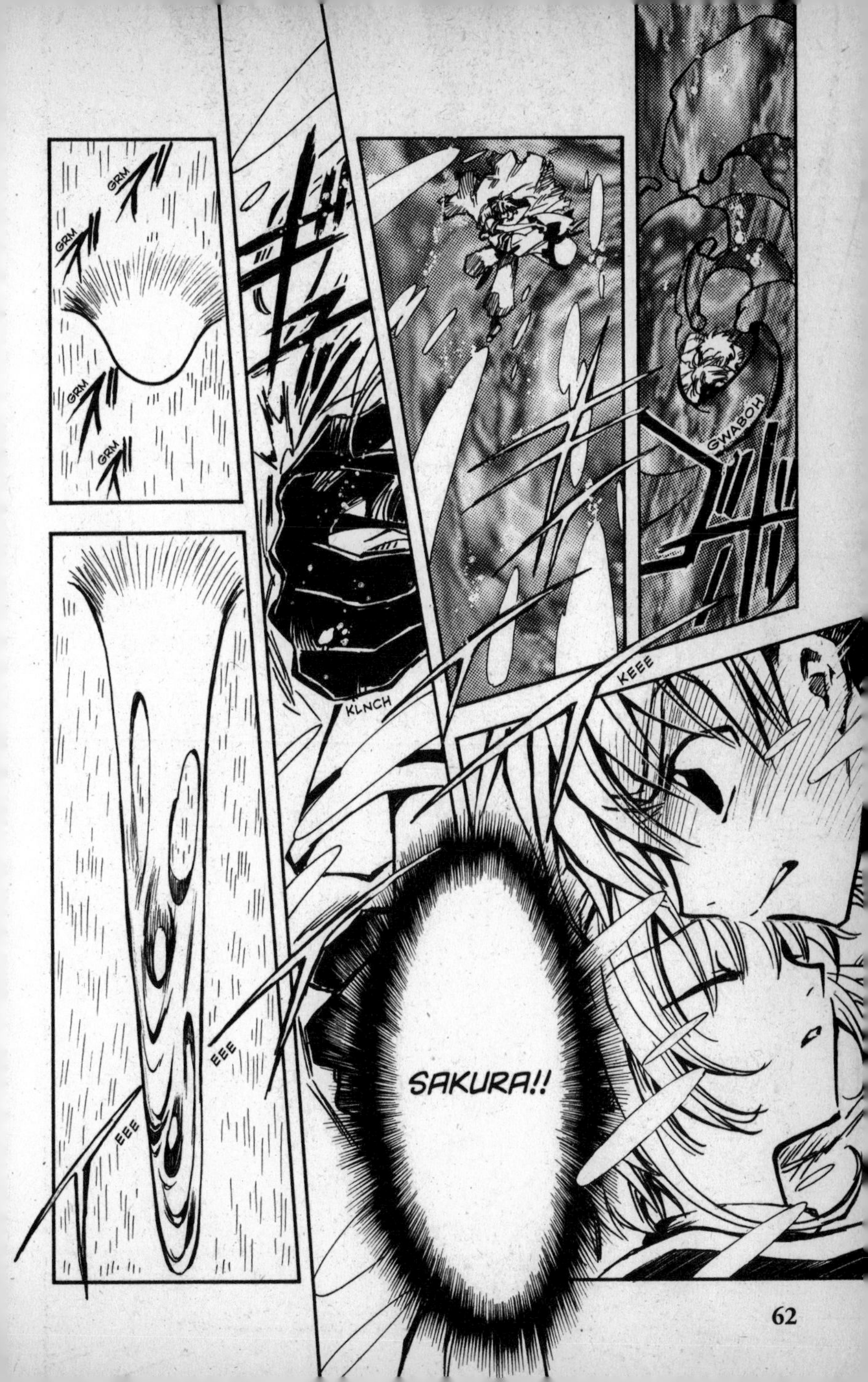
GWABOH
KLNCH
GRM
GRM
GRM
GRM
KEEE
SAKURA!!
EEE
EEE

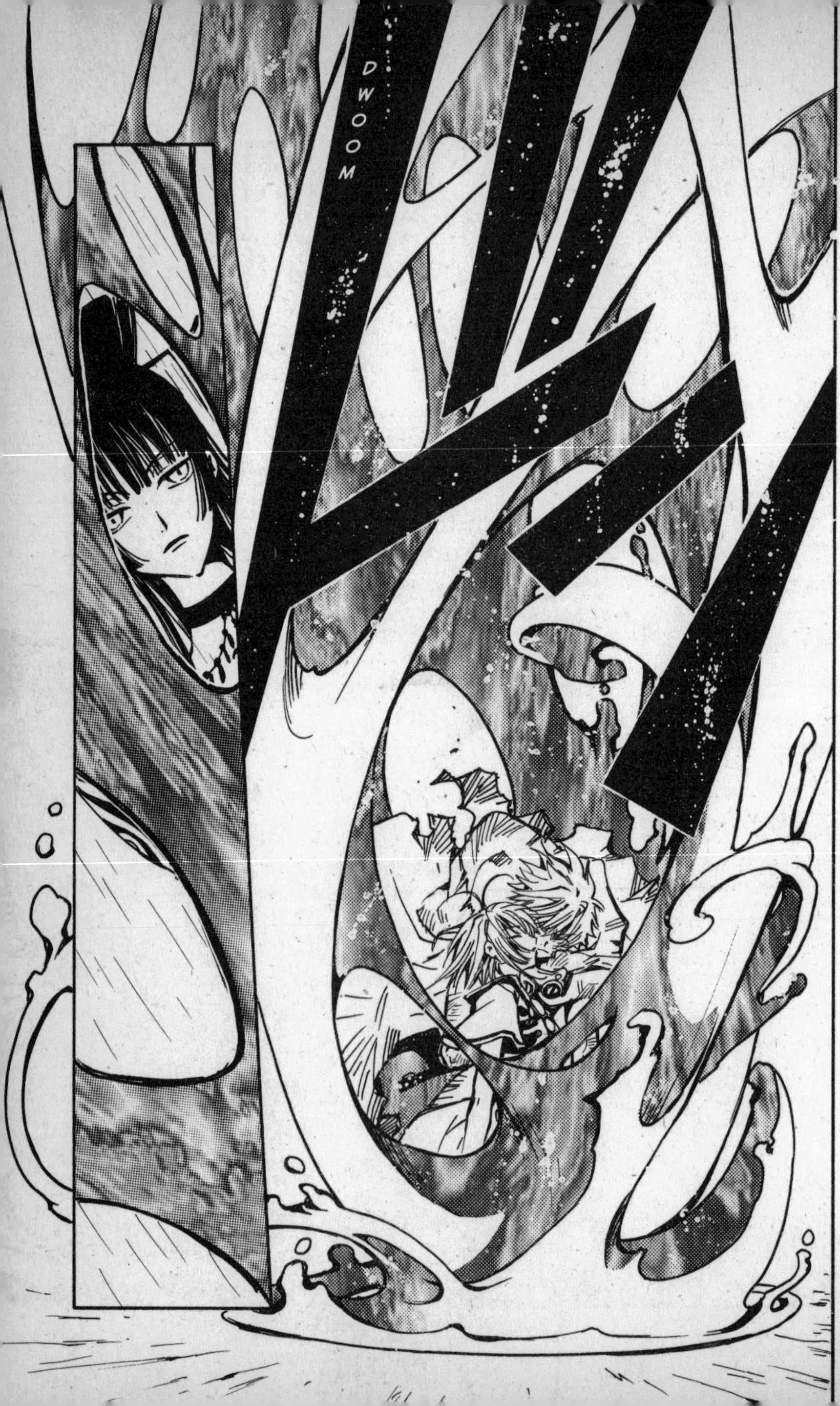
DWOOM

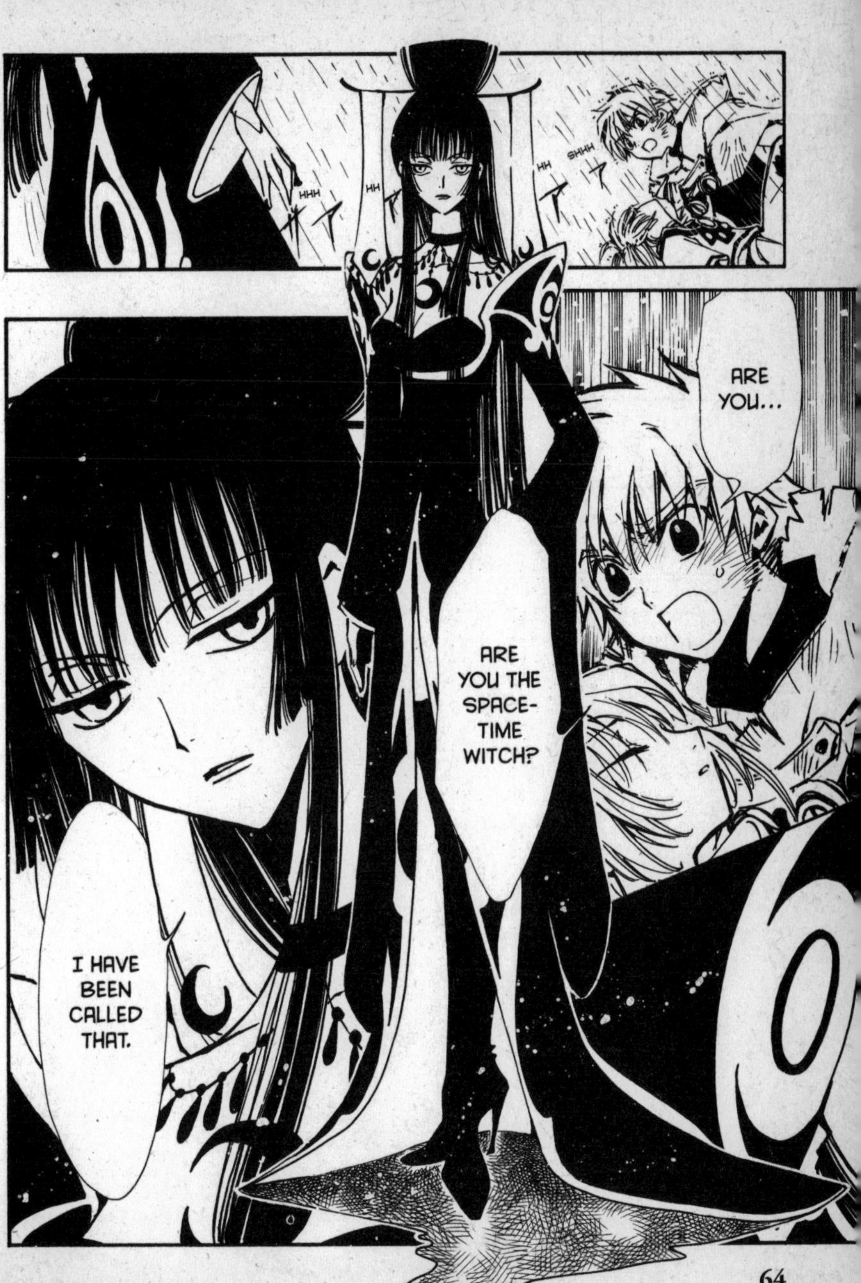
SHHH
HH
HH
HHH
ARE YOU...
ARE YOU THE SPACE-TIME WITCH?
I HAVE BEEN CALLED THAT.

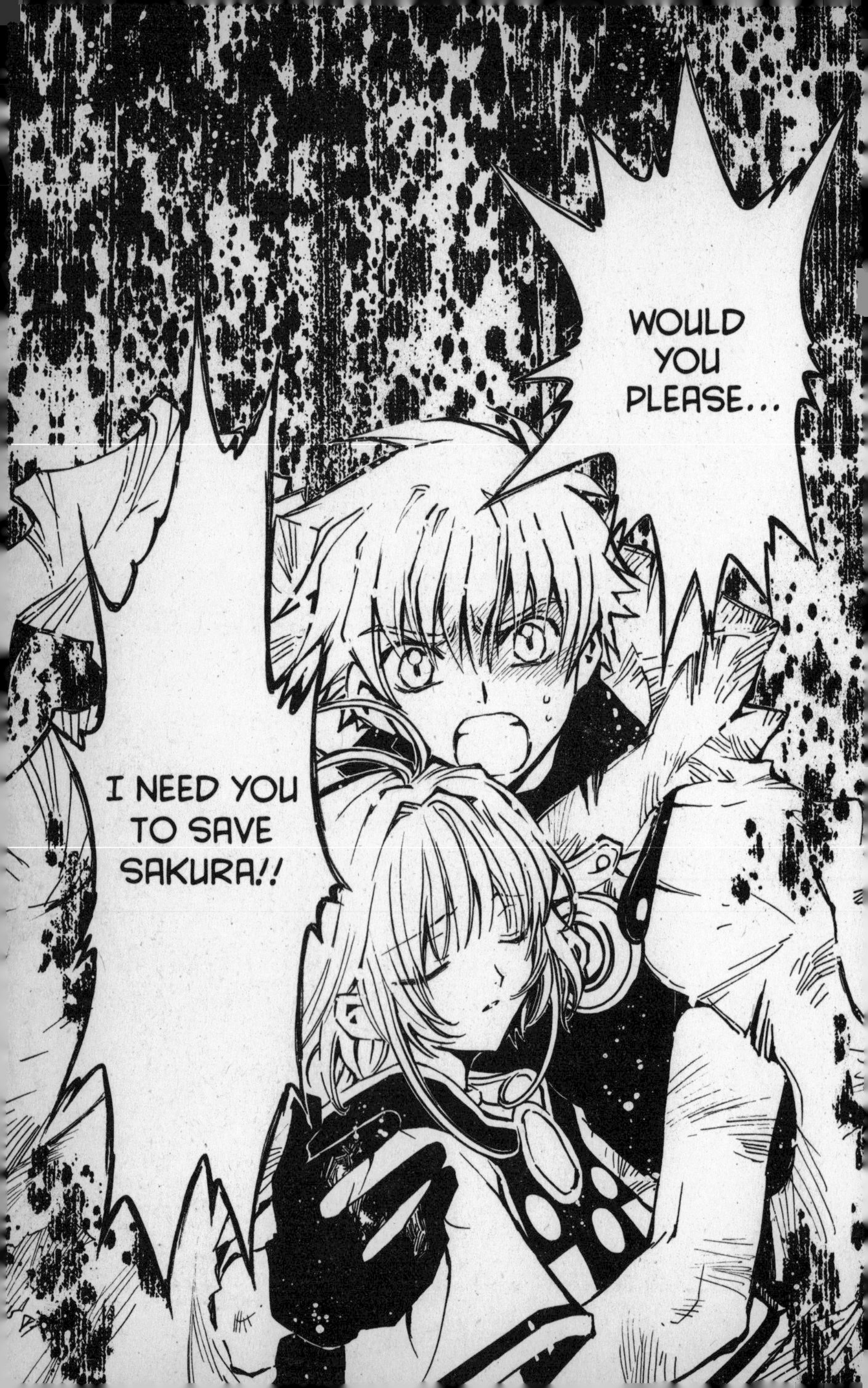
WOULD YOU PLEASE...
I NEED YOU TO SAVE SAKURA!!

RESERVoir CHRoNiCLE

Chapitre.2
The Price of Memory

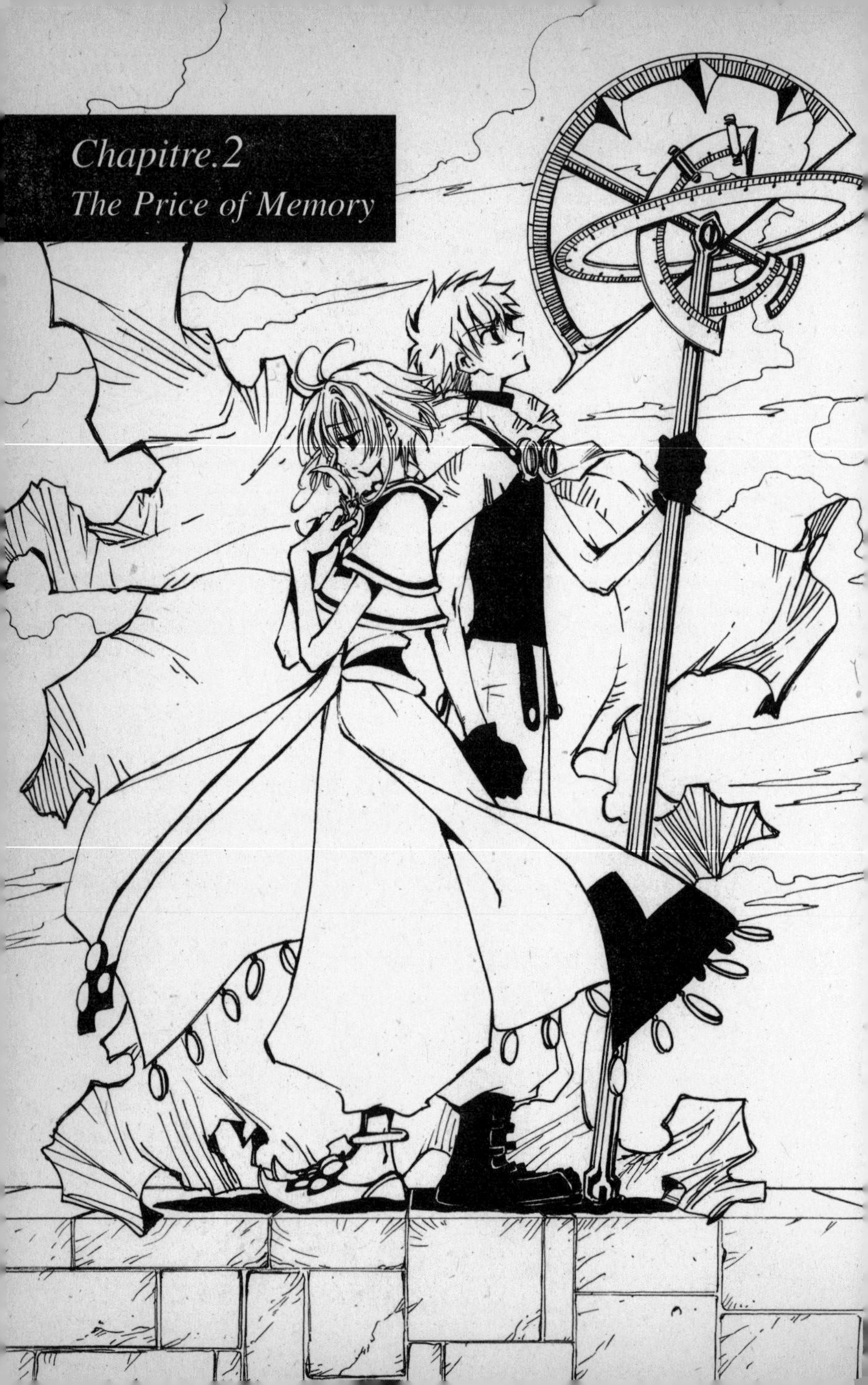

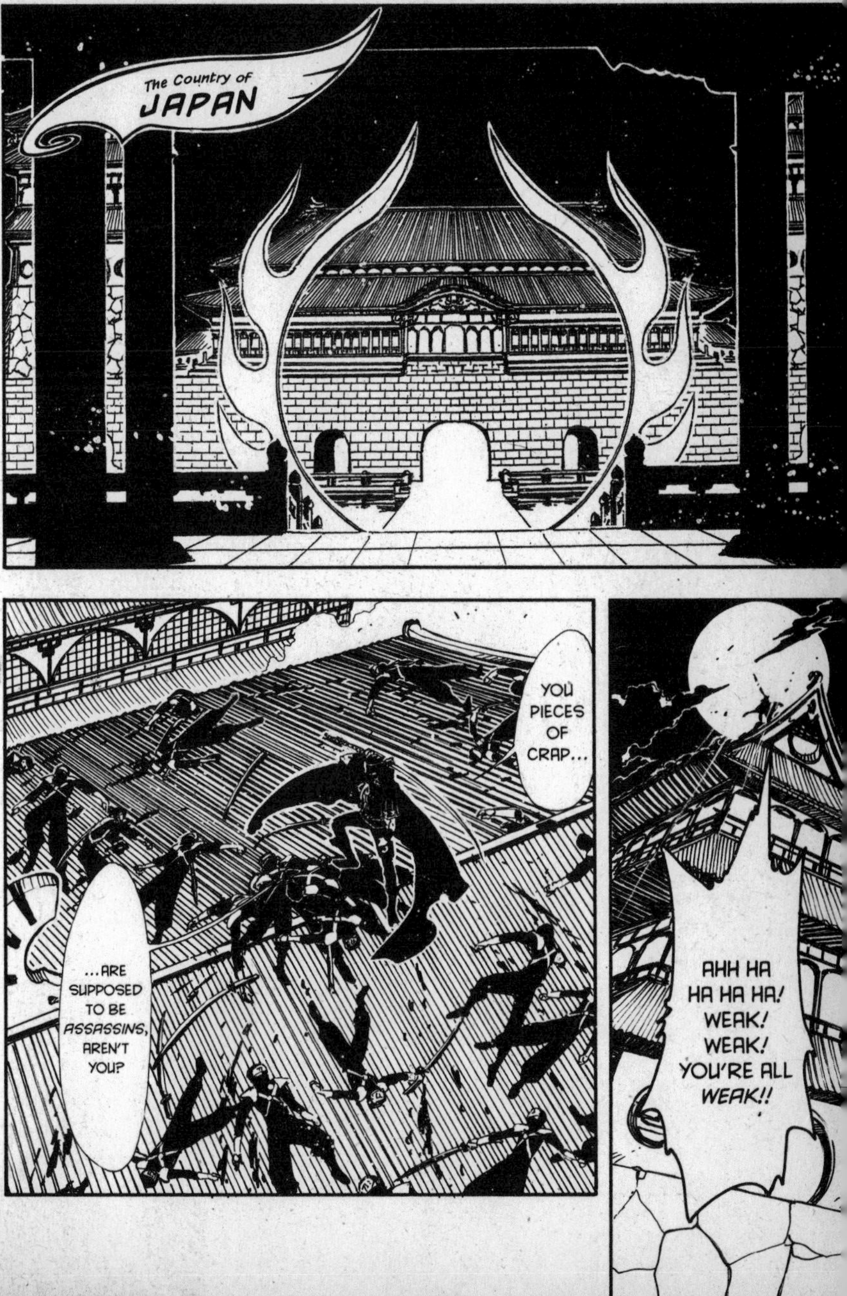
The Country of JAPAN
AHH HA HA HA HA! WEAK! WEAK! YOU'RE ALL *WEAK!!*
YOU PIECES OF CRAP...
...ARE SUPPOSED TO BE *ASSASSINS,* AREN'T YOU?

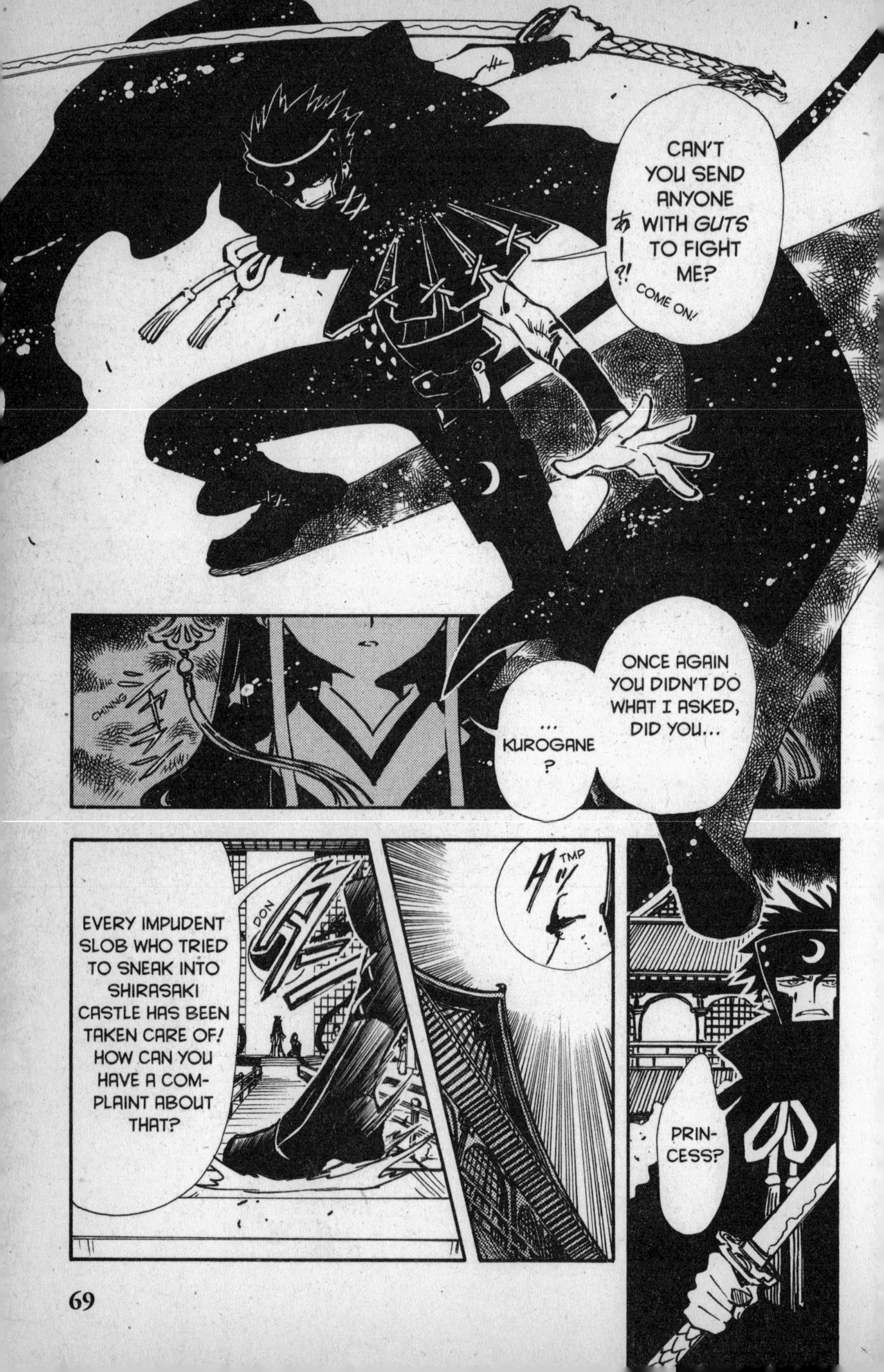
CAN'T YOU SEND ANYONE WITH *GUTS* TO FIGHT ME?
あー?!
COME ON!
ONCE AGAIN YOU DIDN'T DO WHAT I ASKED, DID YOU...
... KUROGANE ?
CHING
PRIN- CESS?
TMP
DON
EVERY IMPUDENT SLOB WHO TRIED TO SNEAK INTO SHIRASAKI CASTLE HAS BEEN TAKEN CARE OF! HOW CAN YOU HAVE A COM- PLAINT ABOUT THAT?

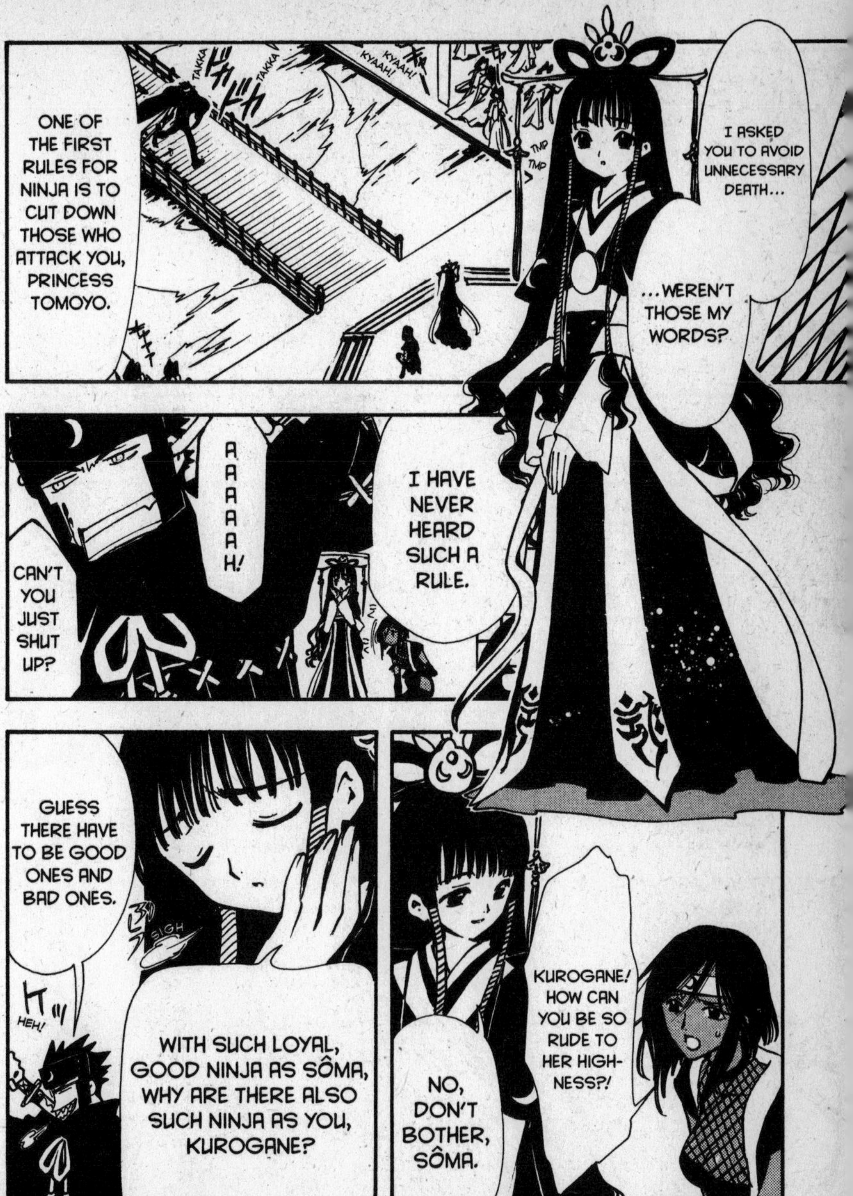
I ASKED YOU TO AVOID UNNECESSARY DEATH...
...WEREN'T THOSE MY WORDS?
TMP TMP
KYAAH! KYAAH!
TAKKA TAKKA
ONE OF THE FIRST RULES FOR NINJA IS TO CUT DOWN THOSE WHO ATTACK YOU, PRINCESS TOMOYO.
I HAVE NEVER HEARD SUCH A RULE.
AAAAAAH!
CAN'T YOU JUST SHUT UP?
KUROGANE! HOW CAN YOU BE SO RUDE TO HER HIGHNESS?!
NO, DON'T BOTHER, SÔMA.
SIGH
WITH SUCH LOYAL, GOOD NINJA AS SÔMA, WHY ARE THERE ALSO SUCH NINJA AS YOU, KUROGANE?
HEH!
GUESS THERE HAVE TO BE GOOD ONES AND BAD ONES.

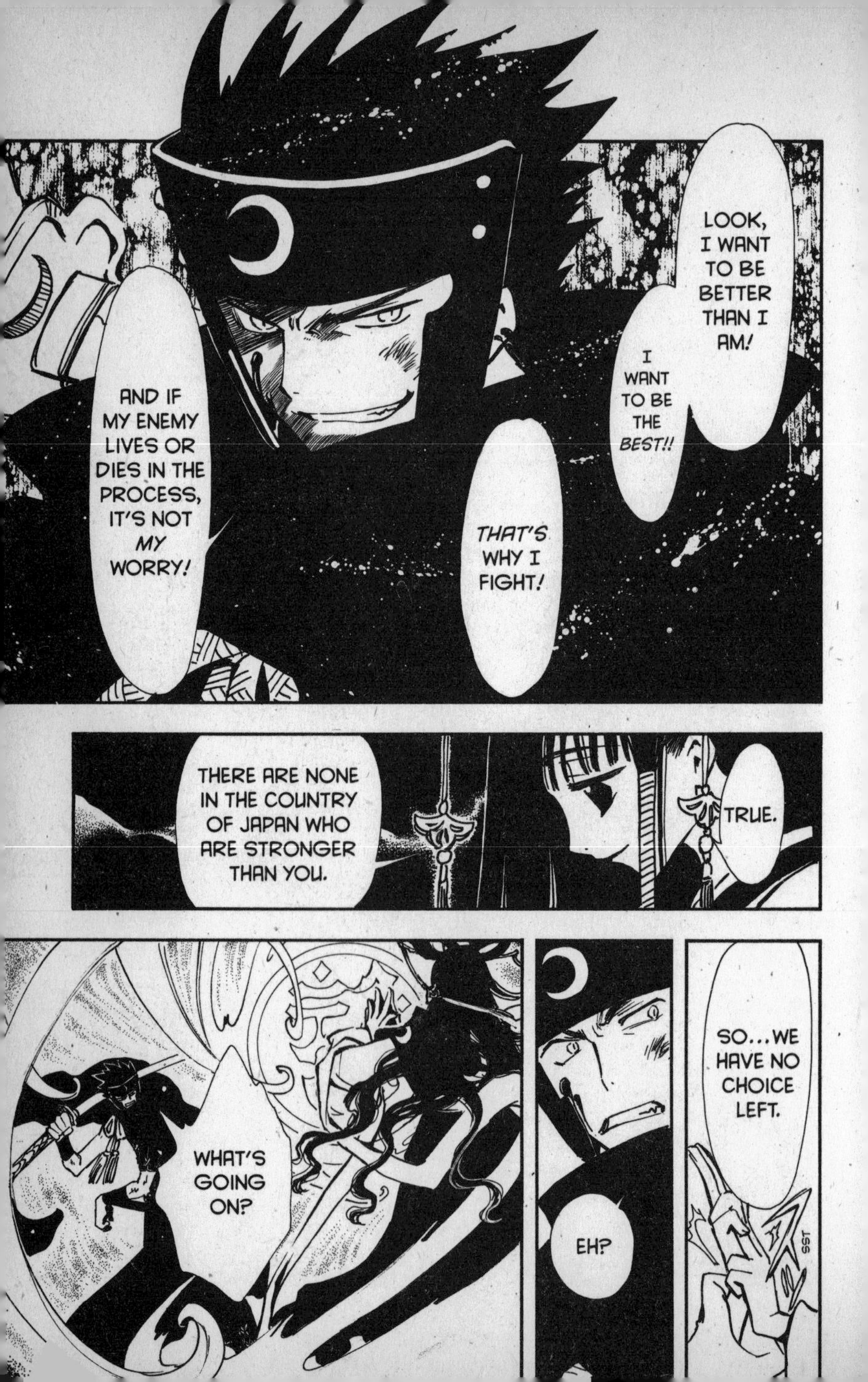
LOOK, I WANT TO BE BETTER THAN I AM!
I WANT TO BE THE *BEST!!*
THAT'S WHY I FIGHT!
AND IF MY ENEMY LIVES OR DIES IN THE PROCESS, IT'S NOT *MY* WORRY!
TRUE.
THERE ARE NONE IN THE COUNTRY OF JAPAN WHO ARE STRONGER THAN YOU.
SO...WE HAVE NO CHOICE LEFT.
SST
EH?
WHAT'S GOING ON?

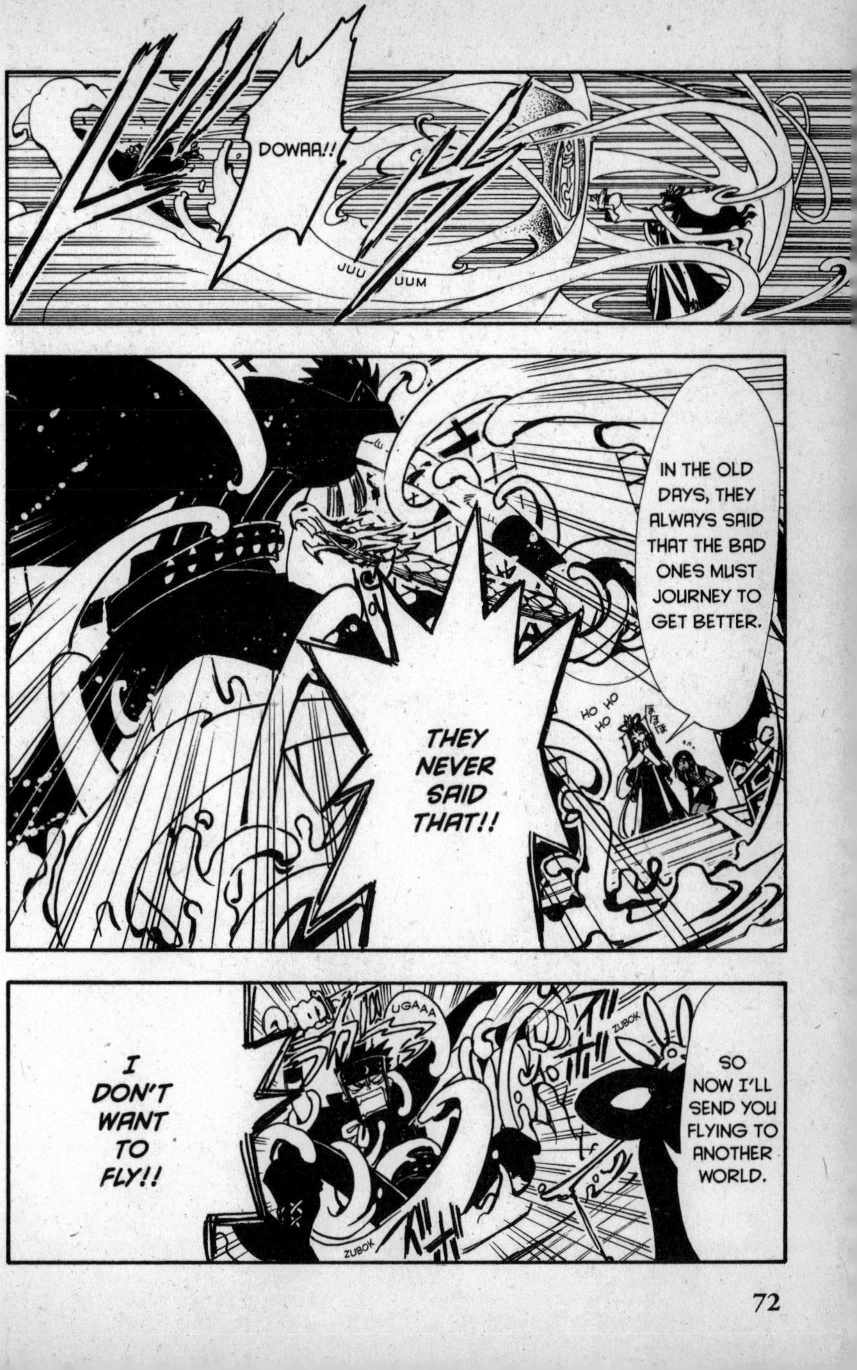
DOWAA!!
JUU UUM
IN THE OLD DAYS, THEY ALWAYS SAID THAT THE BAD ONES MUST JOURNEY TO GET BETTER.
HO HO HO
THEY NEVER SAID THAT!!
SO NOW I'LL SEND YOU FLYING TO ANOTHER WORLD.
ZUBOK
UGAAA
I DON'T WANT TO FLY!!
ZUBOK

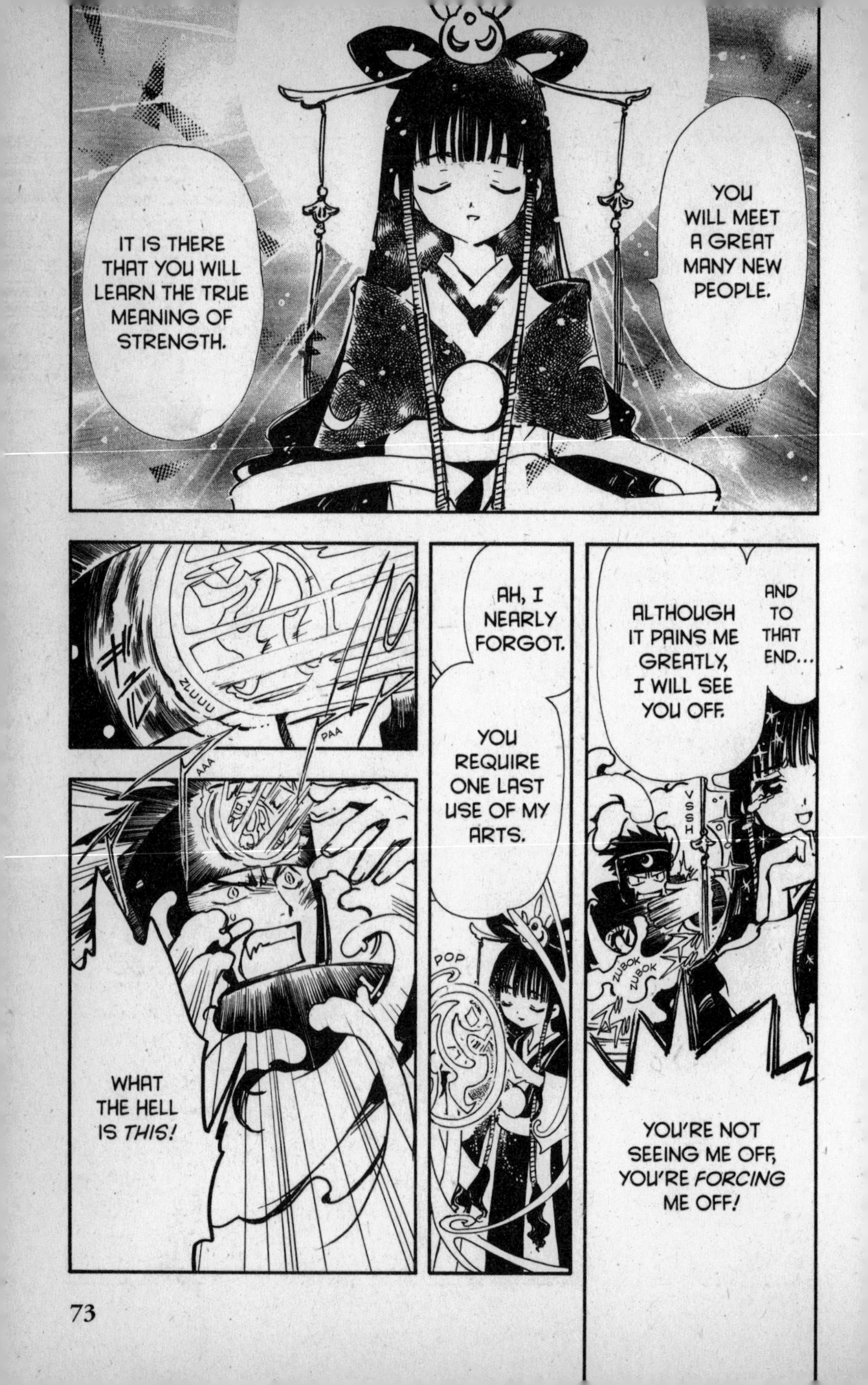
YOU WILL MEET A GREAT MANY NEW PEOPLE.
IT IS THERE THAT YOU WILL LEARN THE TRUE MEANING OF STRENGTH.
AND TO THAT END...
ALTHOUGH IT PAINS ME GREATLY, I WILL SEE YOU OFF.
VSSH
ZUBOK ZUBOK
YOU'RE NOT SEEING ME OFF, YOU'RE *FORCING* ME OFF!
AH, I NEARLY FORGOT.
YOU REQUIRE ONE LAST USE OF MY ARTS.
POP
ZLUUU
PAA
AAA
WHAT THE HELL IS *THIS!*

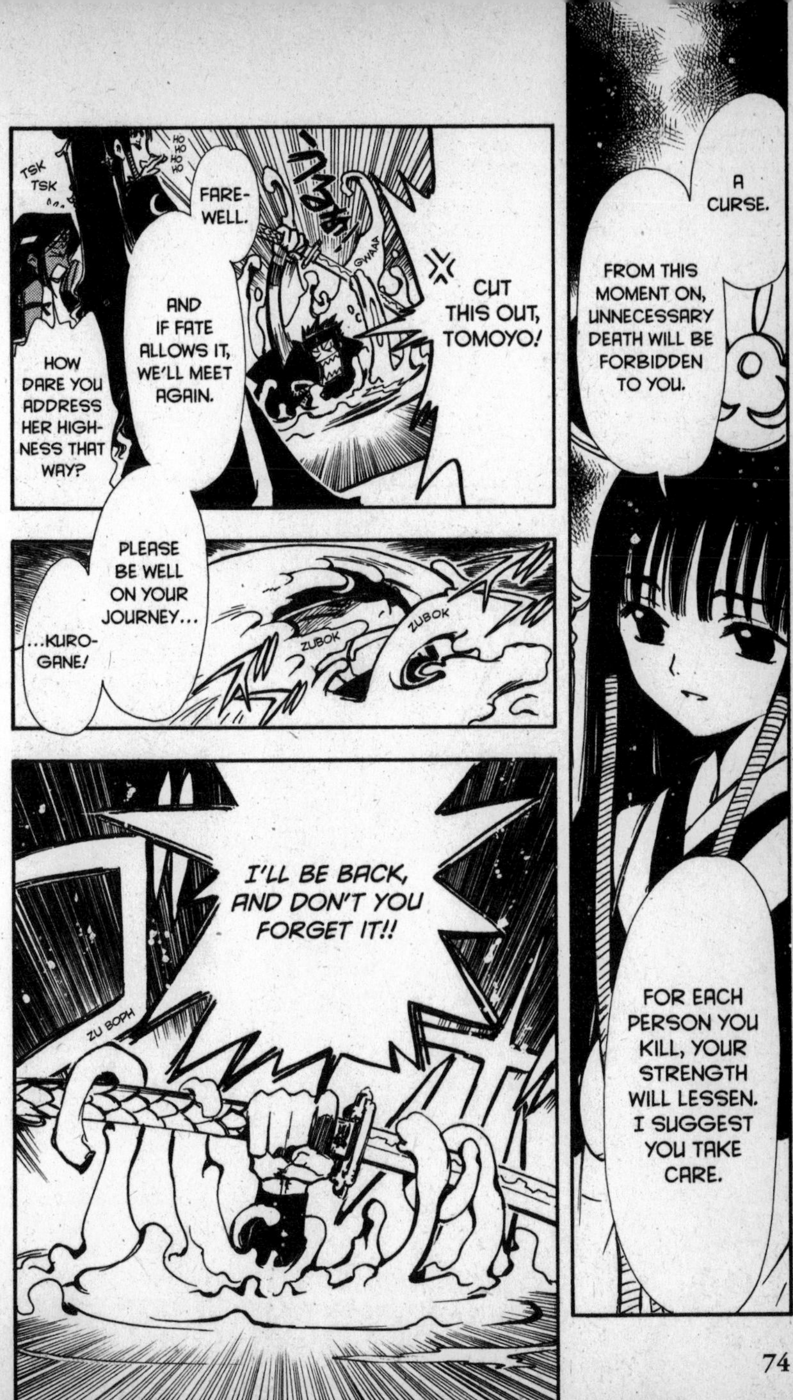
A CURSE.
FROM THIS MOMENT ON, UNNECESSARY DEATH WILL BE FORBIDDEN TO YOU.
FOR EACH PERSON YOU KILL, YOUR STRENGTH WILL LESSEN. I SUGGEST YOU TAKE CARE.
CUT THIS OUT, TOMOYO!
GWAAA
FARE-WELL.
HO HO HO HO
AND IF FATE ALLOWS IT, WE'LL MEET AGAIN.
TSK TSK
HOW DARE YOU ADDRESS HER HIGHNESS THAT WAY?
ZUBOK
ZUBOK
PLEASE BE WELL ON YOUR JOURNEY...
...KURO-GANE!
I'LL BE BACK, AND DON'T YOU FORGET IT!!
ZU BOPH

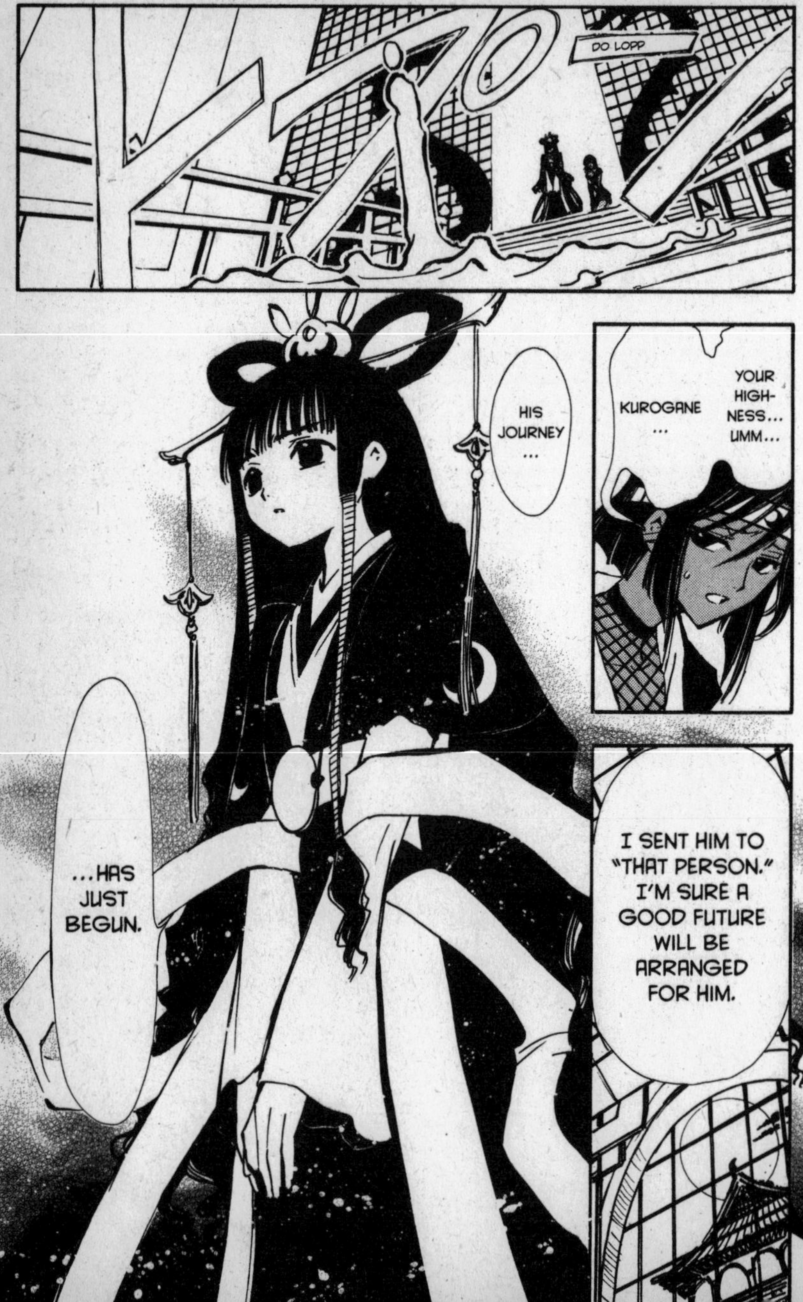
DO LOPP
YOUR HIGH-NESS... UMM...
KUROGANE ...
I SENT HIM TO "THAT PERSON." I'M SURE A GOOD FUTURE WILL BE ARRANGED FOR HIM.
HIS JOURNEY ...
...HAS JUST BEGUN.

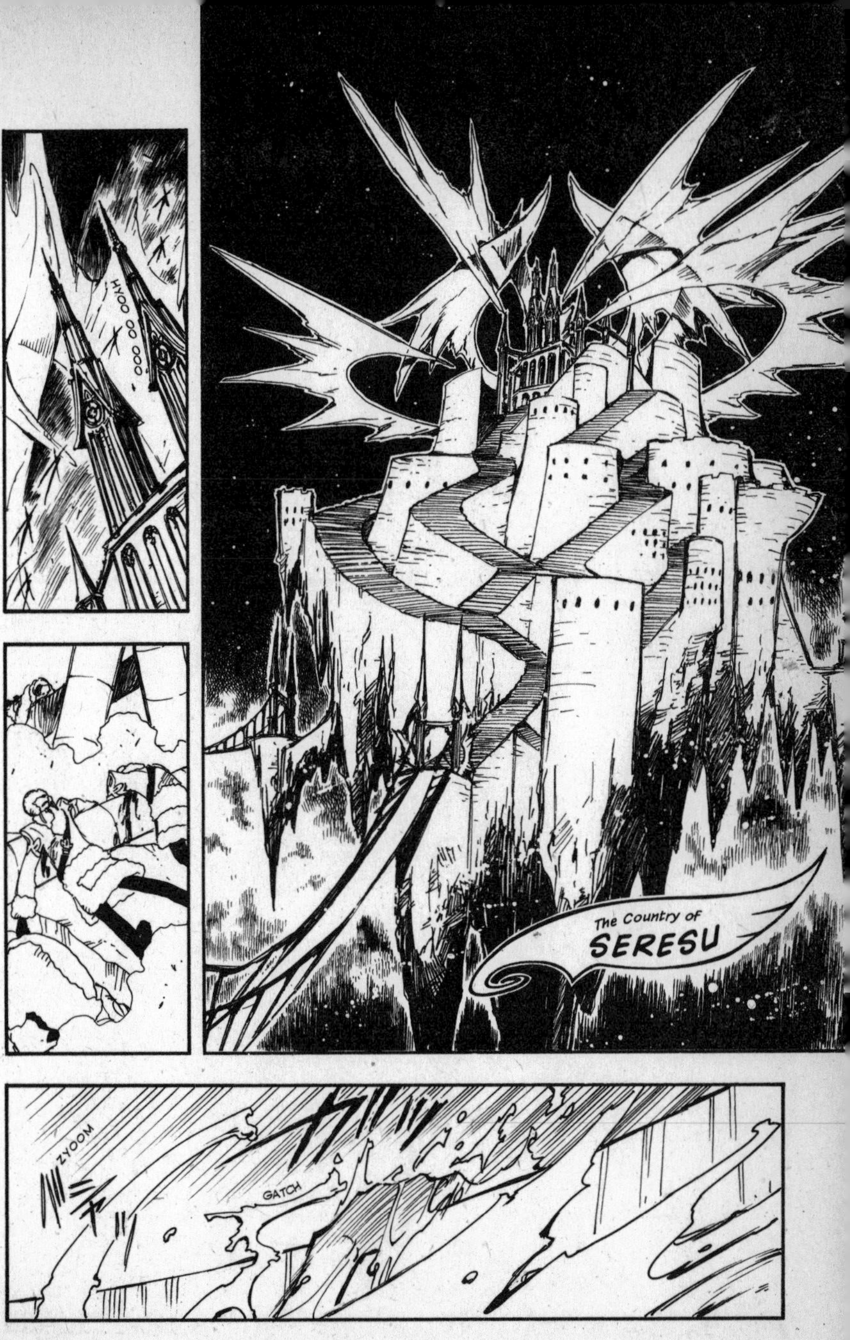
The Country of
SERESU
HYOO OO OOO
ZYOOM
GATCH

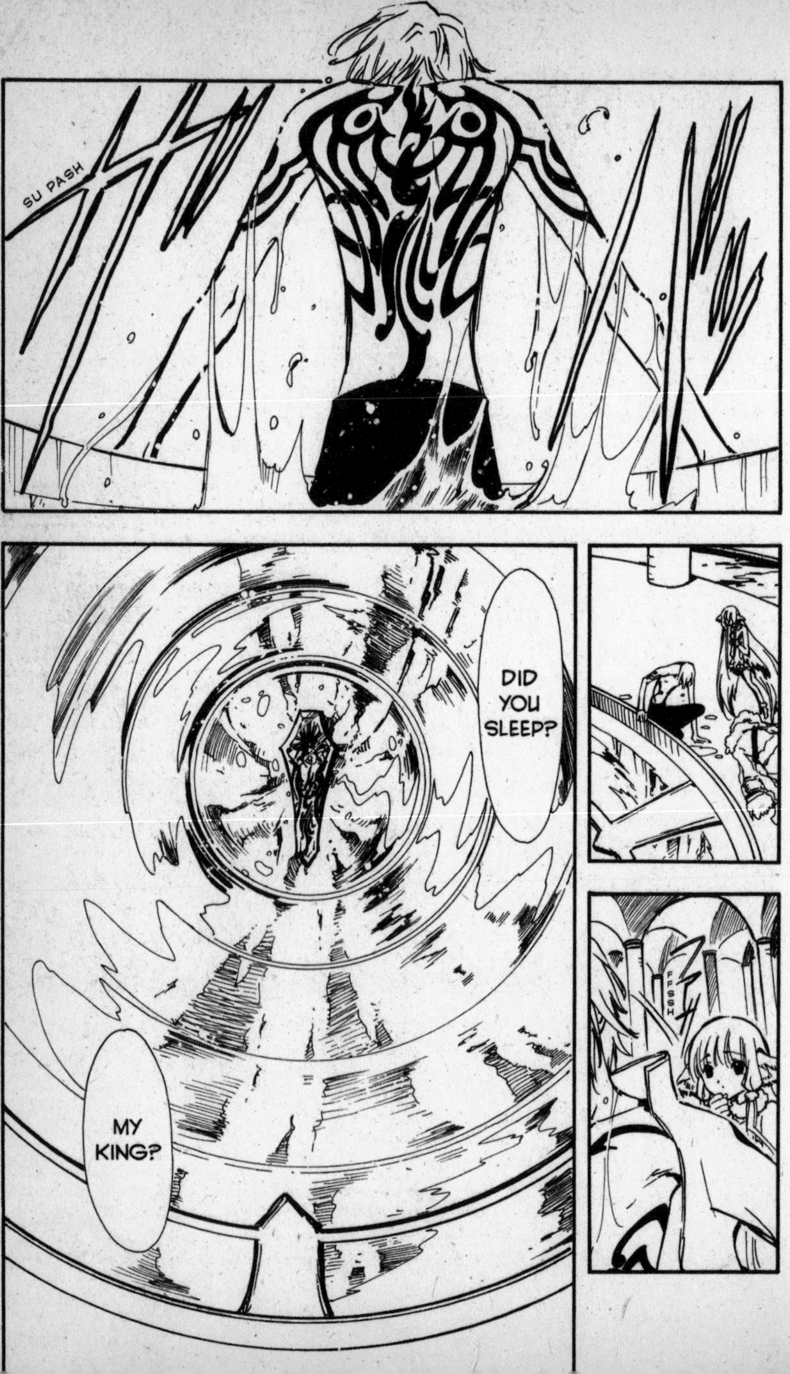
SU PASH
FFSSH
DID YOU SLEEP?
MY KING?

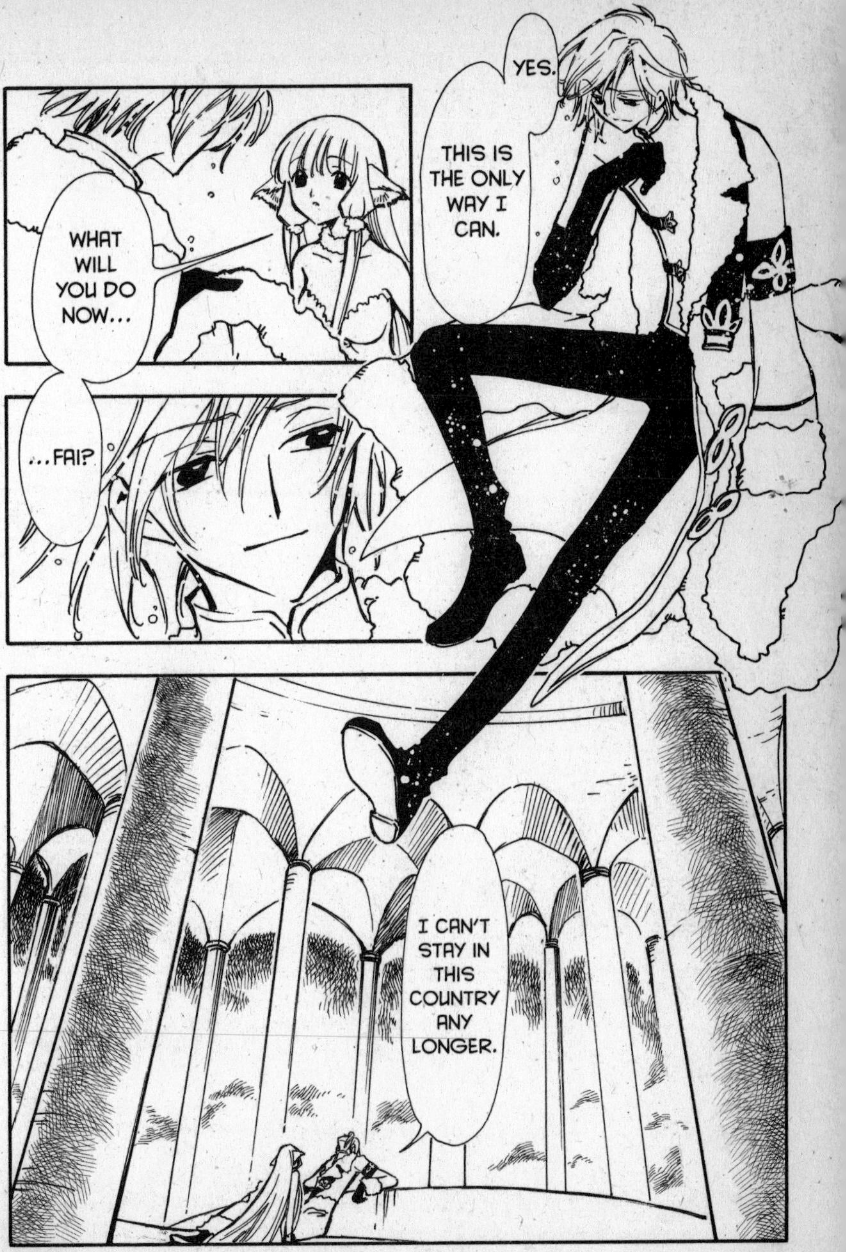
YES.
THIS IS THE ONLY WAY I CAN.
WHAT WILL YOU DO NOW...
...FAI?
I CAN'T STAY IN THIS COUNTRY ANY LONGER.

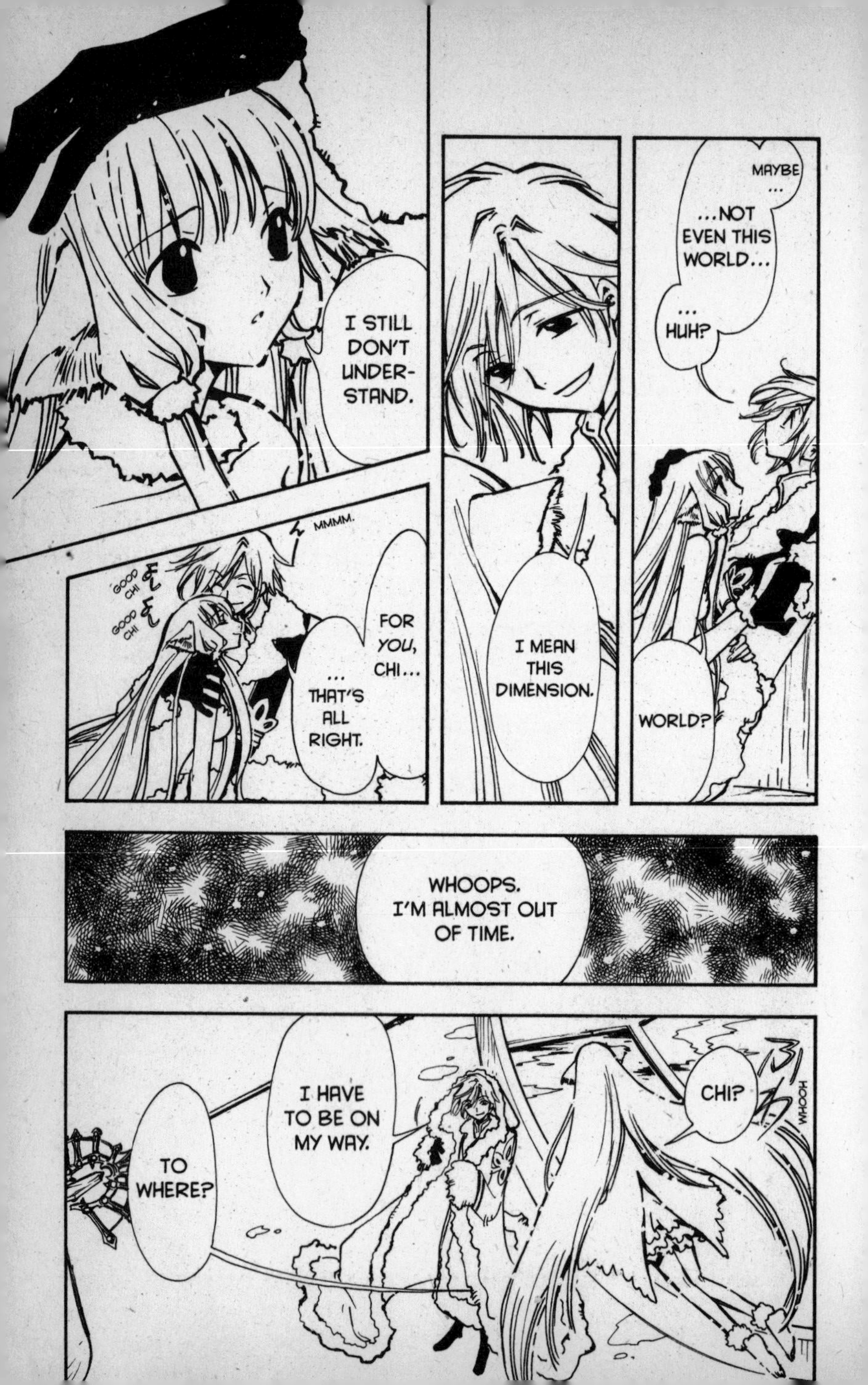
MAYBE ...
...NOT EVEN THIS WORLD...
... HUH?
WORLD?
I MEAN THIS DIMENSION.
I STILL DON'T UNDERSTAND.
MMMM.
GOOD CHI GOOD CHI
FOR *YOU*, CHI...
... THAT'S ALL RIGHT.
WHOOPS. I'M ALMOST OUT OF TIME.
WHOOSH
CHI?
I HAVE TO BE ON MY WAY.
TO WHERE?

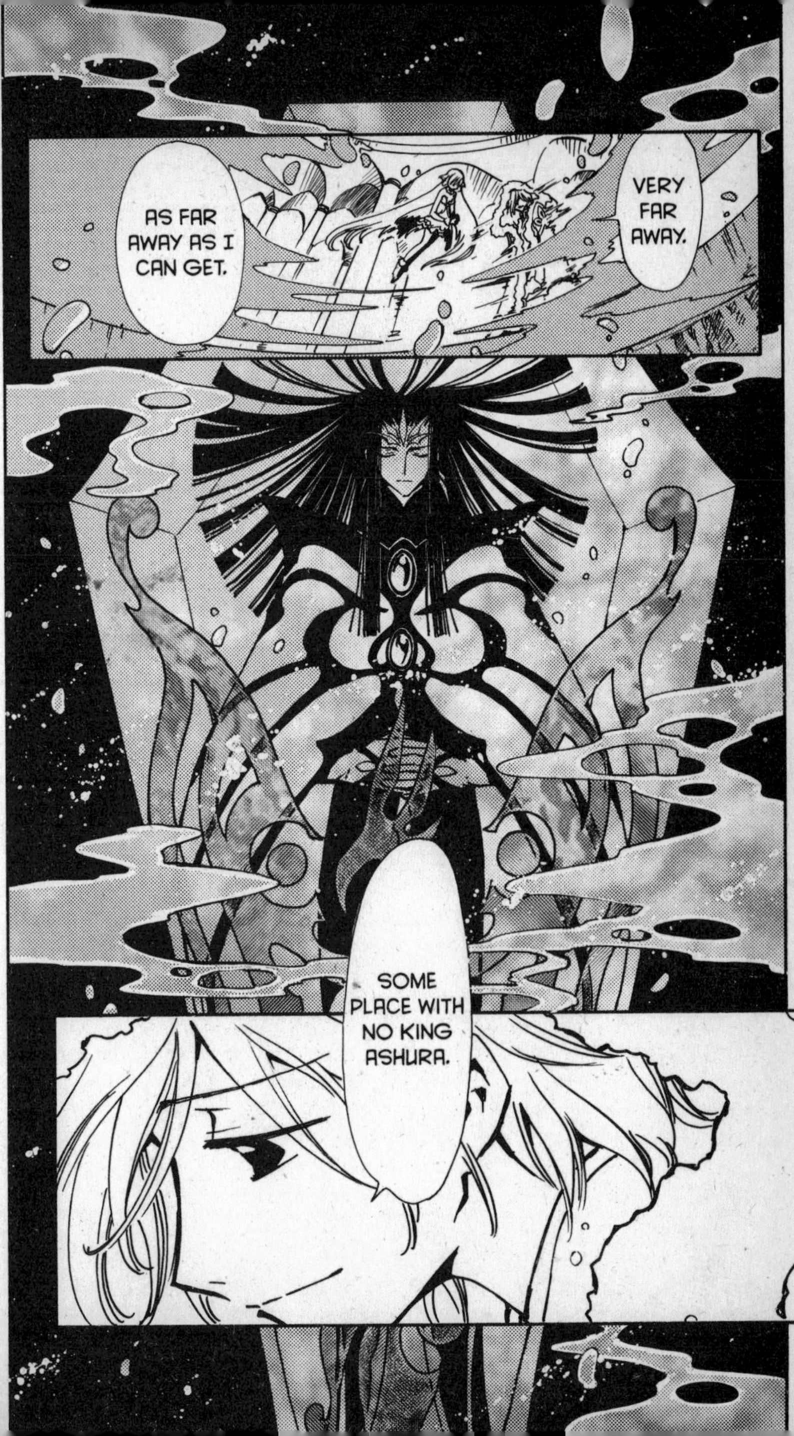
VERY FAR AWAY.
AS FAR AWAY AS I CAN GET.
SOME PLACE WITH NO KING ASHURA.

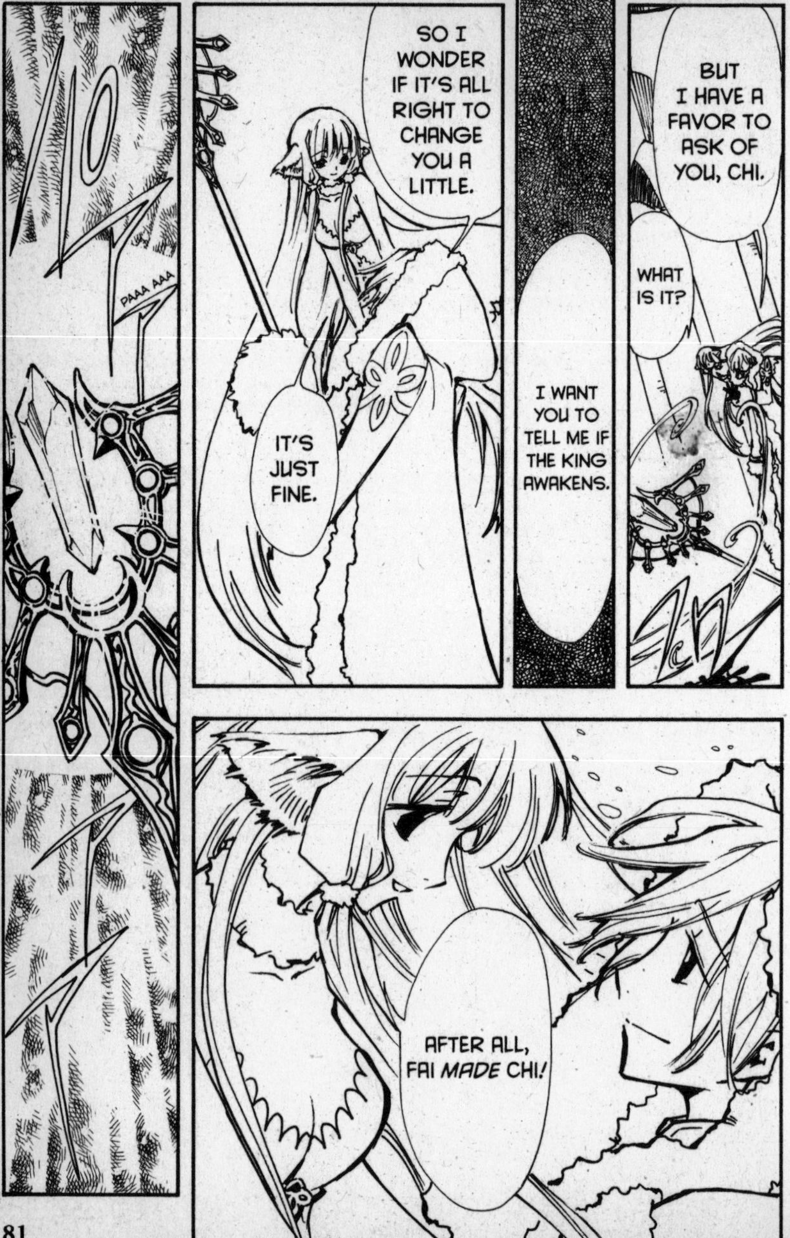
BUT I HAVE A FAVOR TO ASK OF YOU, CHI.
WHAT IS IT?
I WANT YOU TO TELL ME IF THE KING AWAKENS.
SO I WONDER IF IT'S ALL RIGHT TO CHANGE YOU A LITTLE.
IT'S JUST FINE.
AFTER ALL, FAI *MADE* CHI!
PAAA AAA

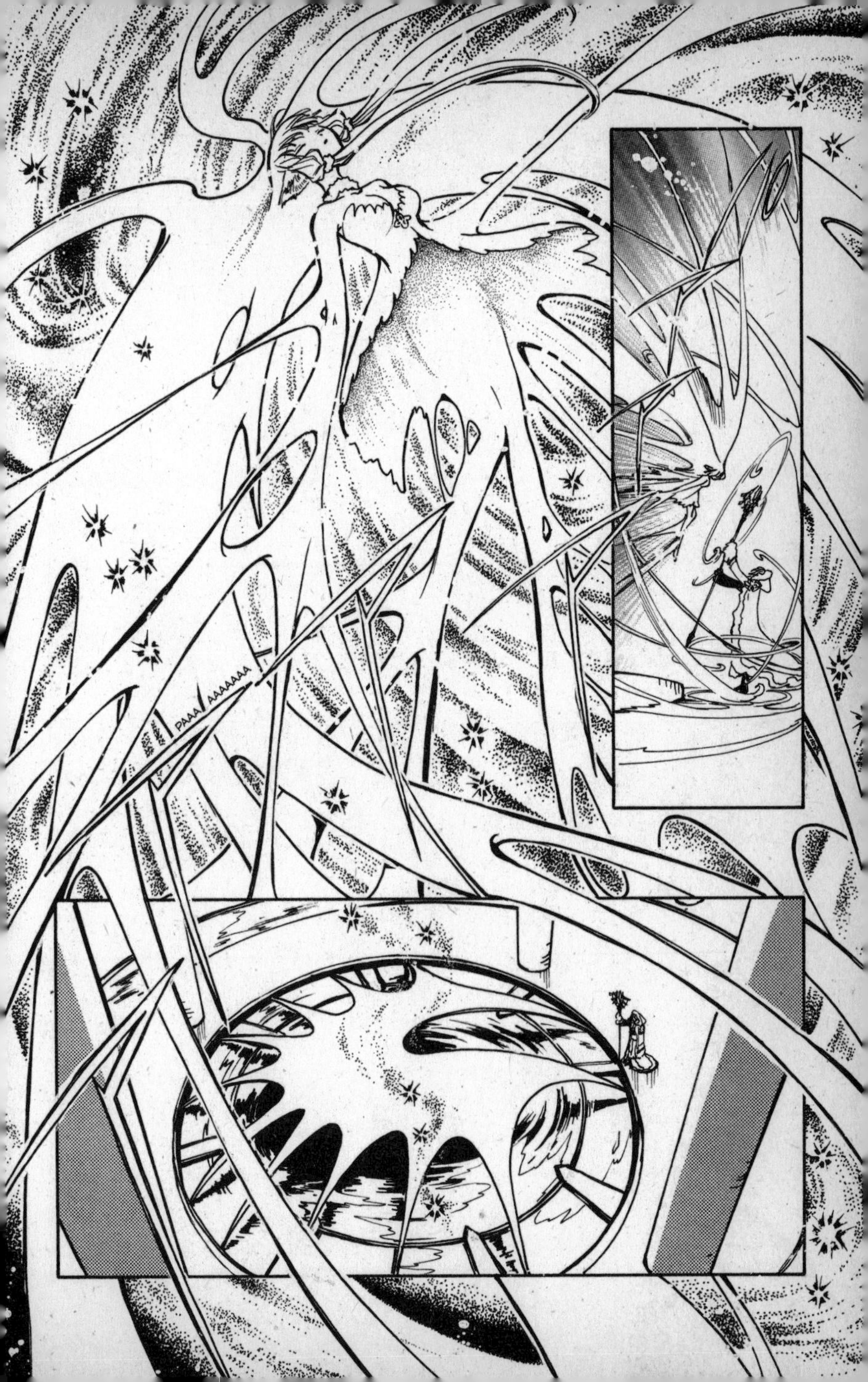
PAAA AAAAAAA

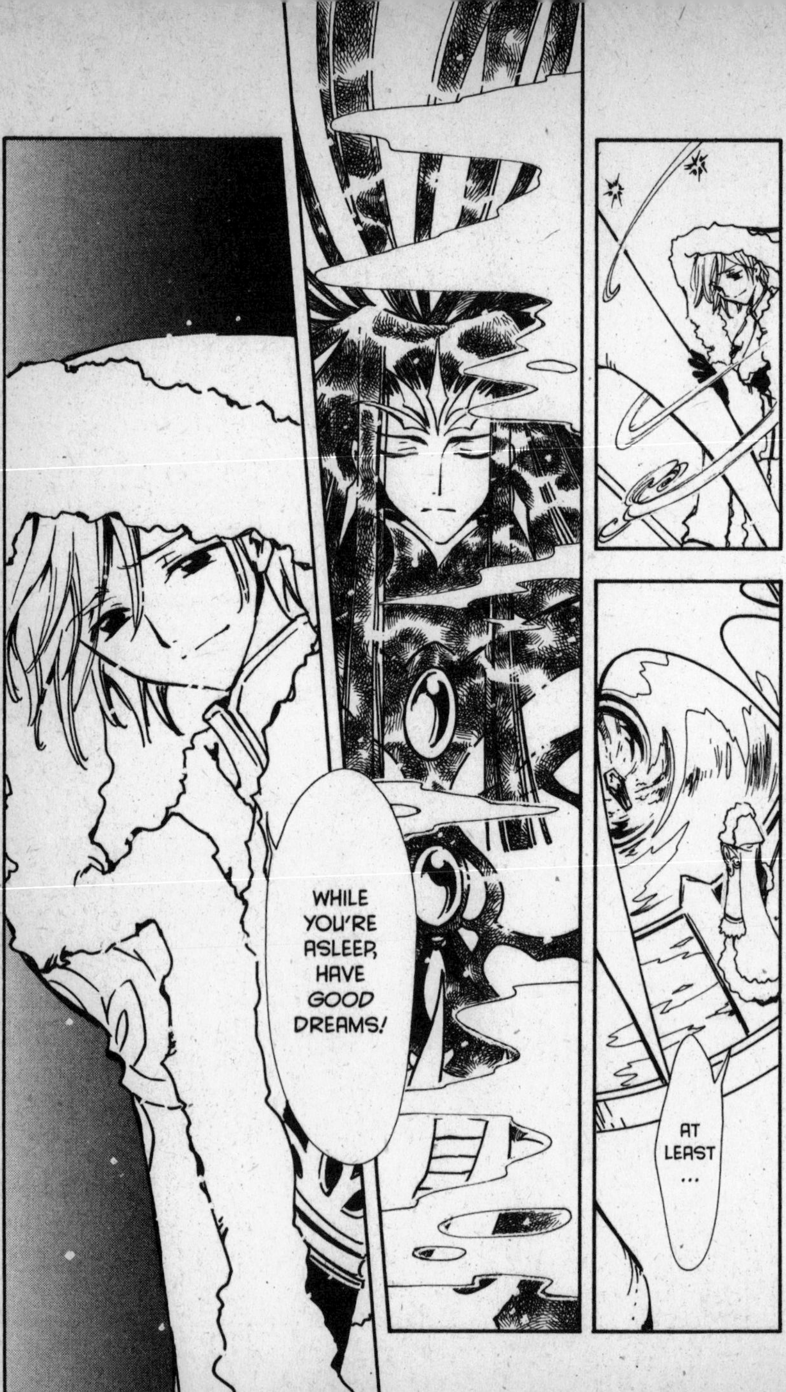
AT LEAST...
WHILE YOU'RE ASLEEP, HAVE *GOOD* DREAMS!

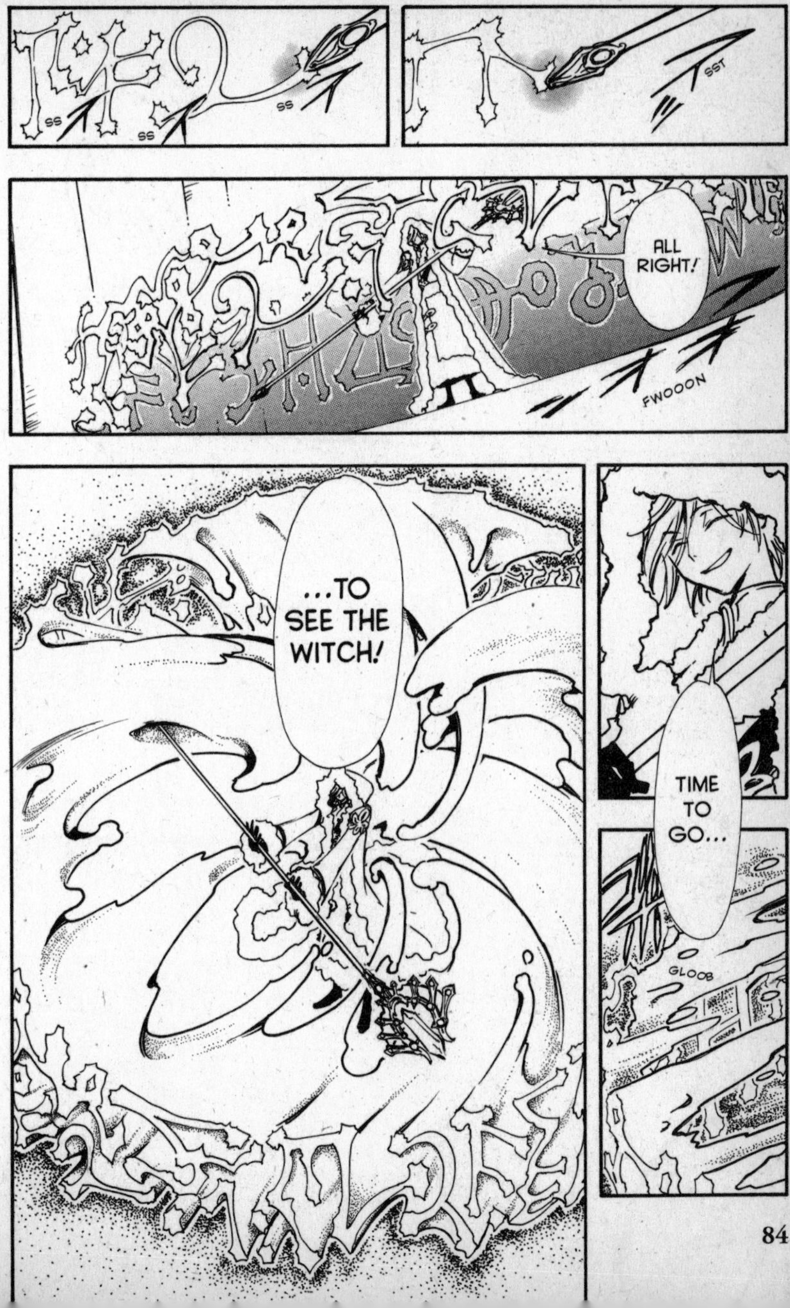
SST
SS
SS
SS
ALL RIGHT!
FWOOON
TIME TO GO...
GLOOB
...TO SEE THE WITCH!

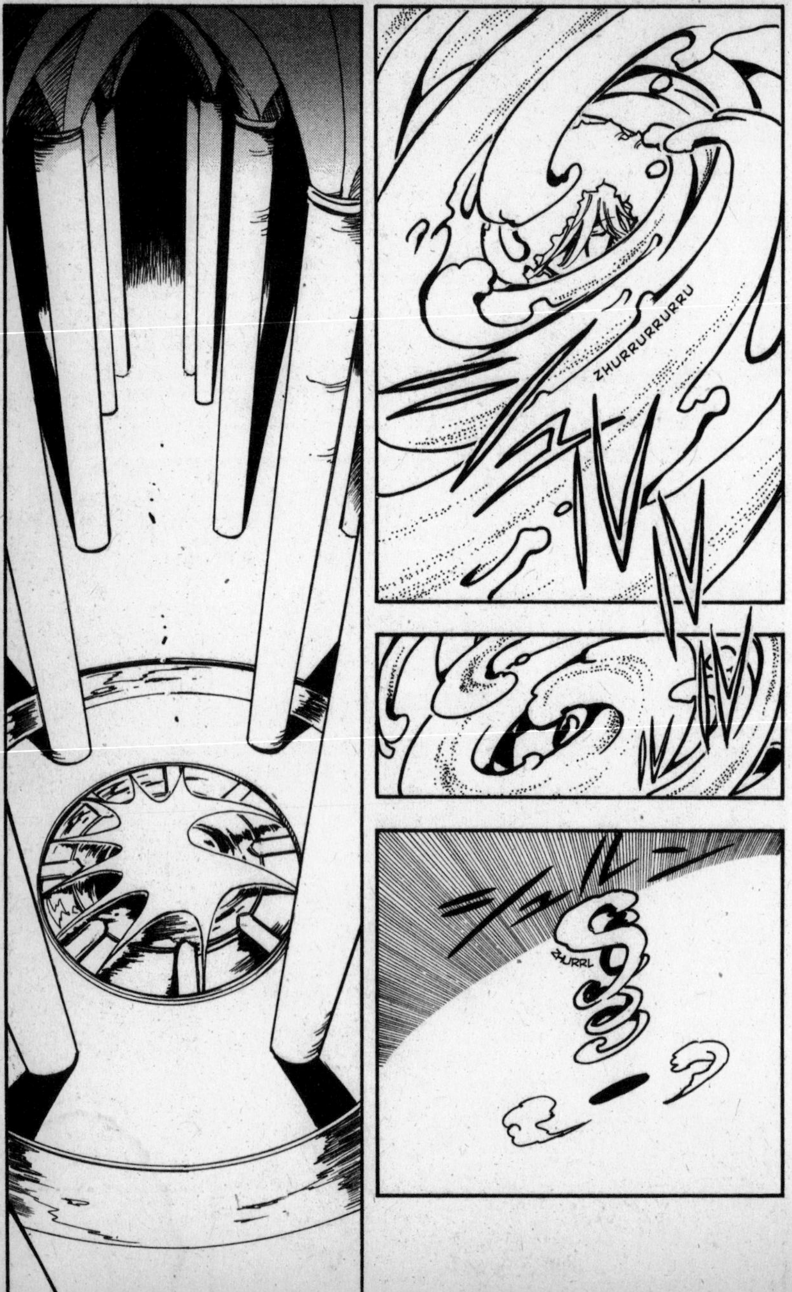
ZHURRURRURRU
ZHURRL

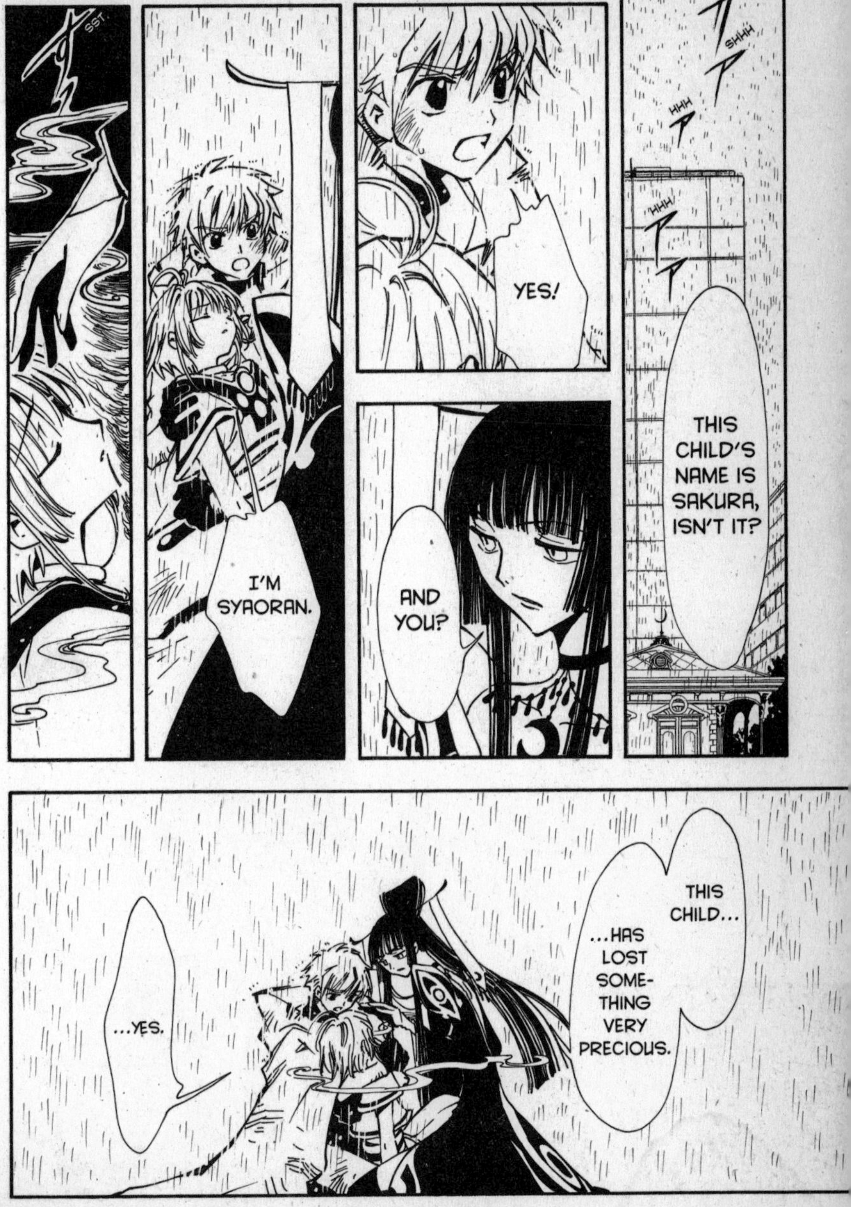
SHHH
HHH
HHH
THIS CHILD'S NAME IS SAKURA, ISN'T IT?
YES!
AND YOU?
I'M SYAORAN.
SST.
THIS CHILD...
...HAS LOST SOME-THING VERY PRECIOUS.
...YES.

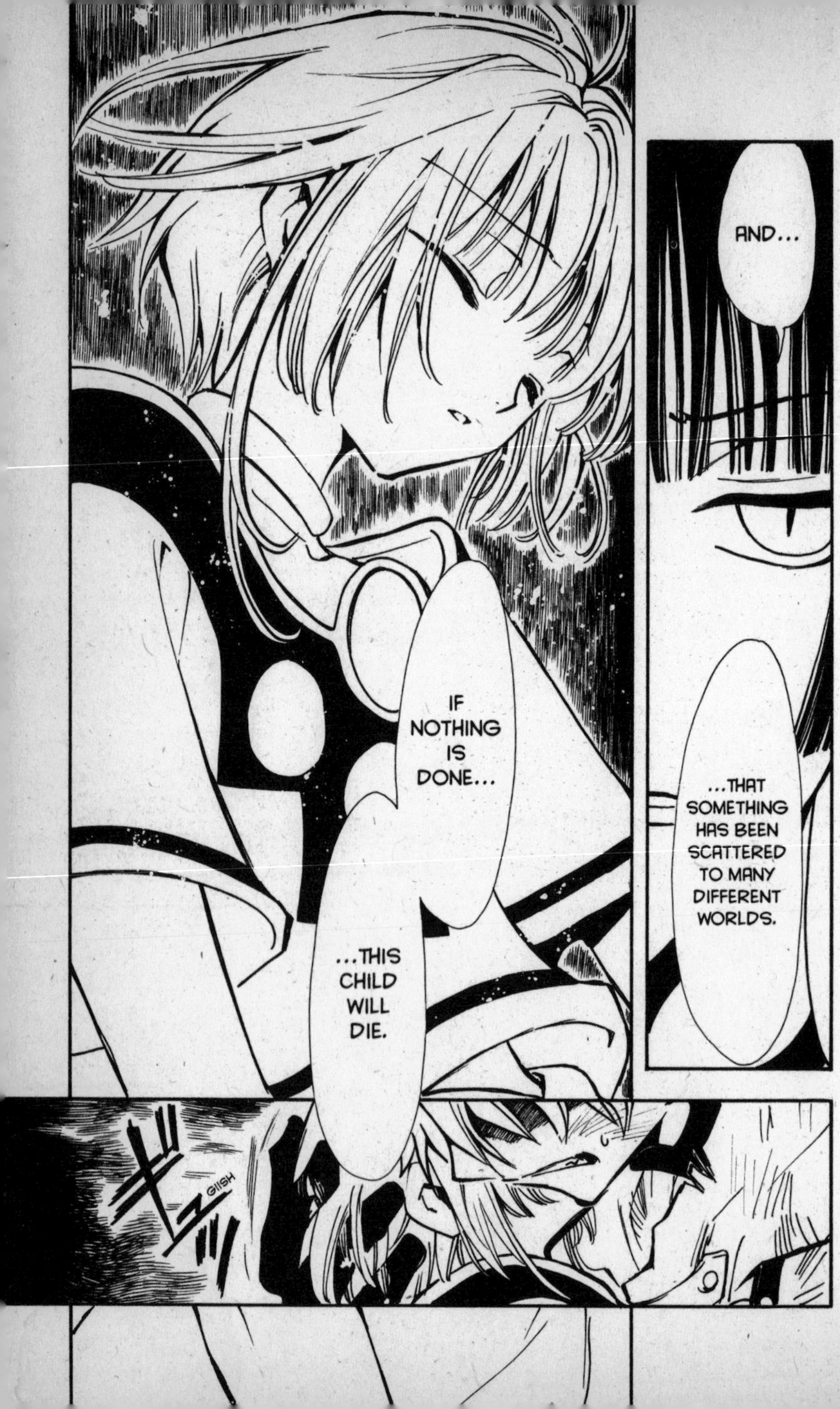
AND...
...THAT SOMETHING HAS BEEN SCATTERED TO MANY DIFFERENT WORLDS.
IF NOTHING IS DONE...
...THIS CHILD WILL DIE.
GIISH

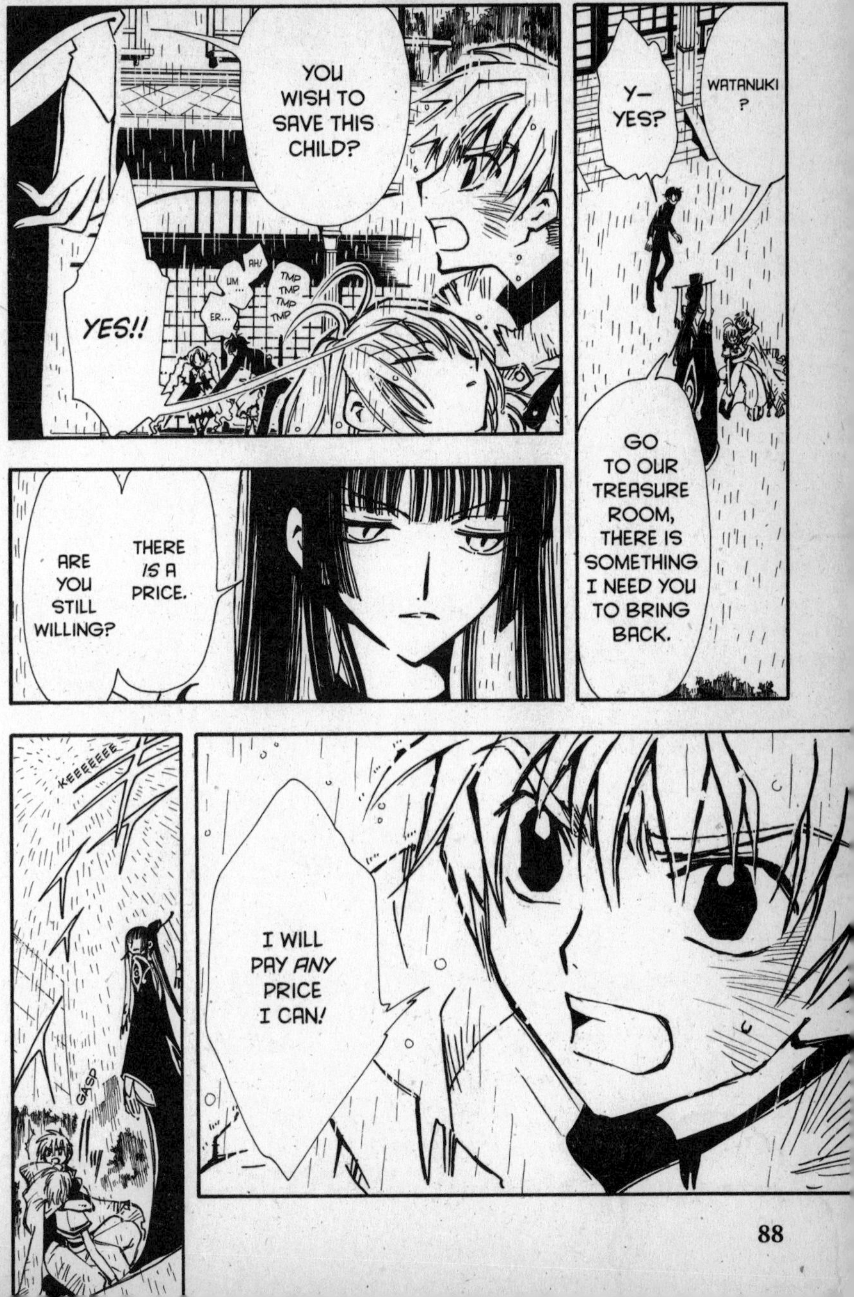
WATANUKI ?
Y— YES?
GO TO OUR TREASURE ROOM, THERE IS SOMETHING I NEED YOU TO BRING BACK.
YOU WISH TO SAVE THIS CHILD?
AH!
UM ...
ER...
TMP TMP TMP TMP
YES!!
THERE *IS* A PRICE.
ARE YOU STILL WILLING?
I WILL PAY *ANY* PRICE I CAN!
KEEEEEEE
GASP

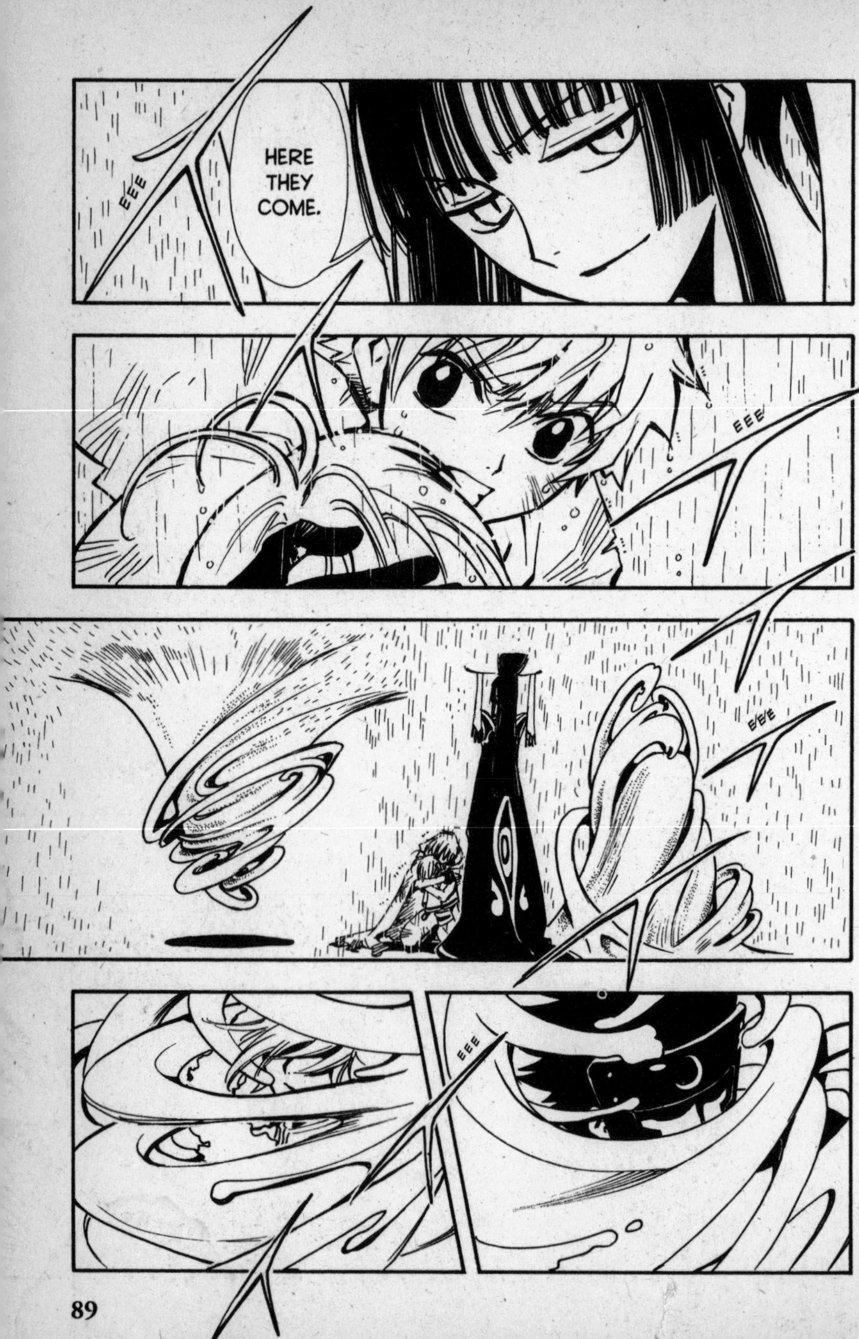
HERE THEY COME.
EEE
EEE
EEE
EEE

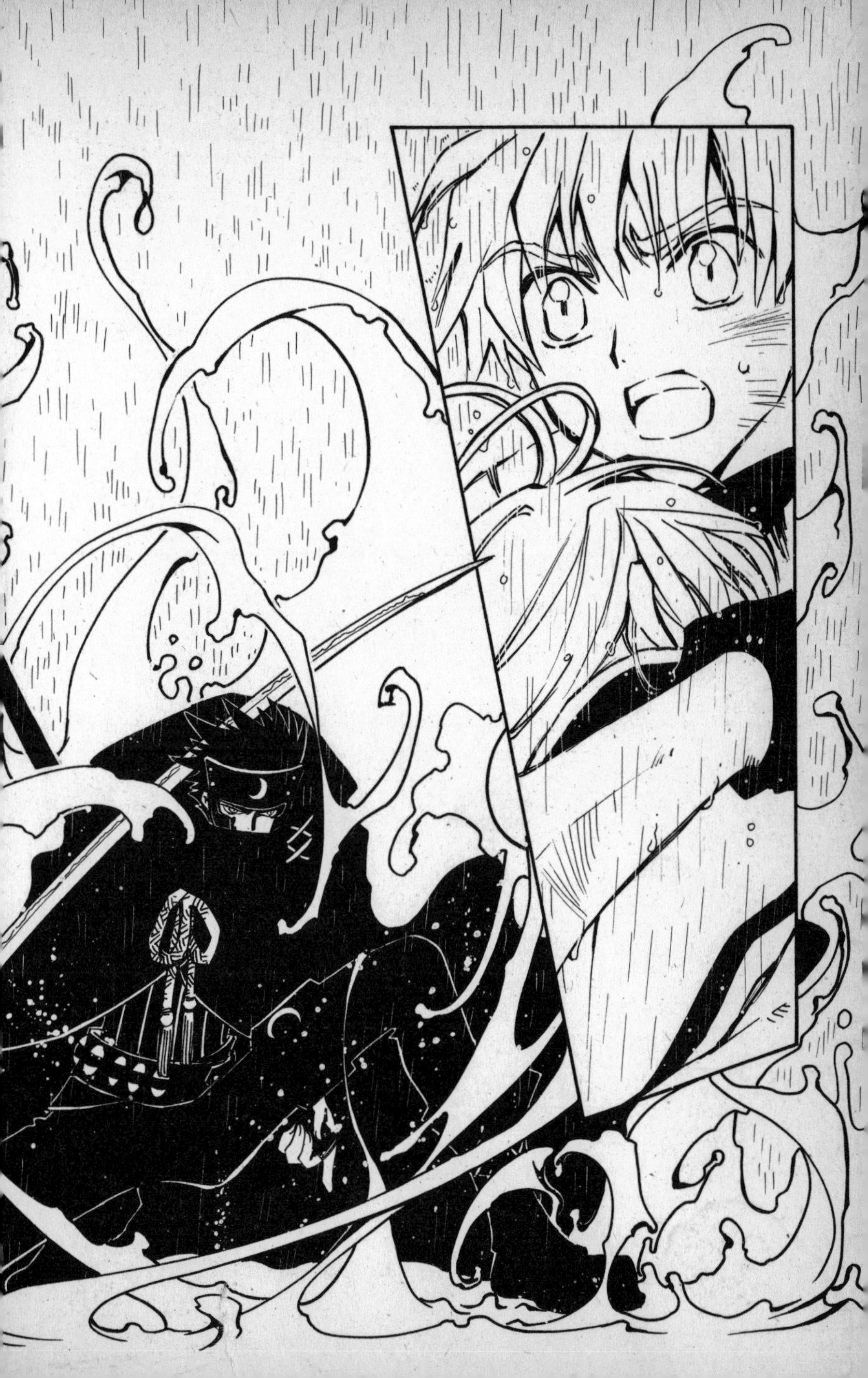

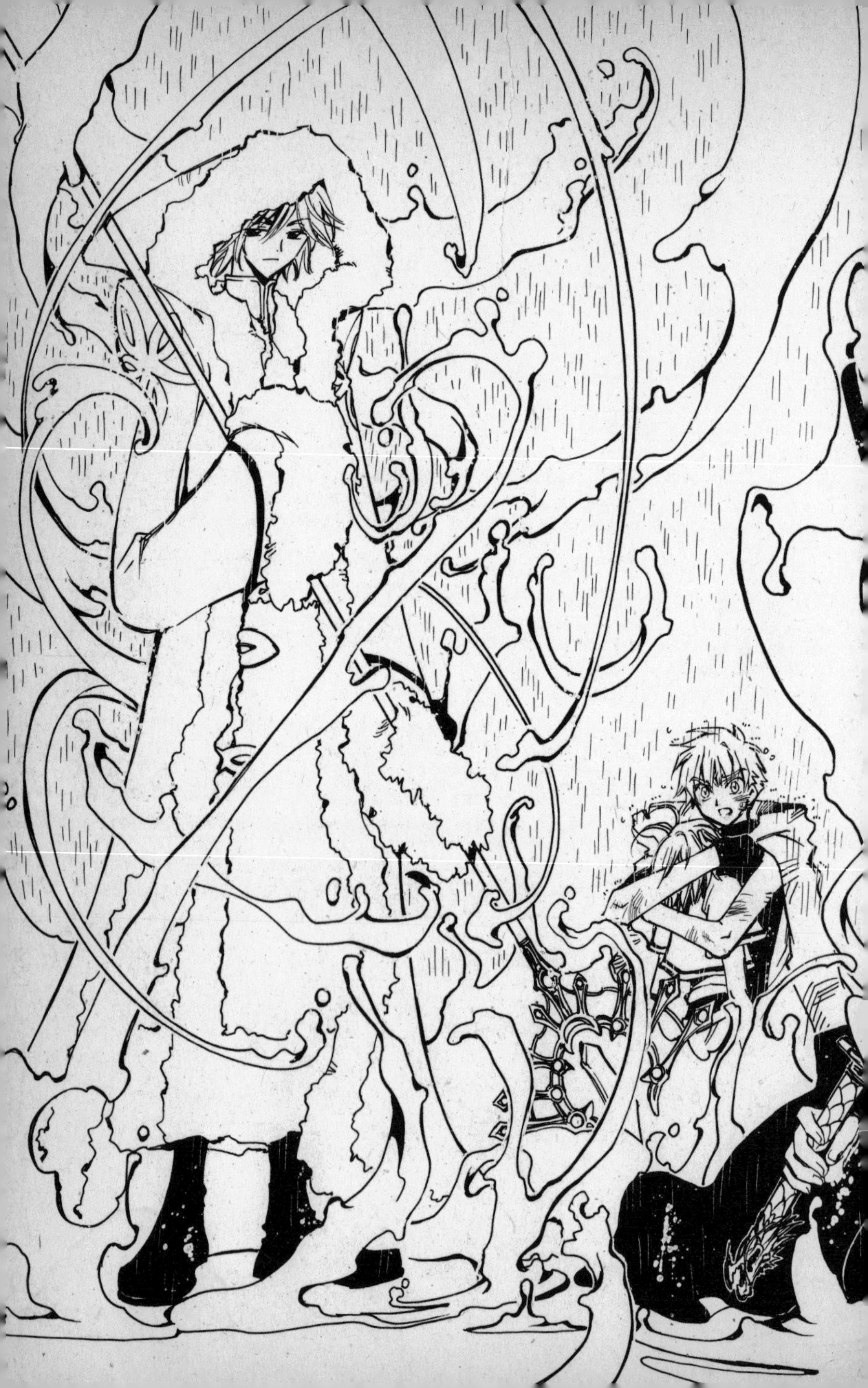

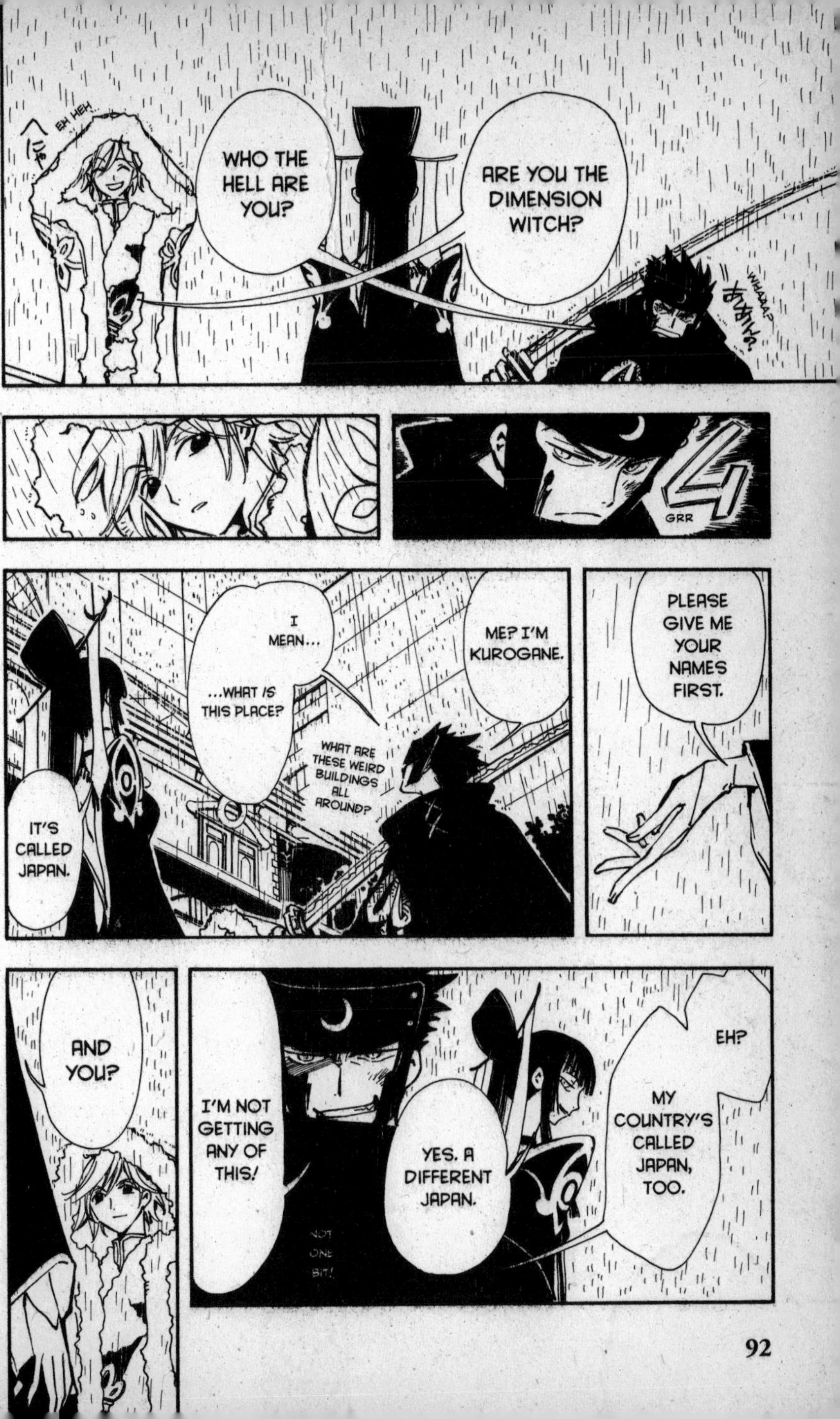
WHAAA?
ARE YOU THE DIMENSION WITCH?
WHO THE HELL ARE YOU?
EH HEH...
GRR
PLEASE GIVE ME YOUR NAMES FIRST.
ME? I'M KUROGANE.
I MEAN...
...WHAT IS THIS PLACE?
WHAT ARE THESE WEIRD BUILDINGS ALL AROUND?
IT'S CALLED JAPAN.
EH?
MY COUNTRY'S CALLED JAPAN, TOO.
YES. A DIFFERENT JAPAN.
I'M NOT GETTING ANY OF THIS!
NOT ONE BIT!
AND YOU?

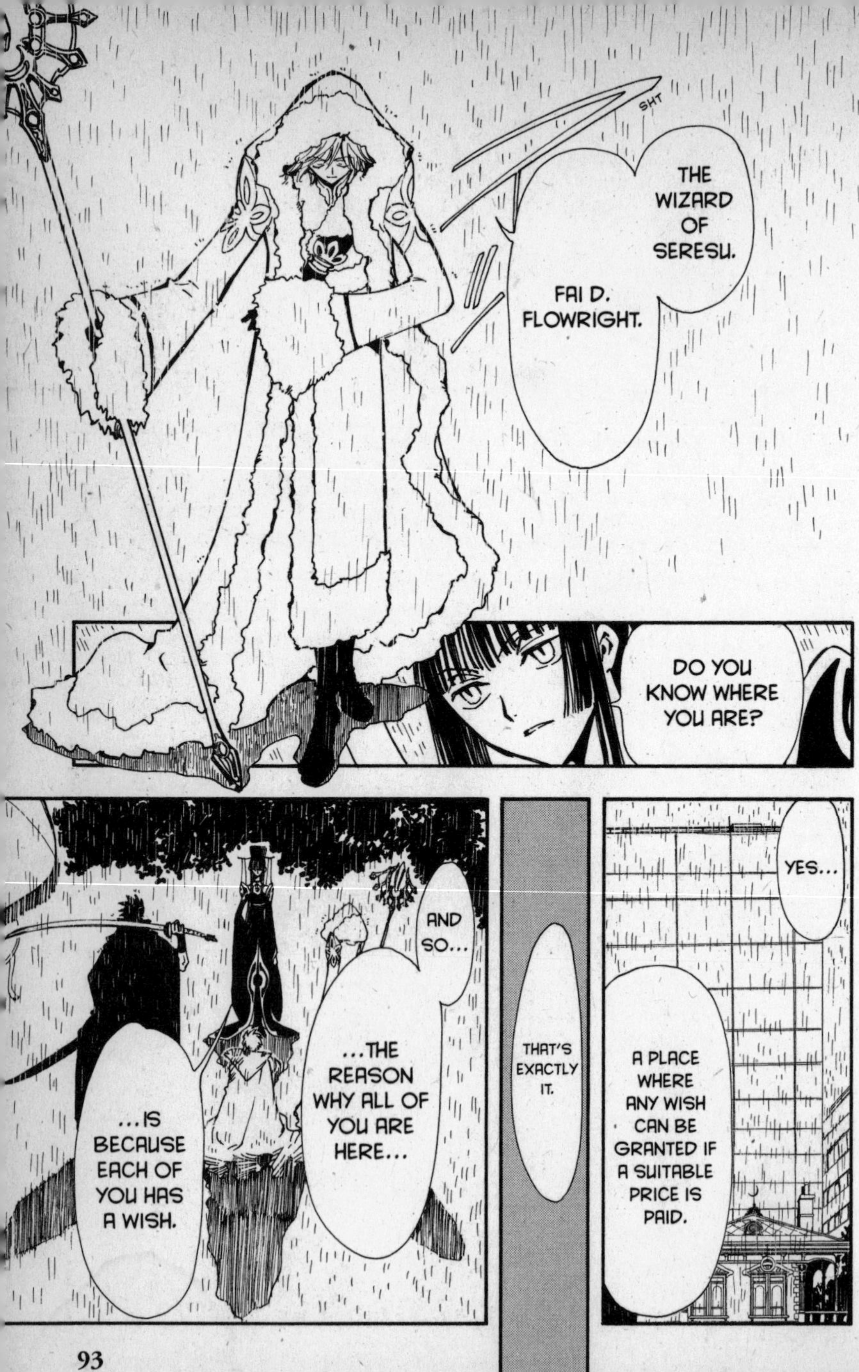
SHT
THE WIZARD OF SERESU.
FAI D. FLOWRIGHT.
DO YOU KNOW WHERE YOU ARE?
YES...
A PLACE WHERE ANY WISH CAN BE GRANTED IF A SUITABLE PRICE IS PAID.
THAT'S EXACTLY IT.
AND SO...
...THE REASON WHY ALL OF YOU ARE HERE...
...IS BECAUSE EACH OF YOU HAS A WISH.

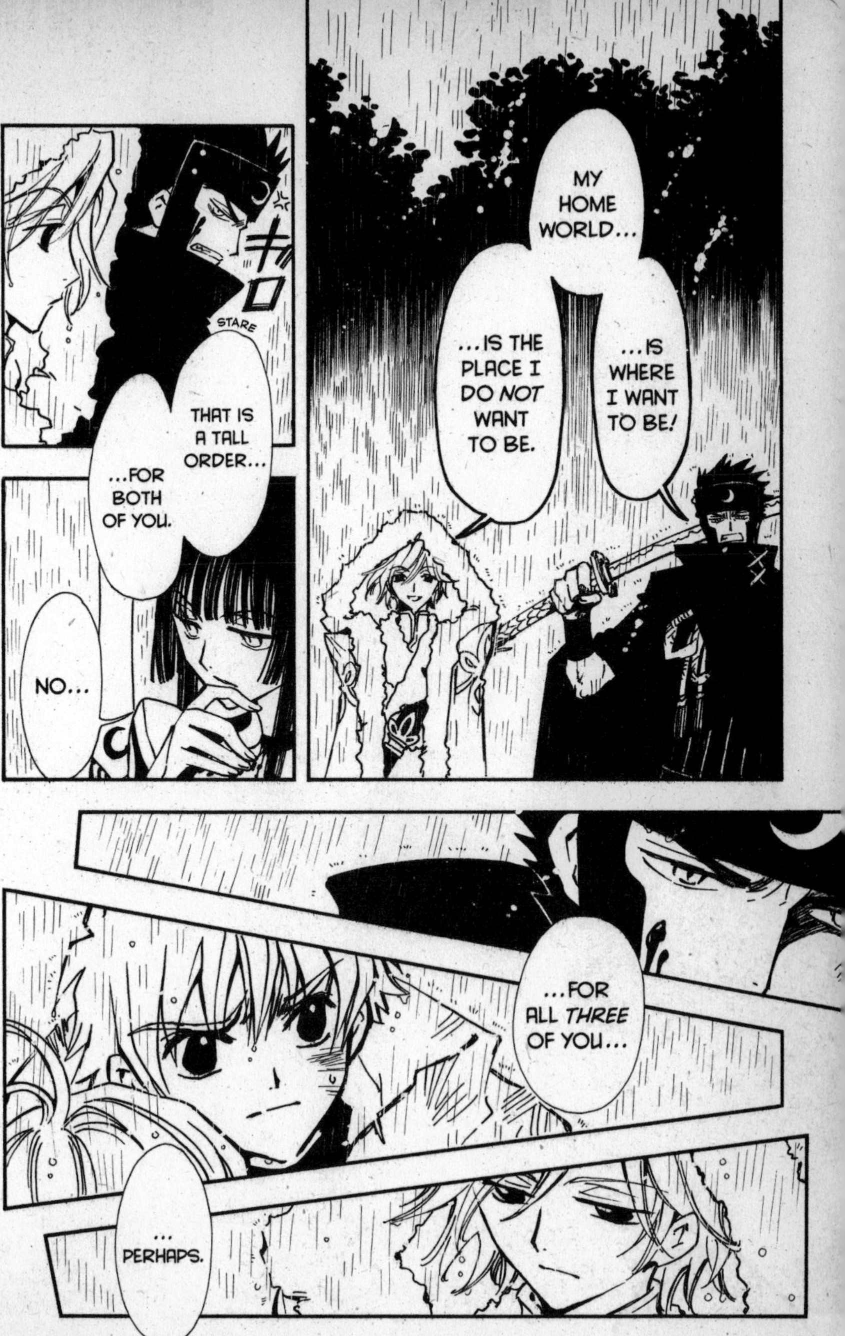
MY HOME WORLD...
...IS WHERE I WANT TO BE!
...IS THE PLACE I DO *NOT* WANT TO BE.
STARE
THAT IS A TALL ORDER...
...FOR BOTH OF YOU.
NO...
...FOR ALL *THREE* OF YOU...
... PERHAPS.

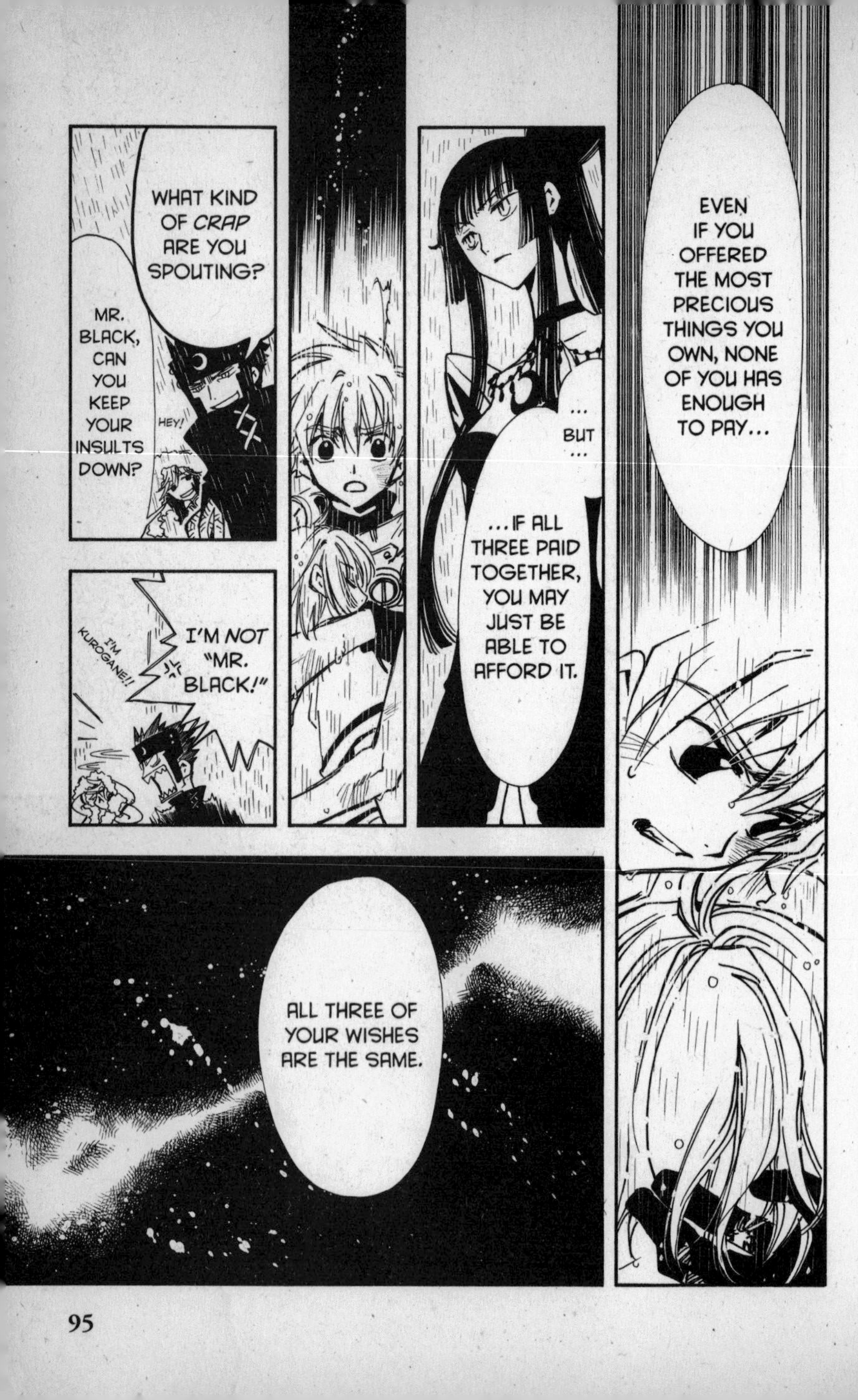
EVEN IF YOU OFFERED THE MOST PRECIOUS THINGS YOU OWN, NONE OF YOU HAS ENOUGH TO PAY...
...BUT...
...IF ALL THREE PAID TOGETHER, YOU MAY JUST BE ABLE TO AFFORD IT.
WHAT KIND OF *CRAP* ARE YOU SPOUTING?
MR. BLACK, CAN YOU KEEP YOUR INSULTS DOWN?
HEY!
I'M *NOT* "MR. BLACK!"
I'M KUROGANE!!
ALL THREE OF YOUR WISHES ARE THE SAME.

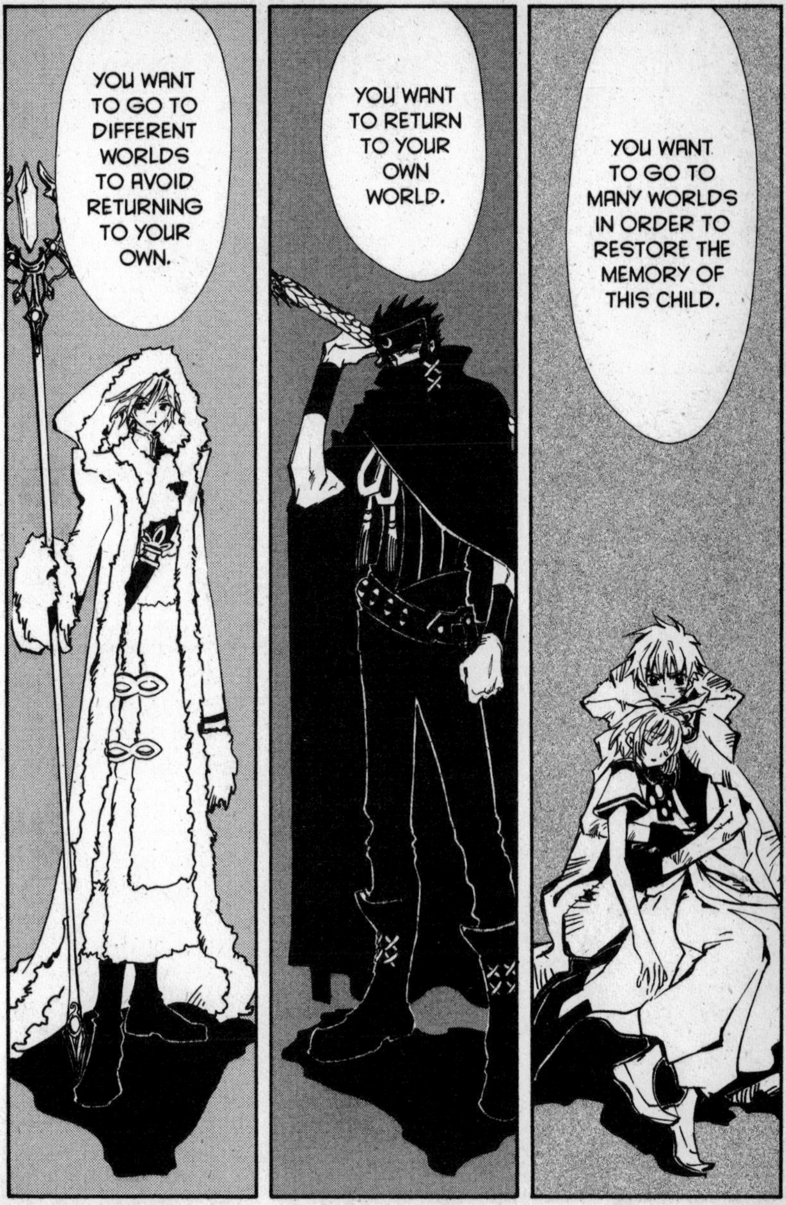
YOU WANT TO GO TO MANY WORLDS IN ORDER TO RESTORE THE MEMORY OF THIS CHILD.
YOU WANT TO RETURN TO YOUR OWN WORLD.
YOU WANT TO GO TO DIFFERENT WORLDS TO AVOID RETURNING TO YOUR OWN.

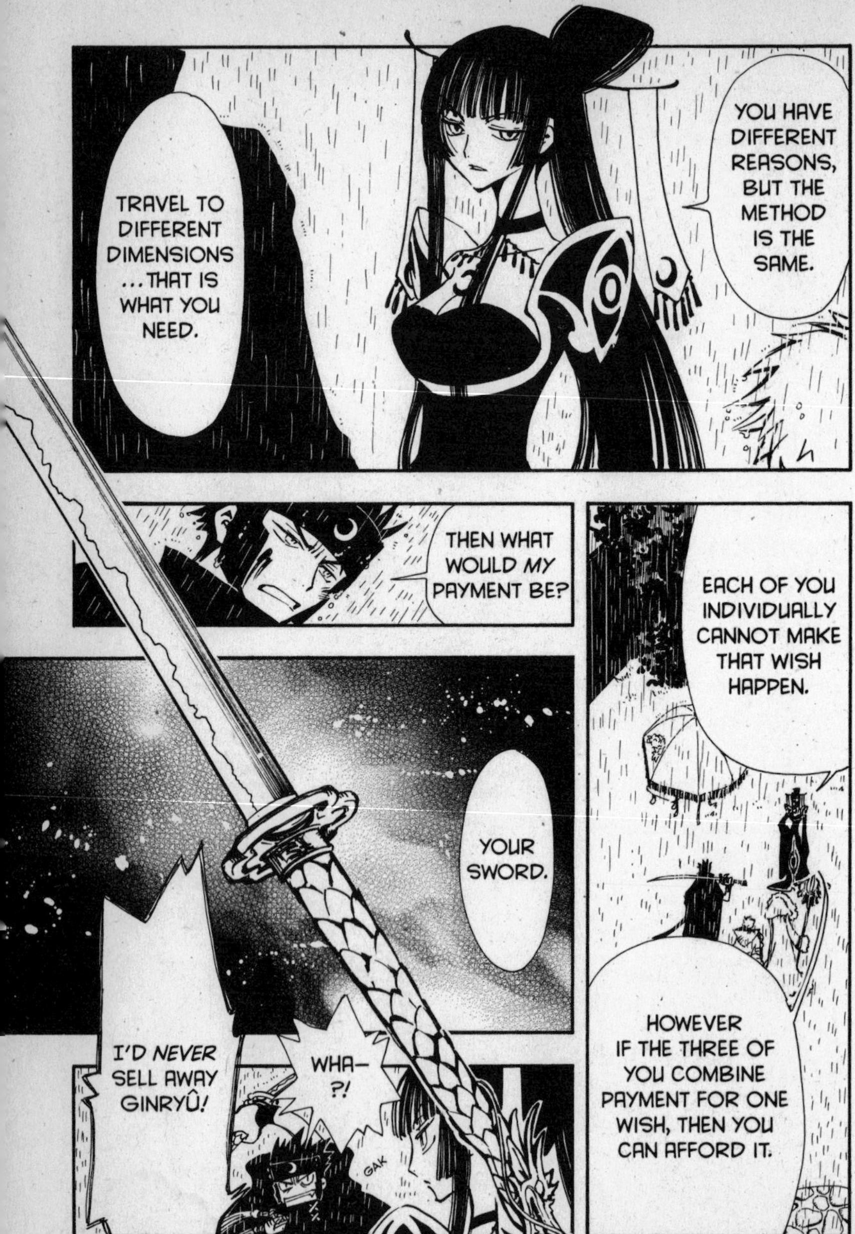
YOU HAVE DIFFERENT REASONS, BUT THE METHOD IS THE SAME.
TRAVEL TO DIFFERENT DIMENSIONS ...THAT IS WHAT YOU NEED.
EACH OF YOU INDIVIDUALLY CANNOT MAKE THAT WISH HAPPEN.
HOWEVER IF THE THREE OF YOU COMBINE PAYMENT FOR ONE WISH, THEN YOU CAN AFFORD IT.
THEN WHAT WOULD *MY* PAYMENT BE?
YOUR SWORD.
WHA--?!
GAK
I'D *NEVER* SELL AWAY GINRYÛ!

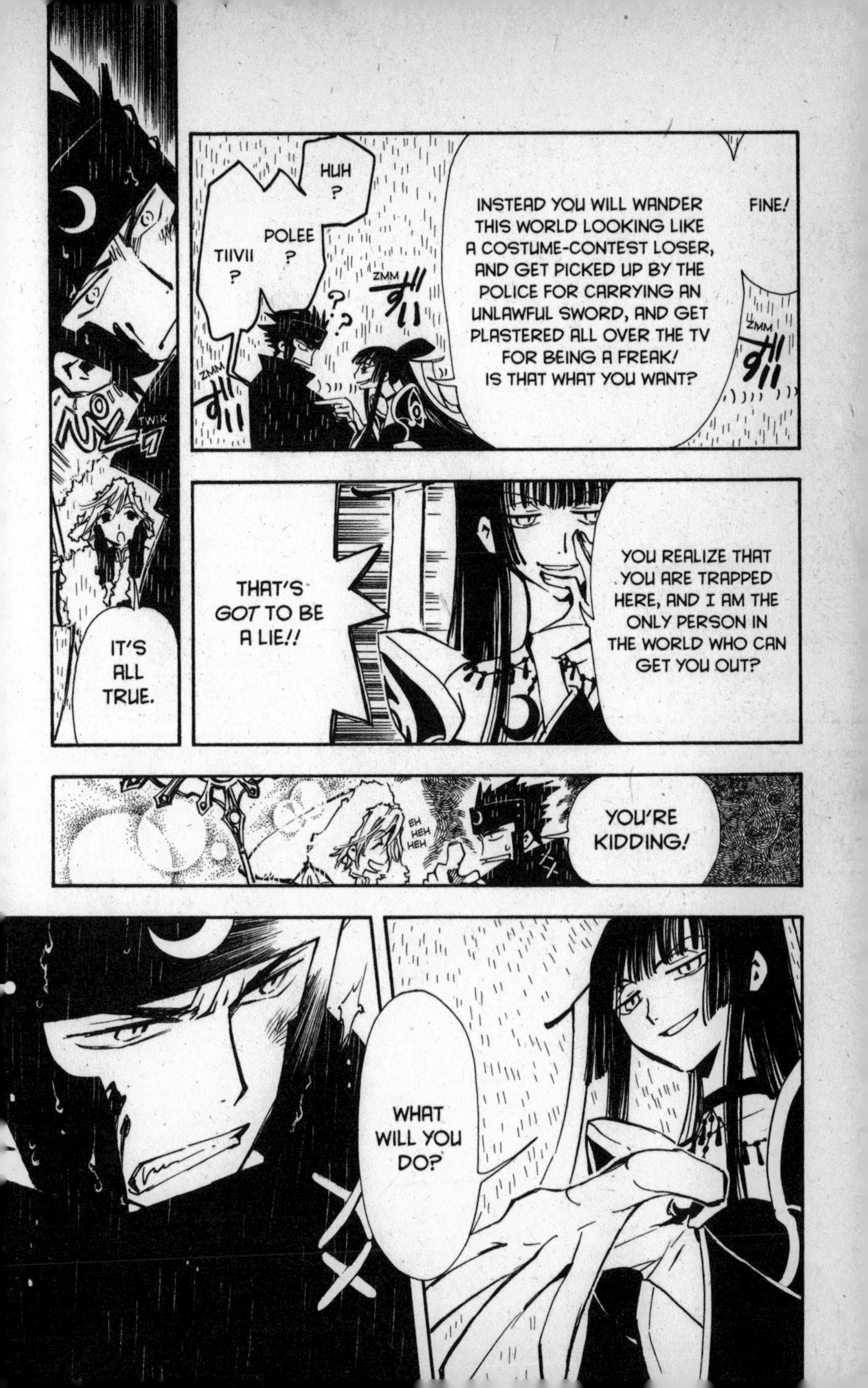
FINE!
ZMM
INSTEAD YOU WILL WANDER THIS WORLD LOOKING LIKE A COSTUME-CONTEST LOSER, AND GET PICKED UP BY THE POLICE FOR CARRYING AN UNLAWFUL SWORD, AND GET PLASTERED ALL OVER THE TV FOR BEING A FREAK! IS THAT WHAT YOU WANT?
HUH?
POLEE?
TIIVII?
ZMM
ZMM
YOU REALIZE THAT YOU ARE TRAPPED HERE, AND I AM THE ONLY PERSON IN THE WORLD WHO CAN GET YOU OUT?
THAT'S *GOT* TO BE A LIE!!
TWIK
IT'S ALL TRUE.
YOU'RE KIDDING!
EH HEH HEH
WHAT WILL YOU DO?

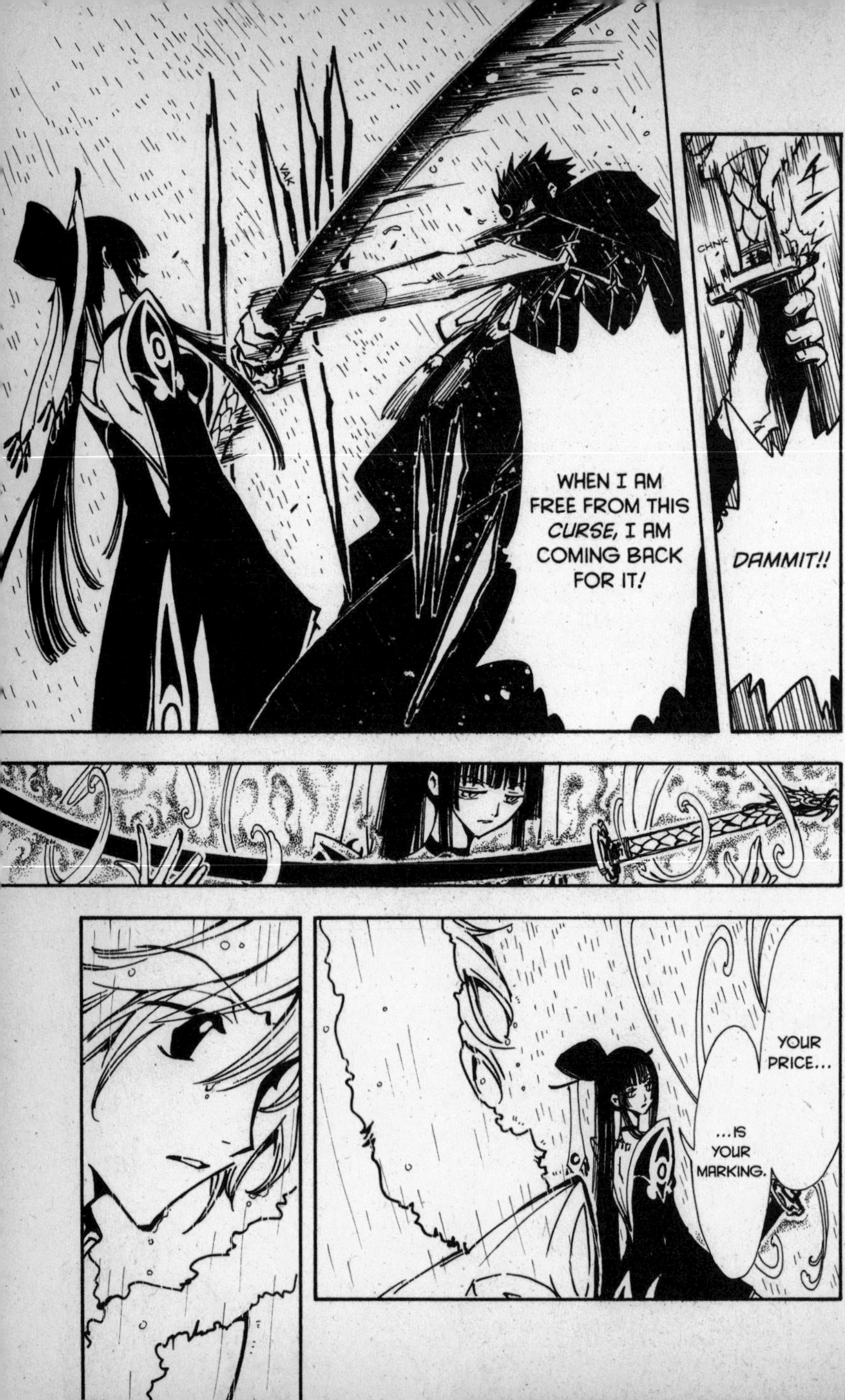
CHNK
DAMMIT!!
VAK
WHEN I AM FREE FROM THIS *CURSE,* I AM COMING BACK FOR IT!
YOUR PRICE...
...IS YOUR MARKING.

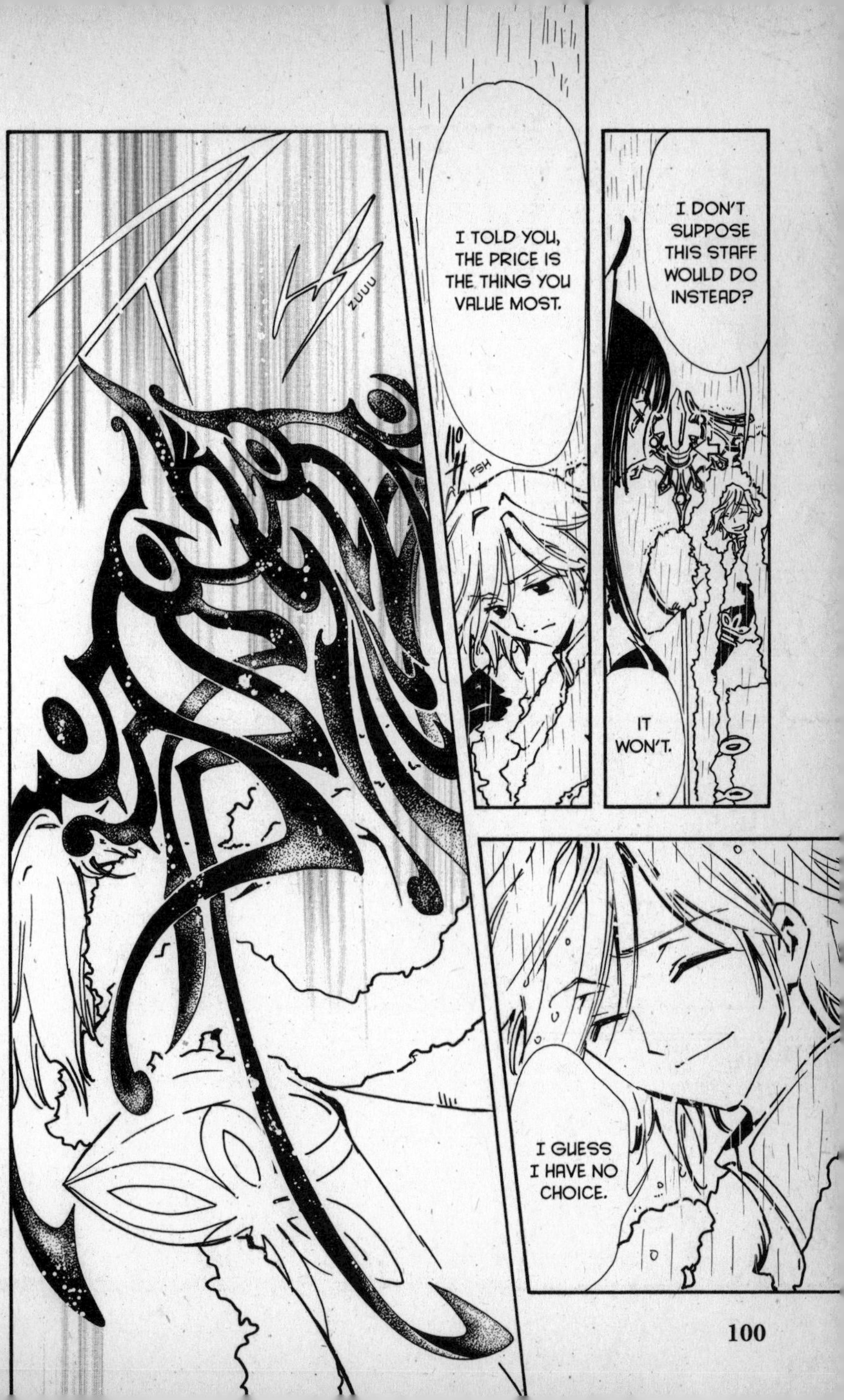
I DON'T SUPPOSE THIS STAFF WOULD DO INSTEAD?
IT WON'T.
I TOLD YOU, THE PRICE IS THE THING YOU VALUE MOST.
FSH
I GUESS I HAVE NO CHOICE.
ZUUU

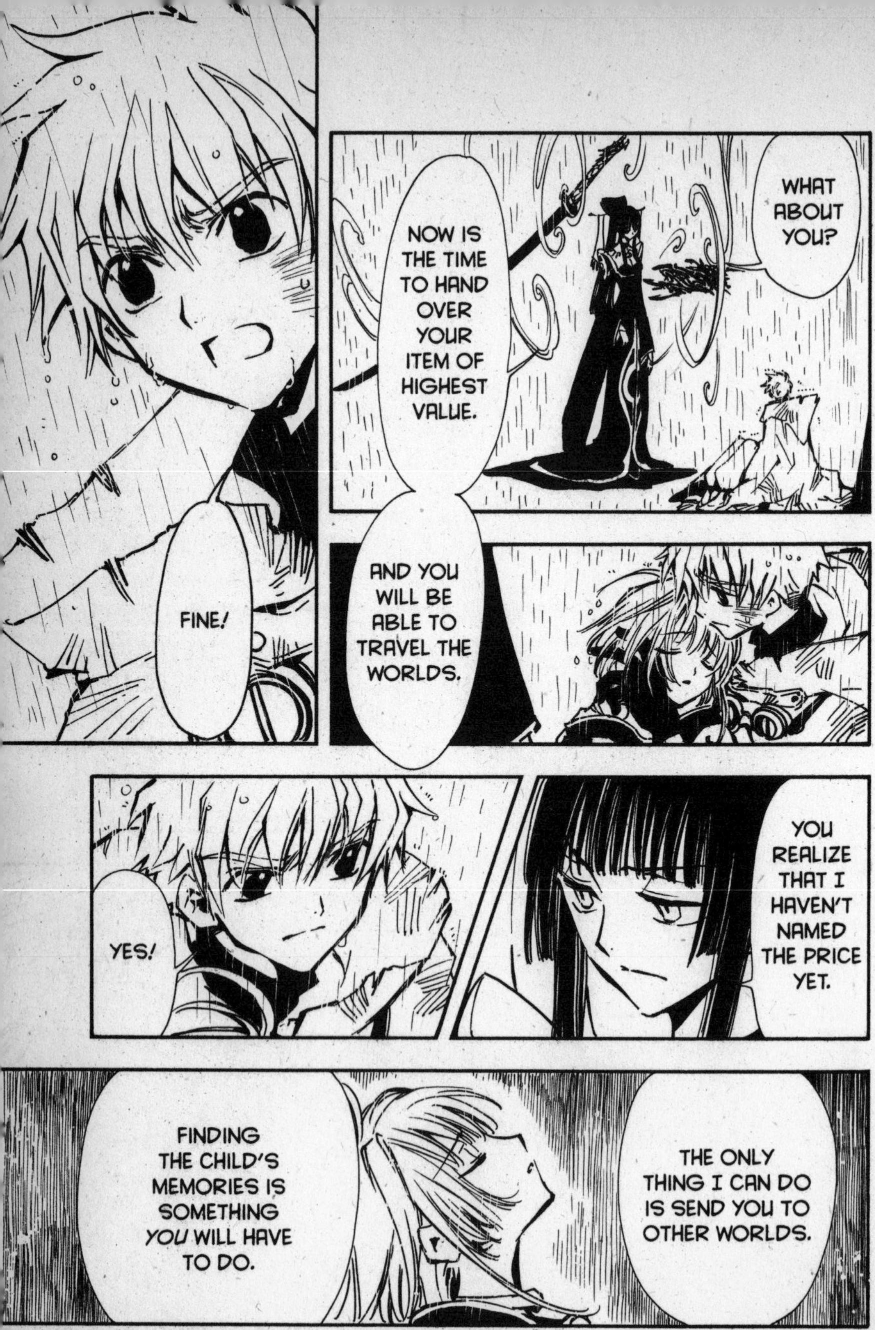
WHAT ABOUT YOU?
NOW IS THE TIME TO HAND OVER YOUR ITEM OF HIGHEST VALUE.
AND YOU WILL BE ABLE TO TRAVEL THE WORLDS.
FINE!
YOU REALIZE THAT I HAVEN'T NAMED THE PRICE YET.
YES!
THE ONLY THING I CAN DO IS SEND YOU TO OTHER WORLDS.
FINDING THE CHILD'S MEMORIES IS SOMETHING *YOU* WILL HAVE TO DO.

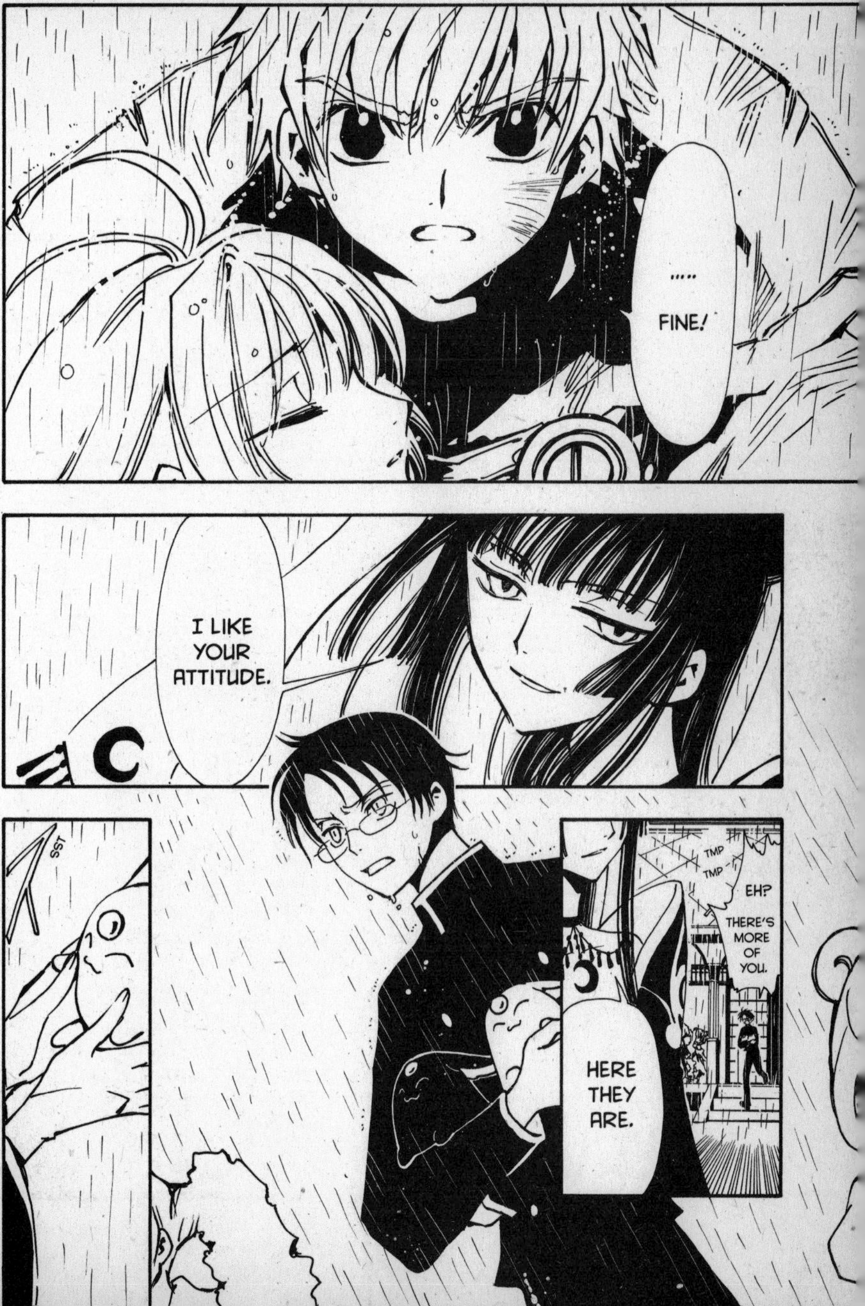
……
FINE!
I LIKE YOUR ATTITUDE.
TMP TMP
EH?
THERE'S MORE OF YOU.
HERE THEY ARE.
SST

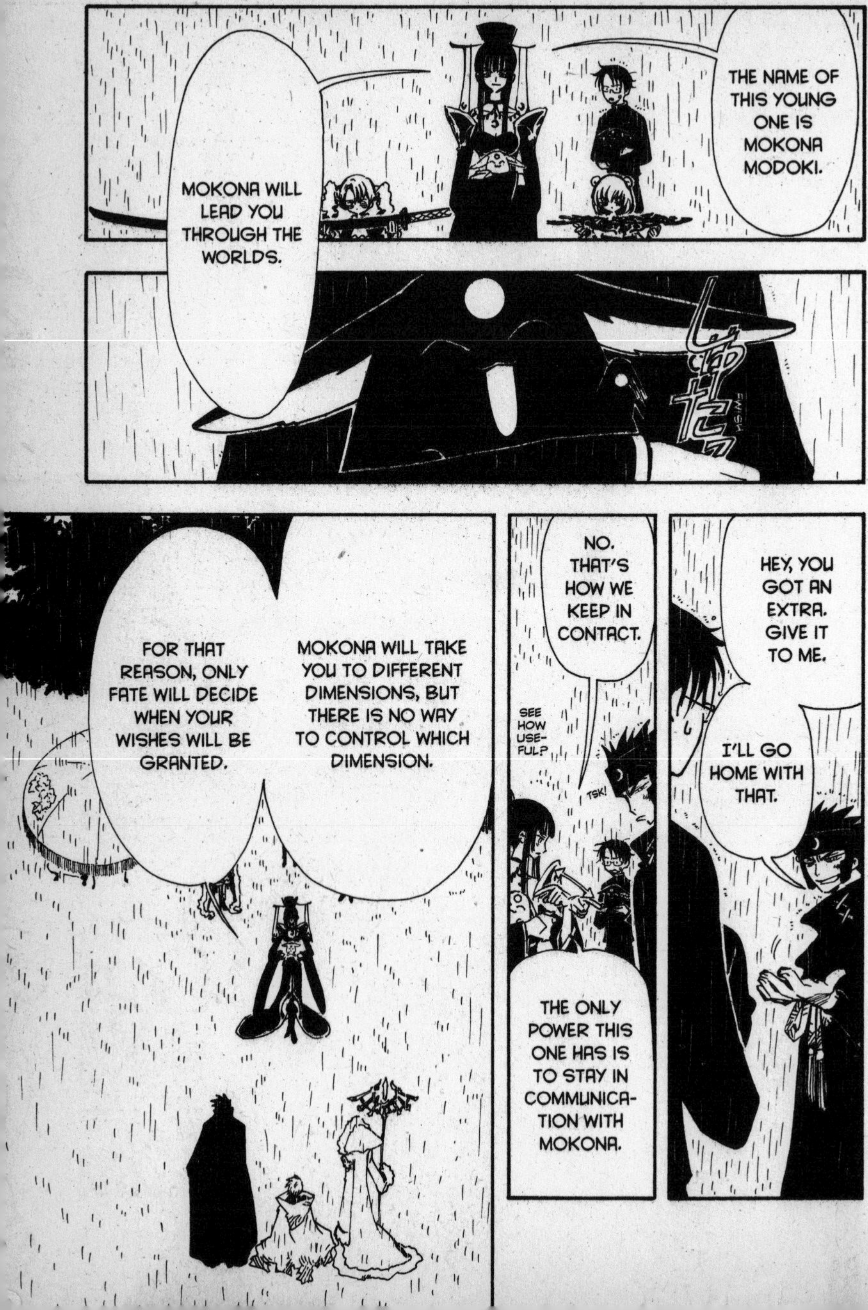
THE NAME OF THIS YOUNG ONE IS MOKONA MODOKI.
MOKONA WILL LEAD YOU THROUGH THE WORLDS.
FWISH
HEY, YOU GOT AN EXTRA. GIVE IT TO ME.
I'LL GO HOME WITH THAT.
NO. THAT'S HOW WE KEEP IN CONTACT.
SEE HOW USE-FUL?
TSK!
THE ONLY POWER THIS ONE HAS IS TO STAY IN COMMUNICA-TION WITH MOKONA.
MOKONA WILL TAKE YOU TO DIFFERENT DIMENSIONS, BUT THERE IS NO WAY TO CONTROL WHICH DIMENSION.
FOR THAT REASON, ONLY FATE WILL DECIDE WHEN YOUR WISHES WILL BE GRANTED.

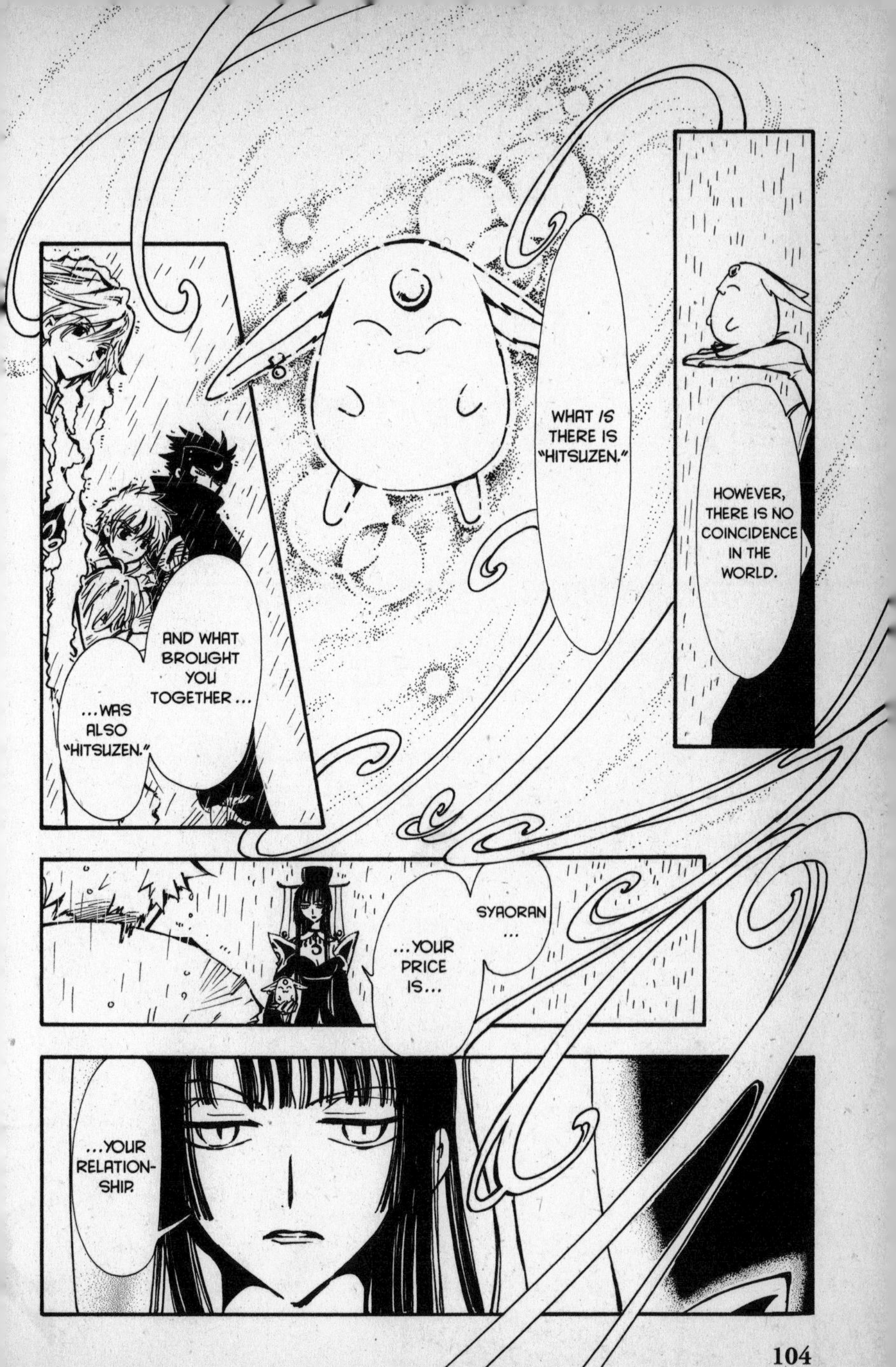
HOWEVER, THERE IS NO COINCIDENCE IN THE WORLD.
WHAT IS THERE IS "HITSUZEN."
AND WHAT BROUGHT YOU TOGETHER...
...WAS ALSO "HITSUZEN."
SYAORAN...
...YOUR PRICE IS...
...YOUR RELATION-SHIP.

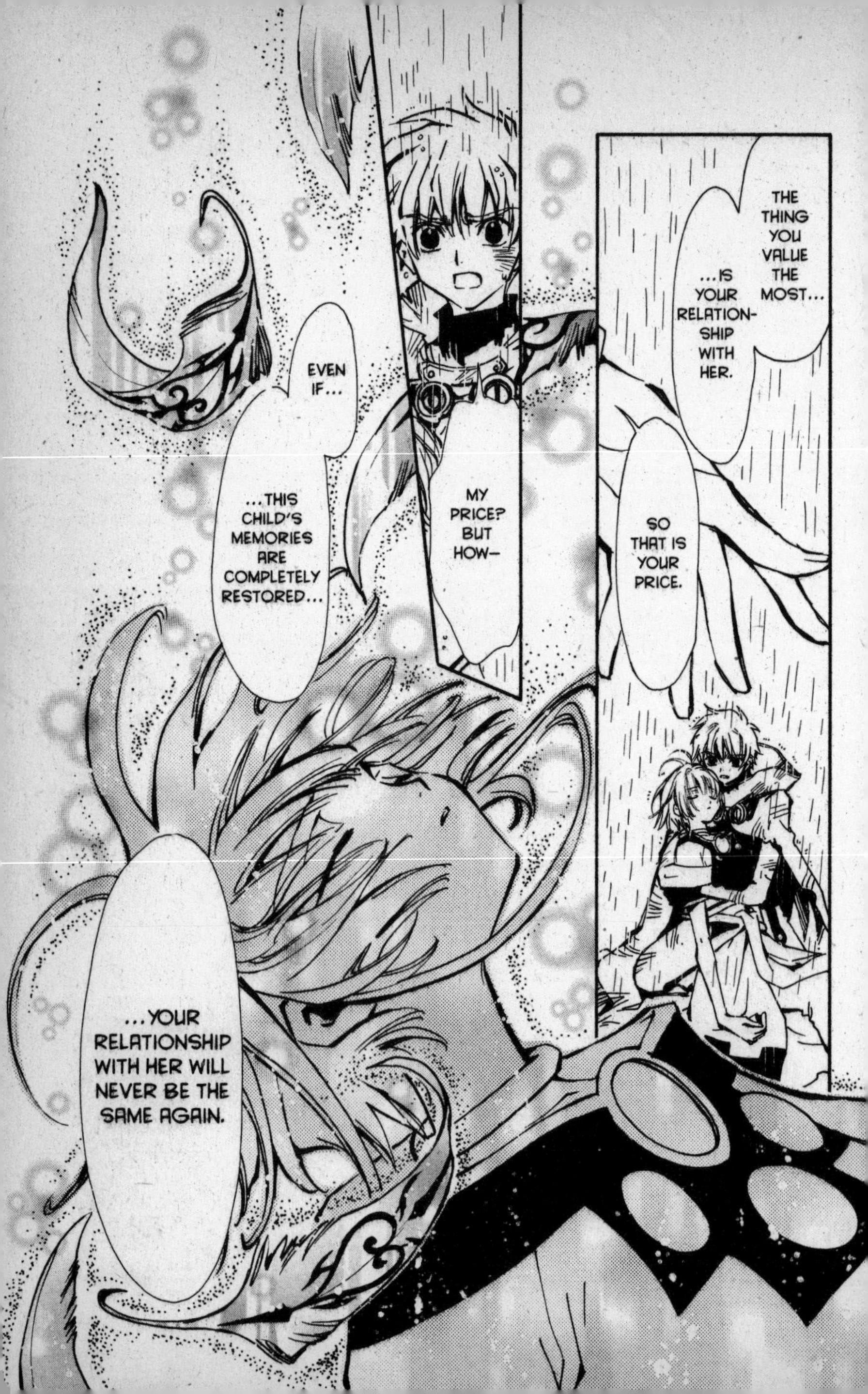

THE THING YOU VALUE THE MOST... ...IS YOUR RELATIONSHIP WITH HER.
SO THAT IS YOUR PRICE.
MY PRICE? BUT HOW-
EVEN IF...
...THIS CHILD'S MEMORIES ARE COMPLETELY RESTORED...
...YOUR RELATIONSHIP WITH HER WILL NEVER BE THE SAME AGAIN.

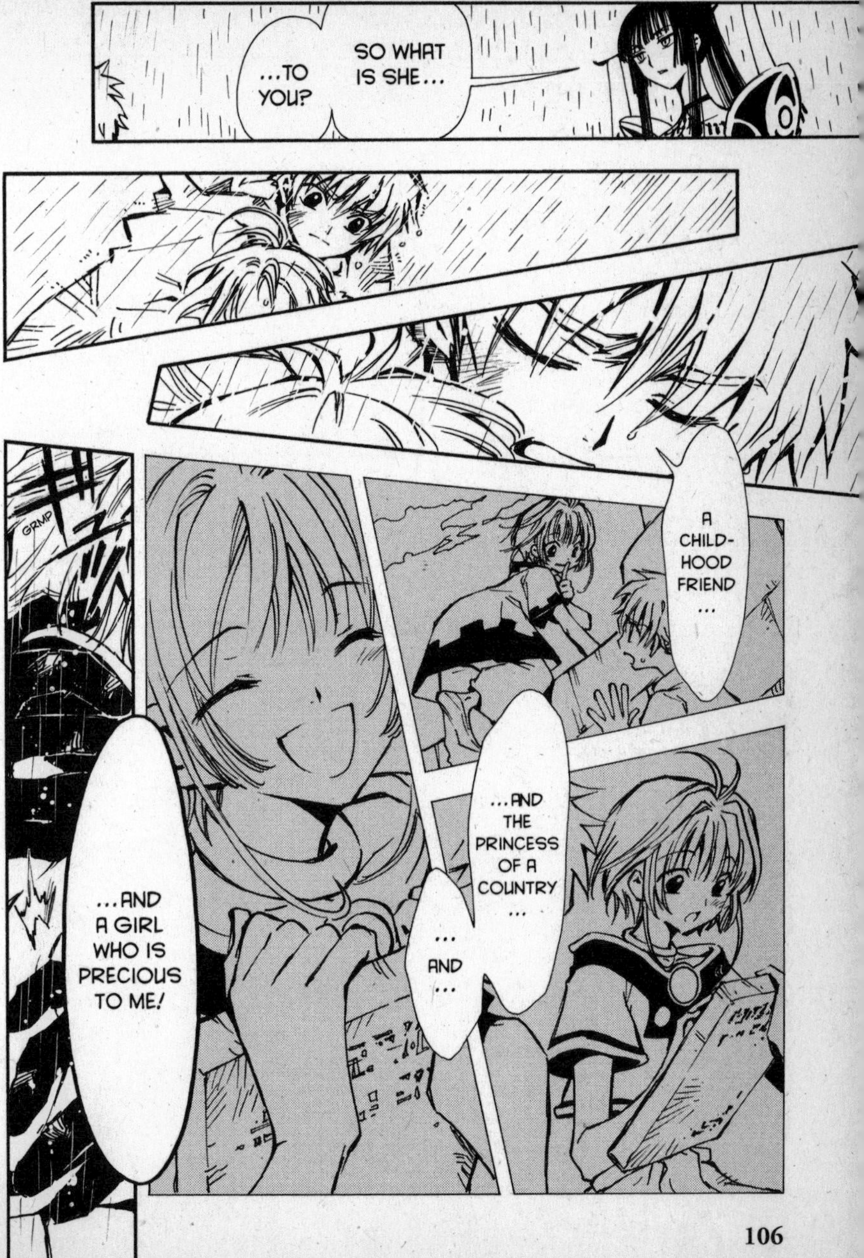
SO WHAT IS SHE...
...TO YOU?
GRMP
A CHILD-HOOD FRIEND ...
...AND THE PRINCESS OF A COUNTRY ...
... AND ...
...AND A GIRL WHO IS PRECIOUS TO ME!

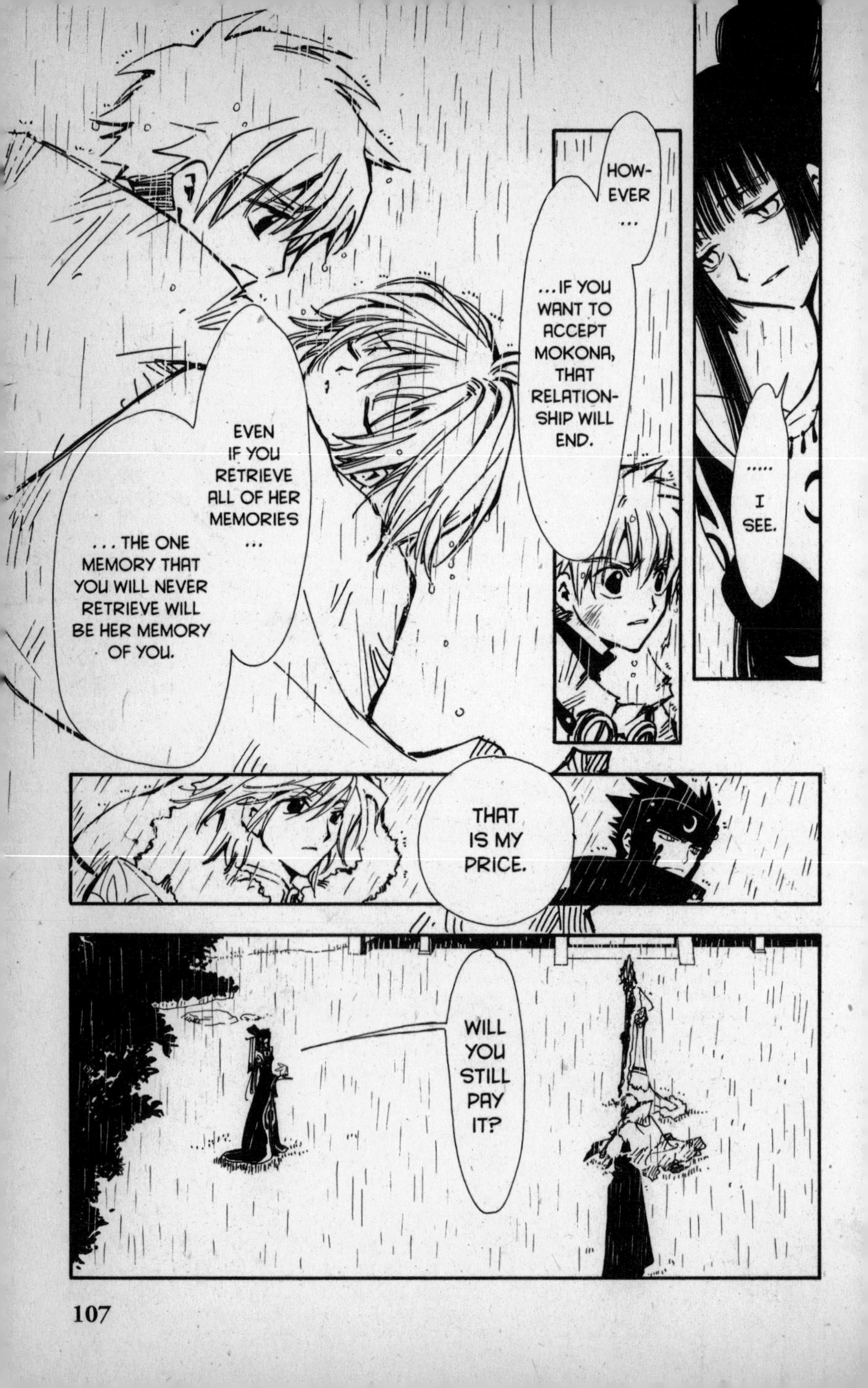
..... I SEE.
HOW-EVER ...
...IF YOU WANT TO ACCEPT MOKONA, THAT RELATIONSHIP WILL END.
EVEN IF YOU RETRIEVE ALL OF HER MEMORIES ...
... THE ONE MEMORY THAT YOU WILL NEVER RETRIEVE WILL BE HER MEMORY OF YOU.
THAT IS MY PRICE.
WILL YOU STILL PAY IT?

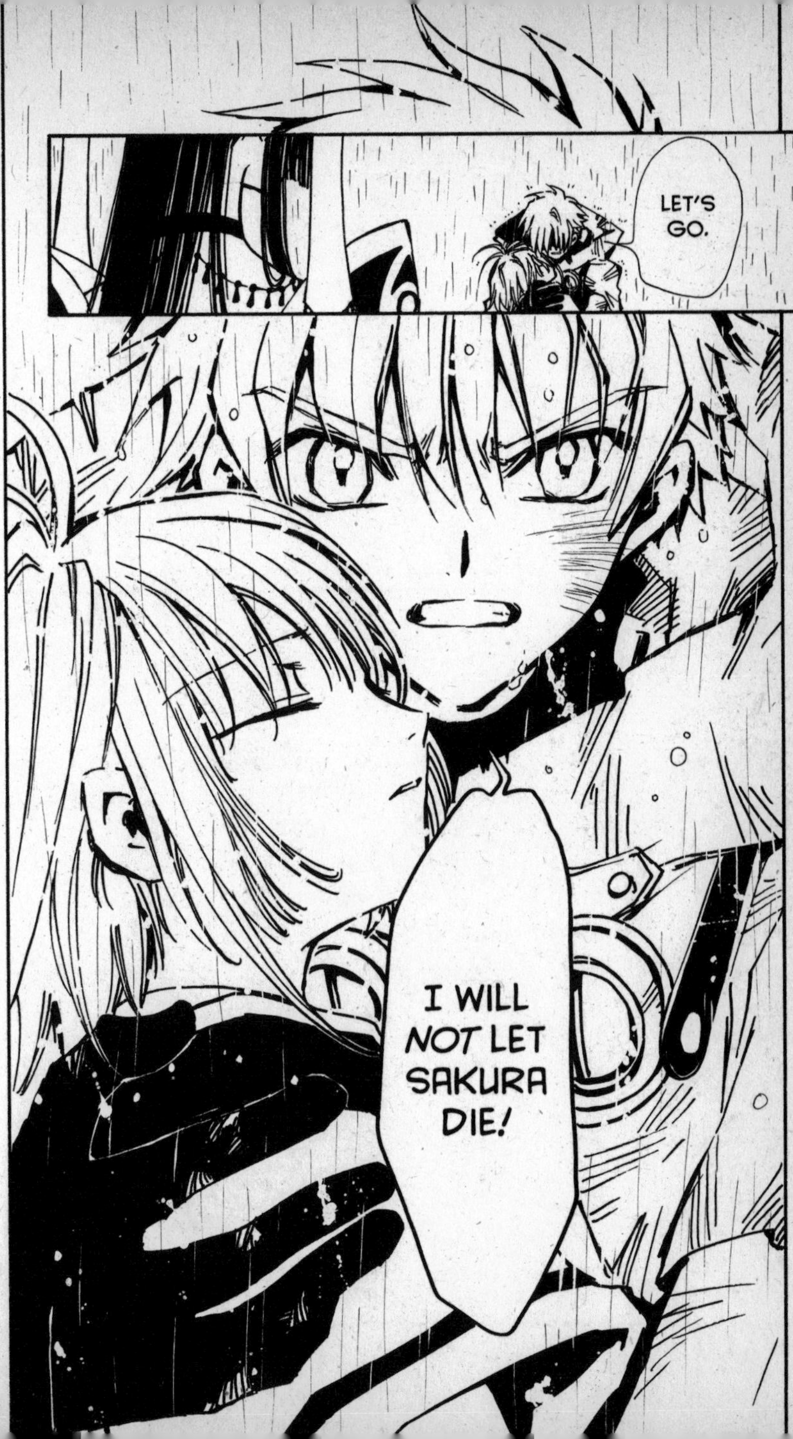
LET'S GO.
I WILL *NOT* LET SAKURA DIE!

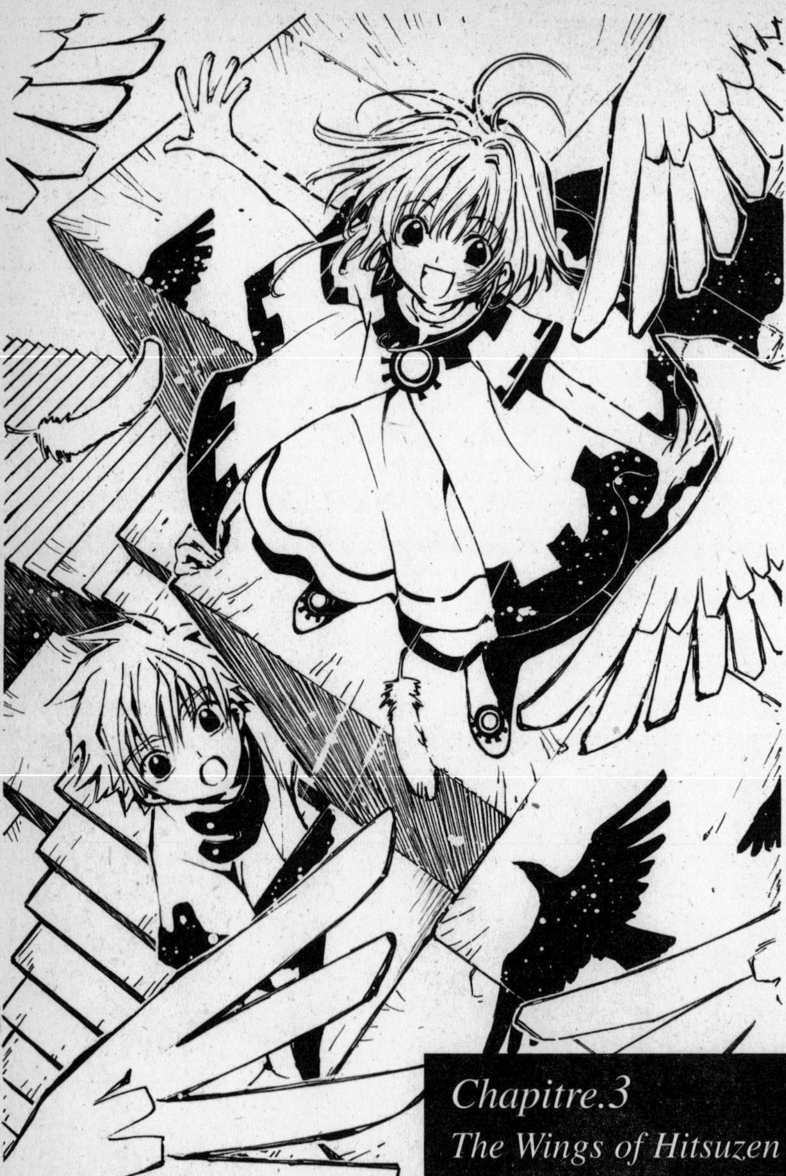

Chapitre.3

The Wings of Hitsuzen

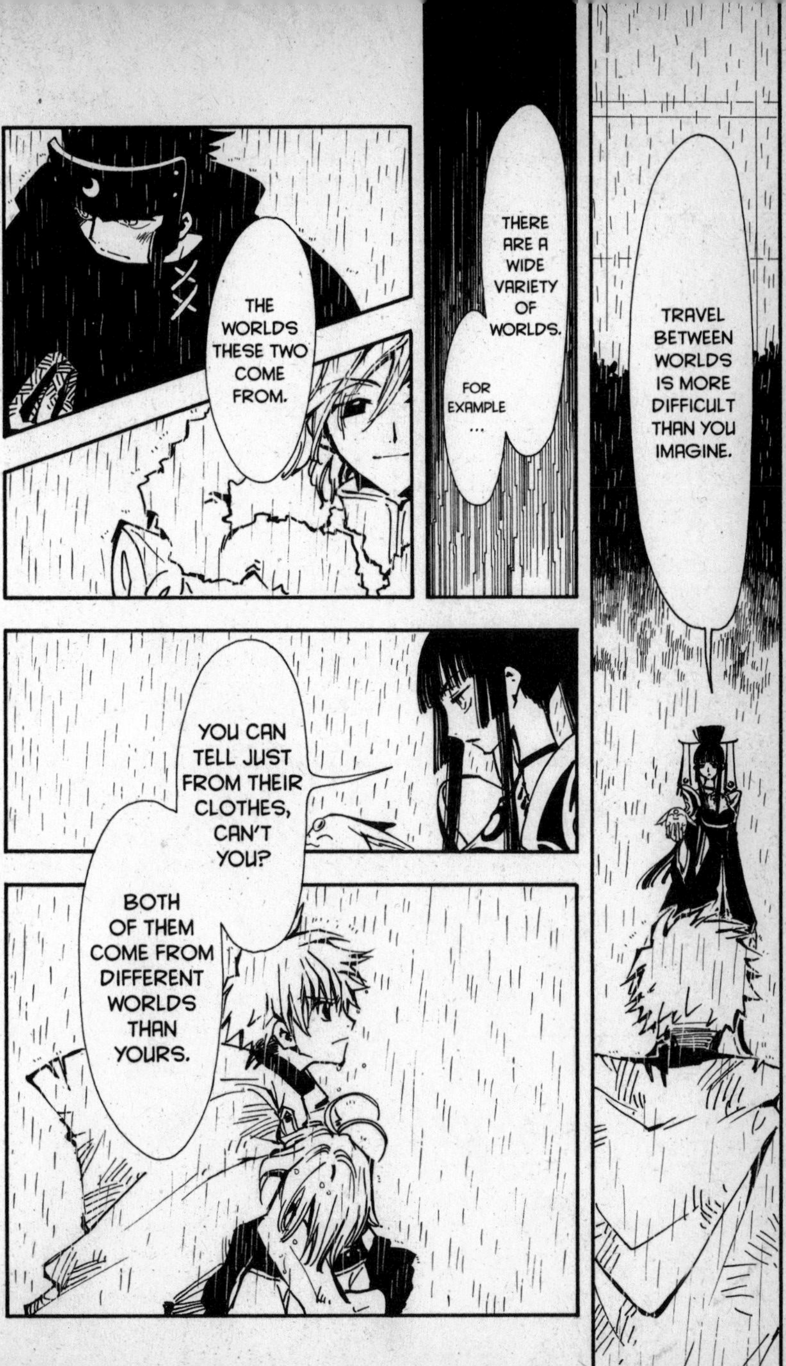
TRAVEL BETWEEN WORLDS IS MORE DIFFICULT THAN YOU IMAGINE.
THERE ARE A WIDE VARIETY OF WORLDS.
FOR EXAMPLE ...
THE WORLDS THESE TWO COME FROM.
YOU CAN TELL JUST FROM THEIR CLOTHES, CAN'T YOU?
BOTH OF THEM COME FROM DIFFERENT WORLDS THAN YOURS.

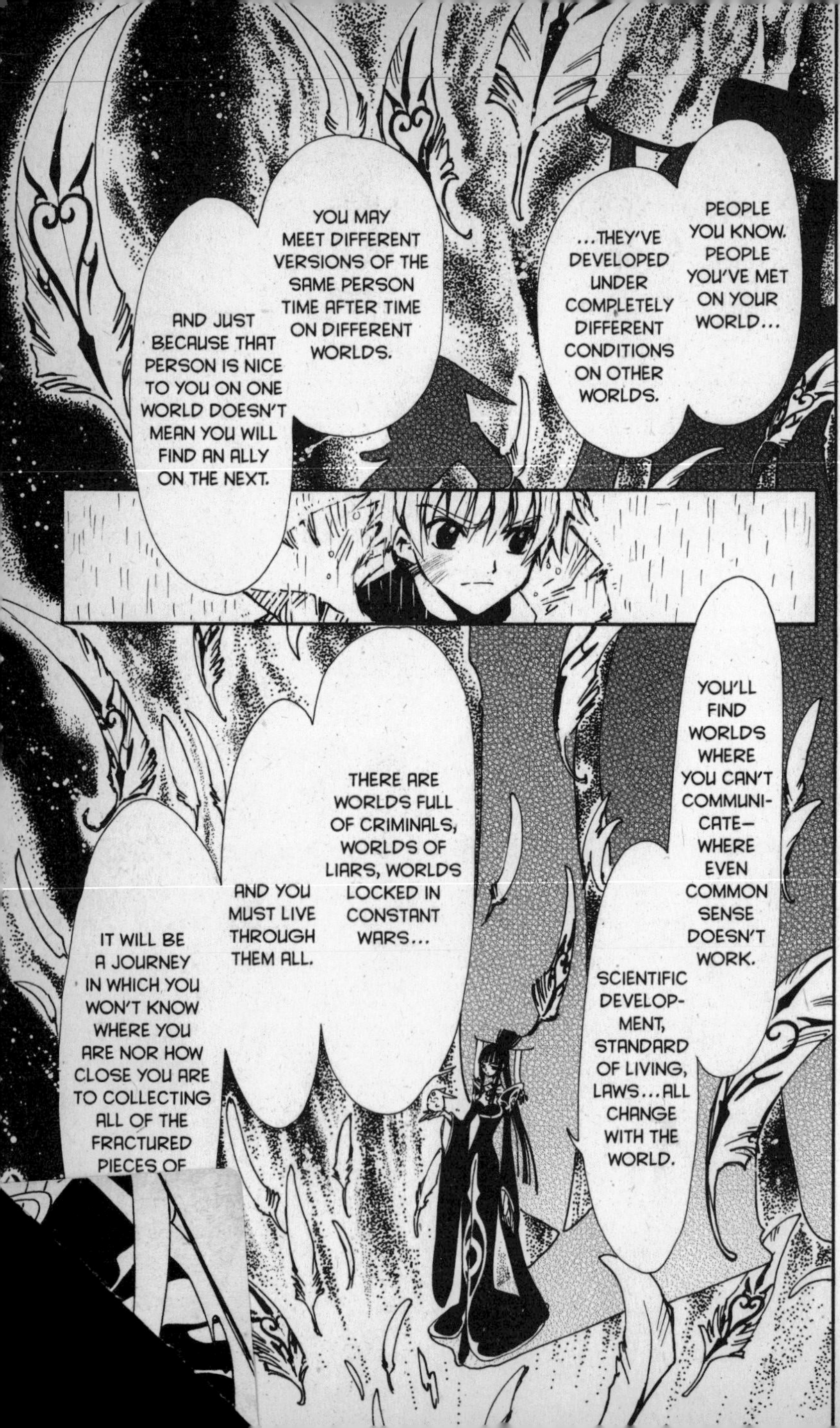
PEOPLE YOU KNOW. PEOPLE YOU'VE MET ON YOUR WORLD...
...THEY'VE DEVELOPED UNDER COMPLETELY DIFFERENT CONDITIONS ON OTHER WORLDS.
YOU MAY MEET DIFFERENT VERSIONS OF THE SAME PERSON TIME AFTER TIME ON DIFFERENT WORLDS.
AND JUST BECAUSE THAT PERSON IS NICE TO YOU ON ONE WORLD DOESN'T MEAN YOU WILL FIND AN ALLY ON THE NEXT.
YOU'LL FIND WORLDS WHERE YOU CAN'T COMMUNI-CATE—WHERE EVEN COMMON SENSE DOESN'T WORK.
SCIENTIFIC DEVELOP-MENT, STANDARD OF LIVING, LAWS...ALL CHANGE WITH THE WORLD.
THERE ARE WORLDS FULL OF CRIMINALS, WORLDS OF LIARS, WORLDS LOCKED IN CONSTANT WARS...
AND YOU MUST LIVE THROUGH THEM ALL.
IT WILL BE A JOURNEY IN WHICH YOU WON'T KNOW WHERE YOU ARE NOR HOW CLOSE YOU ARE TO COLLECTING ALL OF THE FRACTURED PIECES OF

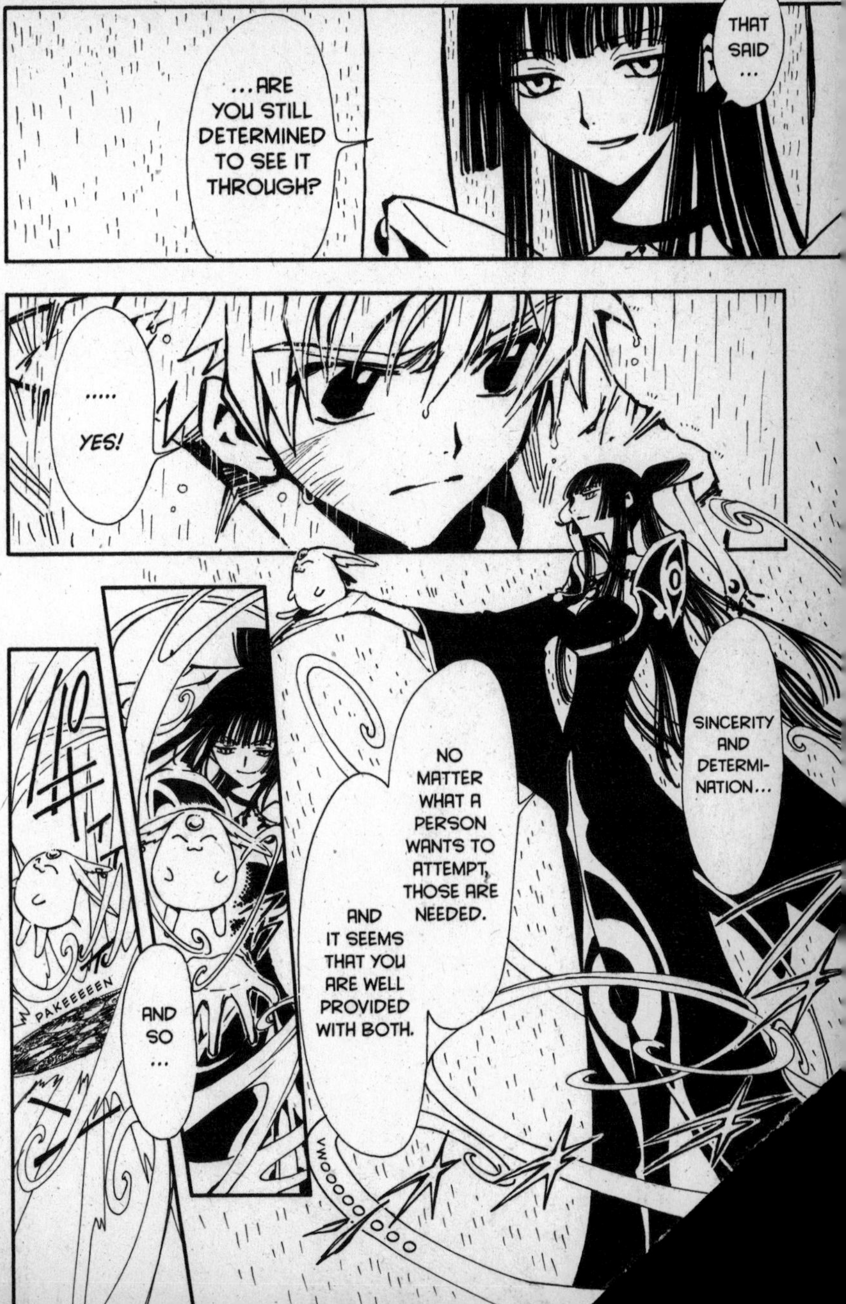
THAT SAID ...
...ARE YOU STILL DETERMINED TO SEE IT THROUGH?
..... YES!
SINCERITY AND DETERMINATION...
NO MATTER WHAT A PERSON WANTS TO ATTEMPT, THOSE ARE NEEDED.
AND IT SEEMS THAT YOU ARE WELL PROVIDED WITH BOTH.
VWOOOOOOOOOO
AND SO ...
PAKEEEEEEN

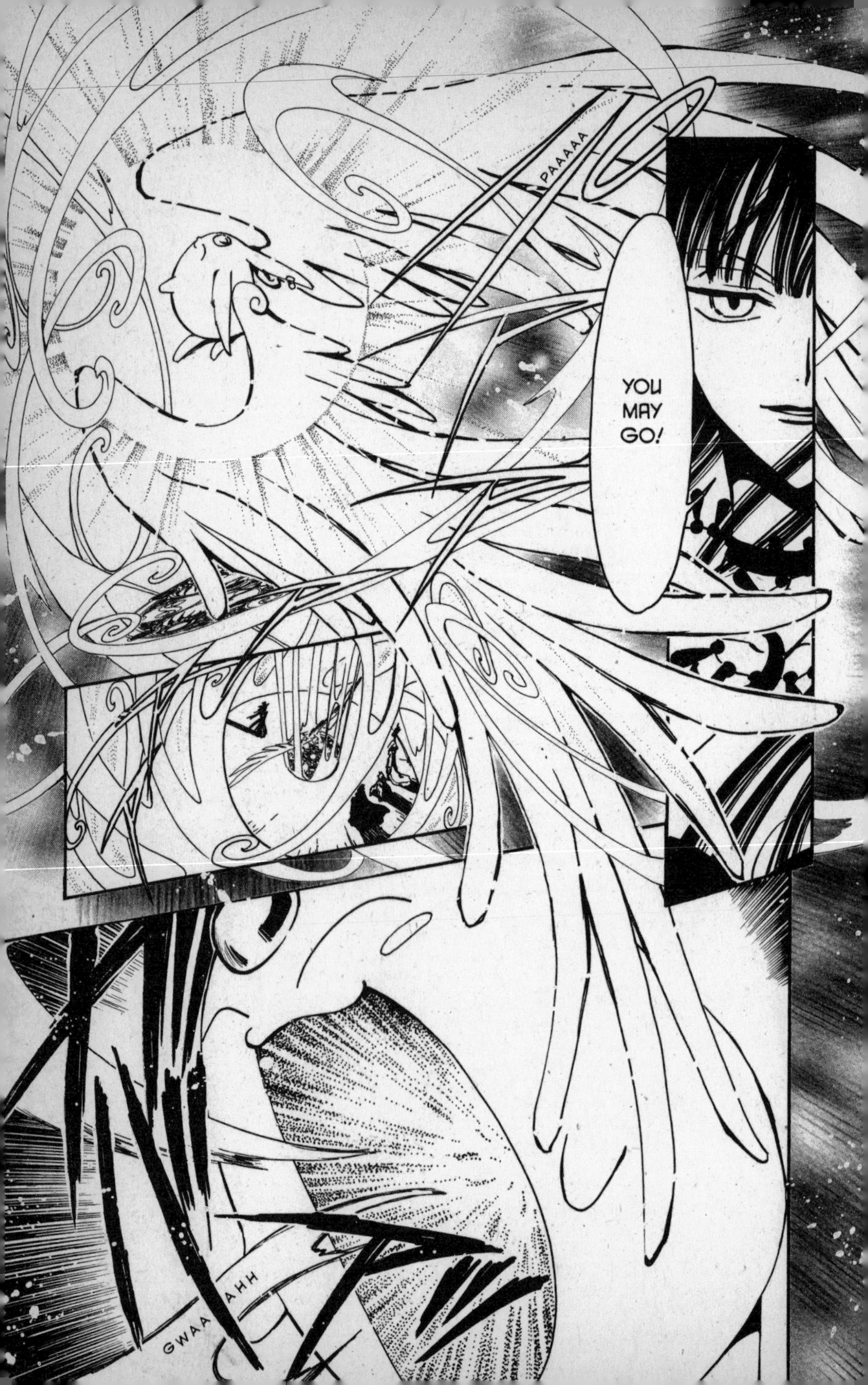
PAAAAA
YOU MAY GO!
GWAAAAHH

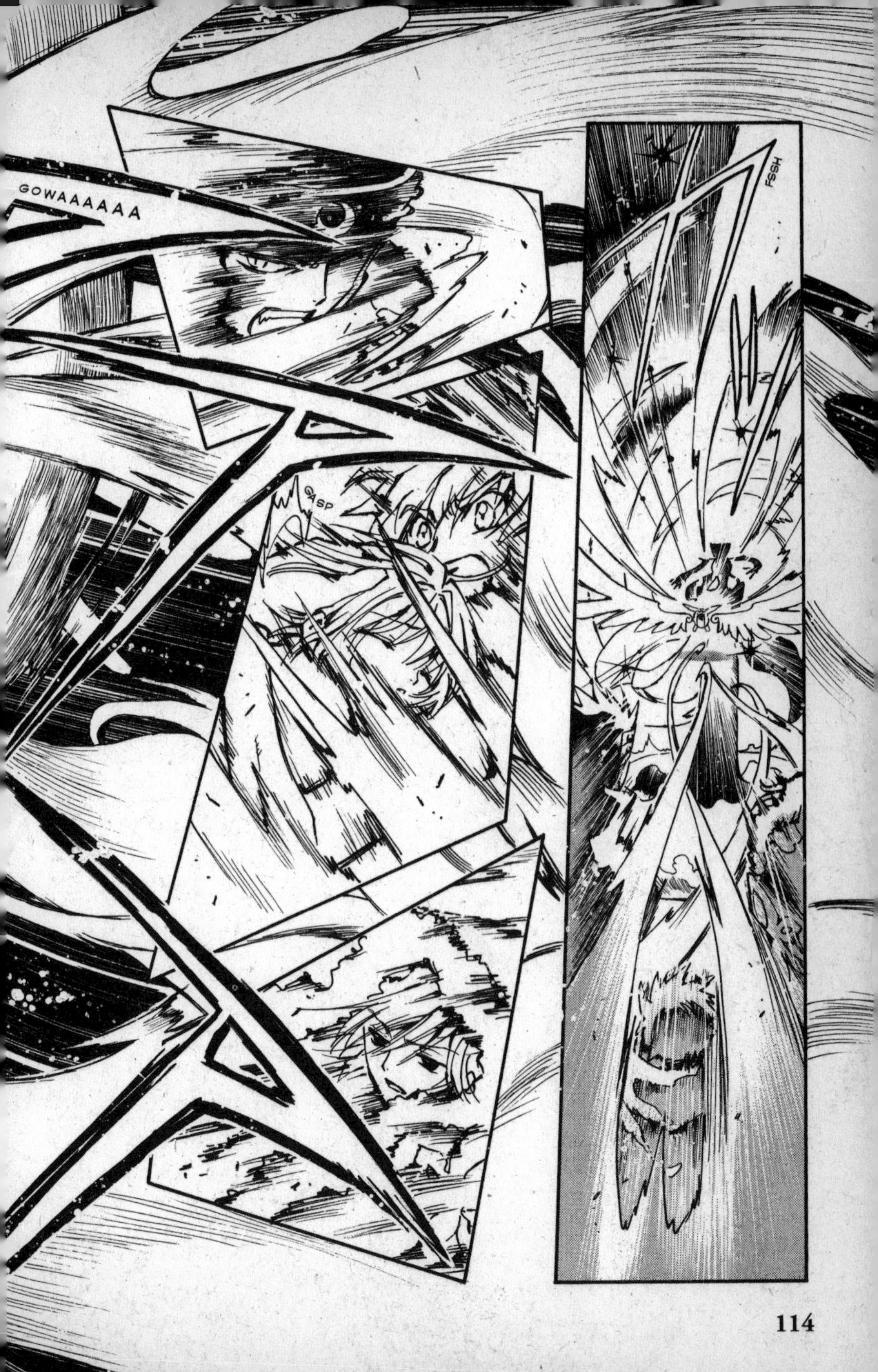
FSSH
GOWAAAAAAA
GASP

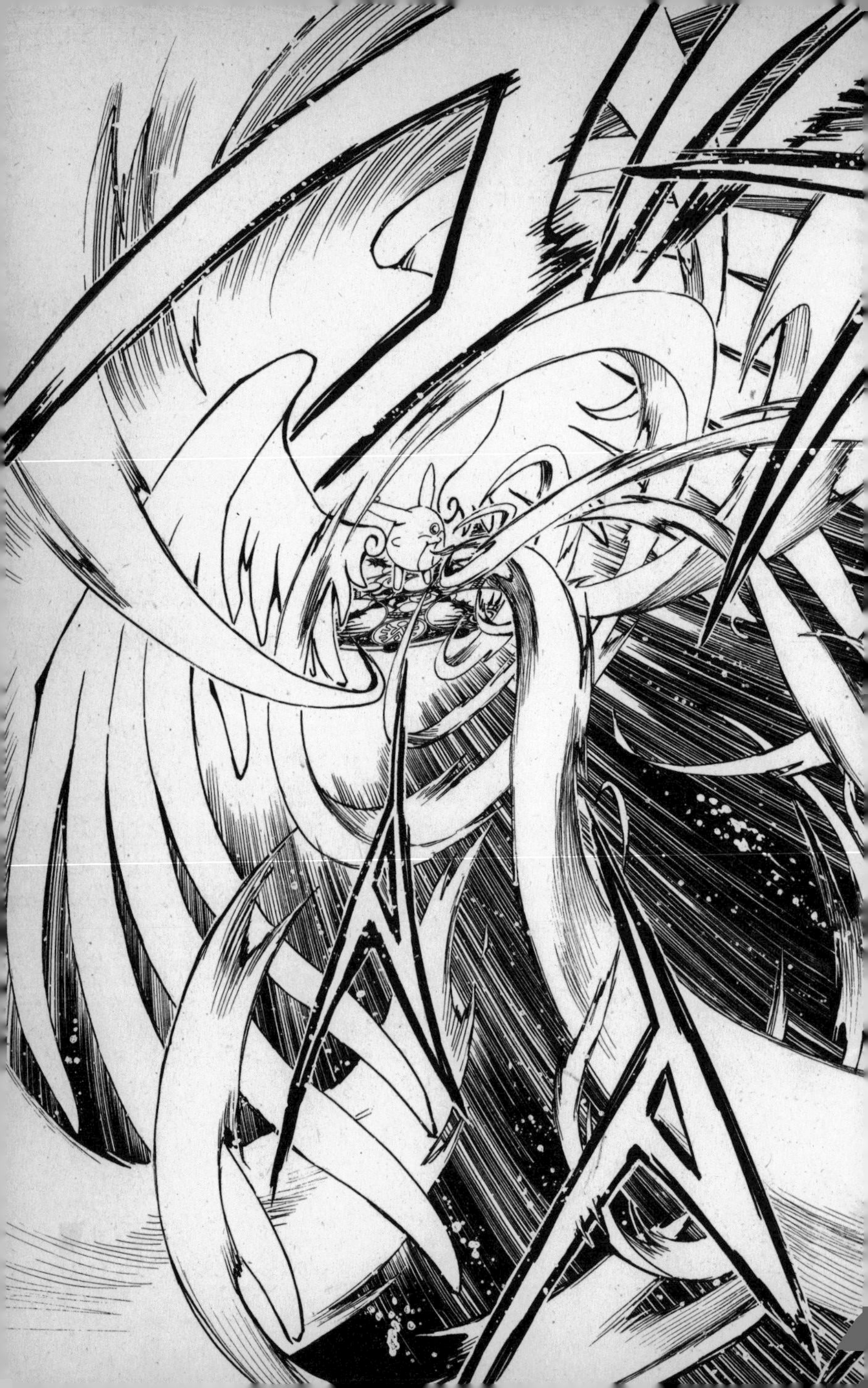

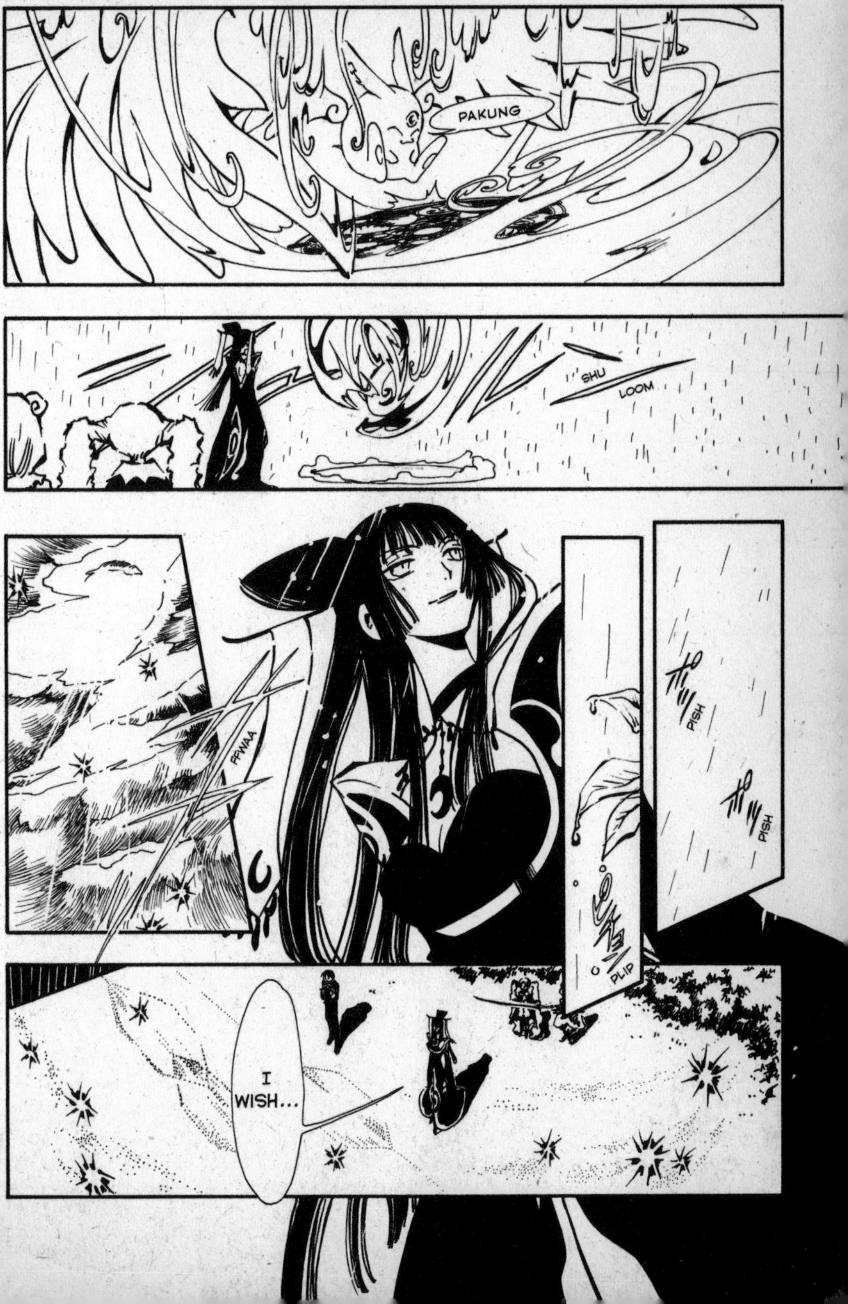
PAKUNG
SHU
LOOM
PISH
PISH
PLIP
FFWAA
I WISH...

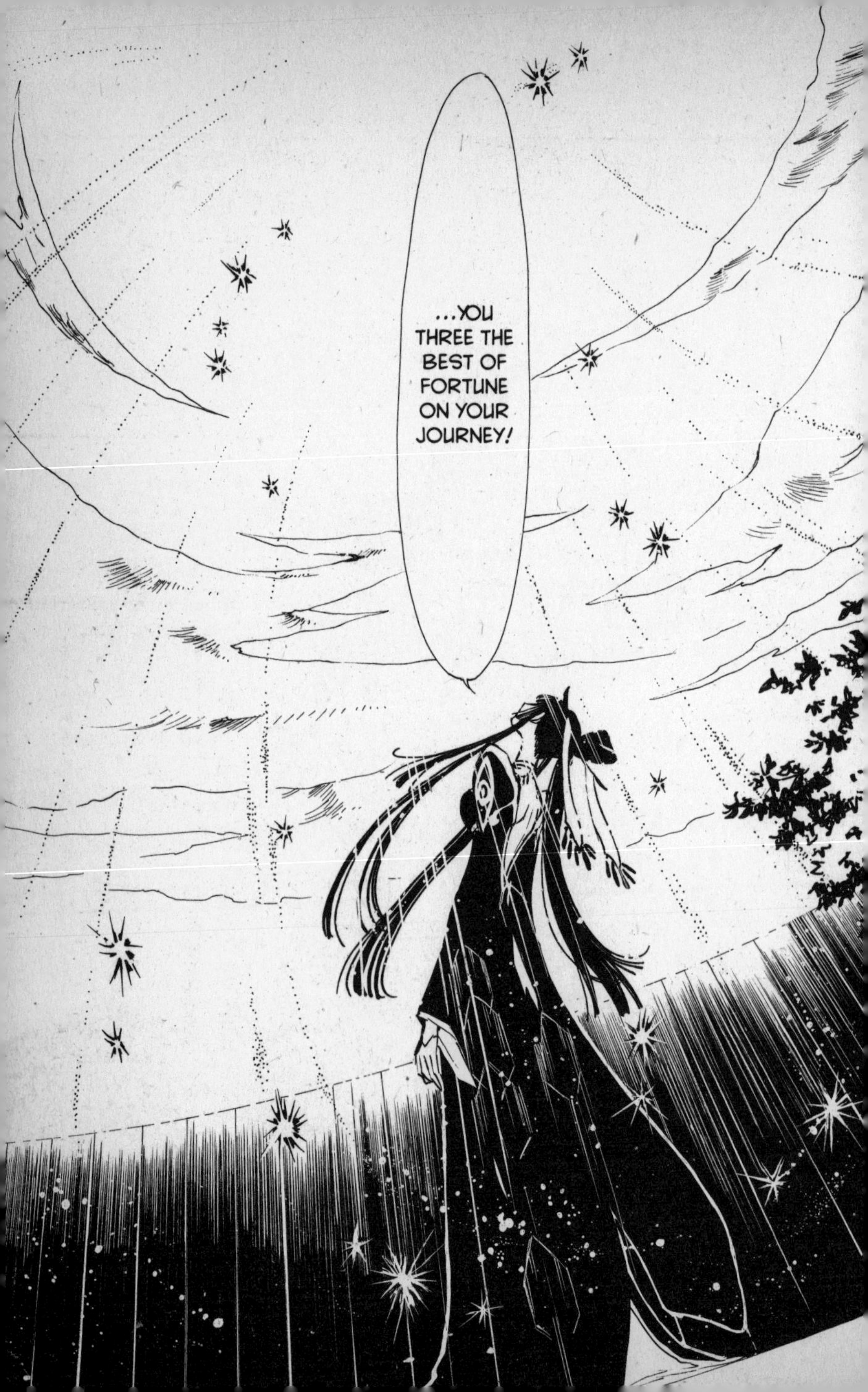
...YOU THREE THE BEST OF FORTUNE ON YOUR JOURNEY!

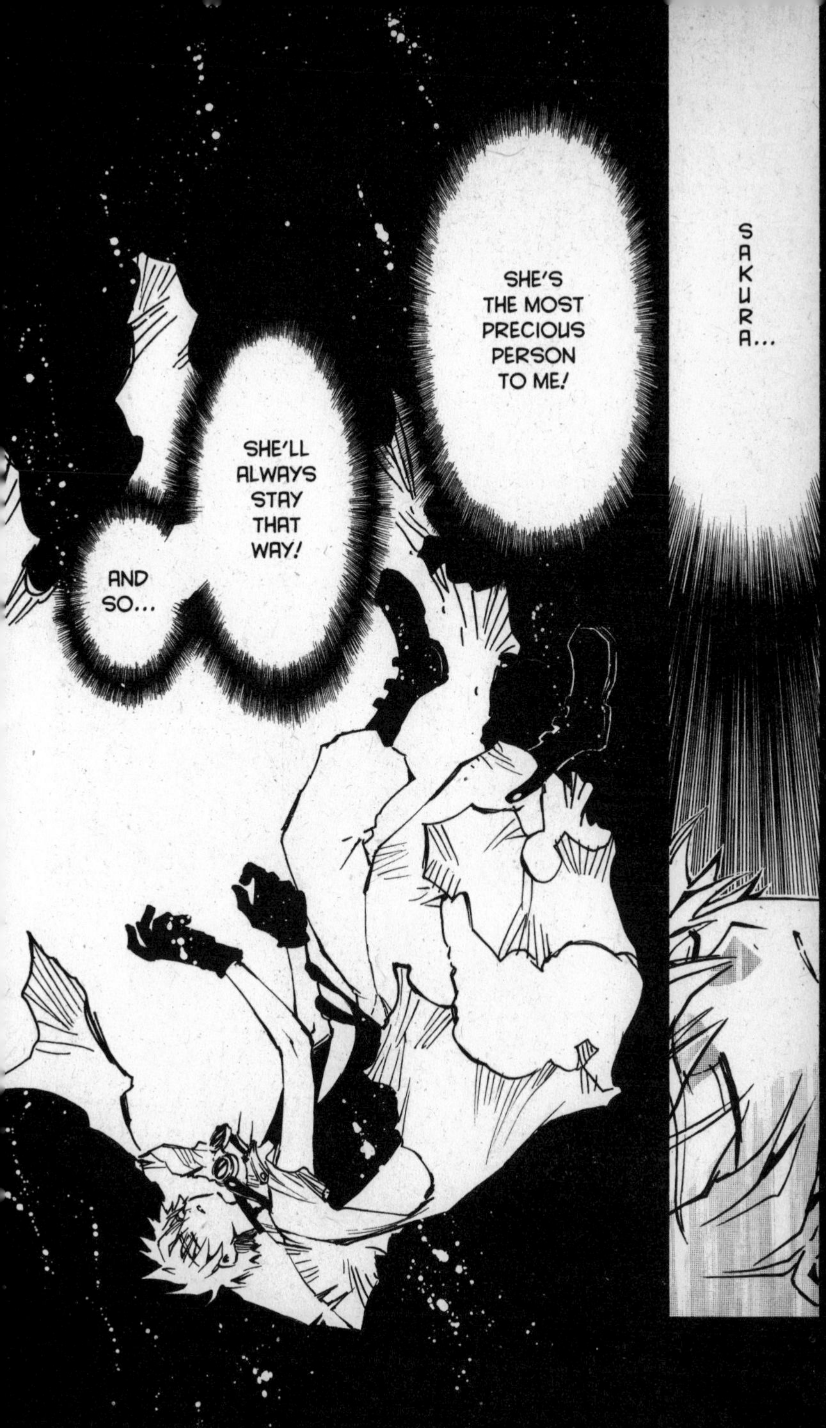
SAKURA...
SHE'S THE MOST PRECIOUS PERSON TO ME!
SHE'LL ALWAYS STAY THAT WAY!
AND SO...

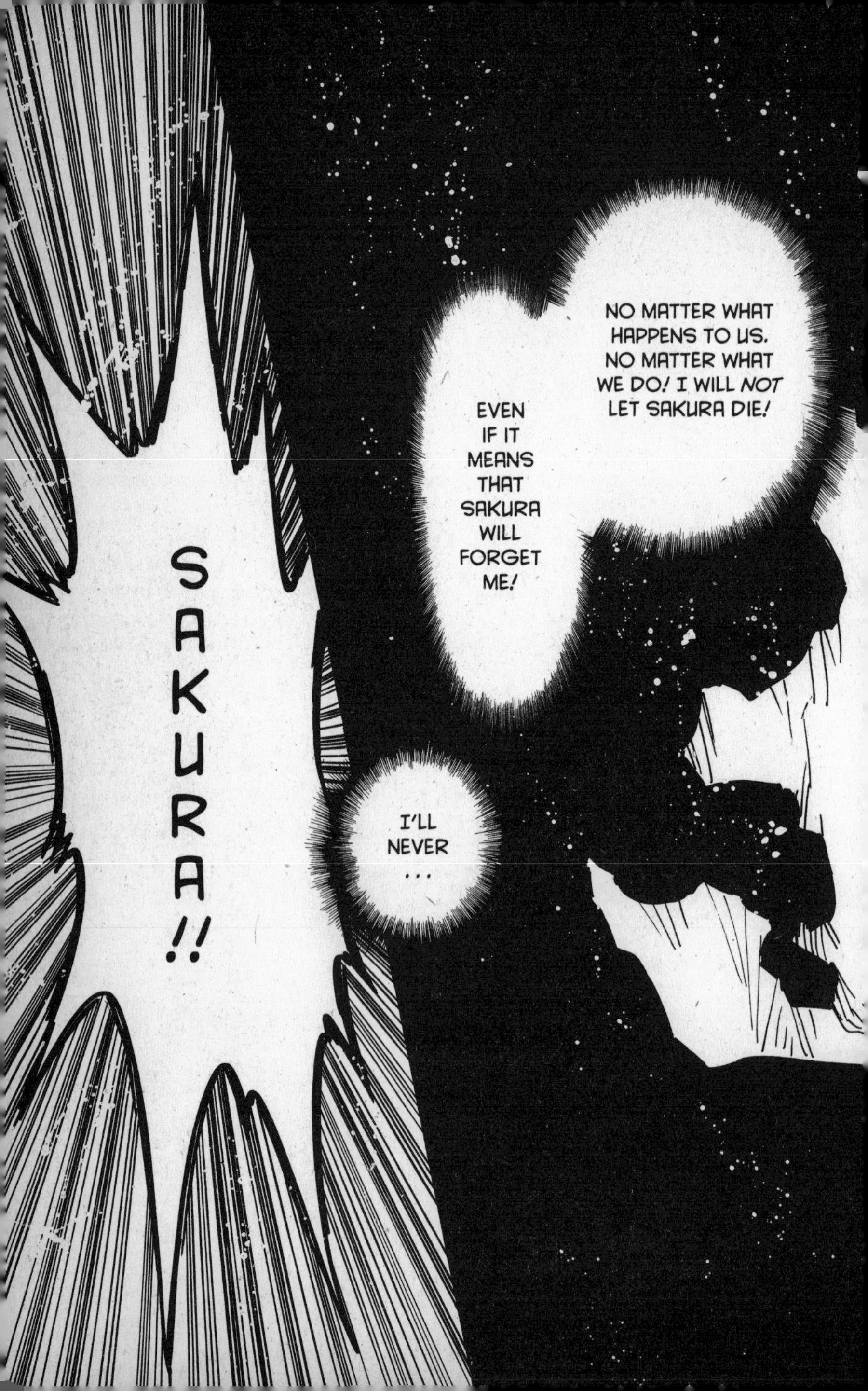
NO MATTER WHAT HAPPENS TO US. NO MATTER WHAT WE DO! I WILL *NOT* LET SAKURA DIE!
EVEN IF IT MEANS THAT SAKURA WILL FORGET ME!
I'LL NEVER . . .
SAKURA!!

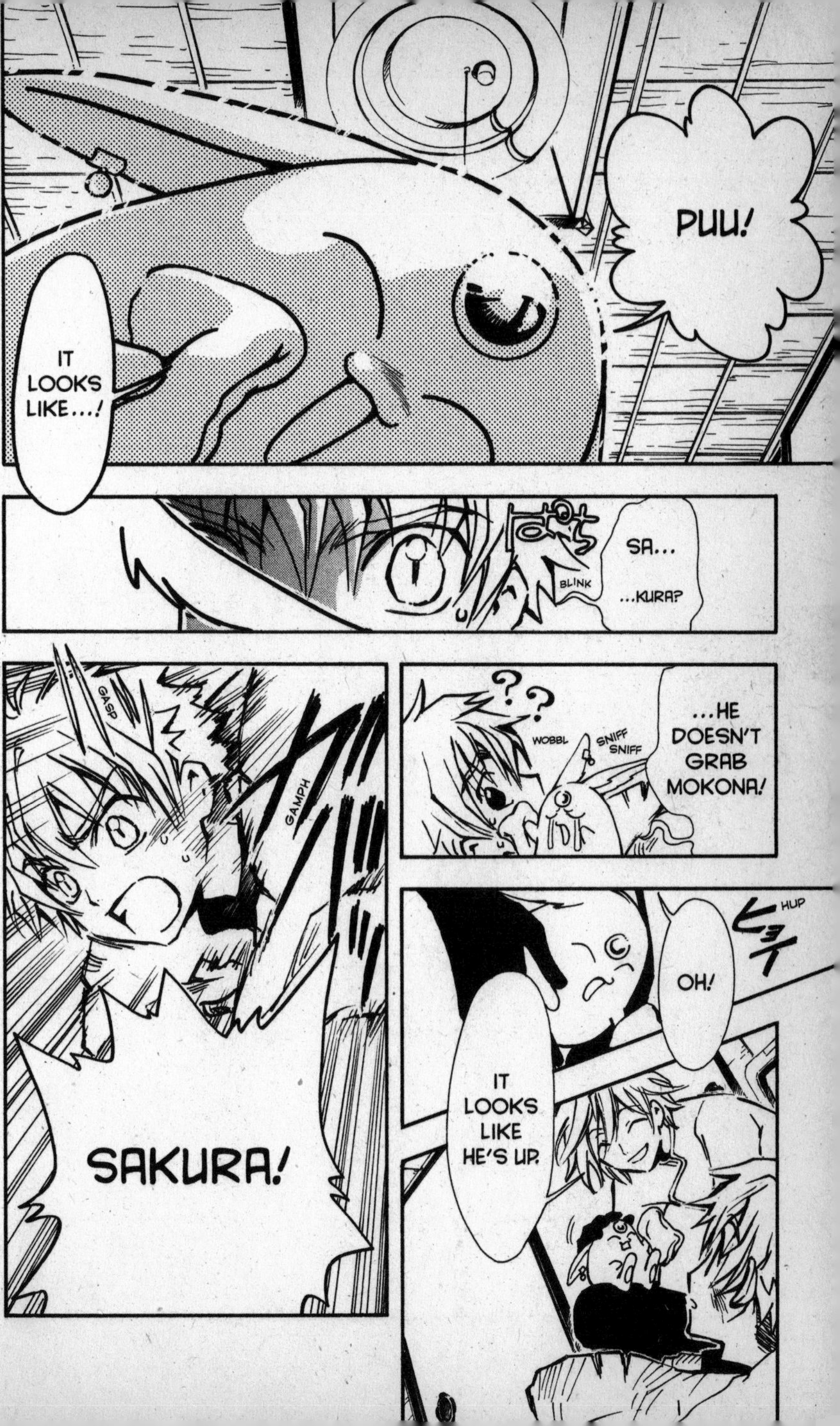
PUU!
IT LOOKS LIKE...!
ぱち
BLINK
SA... ...KURA?
WOBBL
SNIFF SNIFF
...HE DOESN'T GRAB MOKONA!
ヒョイ
HUP
OH!
IT LOOKS LIKE HE'S UP.
GASP
GAMPH
SAKURA!

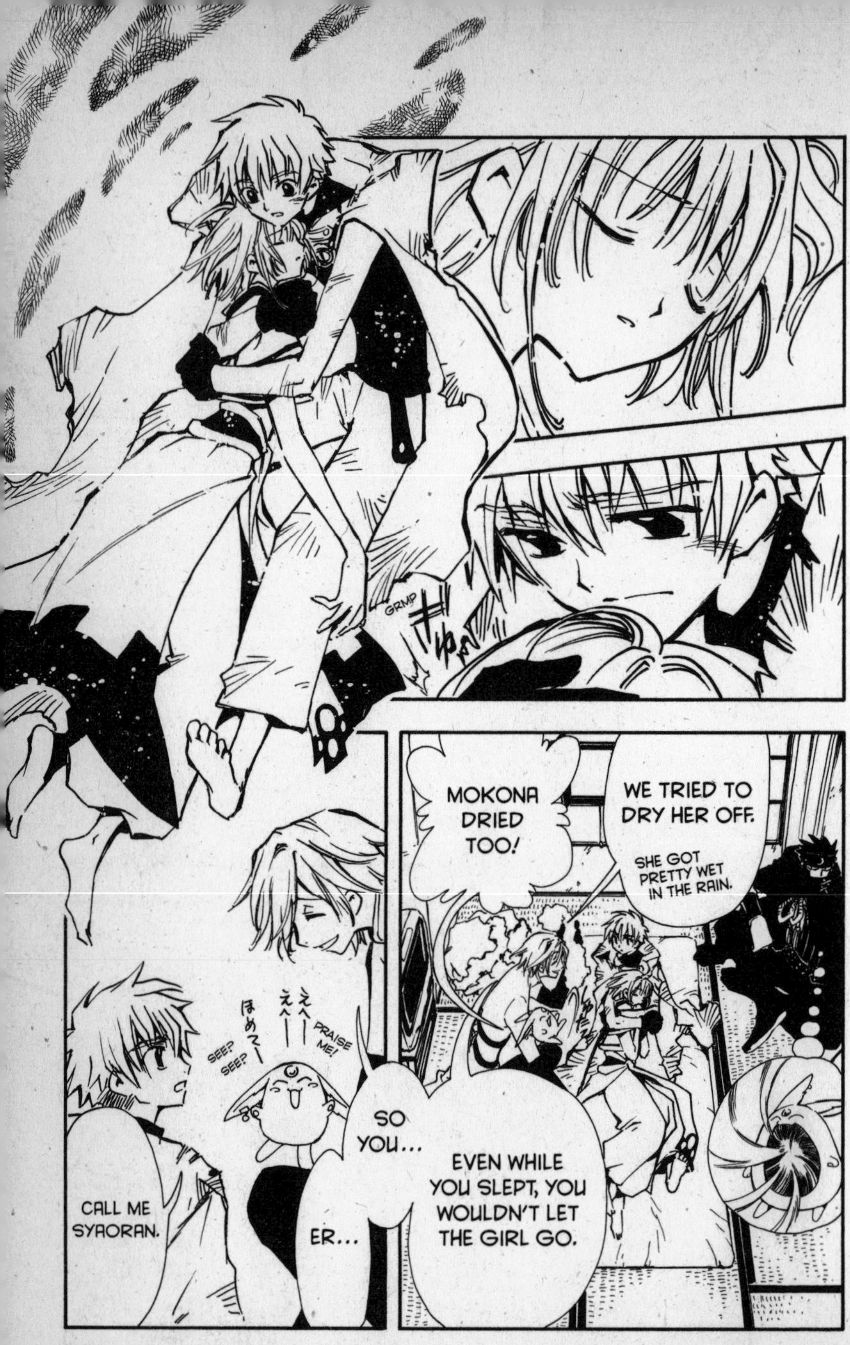
GRMP
WE TRIED TO DRY HER OFF.
SHE GOT PRETTY WET IN THE RAIN.
MOKONA DRIED TOO!
SO YOU...
EVEN WHILE YOU SLEPT, YOU WOULDN'T LET THE GIRL GO.
ER...
えへ〜
えへ〜
PRAISE ME!
ほめて〜
SEE? SEE?
CALL ME SYAORAN.

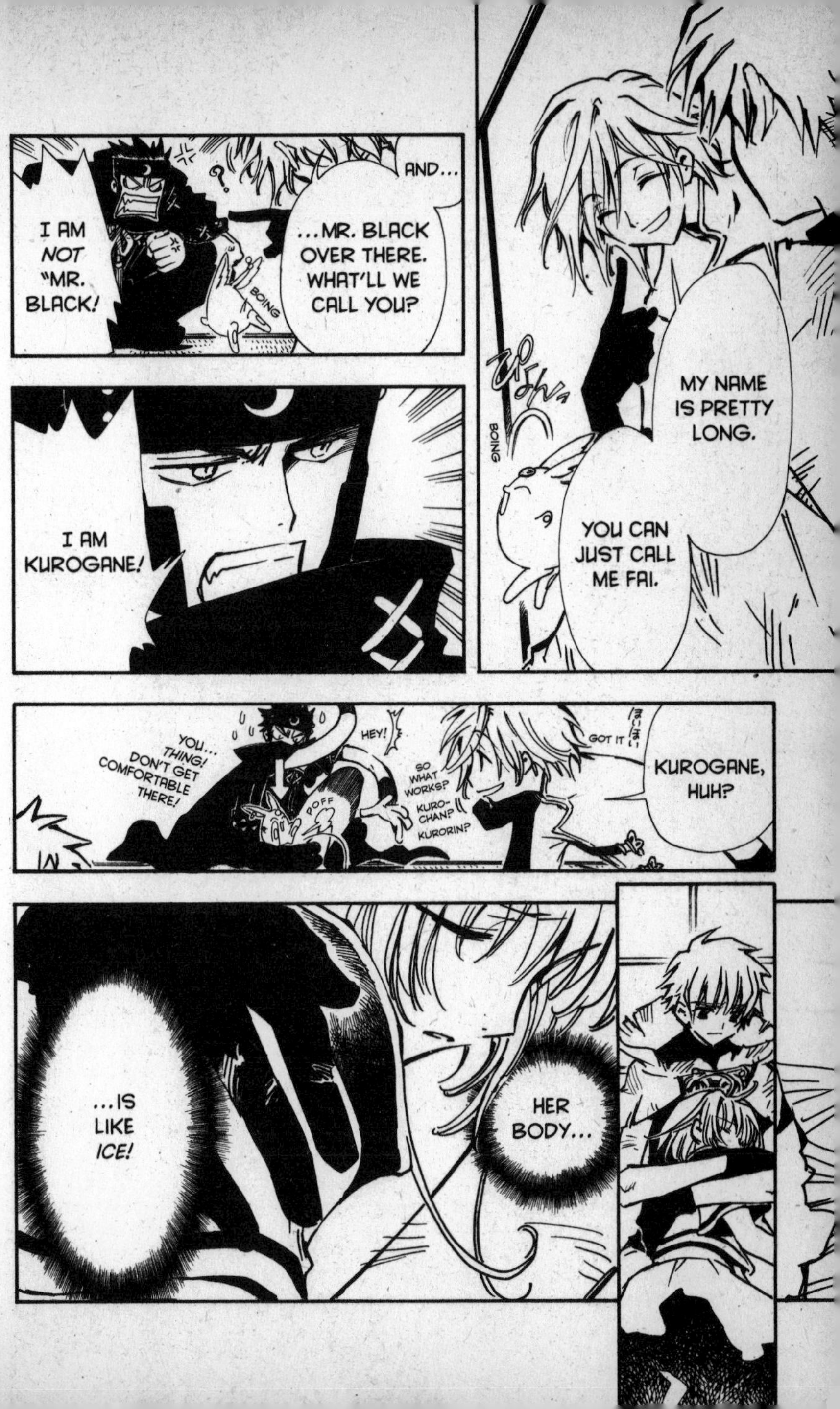
MY NAME IS PRETTY LONG.
ぴょん
BOING
YOU CAN JUST CALL ME FAI.
AND...
...MR. BLACK OVER THERE. WHAT'LL WE CALL YOU?
BOING
I AM *NOT* "MR. BLACK!
I AM KUROGANE!
KUROGANE, HUH?
ほいほい
GOT IT
SO WHAT WORKS? KURO-CHAN? KURORIN?
HEY!
POFF
YOU... *THING!* DON'T GET COMFORTABLE THERE!
HER BODY...
...IS LIKE *ICE!*

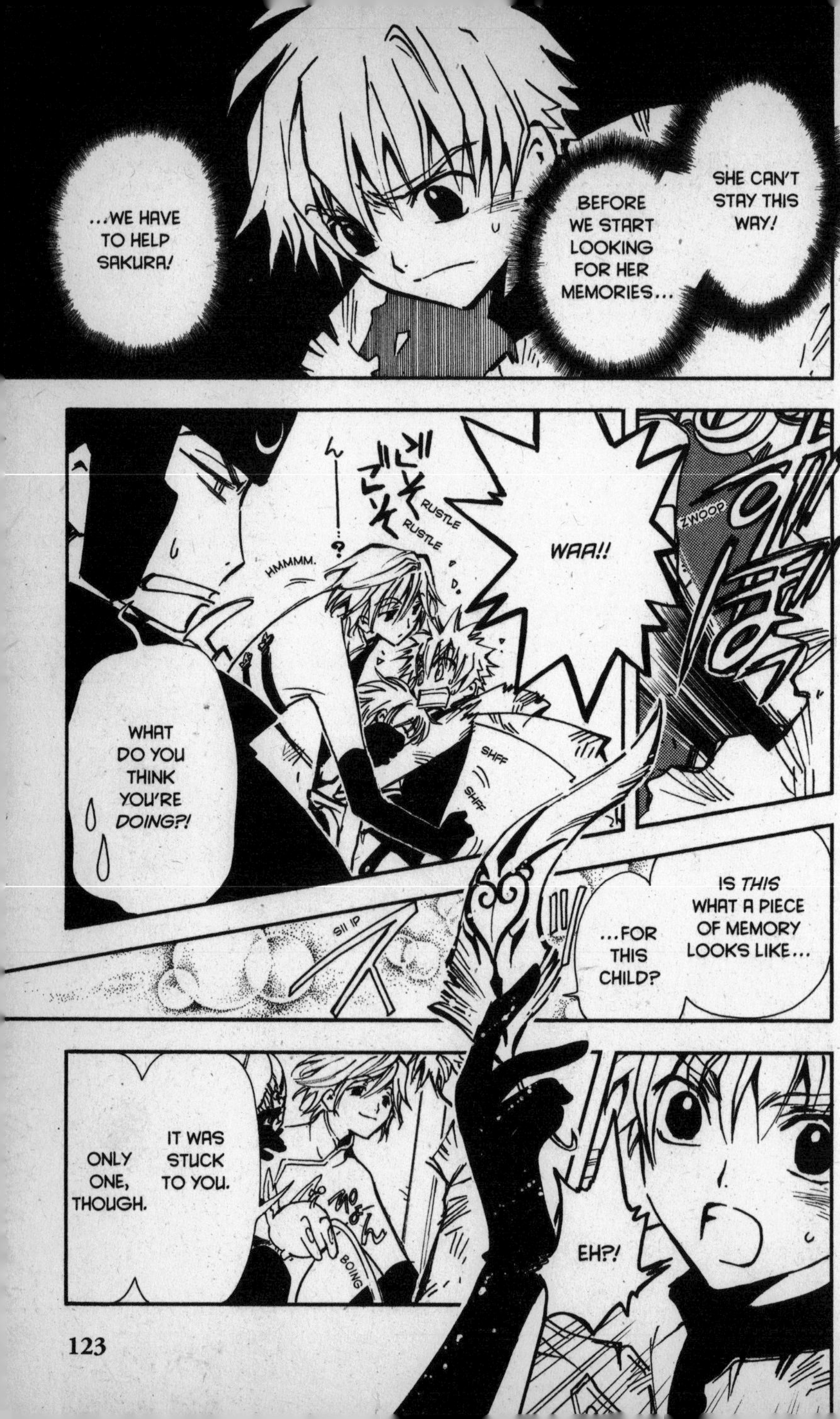
SHE CAN'T STAY THIS WAY!
BEFORE WE START LOOKING FOR HER MEMORIES...
...WE HAVE TO HELP SAKURA!
ZWOOP
WAA!!
RUSTLE RUSTLE
HMMMM.
WHAT DO YOU THINK YOU'RE DOING?!
SHFF SHFF
IS THIS WHAT A PIECE OF MEMORY LOOKS LIKE...
...FOR THIS CHILD?
EH?!
IT WAS STUCK TO YOU.
ONLY ONE, THOUGH.
BOING

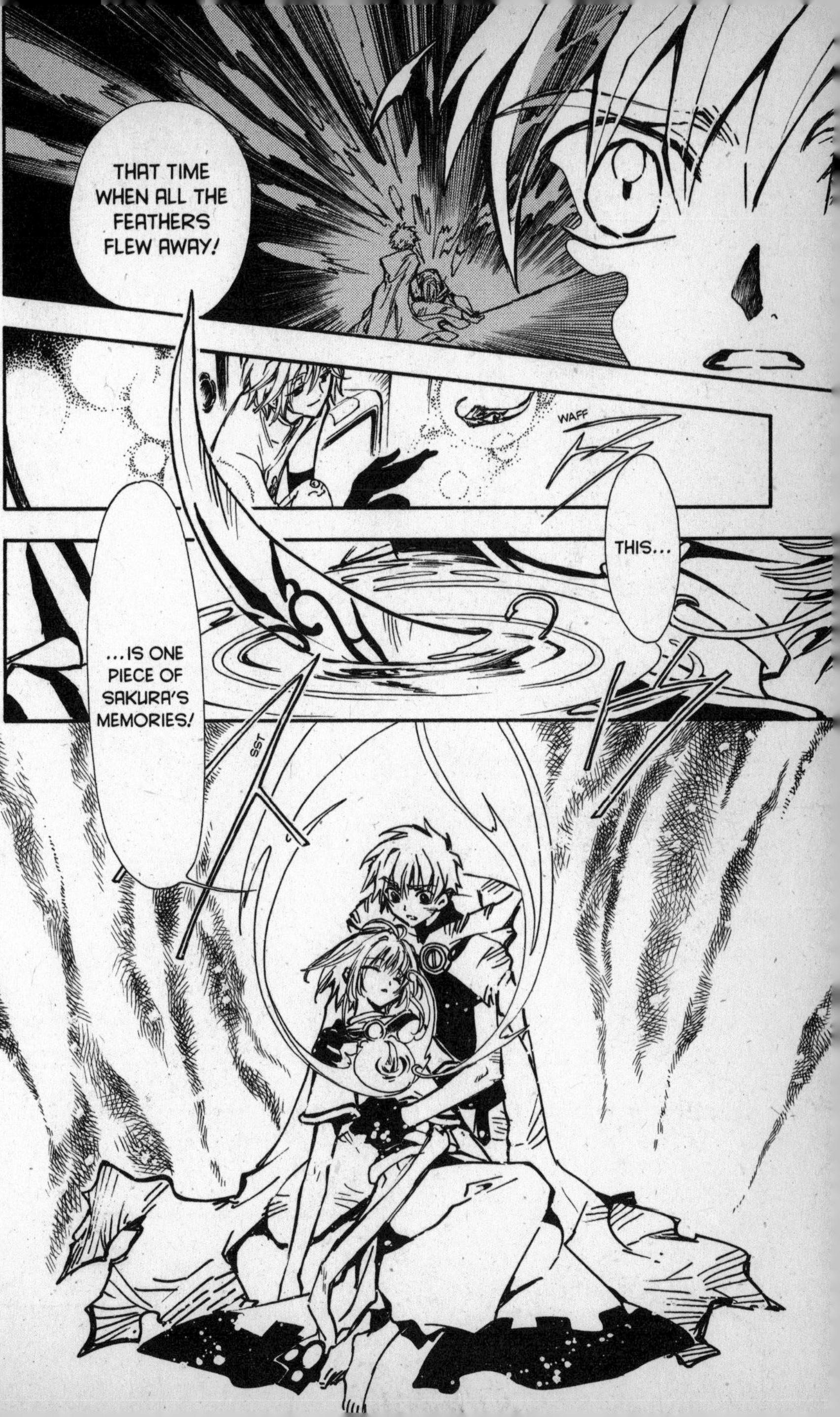
THAT TIME WHEN ALL THE FEATHERS FLEW AWAY!
WAFF
THIS...
...IS ONE PIECE OF SAKURA'S MEMORIES!
SST

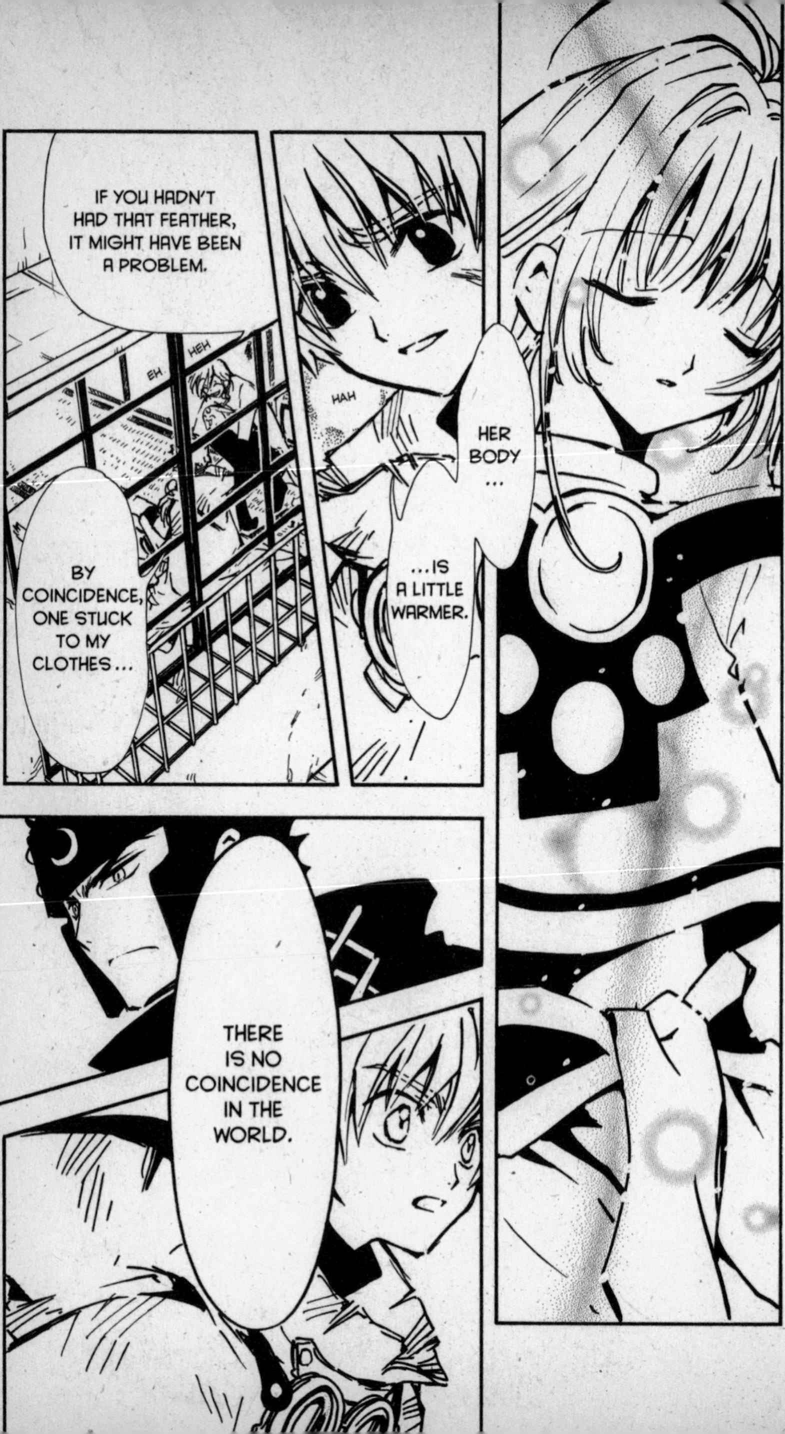
HER BODY ...
...IS A LITTLE WARMER.
HAH
IF YOU HADN'T HAD THAT FEATHER, IT MIGHT HAVE BEEN A PROBLEM.
HEH
EH
BY COINCIDENCE, ONE STUCK TO MY CLOTHES ...
THERE IS NO COINCIDENCE IN THE WORLD.

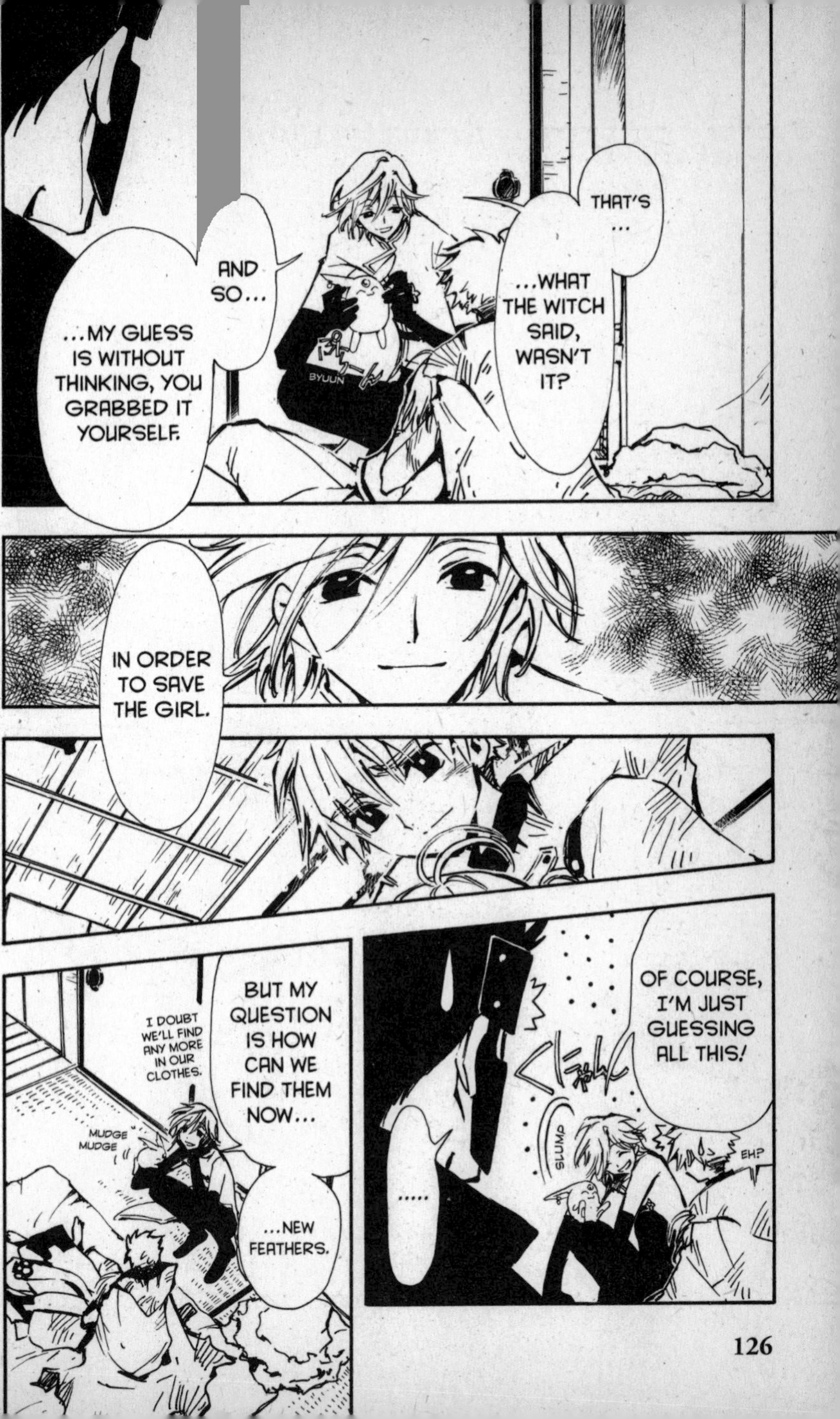
THAT'S...
...WHAT THE WITCH SAID, WASN'T IT?
AND SO...
...MY GUESS IS WITHOUT THINKING, YOU GRABBED IT YOURSELF.
BYUUN
IN ORDER TO SAVE THE GIRL.
OF COURSE, I'M JUST GUESSING ALL THIS!
EH?
SLUMP
.....
BUT MY QUESTION IS HOW CAN WE FIND THEM NOW...
...NEW FEATHERS.
I DOUBT WE'LL FIND ANY MORE IN OUR CLOTHES.
MUDGE MUDGE

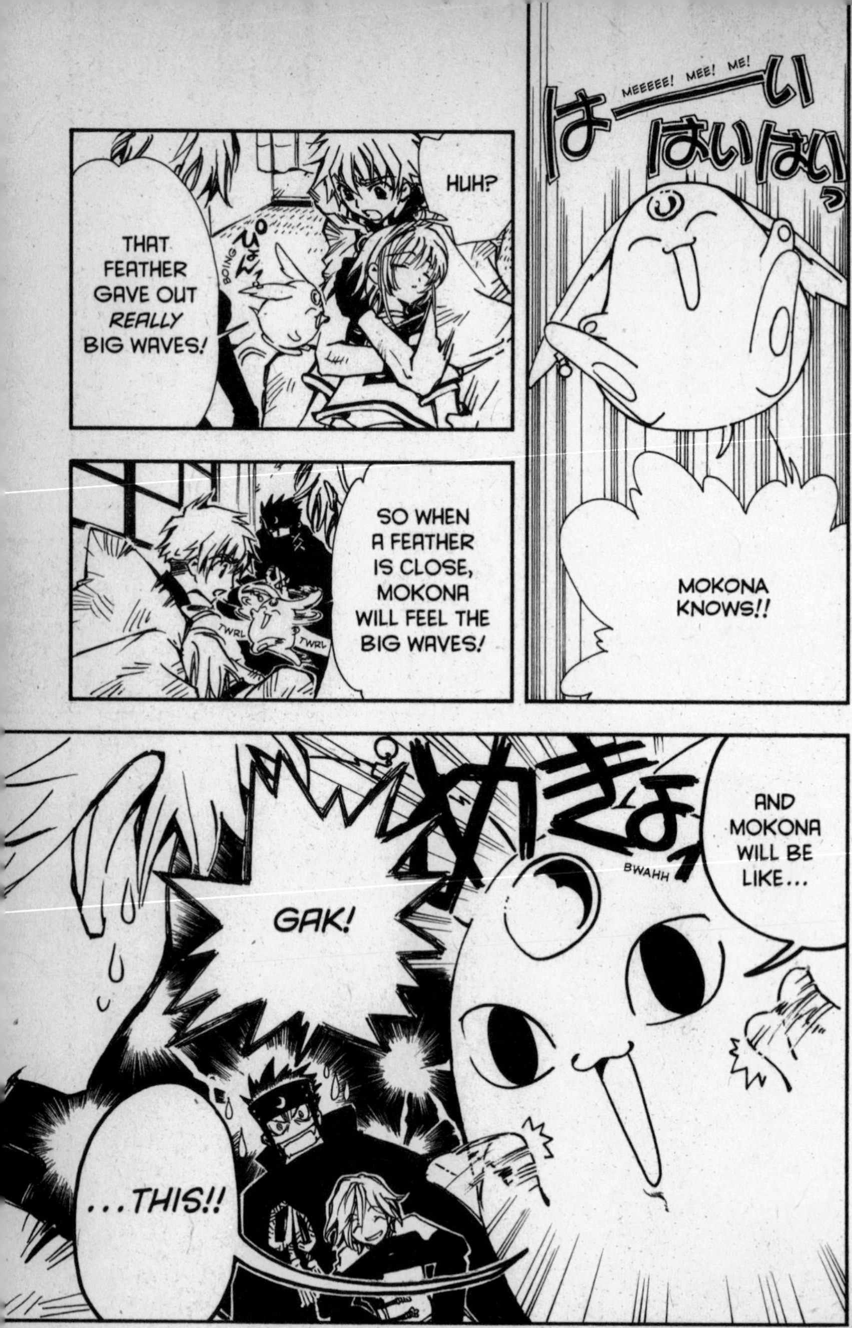
はーーい はいはいっ
MEEEEE! MEE! ME!
MOKONA KNOWS!!
HUH?
THAT FEATHER GAVE OUT *REALLY* BIG WAVES!
ぴょん
BOING
SO WHEN A FEATHER IS CLOSE, MOKONA WILL FEEL THE BIG WAVES!
TWRL
TWRL
AND MOKONA WILL BE LIKE...
かきょっ
BWAHH
GAK!
...THIS!!

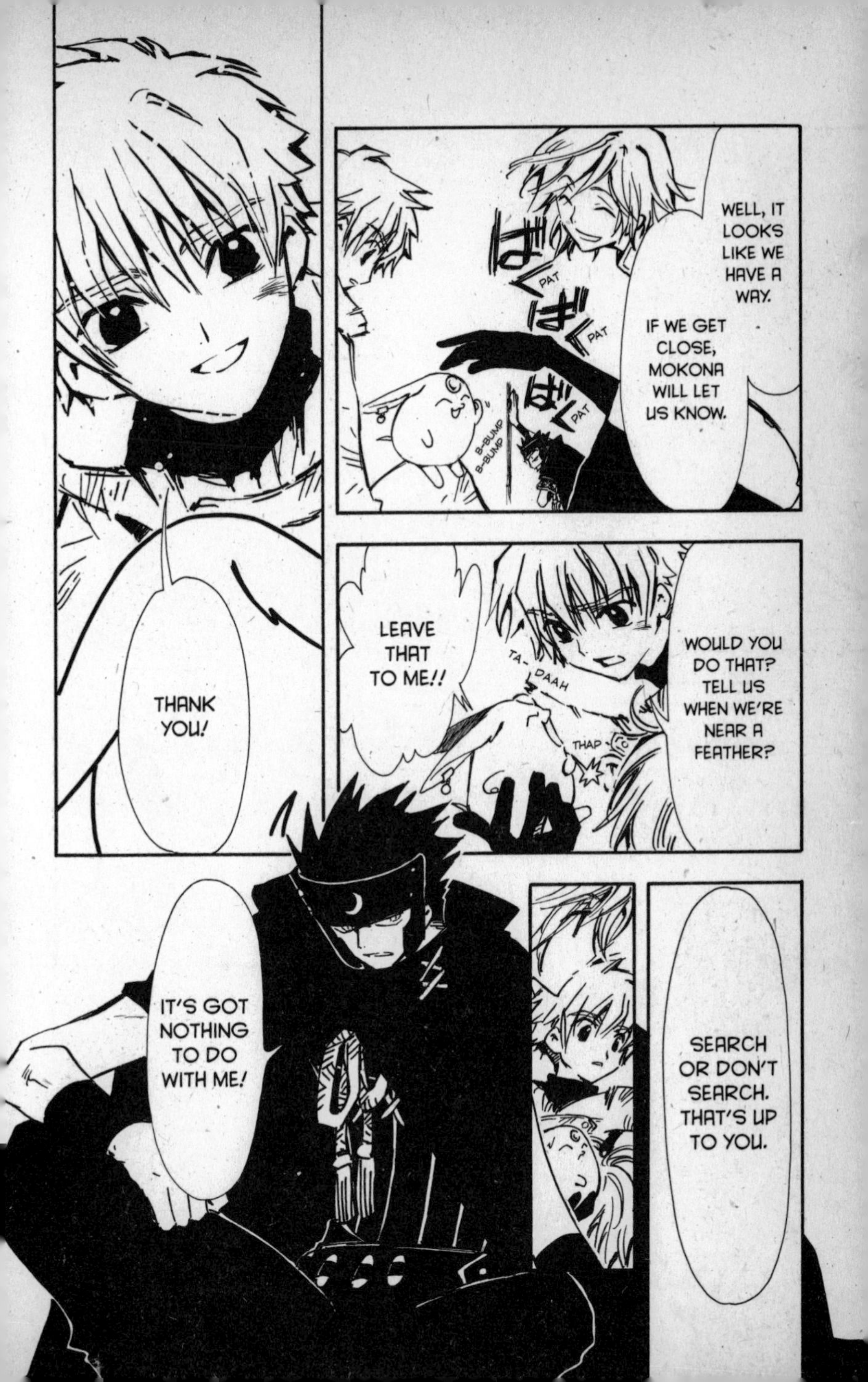
WELL, IT LOOKS LIKE WE HAVE A WAY.
IF WE GET CLOSE, MOKONA WILL LET US KNOW.
PAT PAT PAT
B-BUMP B-BUMP
WOULD YOU DO THAT? TELL US WHEN WE'RE NEAR A FEATHER?
LEAVE THAT TO ME!!
TA-DAAH
THAP
THANK YOU!
SEARCH OR DON'T SEARCH. THAT'S UP TO YOU.
IT'S GOT NOTHING TO DO WITH ME!

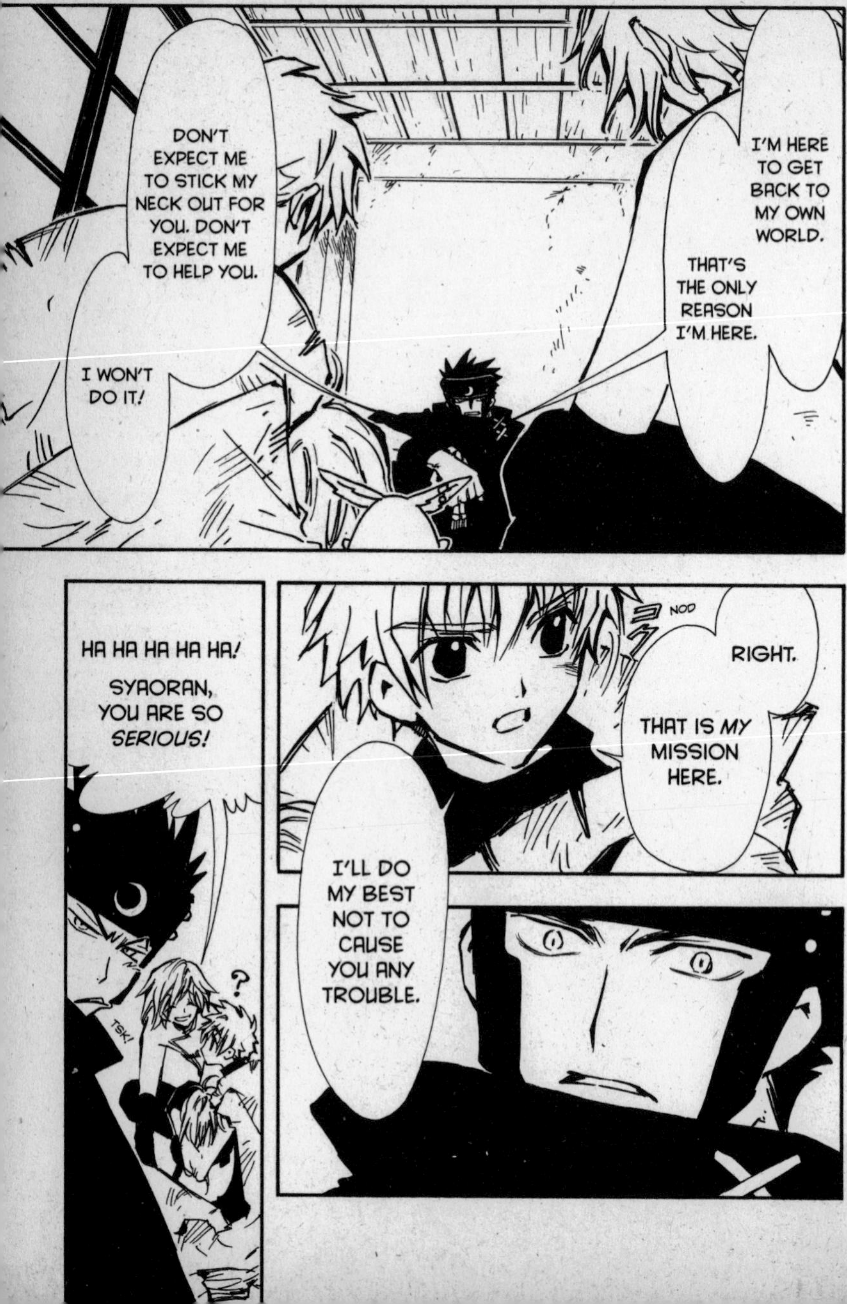
I'M HERE TO GET BACK TO MY OWN WORLD.
THAT'S THE ONLY REASON I'M HERE.
DON'T EXPECT ME TO STICK MY NECK OUT FOR YOU. DON'T EXPECT ME TO HELP YOU.
I WON'T DO IT!
NOD
RIGHT.
THAT IS *MY* MISSION HERE.
I'LL DO MY BEST NOT TO CAUSE YOU ANY TROUBLE.
HA HA HA HA HA!
SYAORAN, YOU ARE SO *SERIOUS!*
?
TSK!

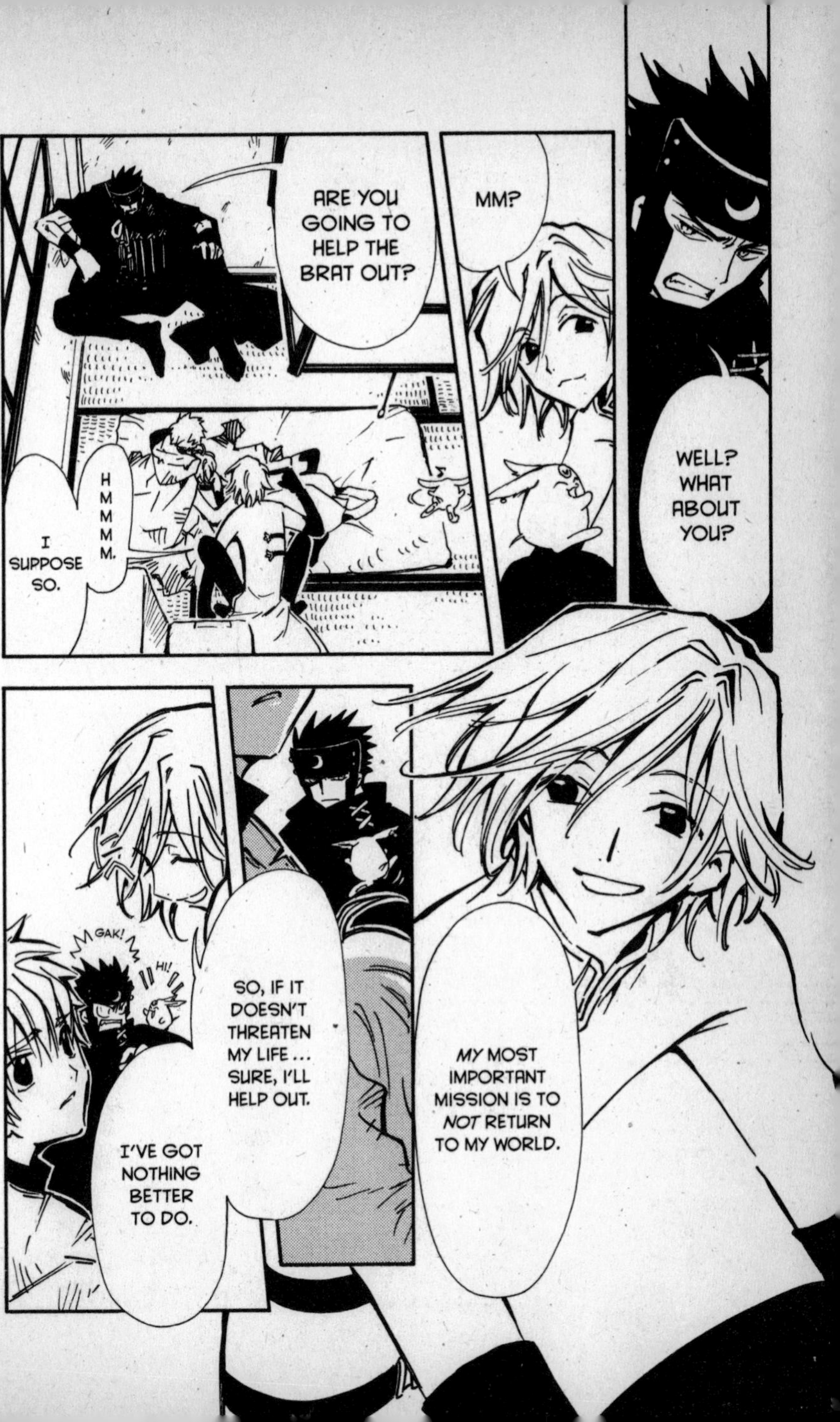
WELL? WHAT ABOUT YOU?
MM?
ARE YOU GOING TO HELP THE BRAT OUT?
HMMMM.
I SUPPOSE SO.
MY MOST IMPORTANT MISSION IS TO *NOT* RETURN TO MY WORLD.
SO, IF IT DOESN'T THREATEN MY LIFE... SURE, I'LL HELP OUT.
GAK!
HI!
I'VE GOT NOTHING BETTER TO DO.

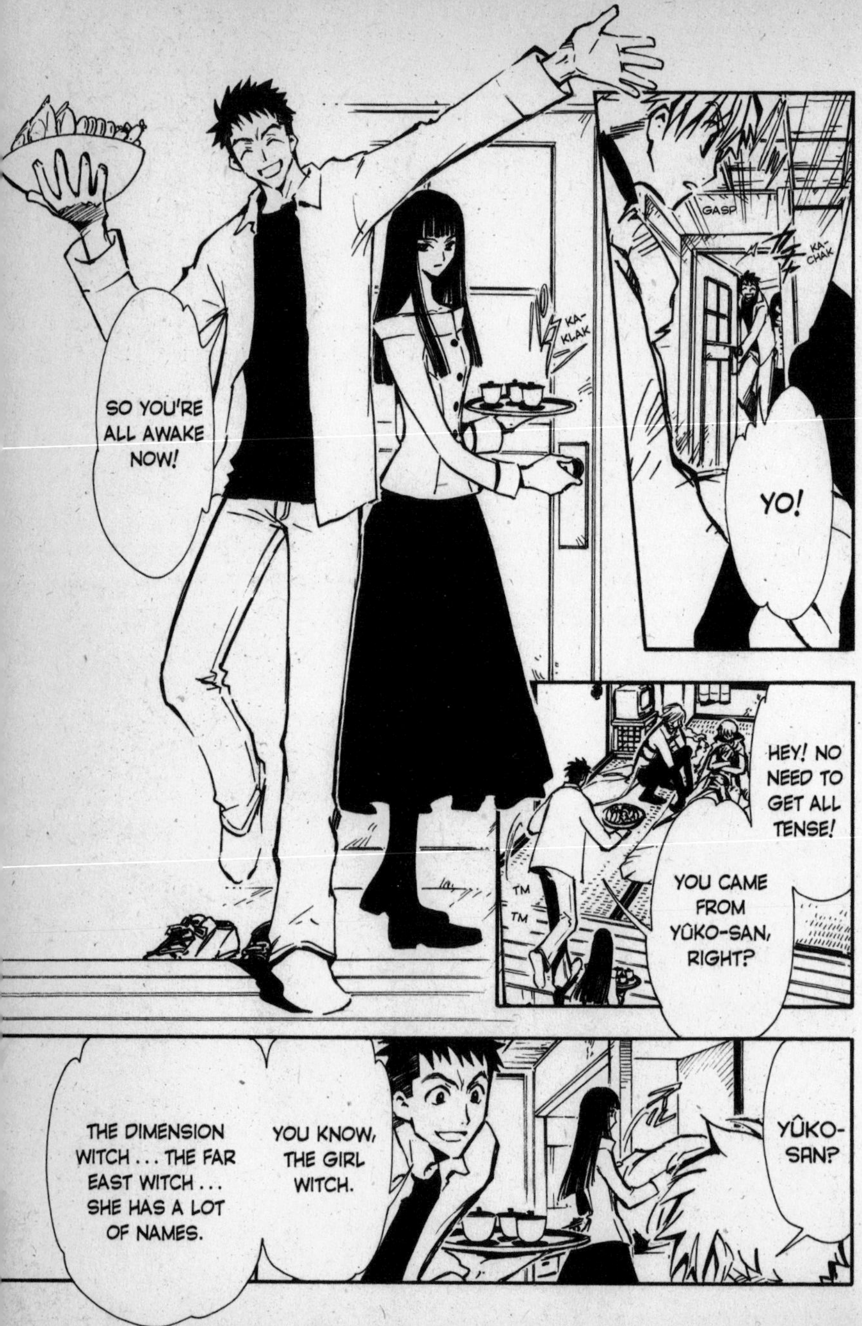
GASP
KA-CHAK
YO!
HEY! NO NEED TO GET ALL TENSE!
YOU CAME FROM YÛKO-SAN, RIGHT?
TM
TM
KA-KLAK
SO YOU'RE ALL AWAKE NOW!
YÛKO-SAN?
YOU KNOW, THE GIRL WITCH.
THE DIMENSION WITCH . . . THE FAR EAST WITCH . . . SHE HAS A LOT OF NAMES.

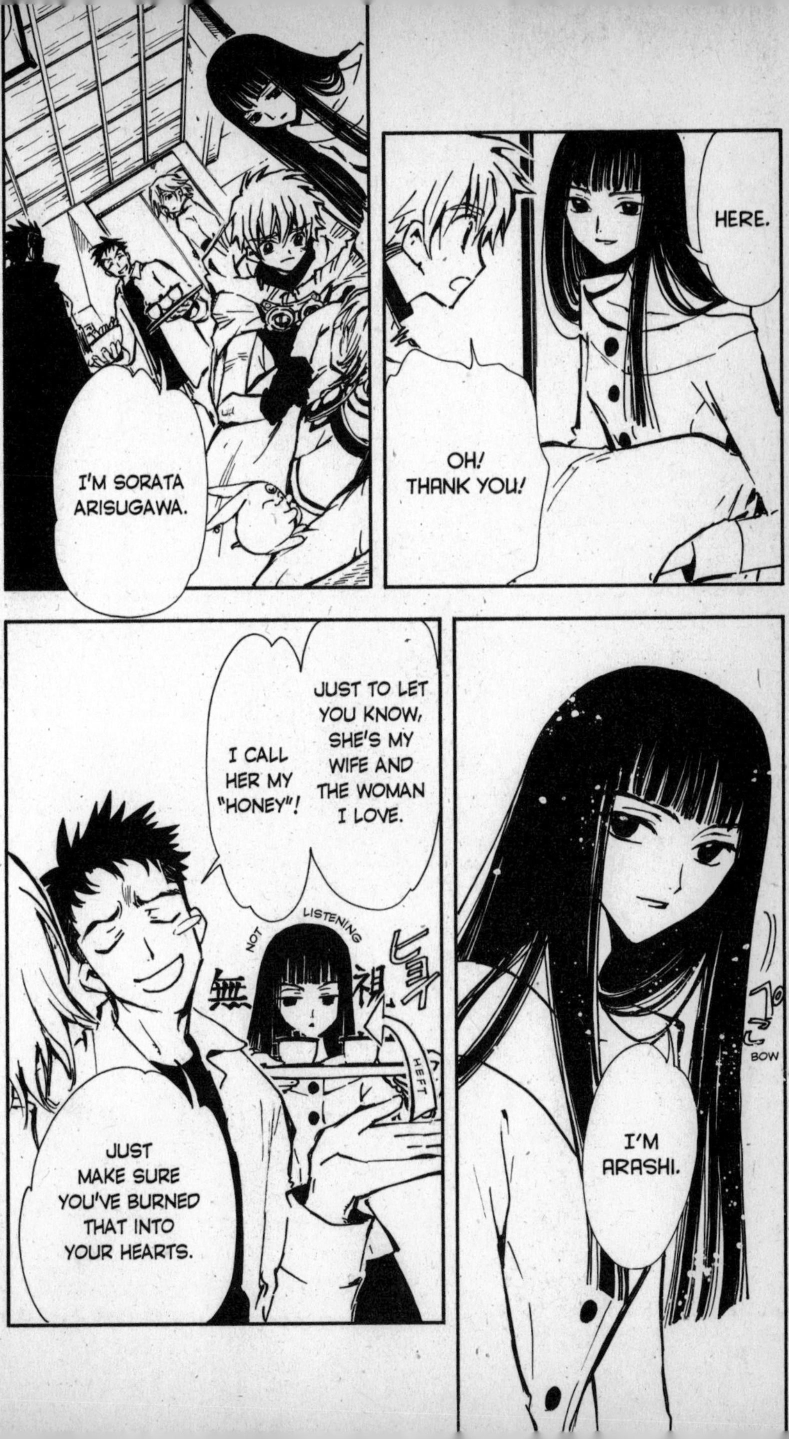
HERE.
OH! THANK YOU!
I'M SORATA ARISUGAWA.
BOW
I'M ARASHI.
JUST TO LET YOU KNOW, SHE'S MY WIFE AND THE WOMAN I LOVE.
I CALL HER MY "HONEY"!
NOT LISTENING
無視
HEFT
JUST MAKE SURE YOU'VE BURNED THAT INTO YOUR HEARTS.

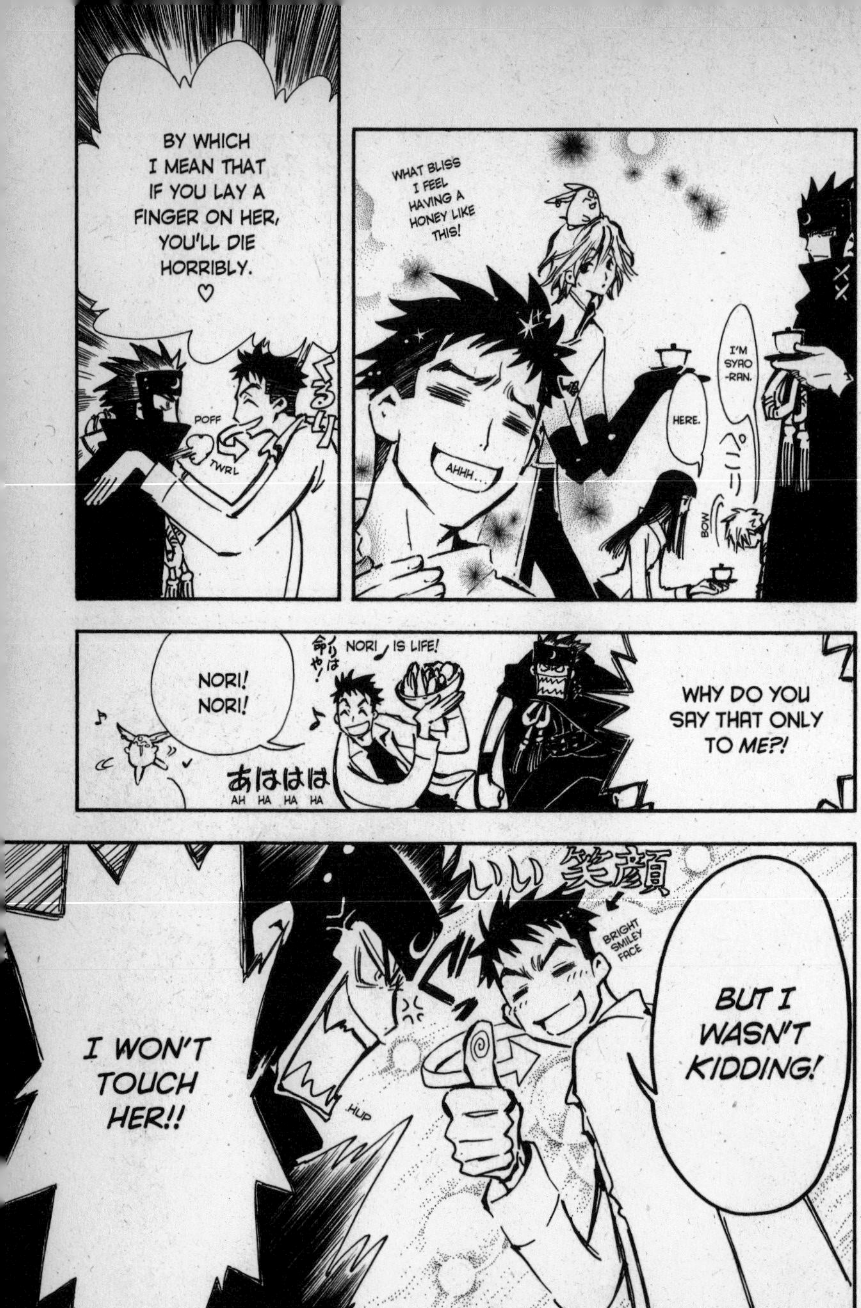
WHAT BLISS I FEEL HAVING A HONEY LIKE THIS!
I'M SYRO-RAN.
HERE.
ぺこり
BOW
AHHH...
BY WHICH I MEAN THAT IF YOU LAY A FINGER ON HER, YOU'LL DIE HORRIBLY. ♡
くるり
POFF
TWRL
WHY DO YOU SAY THAT ONLY TO ME?!
のりは命や!
NORI IS LIFE!
NORI! NORI!
あははは
AH HA HA HA
BUT I WASN'T KIDDING!
いい笑顔
BRIGHT SMILEY FACE
HUP
I WON'T TOUCH HER!!

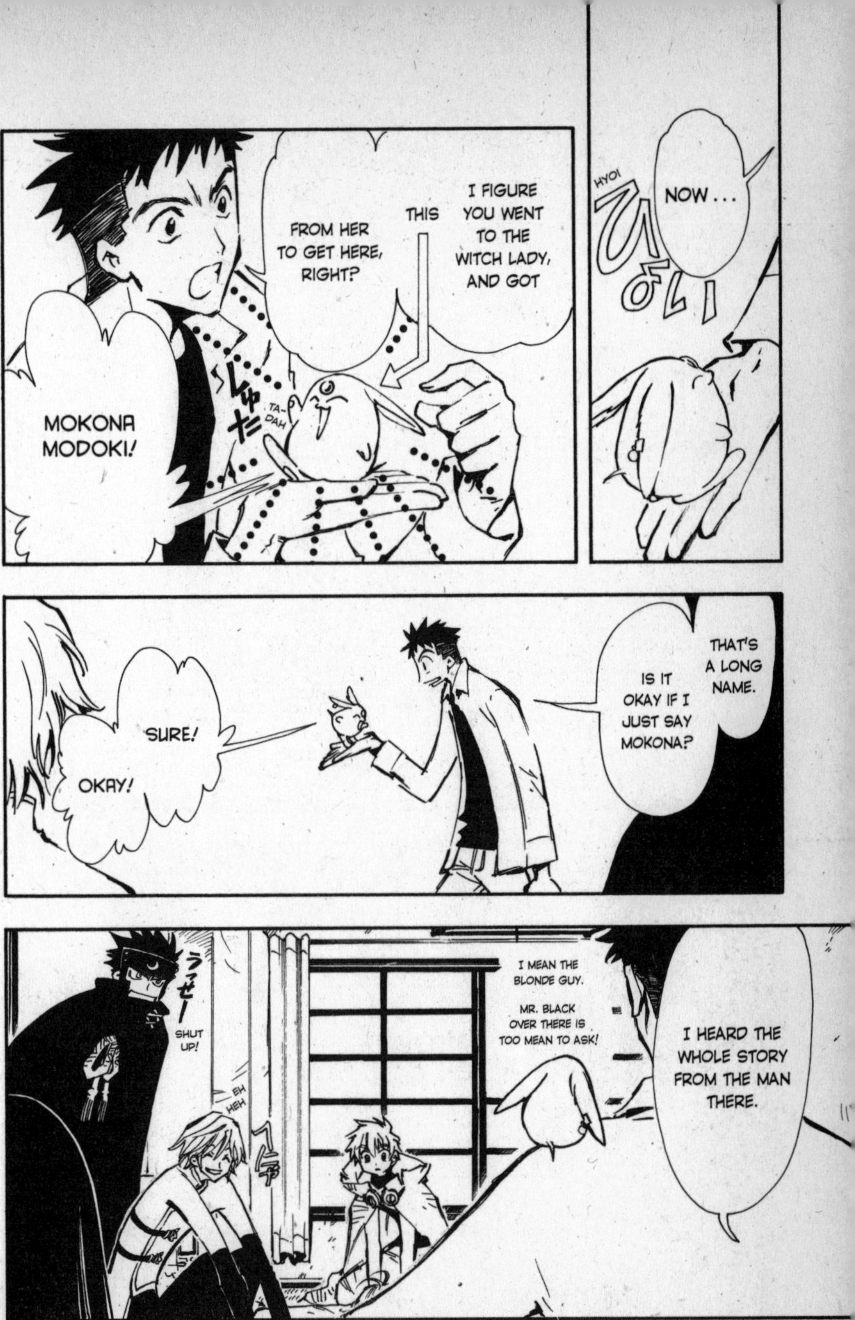
HYOI
NOW...
I FIGURE YOU WENT TO THE WITCH LADY, AND GOT
THIS
FROM HER TO GET HERE, RIGHT?
TA-DAH
MOKONA MODOKI!
THAT'S A LONG NAME.
IS IT OKAY IF I JUST SAY MOKONA?
SURE!
OKAY!
I HEARD THE WHOLE STORY FROM THE MAN THERE.
I MEAN THE BLONDE GUY.
MR. BLACK OVER THERE IS TOO MEAN TO ASK!
EH HEH
SHUT UP!

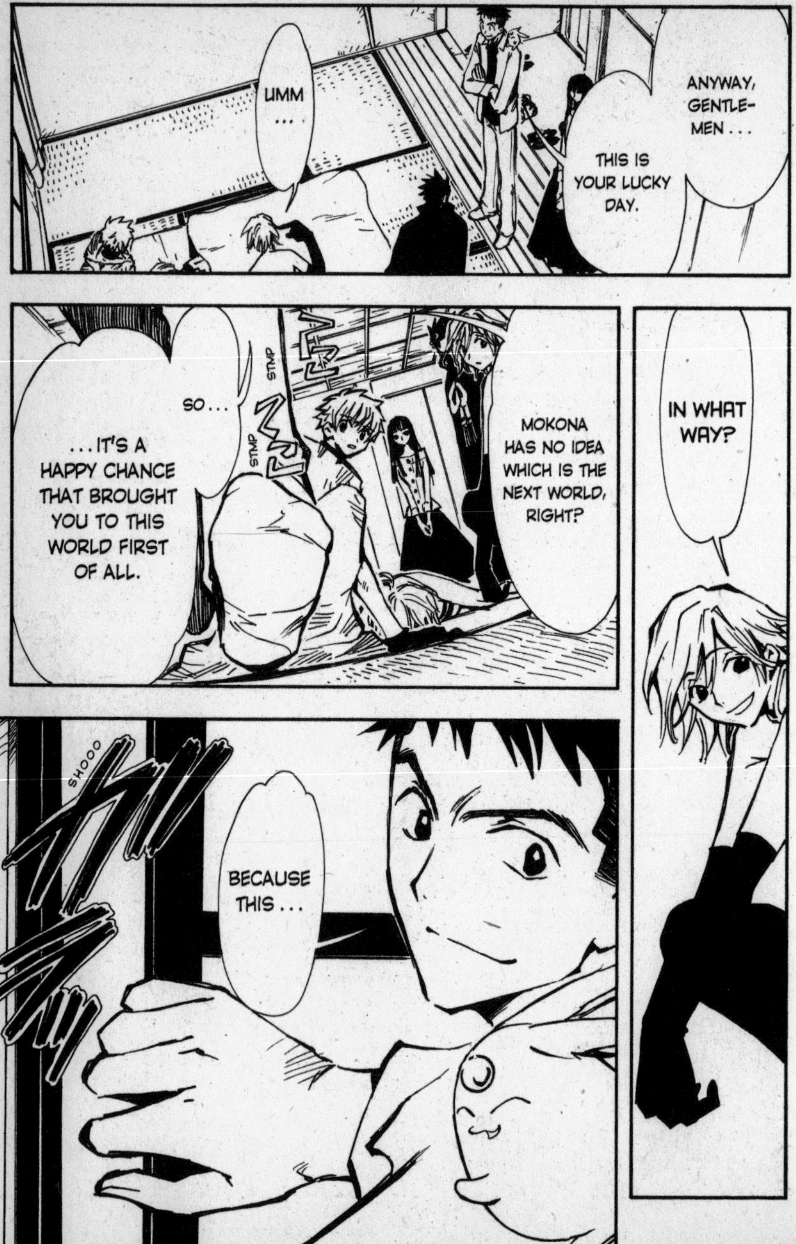
ANYWAY, GENTLE-MEN . . .
THIS IS YOUR LUCKY DAY.
UMM . . .
IN WHAT WAY?
MOKONA HAS NO IDEA WHICH IS THE NEXT WORLD, RIGHT?
SO . . .
STMP
STMP
. . . IT'S A HAPPY CHANCE THAT BROUGHT YOU TO THIS WORLD FIRST OF ALL.
SHOOO
BECAUSE THIS . . .

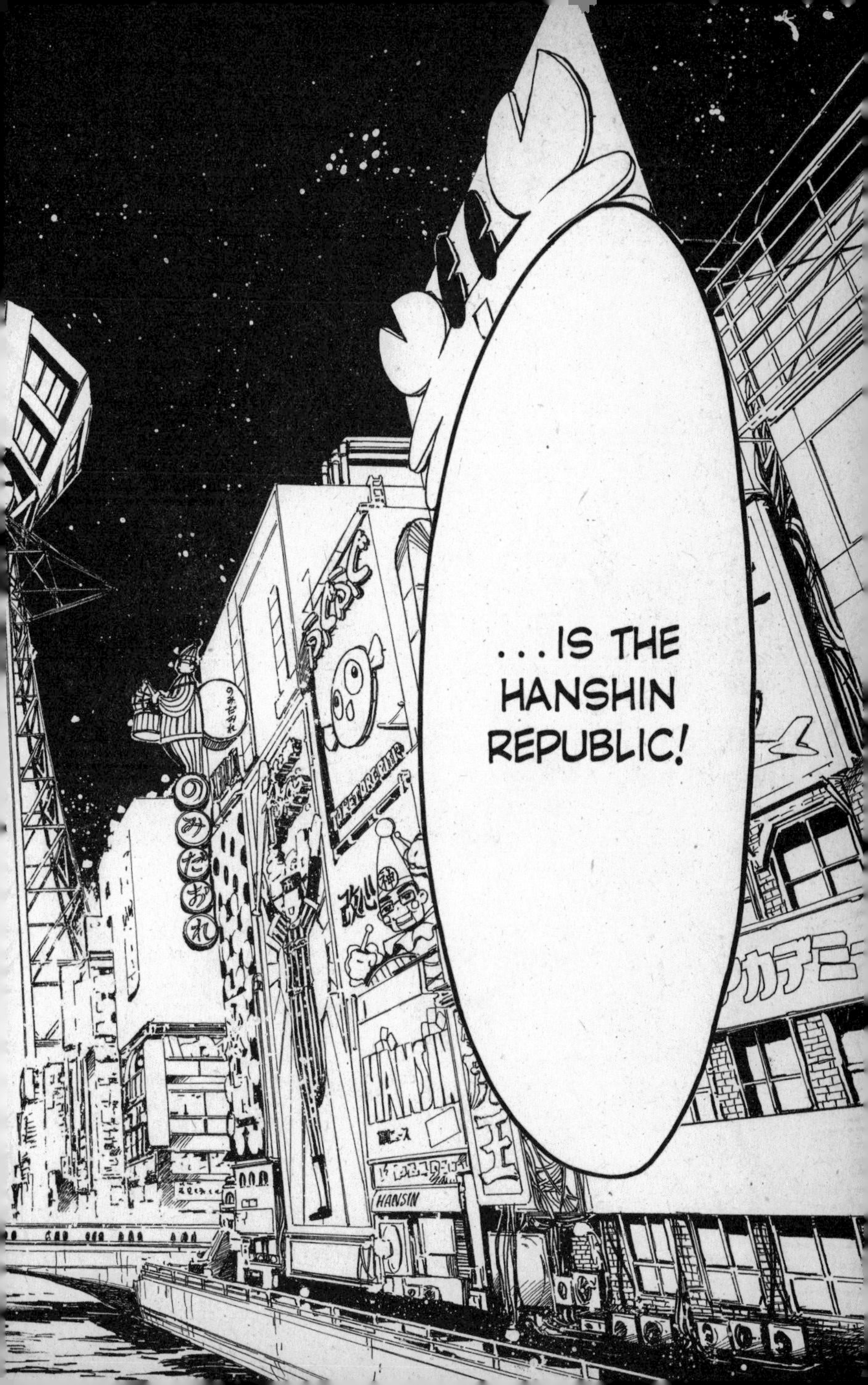
...IS THE HANSHIN REPUBLIC!
のみだおれ
HANSHIN
HANSIN

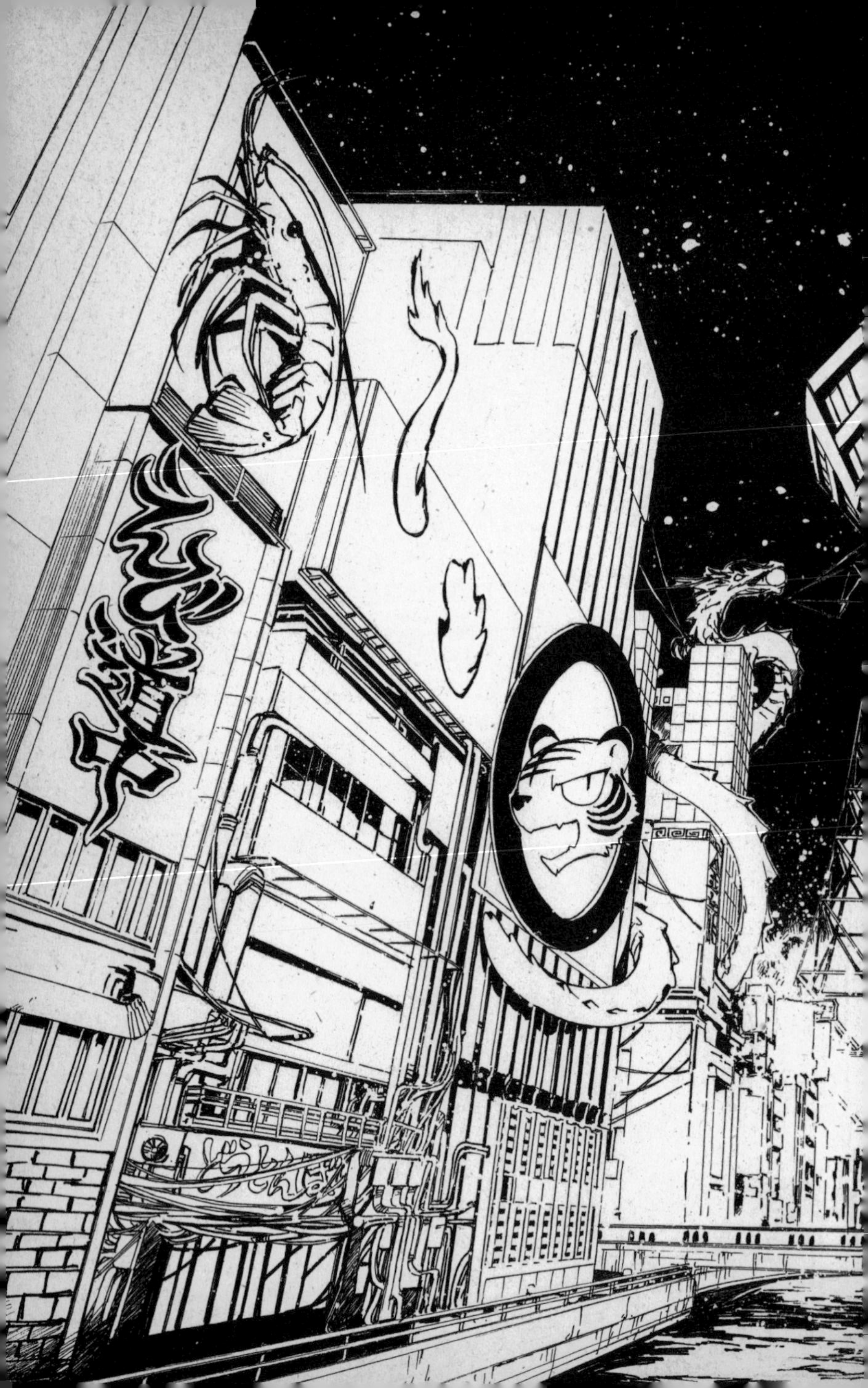
えび道中

RESERVoir CHRoNiCLE

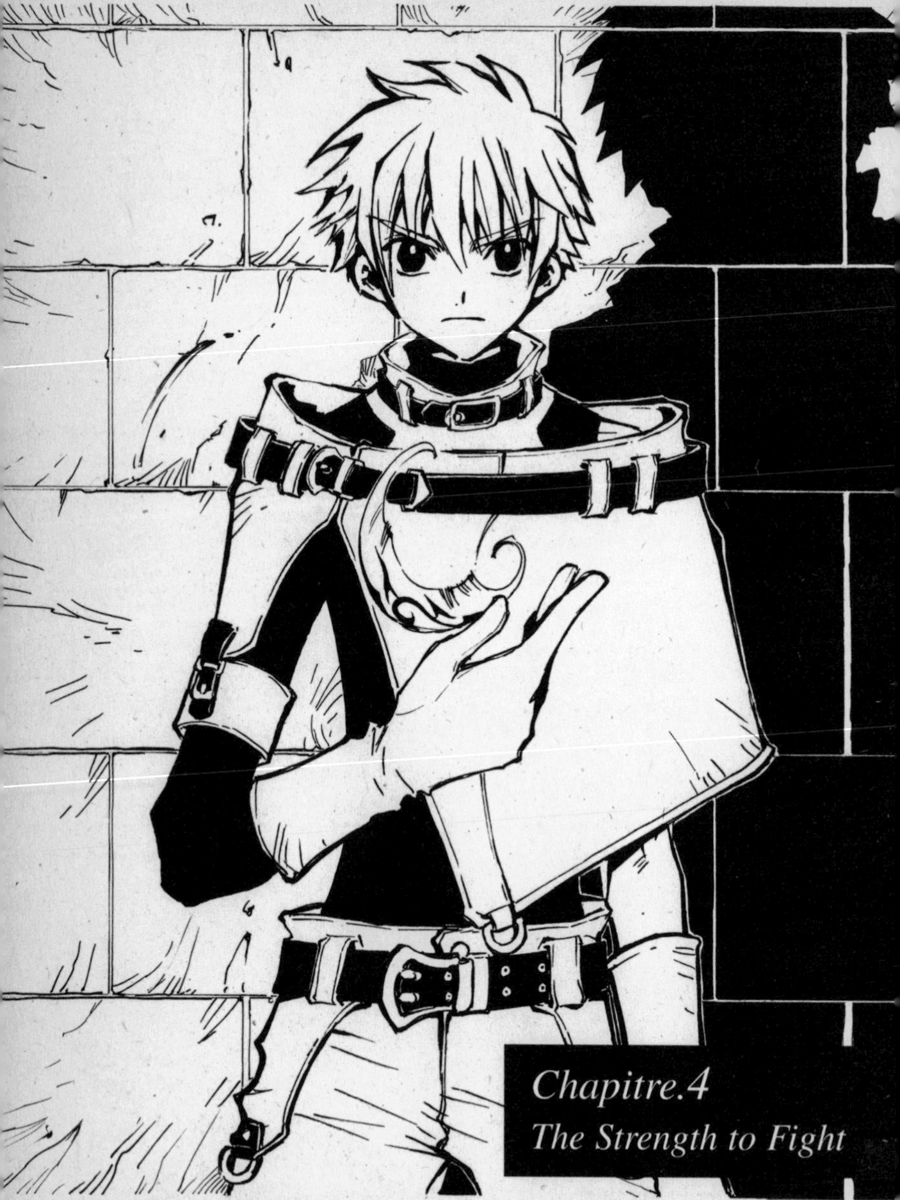
Chapitre.4
The Strength to Fight

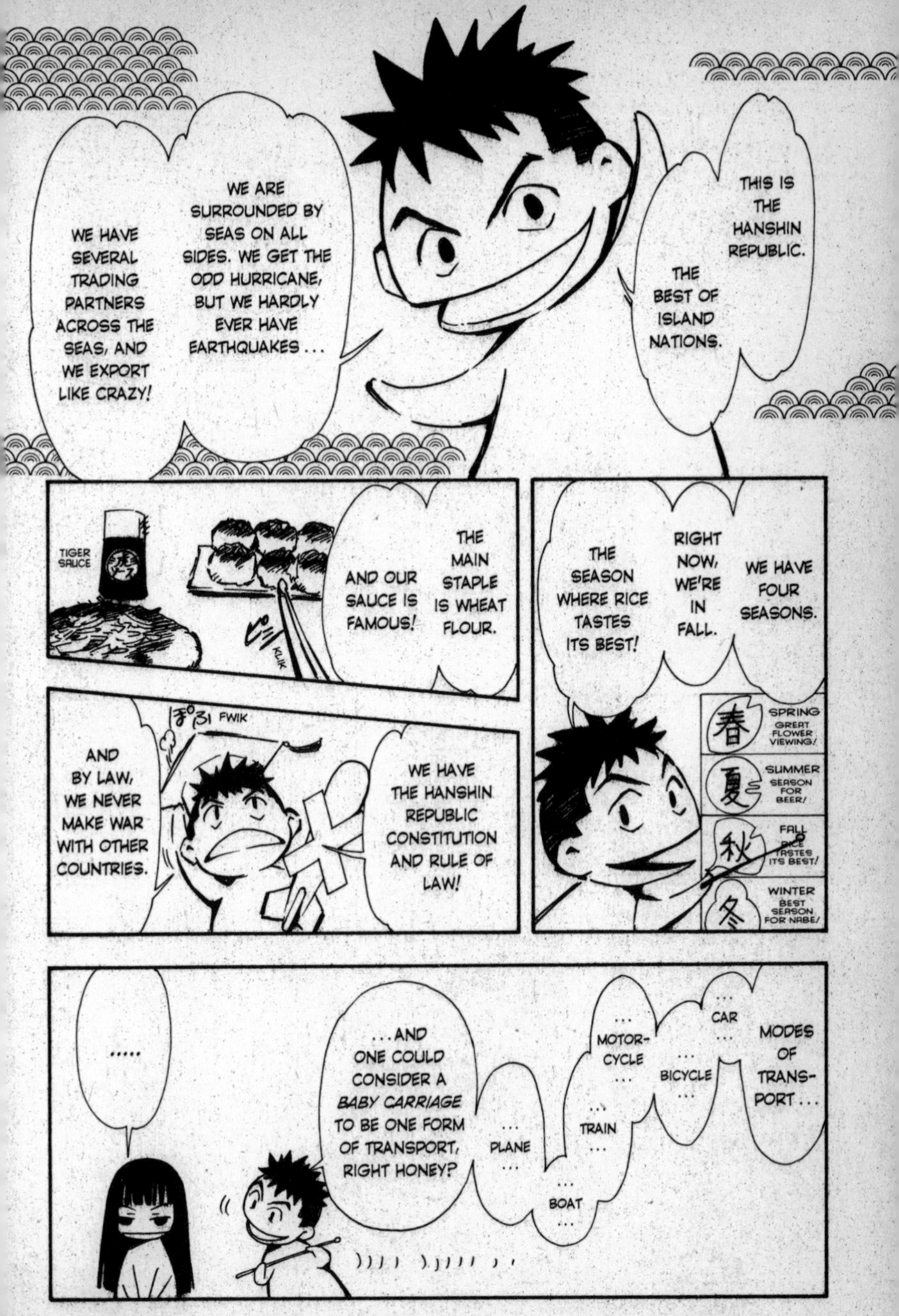

THIS IS THE HANSHIN REPUBLIC.
THE BEST OF ISLAND NATIONS.
WE ARE SURROUNDED BY SEAS ON ALL SIDES. WE GET THE ODD HURRICANE, BUT WE HARDLY EVER HAVE EARTHQUAKES . . .
WE HAVE SEVERAL TRADING PARTNERS ACROSS THE SEAS, AND WE EXPORT LIKE CRAZY!
WE HAVE FOUR SEASONS.
RIGHT NOW, WE'RE IN FALL.
THE SEASON WHERE RICE TASTES ITS BEST!
春 SPRING GREAT FLOWER VIEWING!
夏 SUMMER SEASON FOR BEER!
秋 FALL RICE TASTES ITS BEST!
冬 WINTER BEST SEASON FOR NABE!
THE MAIN STAPLE IS WHEAT FLOUR.
AND OUR SAUCE IS FAMOUS!
KLIK
TIGER SAUCE
WE HAVE THE HANSHIN REPUBLIC CONSTITUTION AND RULE OF LAW!
FWIK
AND BY LAW, WE NEVER MAKE WAR WITH OTHER COUNTRIES.
MODES OF TRANS-PORT . . .
. . . CAR . . .
. . . BICYCLE . . .
. . . MOTOR-CYCLE . . .
. . . TRAIN . . .
. . . BOAT . . .
. . . PLANE . . .
. . . AND ONE COULD CONSIDER A *BABY CARRIAGE* TO BE ONE FORM OF TRANSPORT, RIGHT HONEY?
. . . . . .

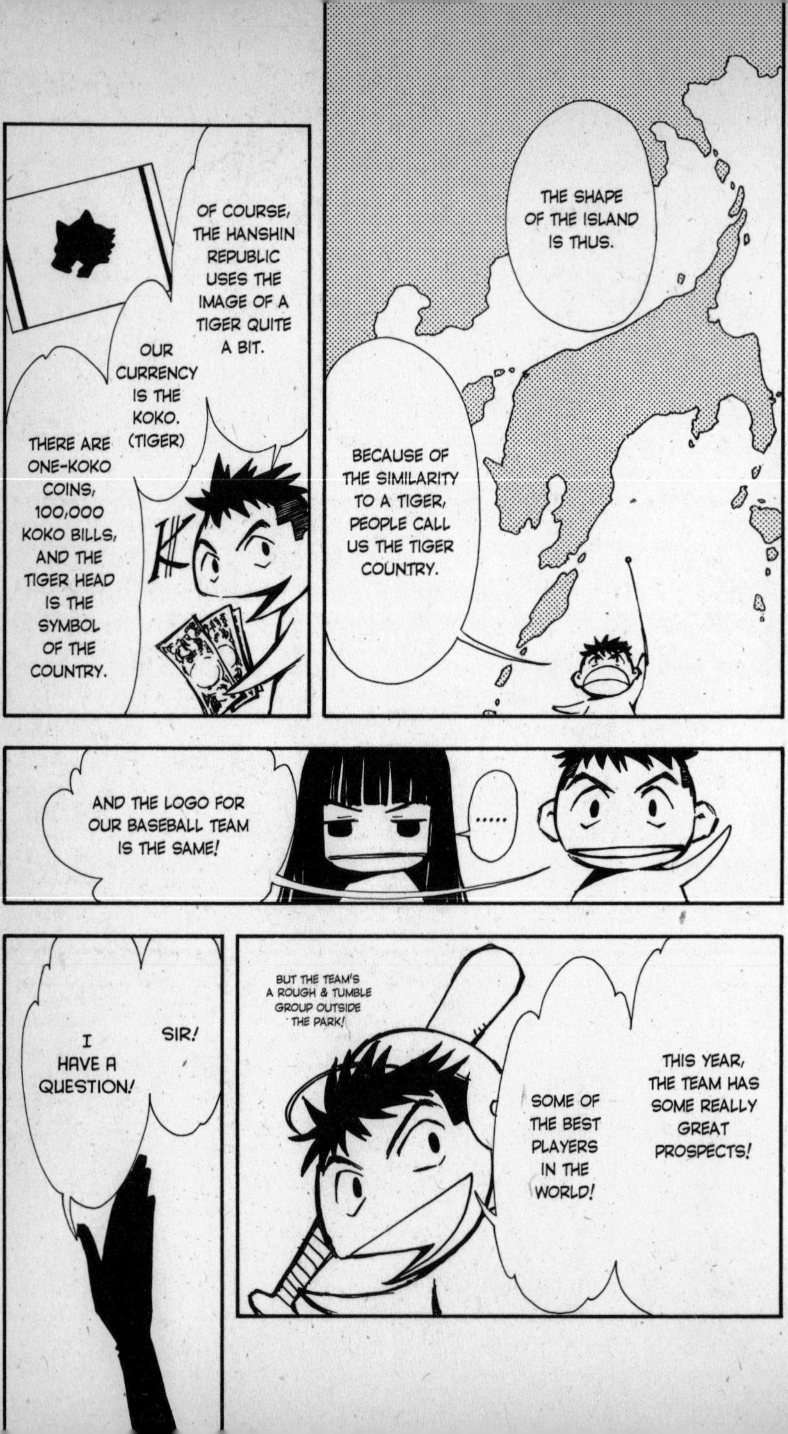
THE SHAPE OF THE ISLAND IS THUS.
BECAUSE OF THE SIMILARITY TO A TIGER, PEOPLE CALL US THE TIGER COUNTRY.
OF COURSE, THE HANSHIN REPUBLIC USES THE IMAGE OF A TIGER QUITE A BIT.
OUR CURRENCY IS THE KOKO. (TIGER)
THERE ARE ONE-KOKO COINS, 100,000 KOKO BILLS, AND THE TIGER HEAD IS THE SYMBOL OF THE COUNTRY.
.....
AND THE LOGO FOR OUR BASEBALL TEAM IS THE SAME!
THIS YEAR, THE TEAM HAS SOME REALLY GREAT PROSPECTS!
SOME OF THE BEST PLAYERS IN THE WORLD!
BUT THE TEAM'S A ROUGH & TUMBLE GROUP OUTSIDE THE PARK!
SIR!
I HAVE A QUESTION!

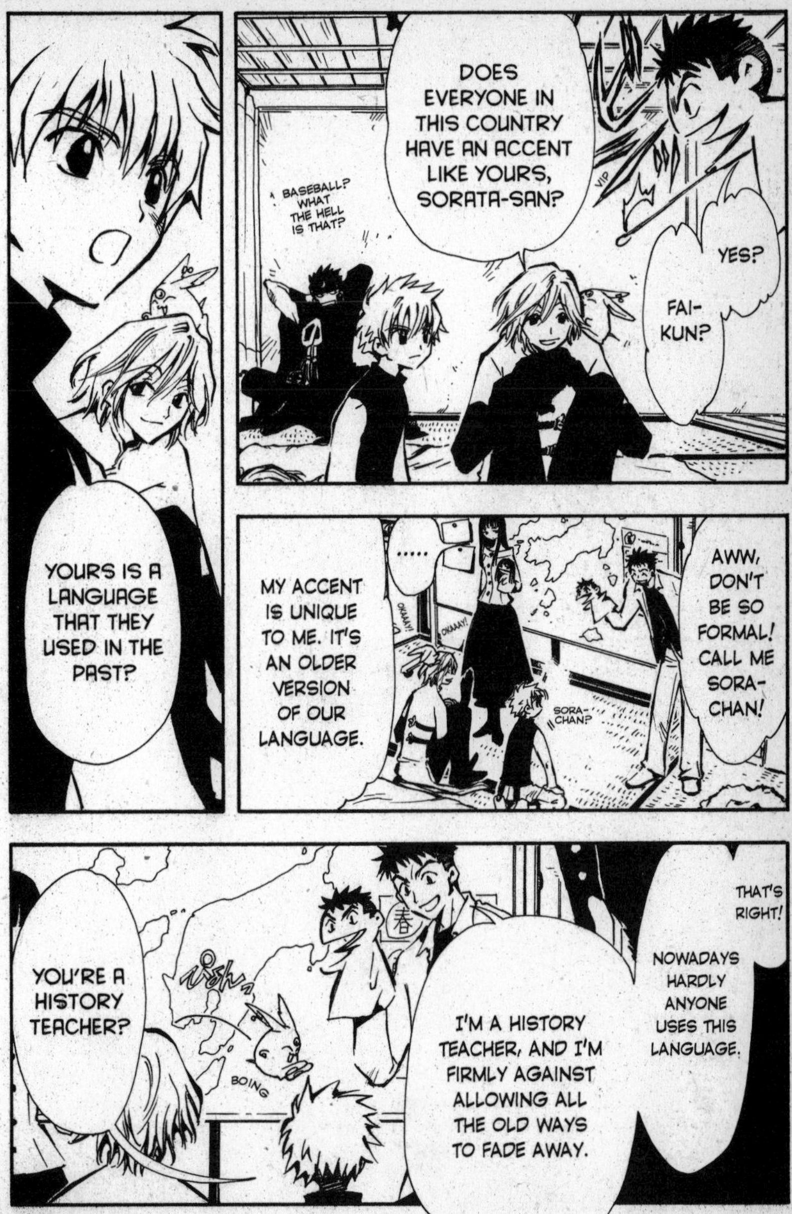
YES?
FAI-KUN?
VIP
DOES EVERYONE IN THIS COUNTRY HAVE AN ACCENT LIKE YOURS, SORATA-SAN?
BASEBALL? WHAT THE HELL IS THAT?
AWW, DON'T BE SO FORMAL! CALL ME SORA-CHAN!
SORA-CHAN?
OKAAAY!
OKAAAY!
.....
MY ACCENT IS UNIQUE TO ME. IT'S AN OLDER VERSION OF OUR LANGUAGE.
YOURS IS A LANGUAGE THAT THEY USED IN THE PAST?
THAT'S RIGHT!
NOWADAYS HARDLY ANYONE USES THIS LANGUAGE.
I'M A HISTORY TEACHER, AND I'M FIRMLY AGAINST ALLOWING ALL THE OLD WAYS TO FADE AWAY.
BOING
YOU'RE A HISTORY TEACHER?

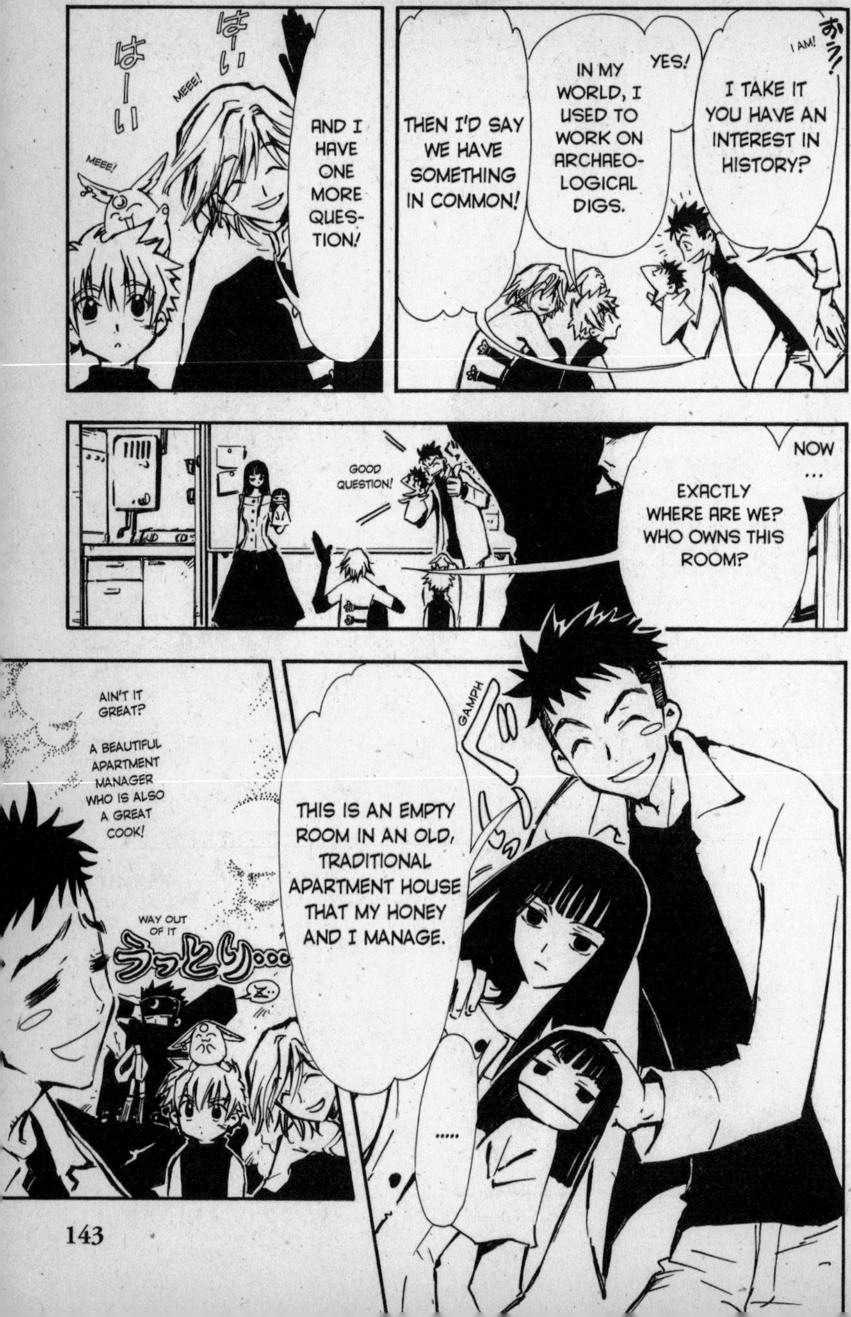
おう!
I AM!
I TAKE IT YOU HAVE AN INTEREST IN HISTORY?
YES!
IN MY WORLD, I USED TO WORK ON ARCHAEO-LOGICAL DIGS.
THEN I'D SAY WE HAVE SOMETHING IN COMMON!
AND I HAVE ONE MORE QUES-TION!
はーい
MEEE!
はーい
MEEE!
NOW ...
EXACTLY WHERE ARE WE? WHO OWNS THIS ROOM?
GOOD QUESTION!
GAMPH
THIS IS AN EMPTY ROOM IN AN OLD, TRADITIONAL APARTMENT HOUSE THAT MY HONEY AND I MANAGE.
......
AIN'T IT GREAT?
A BEAUTIFUL APARTMENT MANAGER WHO IS ALSO A GREAT COOK!
WAY OUT OF IT
うっとり...

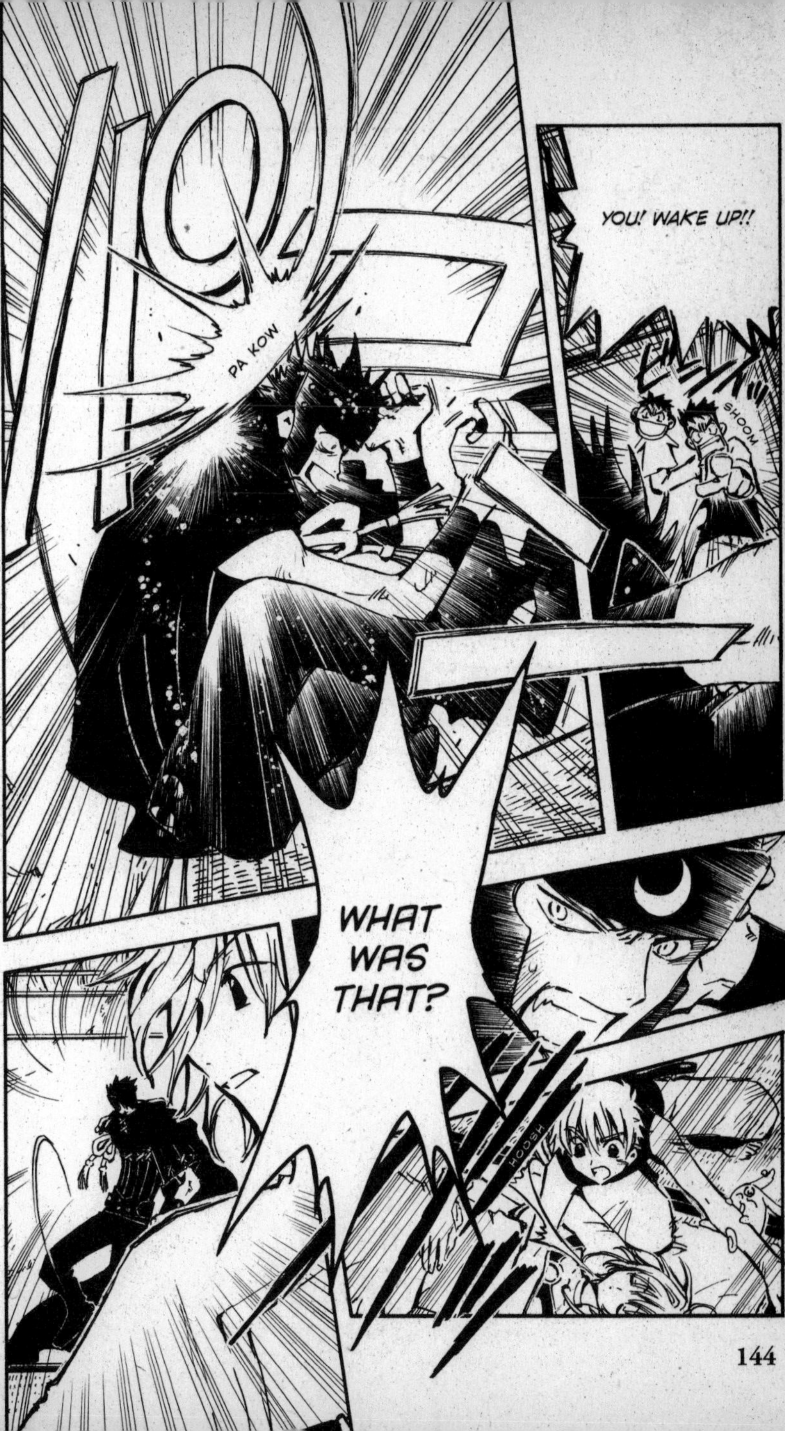
YOU! WAKE UP!!
SHOOM
PA KOW
WHAT WAS THAT?
HOOSH

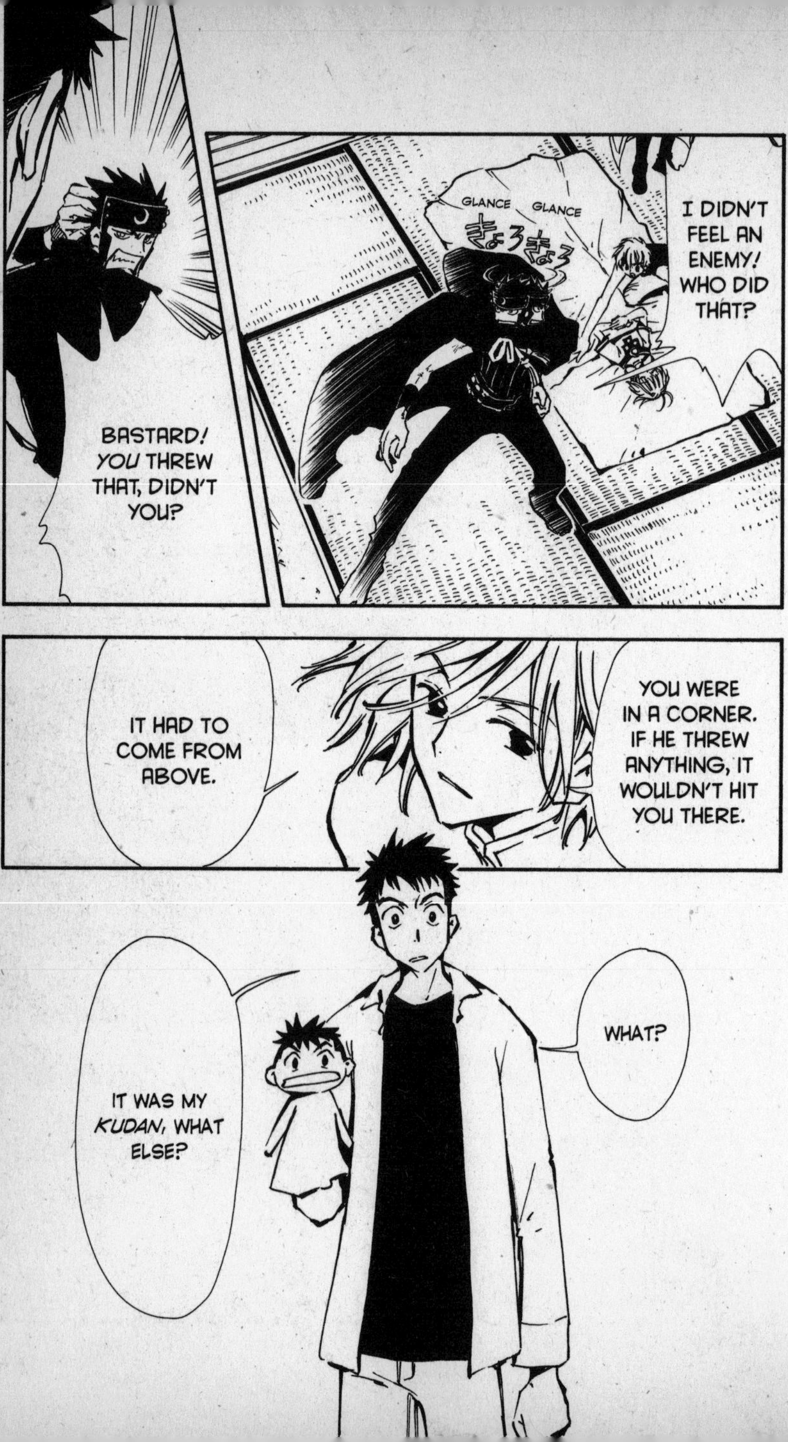

I DIDN'T FEEL AN ENEMY! WHO DID THAT?
GLANCE GLANCE
きょろきょろ
BASTARD! *YOU* THREW THAT, DIDN'T YOU?
YOU WERE IN A CORNER. IF HE THREW ANYTHING, IT WOULDN'T HIT YOU THERE.
IT HAD TO COME FROM ABOVE.
WHAT?
IT WAS MY *KUDAN*, WHAT ELSE?

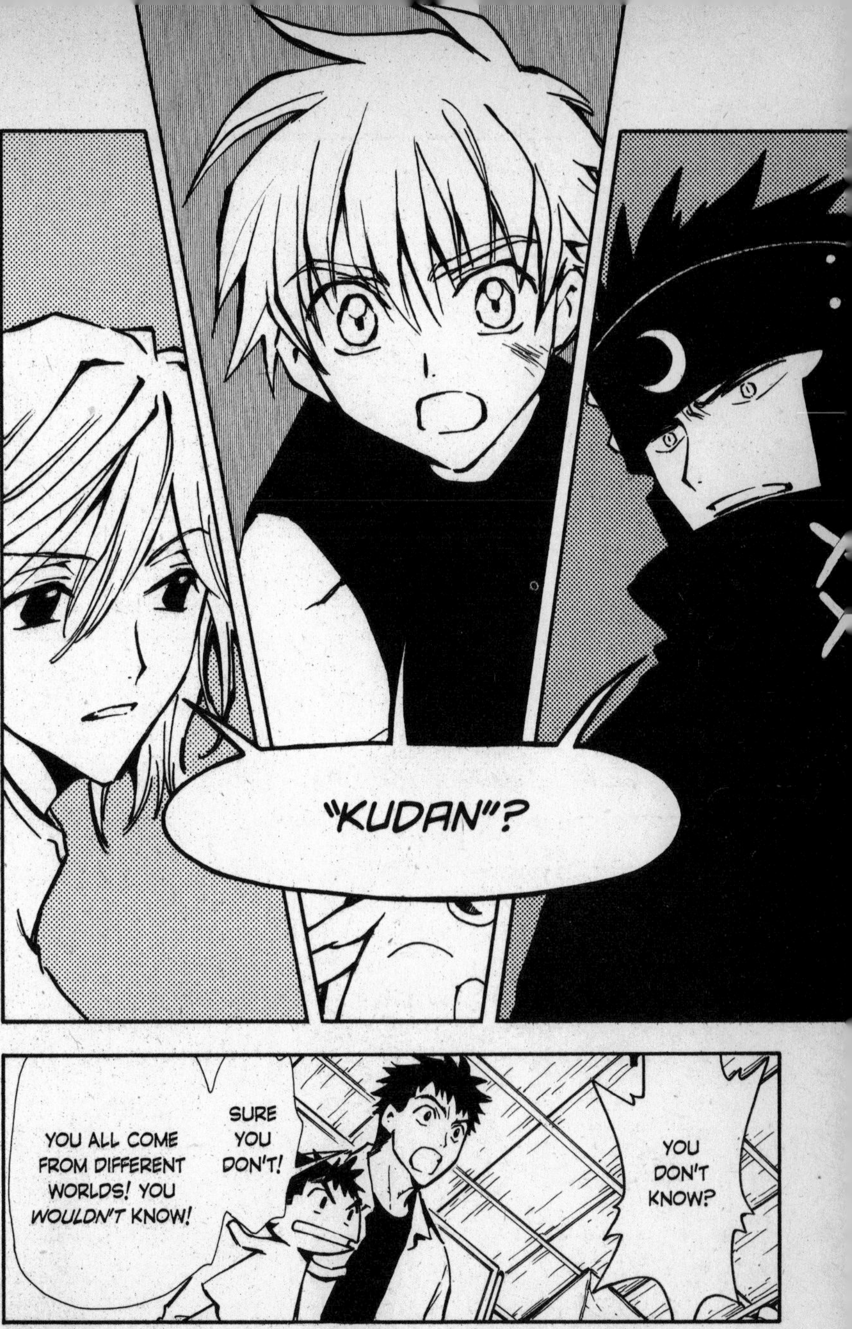
"KUDAN"?
YOU DON'T KNOW?
SURE YOU DON'T!
YOU ALL COME FROM DIFFERENT WORLDS! YOU WOULDN'T KNOW!

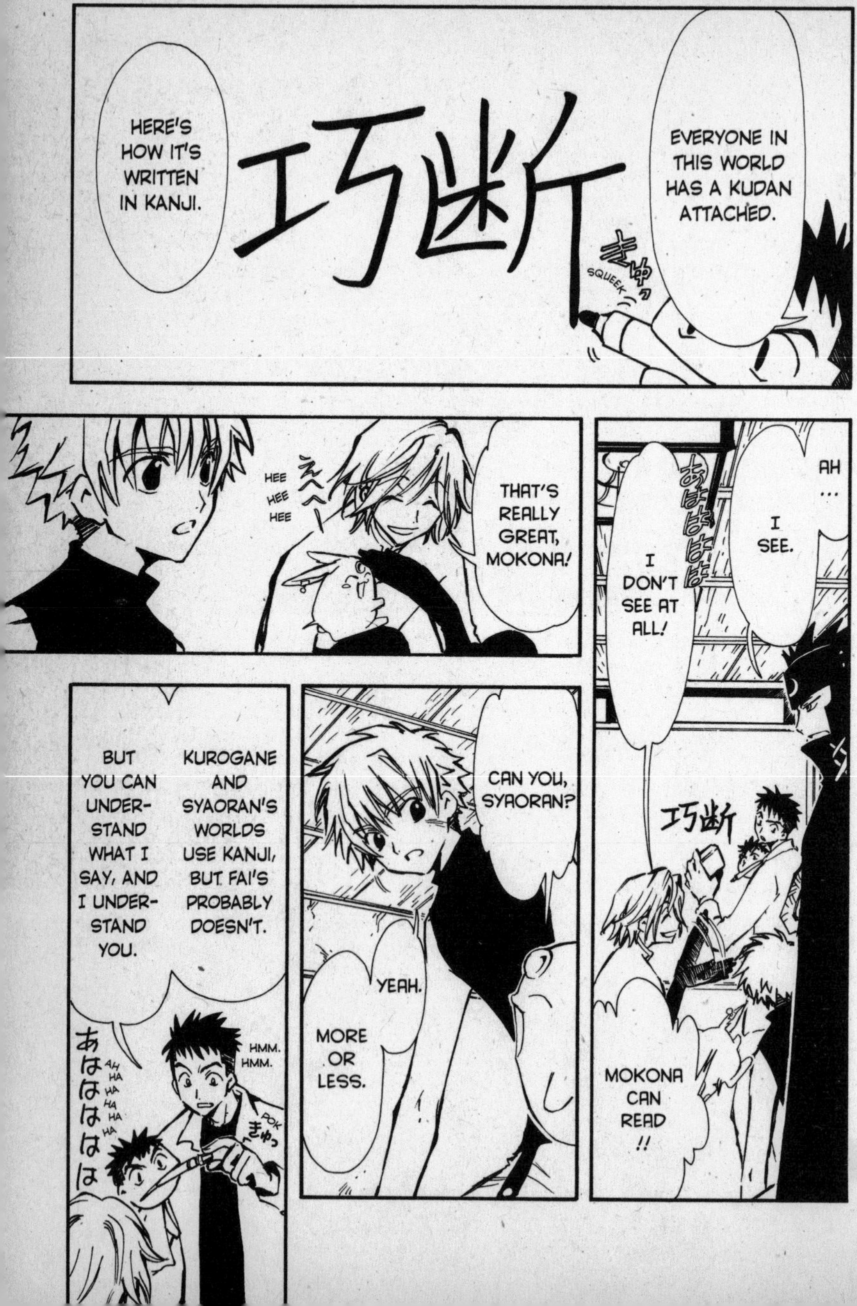
EVERYONE IN THIS WORLD HAS A KUDAN ATTACHED.
巧断
きゅっ
SQUEEK
HERE'S HOW IT'S WRITTEN IN KANJI.
AH … I SEE.
あははは
I DON'T SEE AT ALL!
巧断
MOKONA CAN READ !!
えへへ
HEE HEE HEE
THAT'S REALLY GREAT, MOKONA!
CAN YOU, SYAORAN?
YEAH.
MORE OR LESS.
KUROGANE AND SYAORAN'S WORLDS USE KANJI, BUT FAI'S PROBABLY DOESN'T.
BUT YOU CAN UNDERSTAND WHAT I SAY, AND I UNDERSTAND YOU.
HMM. HMM.
きゅっ
POK
あははは
AH HA HA HA HA

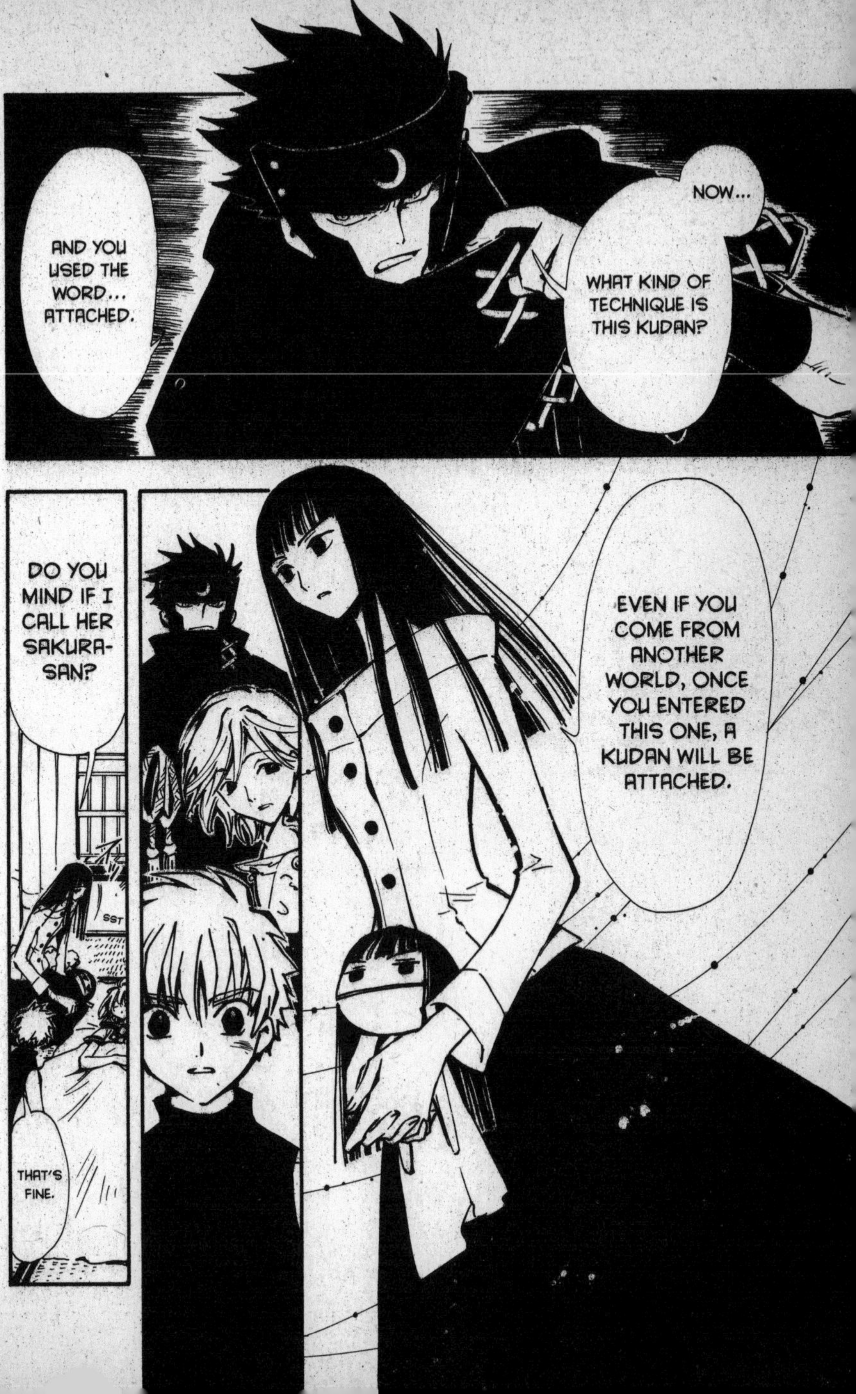
NOW...
WHAT KIND OF TECHNIQUE IS THIS KUDAN?
AND YOU USED THE WORD... ATTACHED.
EVEN IF YOU COME FROM ANOTHER WORLD, ONCE YOU ENTERED THIS ONE, A KUDAN WILL BE ATTACHED.
DO YOU MIND IF I CALL HER SAKURA-SAN?
SST
THAT'S FINE.

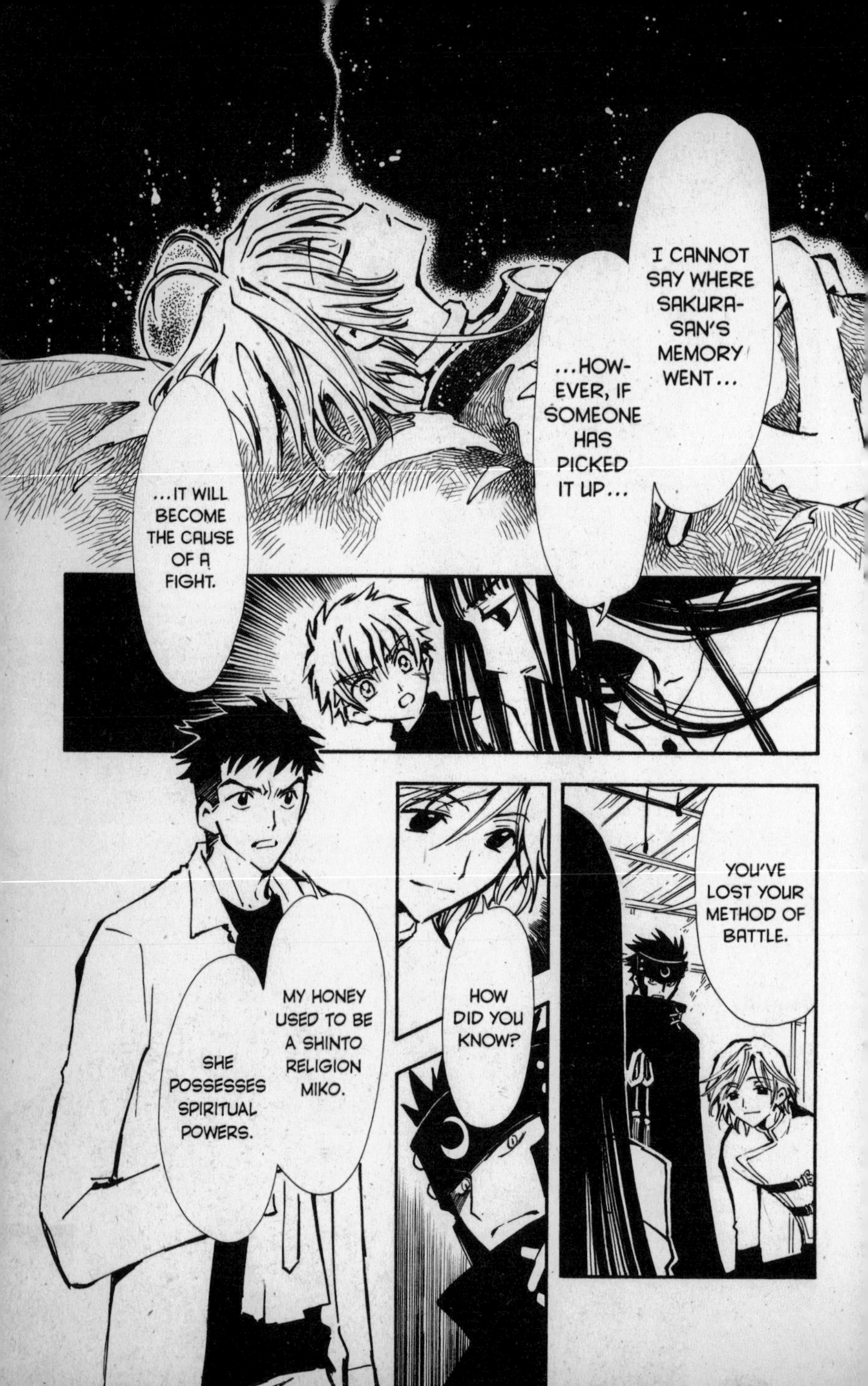
I CANNOT SAY WHERE SAKURA-SAN'S MEMORY WENT...
...HOW-EVER, IF SOMEONE HAS PICKED IT UP...
...IT WILL BECOME THE CAUSE OF A FIGHT.
YOU'VE LOST YOUR METHOD OF BATTLE.
HOW DID YOU KNOW?
MY HONEY USED TO BE A SHINTO RELIGION MIKO.
SHE POSSESSES SPIRITUAL POWERS.

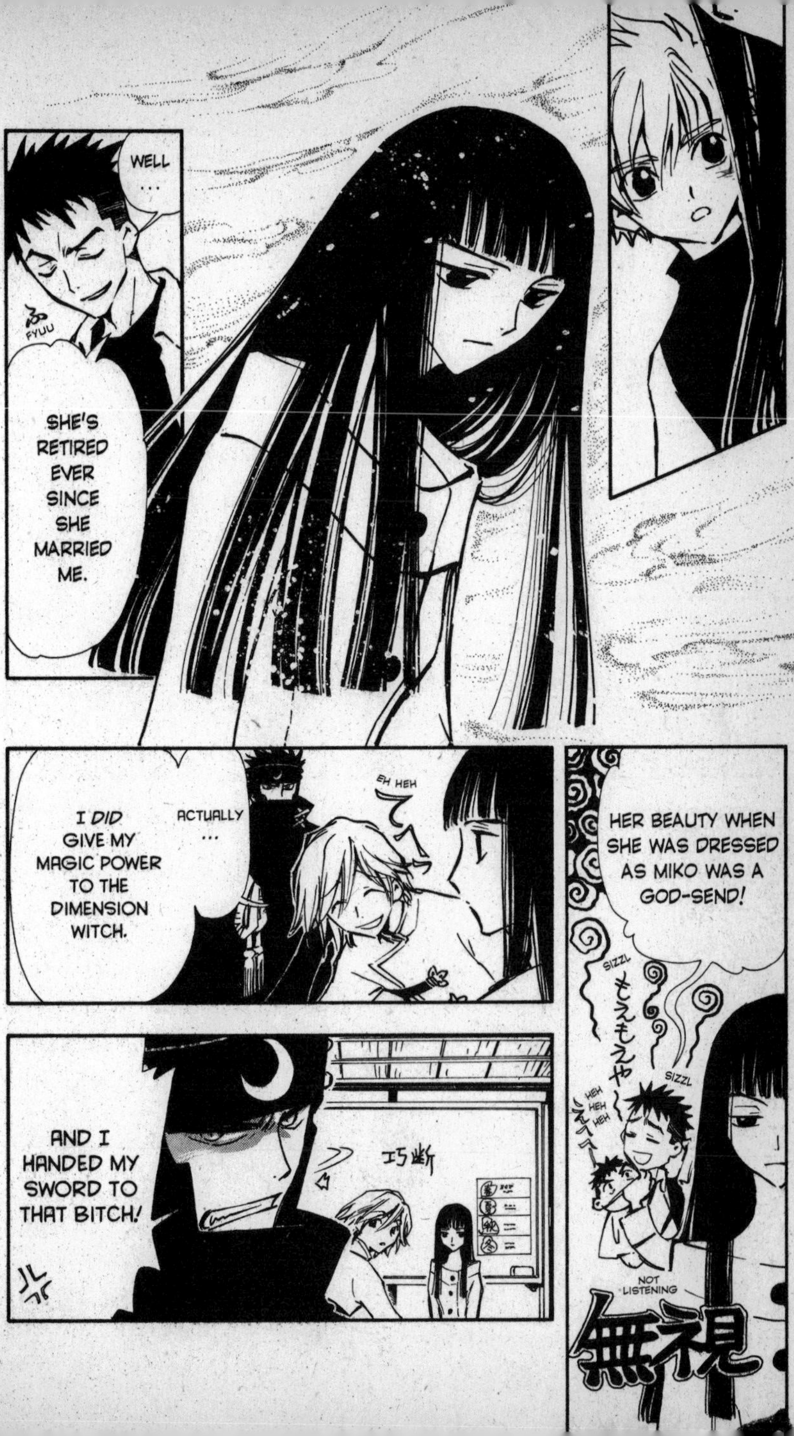
WELL ...
FYUU
SHE'S RETIRED EVER SINCE SHE MARRIED ME.
HER BEAUTY WHEN SHE WAS DRESSED AS MIKO WAS A GOD-SEND!
SIZZL
もえもえや~
SIZZL
HEH HEH HEH
NOT LISTENING
無視
ACTUALLY ...
I DID GIVE MY MAGIC POWER TO THE DIMENSION WITCH.
EH HEH
AND I HANDED MY SWORD TO THAT BITCH!

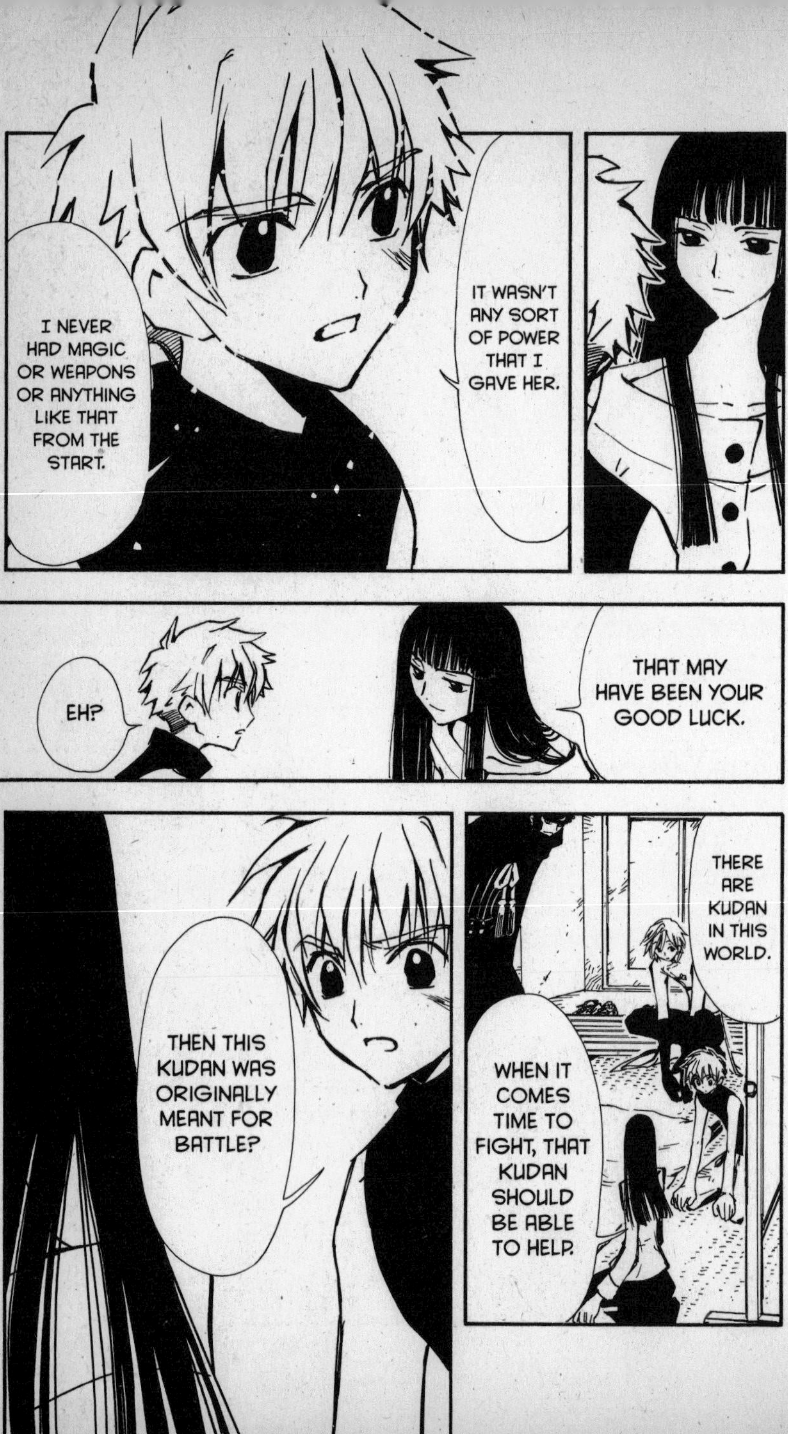
IT WASN'T ANY SORT OF POWER THAT I GAVE HER.
I NEVER HAD MAGIC OR WEAPONS OR ANYTHING LIKE THAT FROM THE START.
THAT MAY HAVE BEEN YOUR GOOD LUCK.
EH?
THERE ARE KUDAN IN THIS WORLD.
WHEN IT COMES TIME TO FIGHT, THAT KUDAN SHOULD BE ABLE TO HELP.
THEN THIS KUDAN WAS ORIGINALLY MEANT FOR BATTLE?

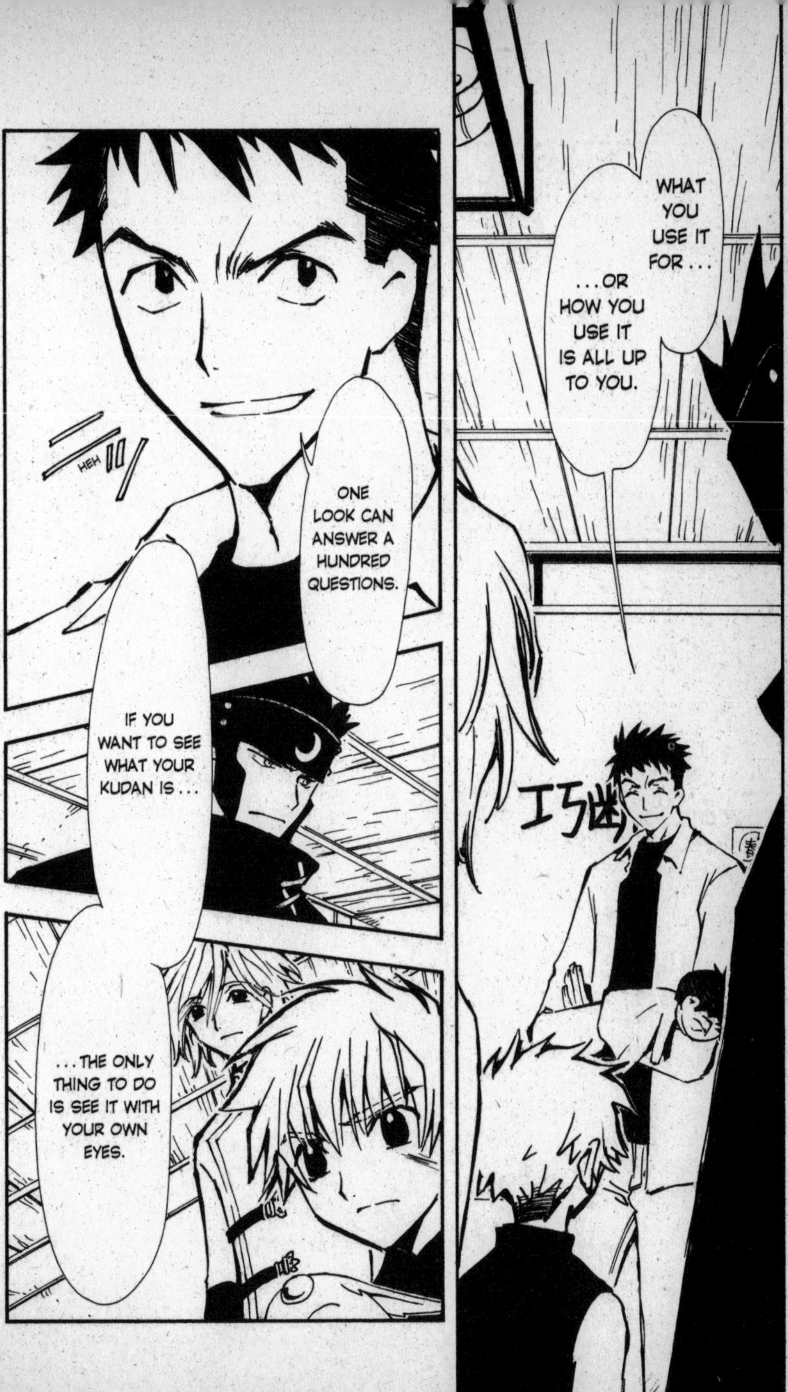
WHAT YOU USE IT FOR . . .
. . . OR HOW YOU USE IT IS ALL UP TO YOU.
HEH
ONE LOOK CAN ANSWER A HUNDRED QUESTIONS.
IF YOU WANT TO SEE WHAT YOUR KUDAN IS . . .
. . . THE ONLY THING TO DO IS SEE IT WITH YOUR OWN EYES.

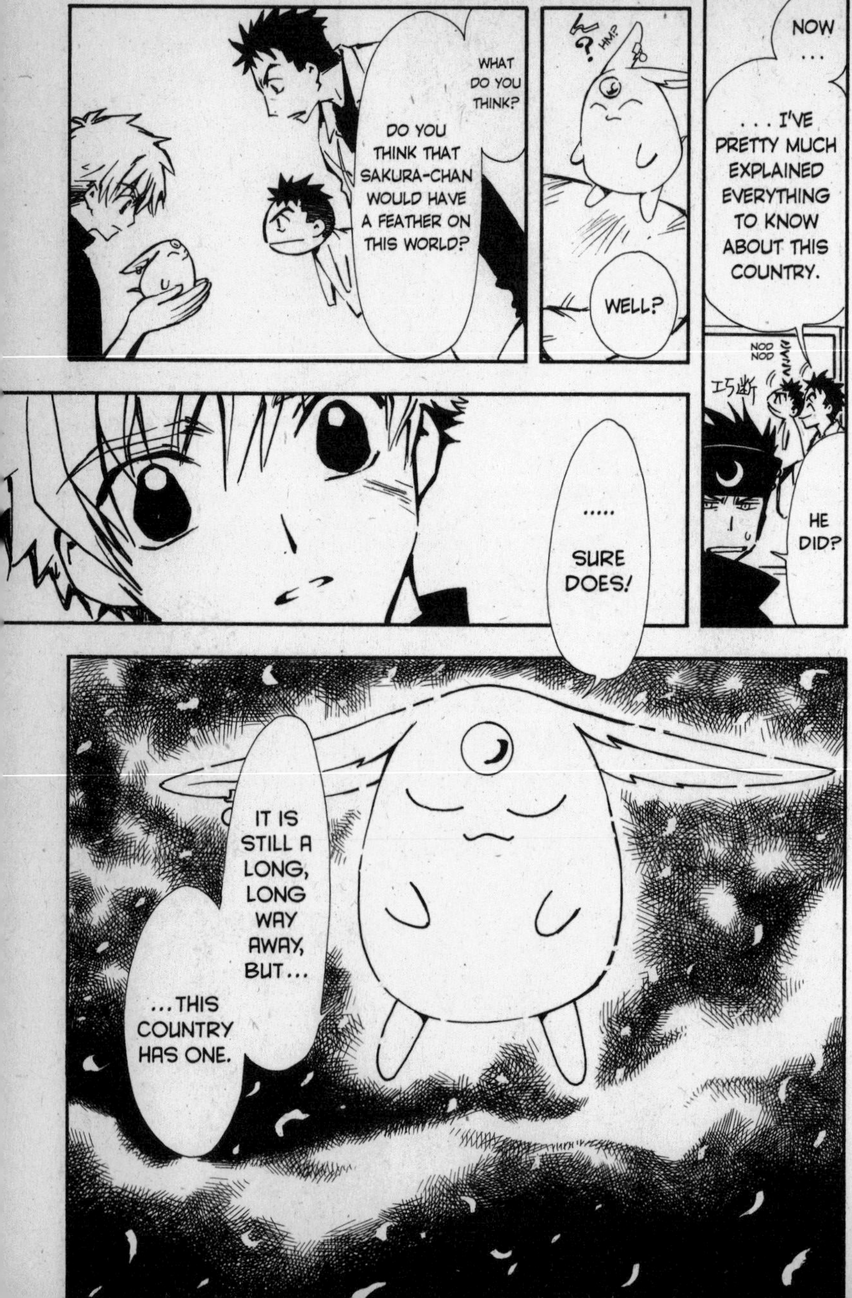
NOW . . .
. . . I'VE PRETTY MUCH EXPLAINED EVERYTHING TO KNOW ABOUT THIS COUNTRY.
NOD NOD
HE DID?
? HM?
WELL?
WHAT DO YOU THINK?
DO YOU THINK THAT SAKURA-CHAN WOULD HAVE A FEATHER ON THIS WORLD?
..... SURE DOES!
IT IS STILL A LONG, LONG WAY AWAY, BUT...
...THIS COUNTRY HAS ONE.

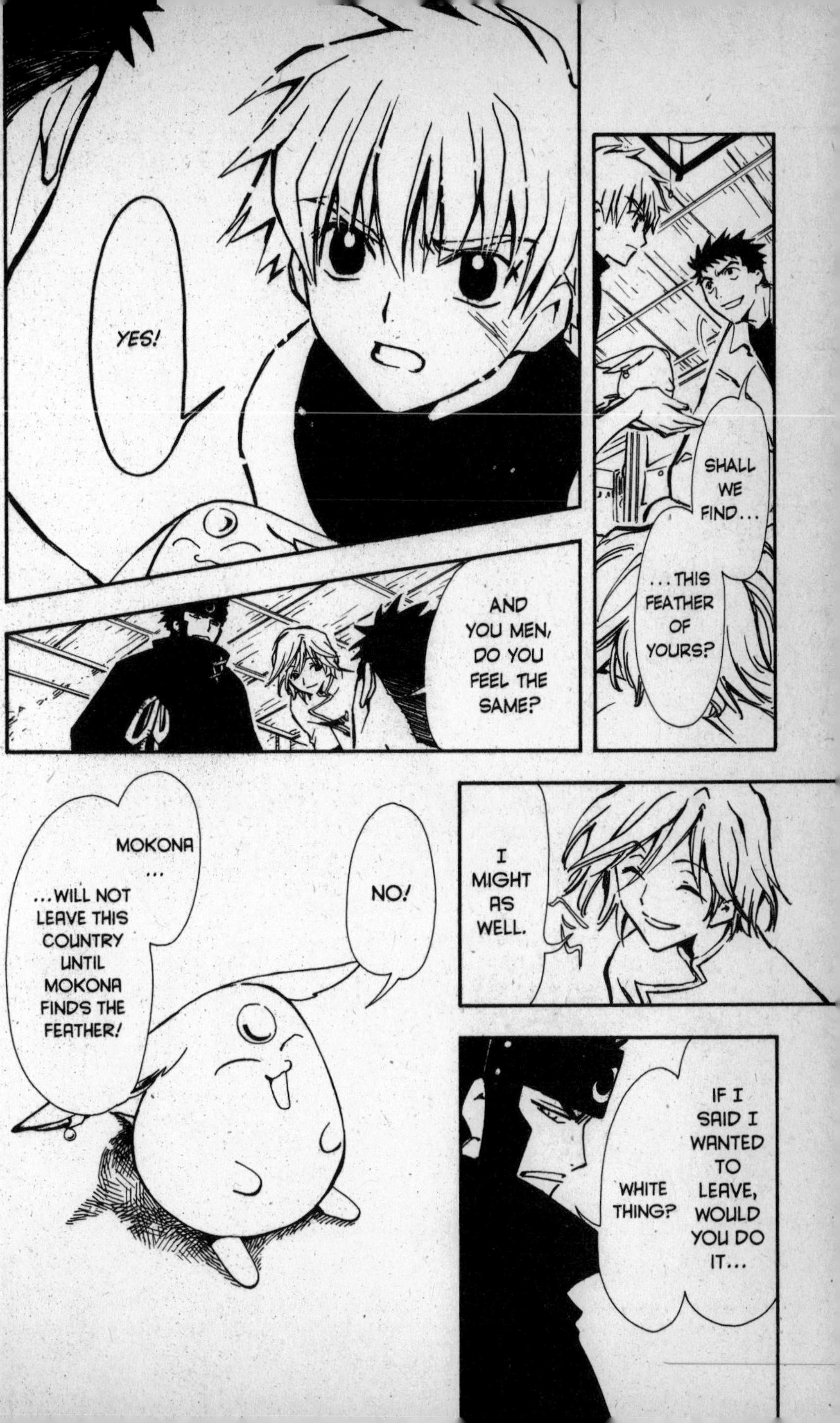
SHALL WE FIND... ...THIS FEATHER OF YOURS?
YES!
AND YOU MEN, DO YOU FEEL THE SAME?
I MIGHT AS WELL.
IF I SAID I WANTED TO LEAVE, WOULD YOU DO IT...
WHITE THING?
NO!
MOKONA ... ...WILL NOT LEAVE THIS COUNTRY UNTIL MOKONA FINDS THE FEATHER!

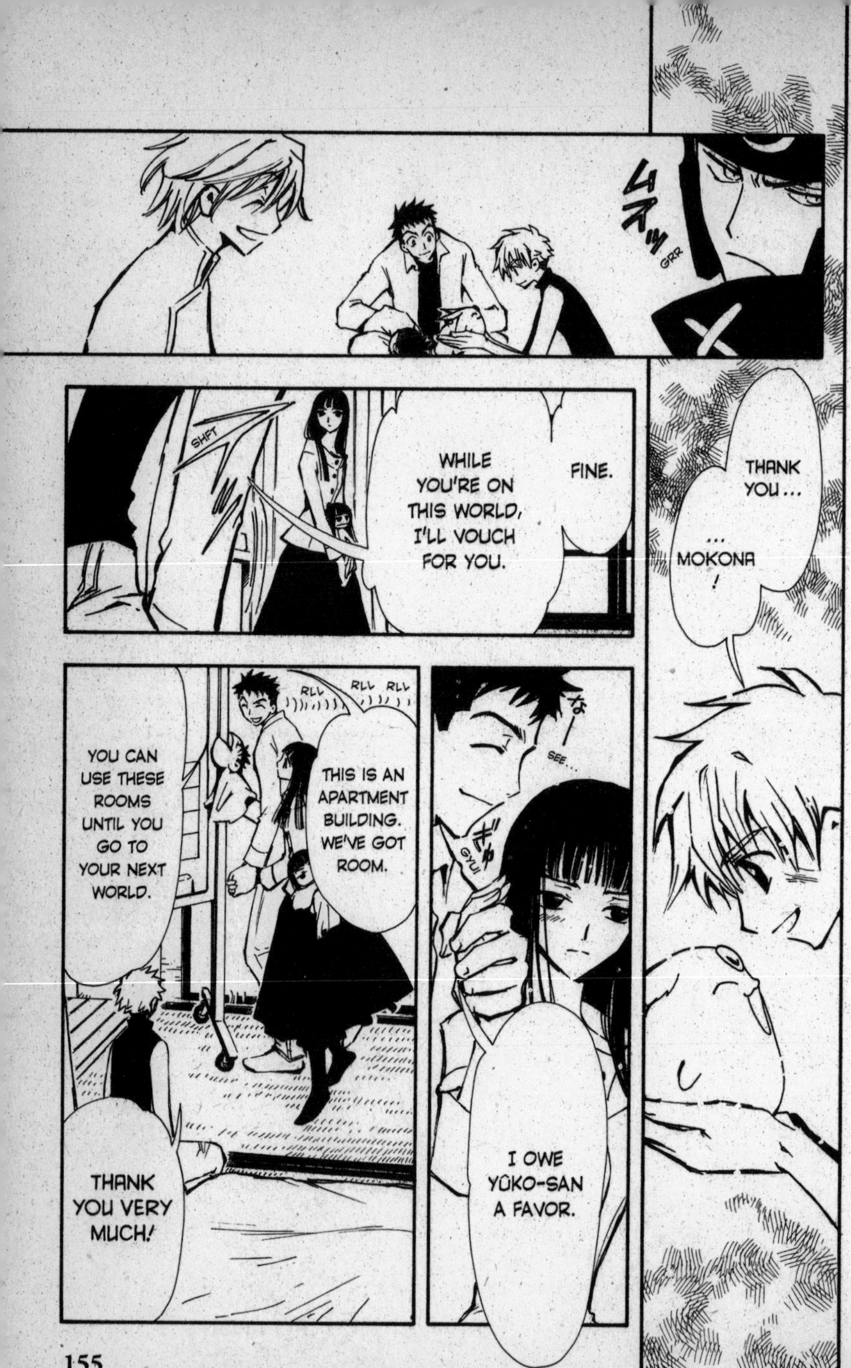
GRR
THANK YOU...
... MOKONA!
FINE.
WHILE YOU'RE ON THIS WORLD, I'LL VOUCH FOR YOU.
SHFT
SEE...
GYU
I OWE YŪKO-SAN A FAVOR.
RLV RLV
RLV
THIS IS AN APARTMENT BUILDING. WE'VE GOT ROOM.
YOU CAN USE THESE ROOMS UNTIL YOU GO TO YOUR NEXT WORLD.
THANK YOU VERY MUCH!

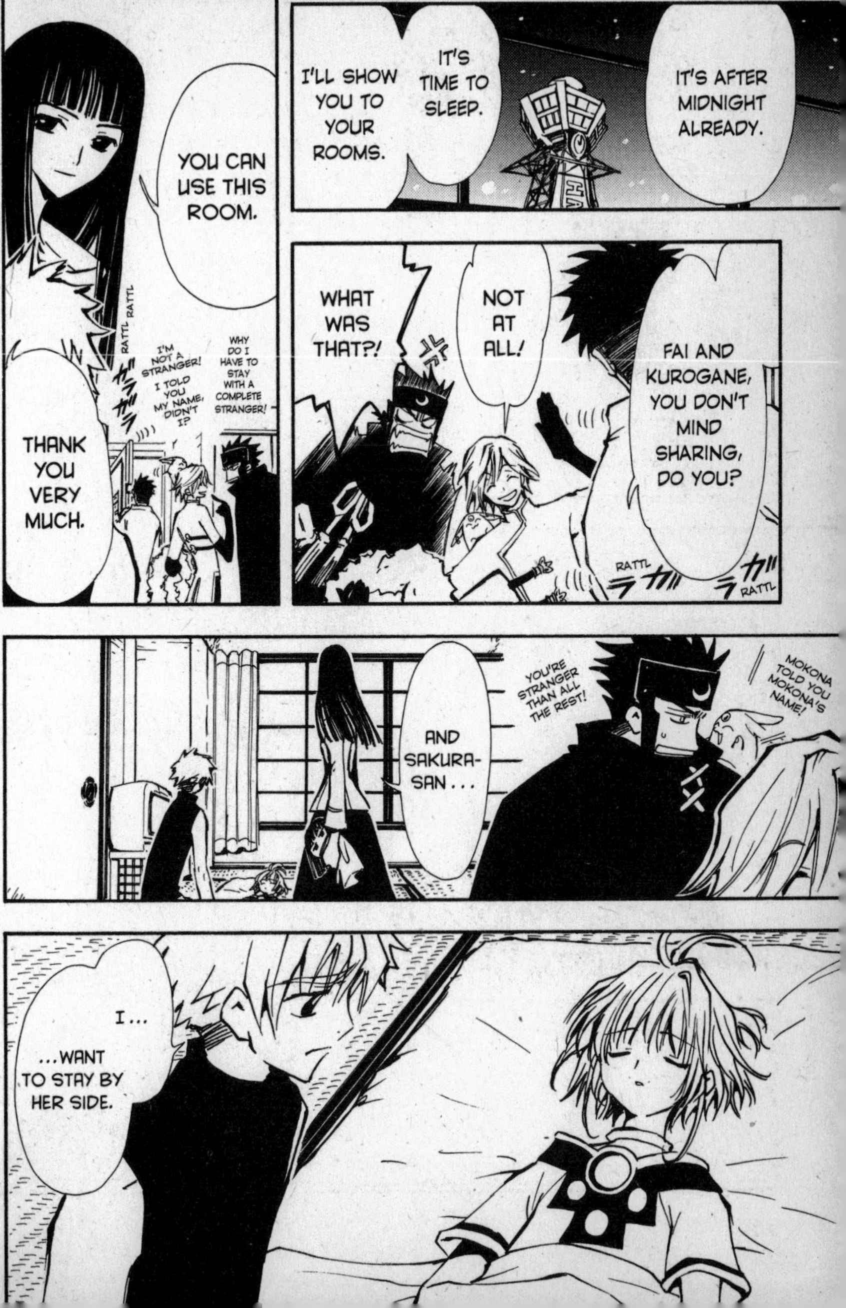
IT'S AFTER MIDNIGHT ALREADY.
IT'S TIME TO SLEEP.
I'LL SHOW YOU TO YOUR ROOMS.
FAI AND KUROGANE, YOU DON'T MIND SHARING, DO YOU?
NOT AT ALL!
WHAT WAS THAT?!
RATTL
RATTL
YOU CAN USE THIS ROOM.
WHY DO I HAVE TO STAY WITH A COMPLETE STRANGER!
I'M NOT A STRANGER! I TOLD YOU MY NAME, DIDN'T I?
RATTL
RATTL
THANK YOU VERY MUCH.
MOKONA TOLD YOU MOKONA'S NAME!
YOU'RE STRANGER THAN ALL THE REST!
AND SAKURA-SAN...
I...
...WANT TO STAY BY HER SIDE.

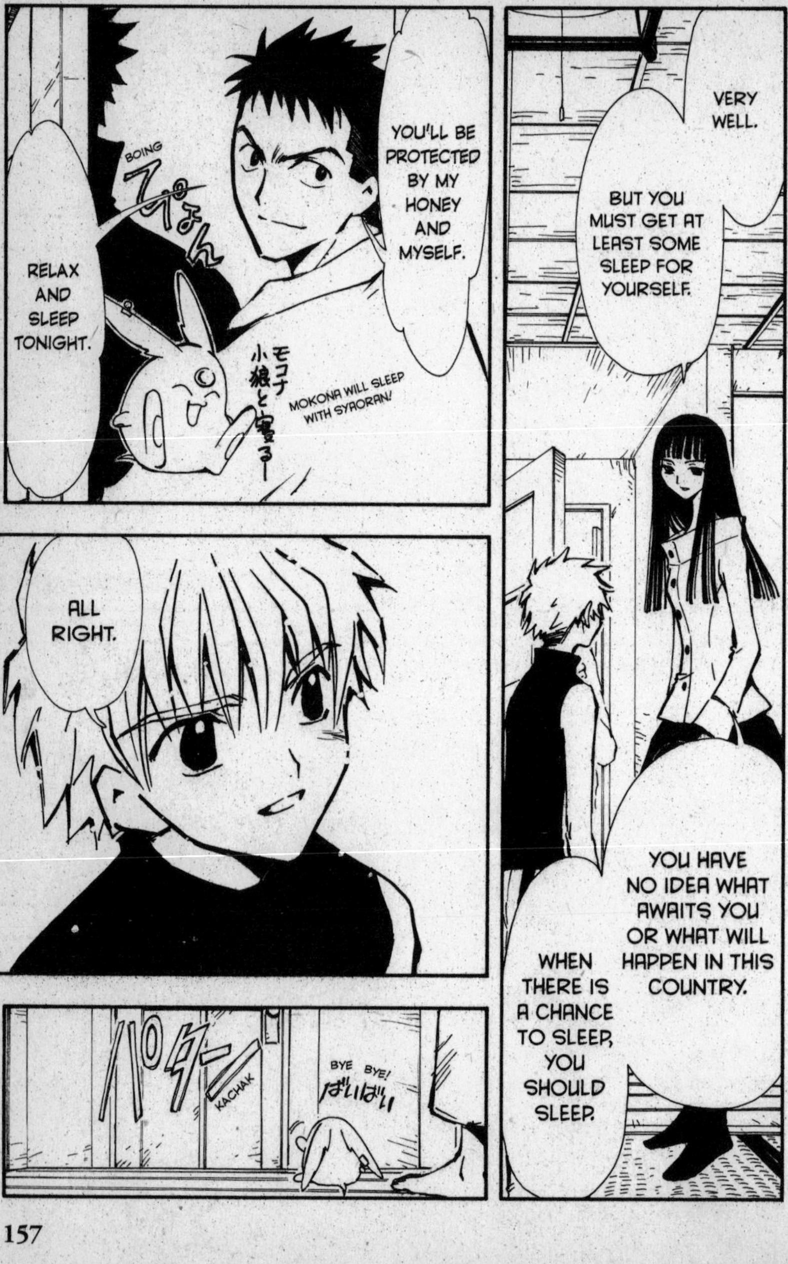
VERY WELL.
BUT YOU MUST GET AT LEAST SOME SLEEP FOR YOURSELF.
YOU HAVE NO IDEA WHAT AWAITS YOU OR WHAT WILL HAPPEN IN THIS COUNTRY.
WHEN THERE IS A CHANCE TO SLEEP, YOU SHOULD SLEEP.
YOU'LL BE PROTECTED BY MY HONEY AND MYSELF.
ぴょん
BOING
RELAX AND SLEEP TONIGHT.
モコナ小狼と寝るー
MOKONA WILL SLEEP WITH SYAORAN!
ALL RIGHT.
パターン
KACHAK
ばいばい
BYE BYE!

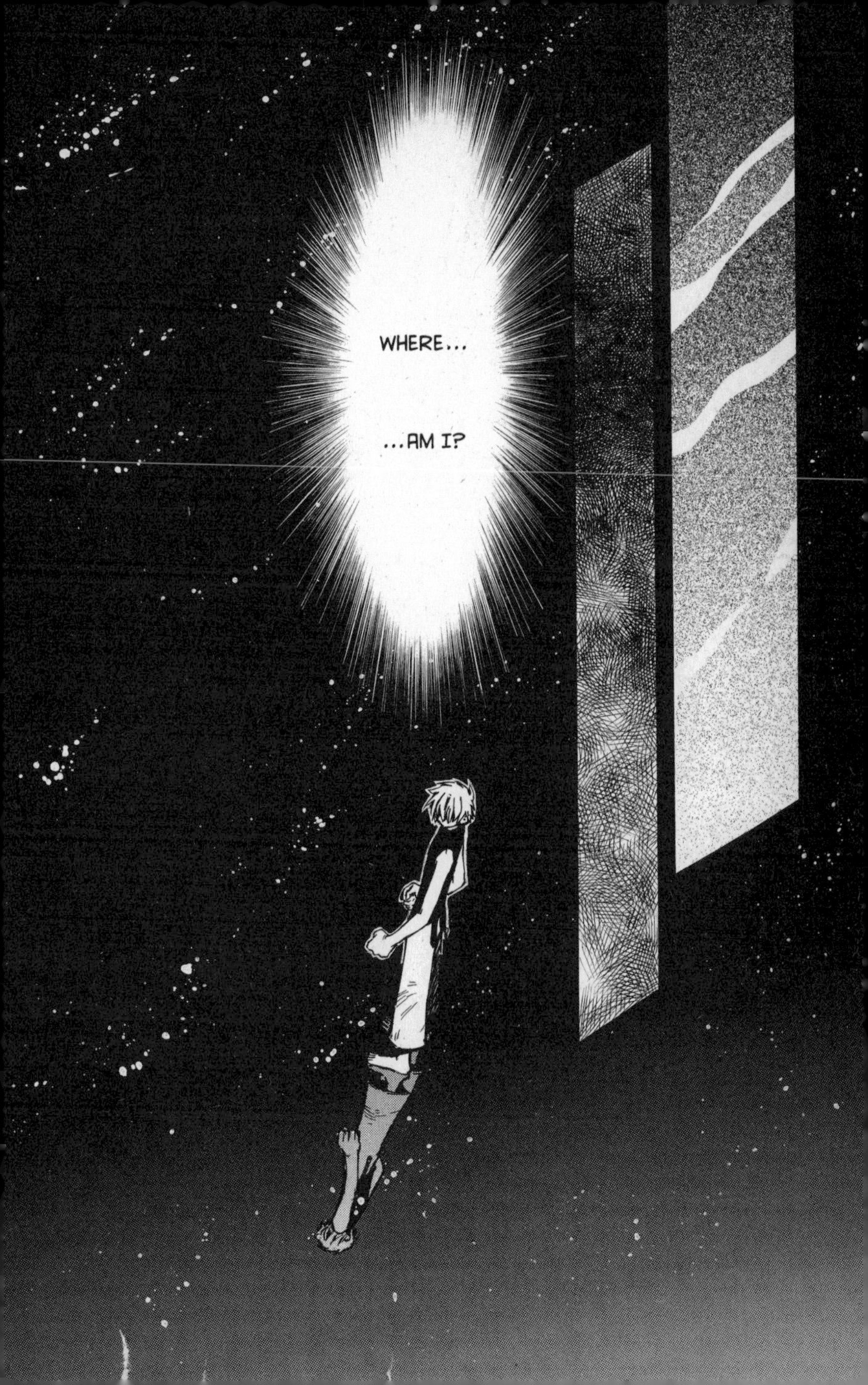
WHERE...
...AM I?

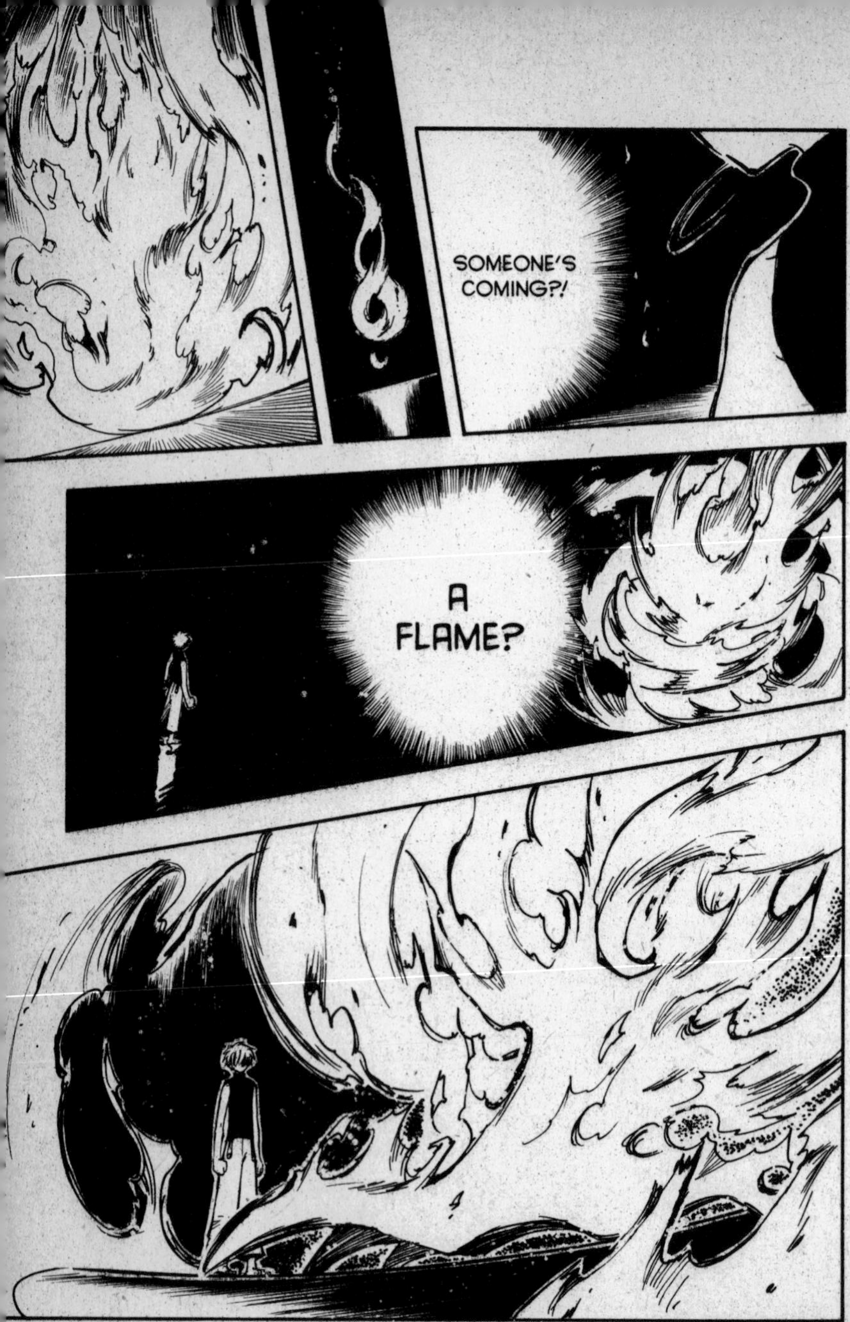
SOMEONE'S COMING?!
A FLAME?

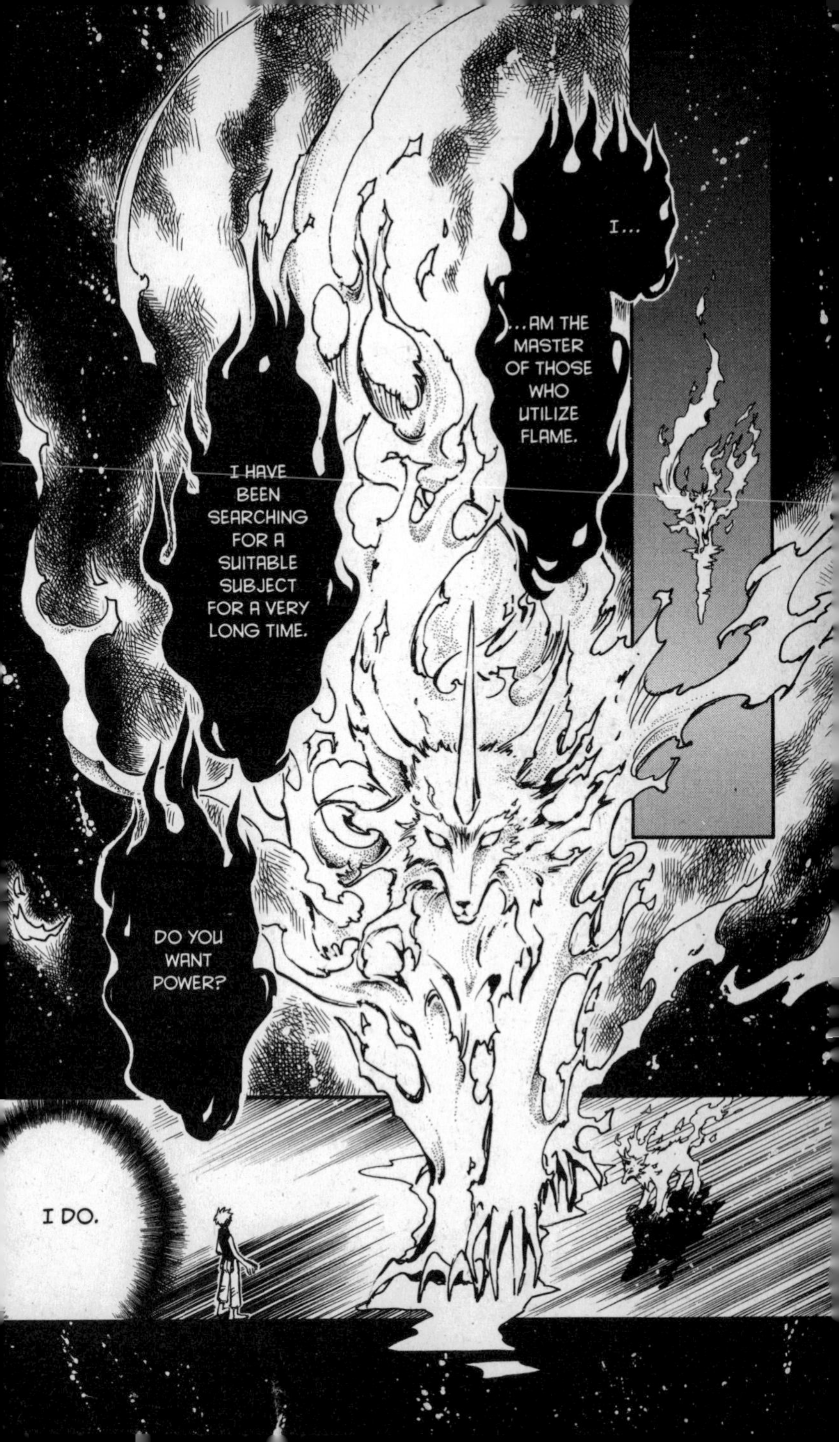
I...
...AM THE MASTER OF THOSE WHO UTILIZE FLAME.
I HAVE BEEN SEARCHING FOR A SUITABLE SUBJECT FOR A VERY LONG TIME.
DO YOU WANT POWER?
I DO.

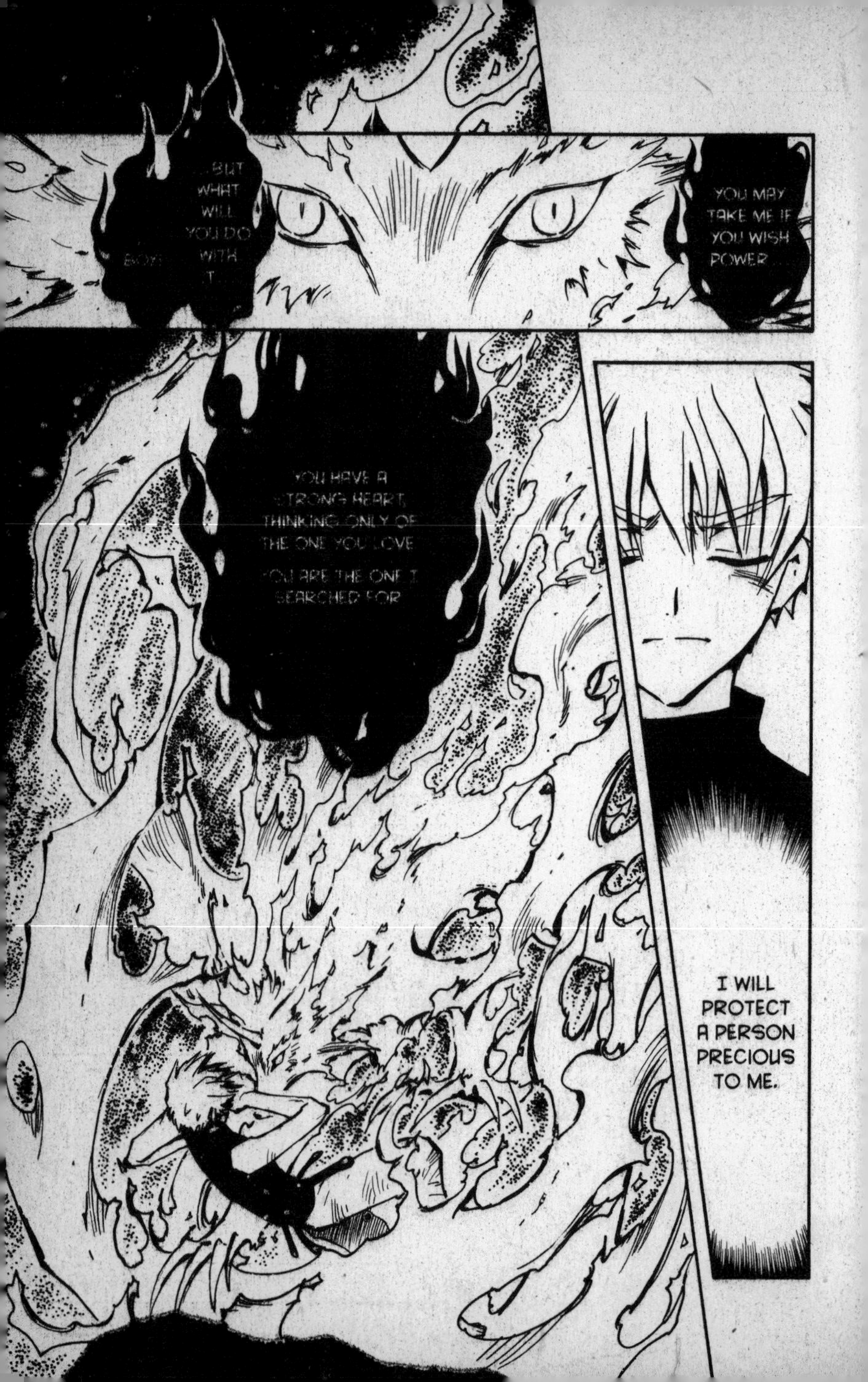
YOU MAY TAKE ME IF YOU WISH POWER...
...BUT WHAT WILL YOU DO WITH IT...
BOY?
I WILL PROTECT A PERSON PRECIOUS TO ME.
YOU HAVE A STRONG HEART, THINKING ONLY OF THE ONE YOU LOVE.
YOU ARE THE ONE I SEARCHED FOR.

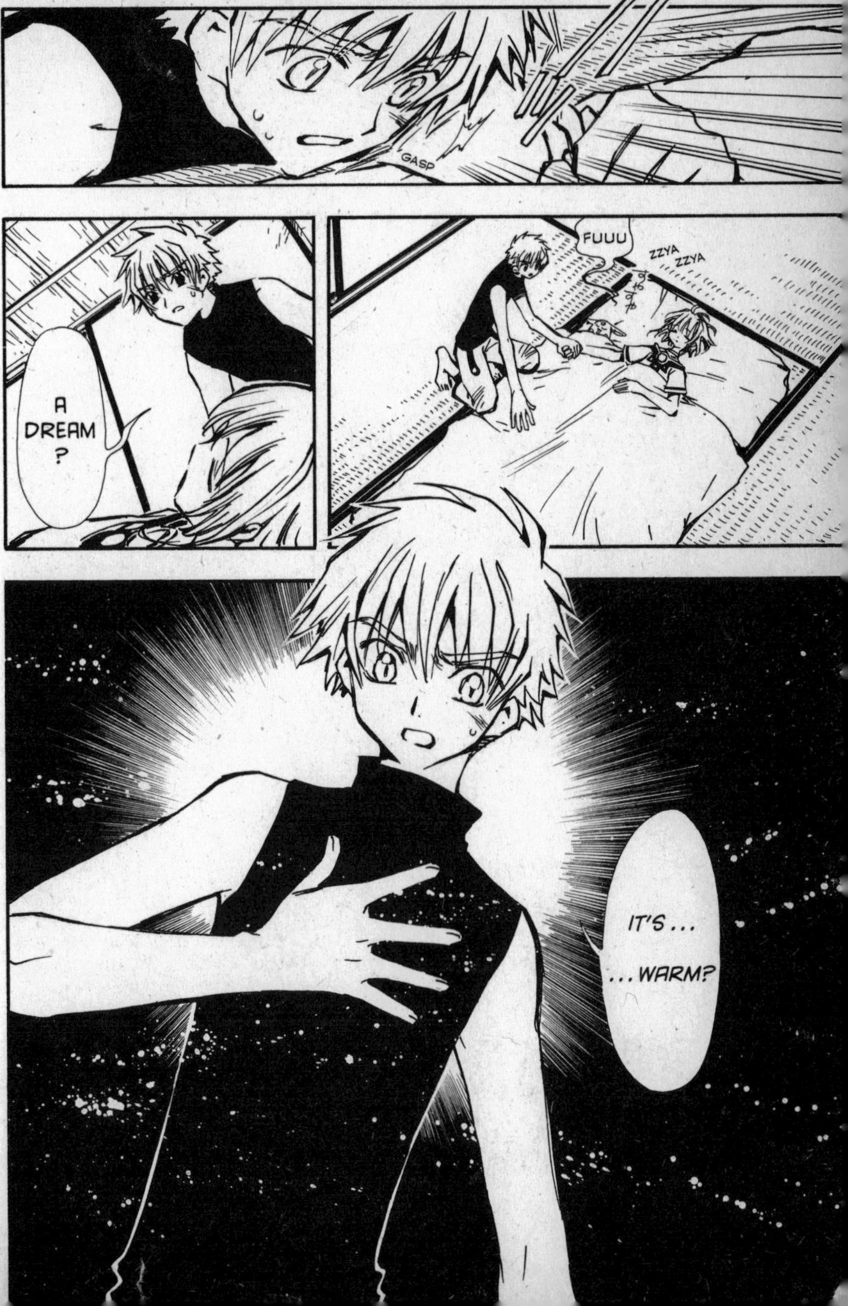
GASP
FUUU
ZZYA ZZYA
A DREAM ?
IT'S . . .
. . . WARM?

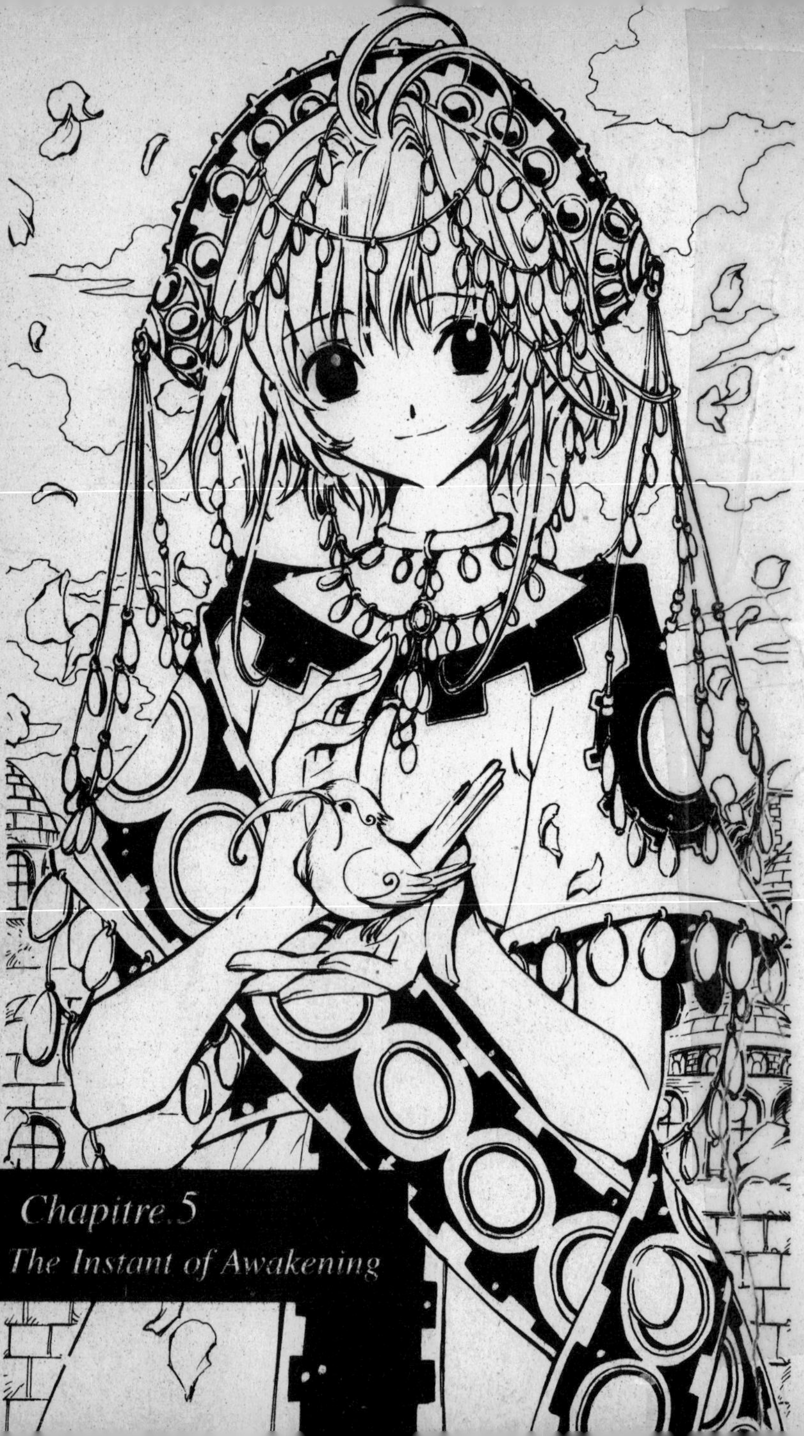

Chapitre.5
The Instant of Awakening

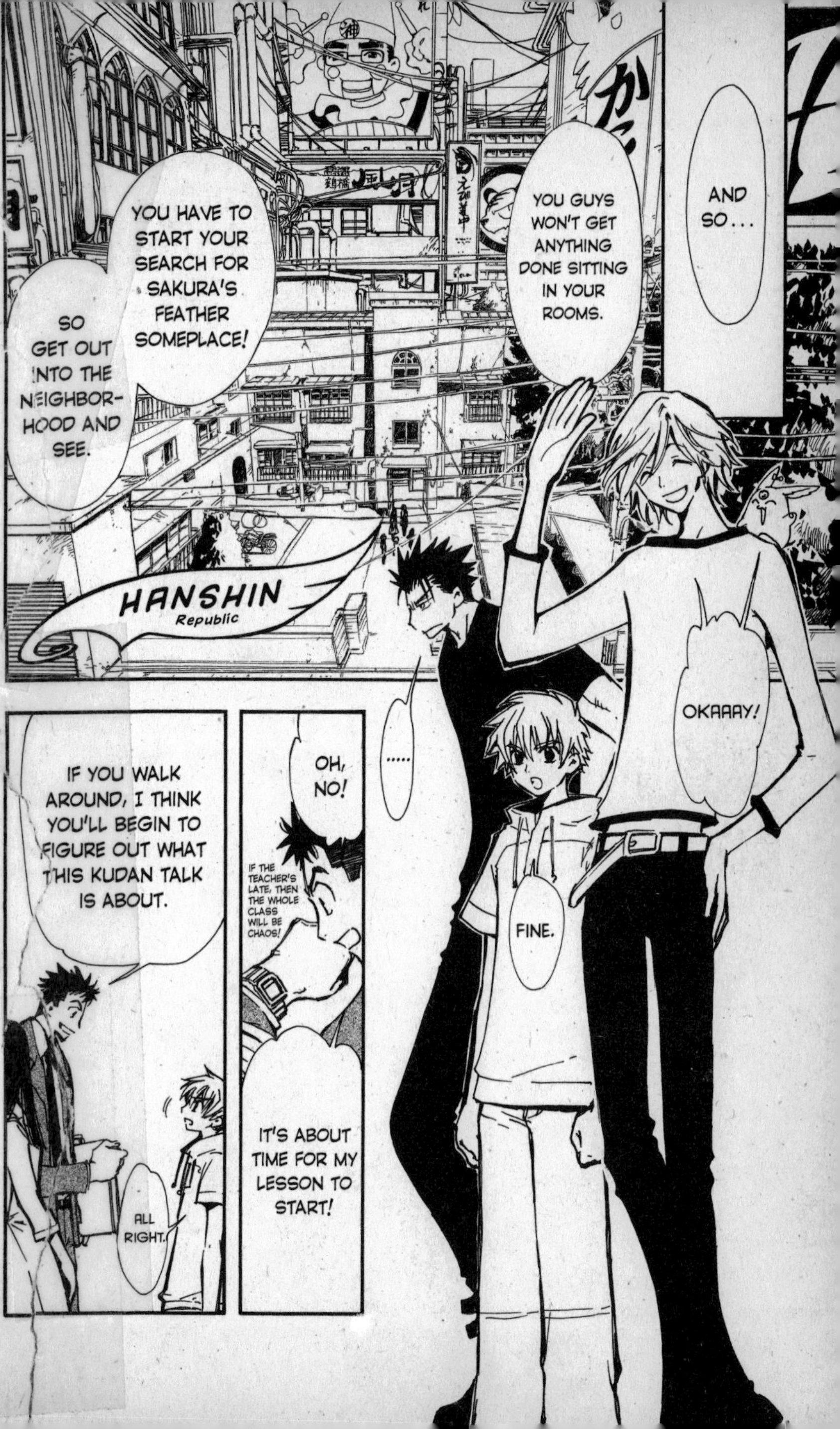
AND SO...
YOU GUYS WON'T GET ANYTHING DONE SITTING IN YOUR ROOMS.
YOU HAVE TO START YOUR SEARCH FOR SAKURA'S FEATHER SOMEPLACE!
SO GET OUT INTO THE NEIGHBOR-HOOD AND SEE.
HANSHIN Republic
OKAAAY!
......
FINE.
OH, NO!
IF THE TEACHER'S LATE, THEN THE WHOLE CLASS WILL BE CHAOS!
IT'S ABOUT TIME FOR MY LESSON TO START!
IF YOU WALK AROUND, I THINK YOU'LL BEGIN TO FIGURE OUT WHAT THIS KUDAN TALK IS ABOUT.
ALL RIGHT.

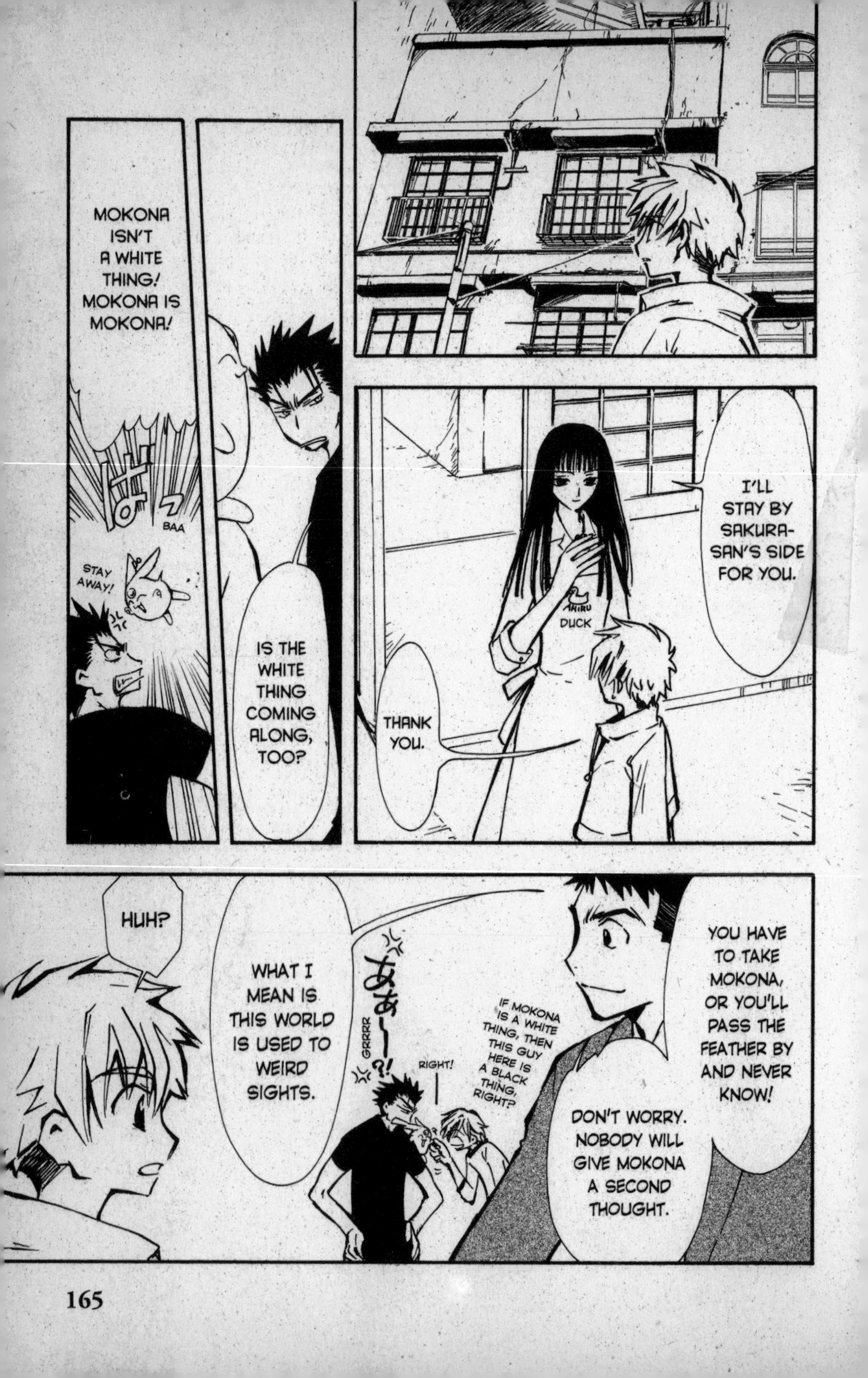
I'LL STAY BY SAKURA-SAN'S SIDE FOR YOU.
AHIRU
DUCK
THANK YOU.
IS THE WHITE THING COMING ALONG, TOO?
MOKONA ISN'T A WHITE THING! MOKONA IS MOKONA!
ばっ
BAA
STAY AWAY!
YOU HAVE TO TAKE MOKONA, OR YOU'LL PASS THE FEATHER BY AND NEVER KNOW!
DON'T WORRY. NOBODY WILL GIVE MOKONA A SECOND THOUGHT.
IF MOKONA IS A WHITE THING, THEN THIS GUY HERE IS A BLACK THING, RIGHT?
RIGHT!
あぁー?!
GRRRR
WHAT I MEAN IS THIS WORLD IS USED TO WEIRD SIGHTS.
HUH?

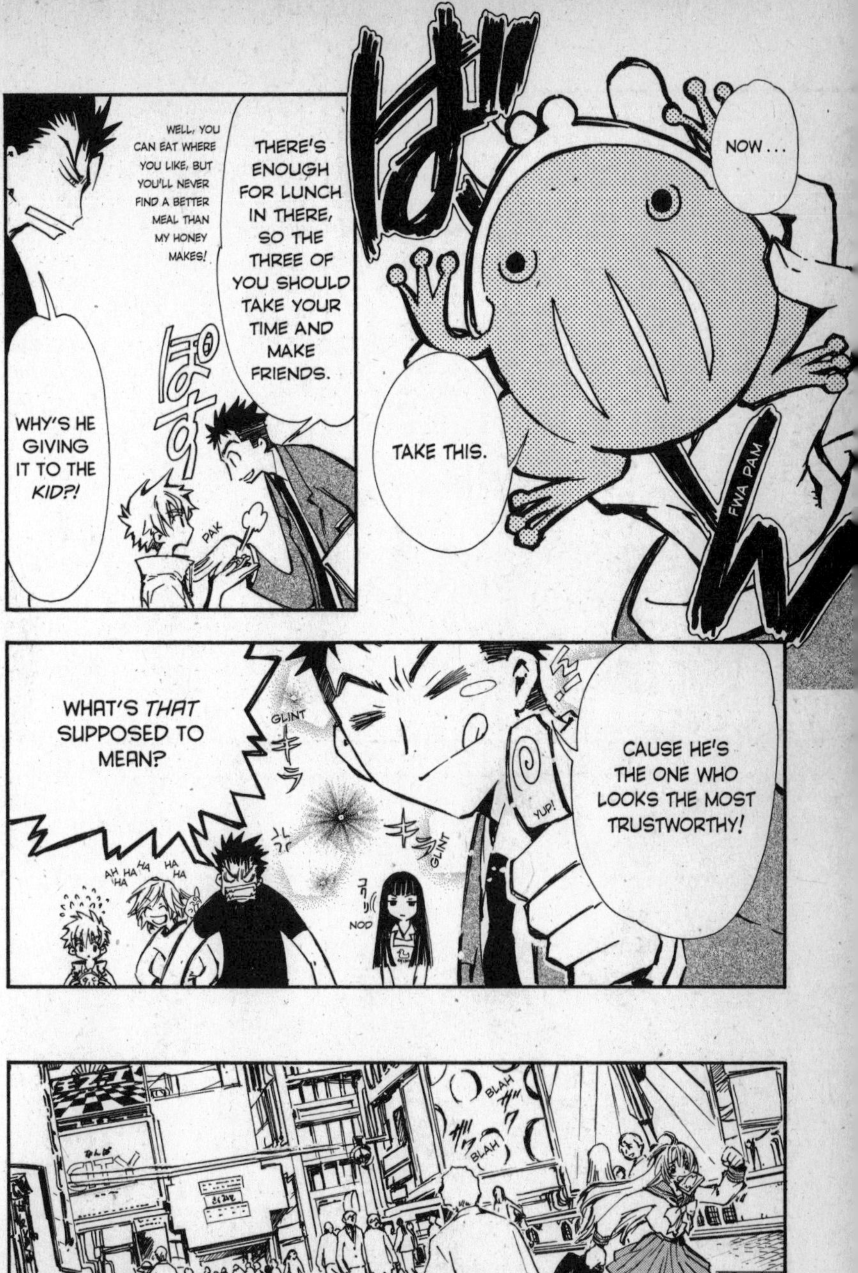
NOW...
TAKE THIS.
FWA PAM
THERE'S ENOUGH FOR LUNCH IN THERE, SO THE THREE OF YOU SHOULD TAKE YOUR TIME AND MAKE FRIENDS.
WELL, YOU CAN EAT WHERE YOU LIKE, BUT YOU'LL NEVER FIND A BETTER MEAL THAN MY HONEY MAKES!
PAK
WHY'S HE GIVING IT TO THE *KID?!*
CAUSE HE'S THE ONE WHO LOOKS THE MOST TRUSTWORTHY!
YUP!
GLINT
GLINT
WHAT'S *THAT* SUPPOSED TO MEAN?
NOD
AH HA HA HA HA HA
BLAH
BLAH

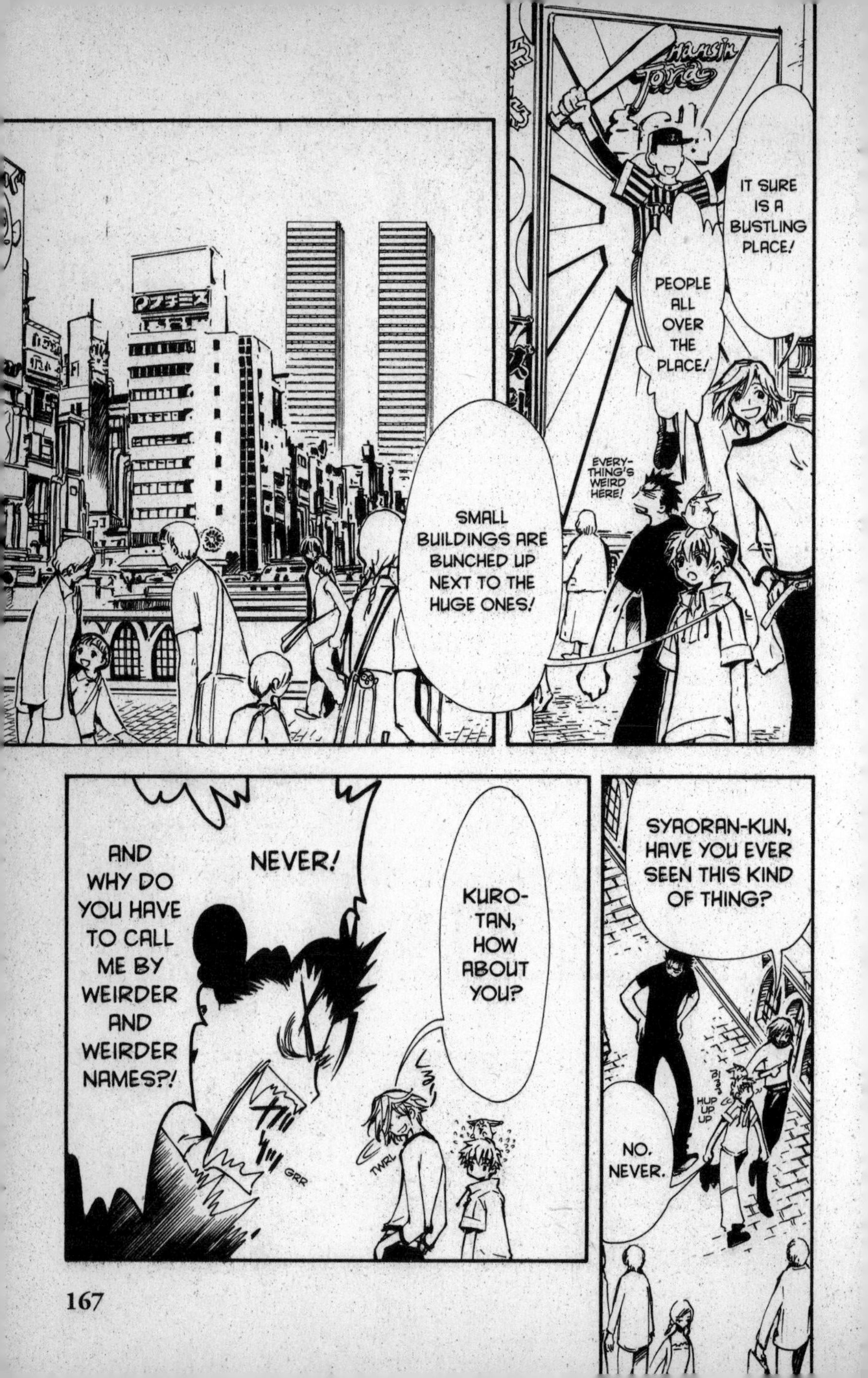
IT SURE IS A BUSTLING PLACE!
PEOPLE ALL OVER THE PLACE!
EVERY-THING'S WEIRD HERE!
SMALL BUILDINGS ARE BUNCHED UP NEXT TO THE HUGE ONES!
SYAORAN-KUN, HAVE YOU EVER SEEN THIS KIND OF THING?
HUP UP UP
NO. NEVER.
KURO-TAN, HOW ABOUT YOU?
TWRL
NEVER!
AND WHY DO YOU HAVE TO CALL ME BY WEIRDER AND WEIRDER NAMES?!
GRR

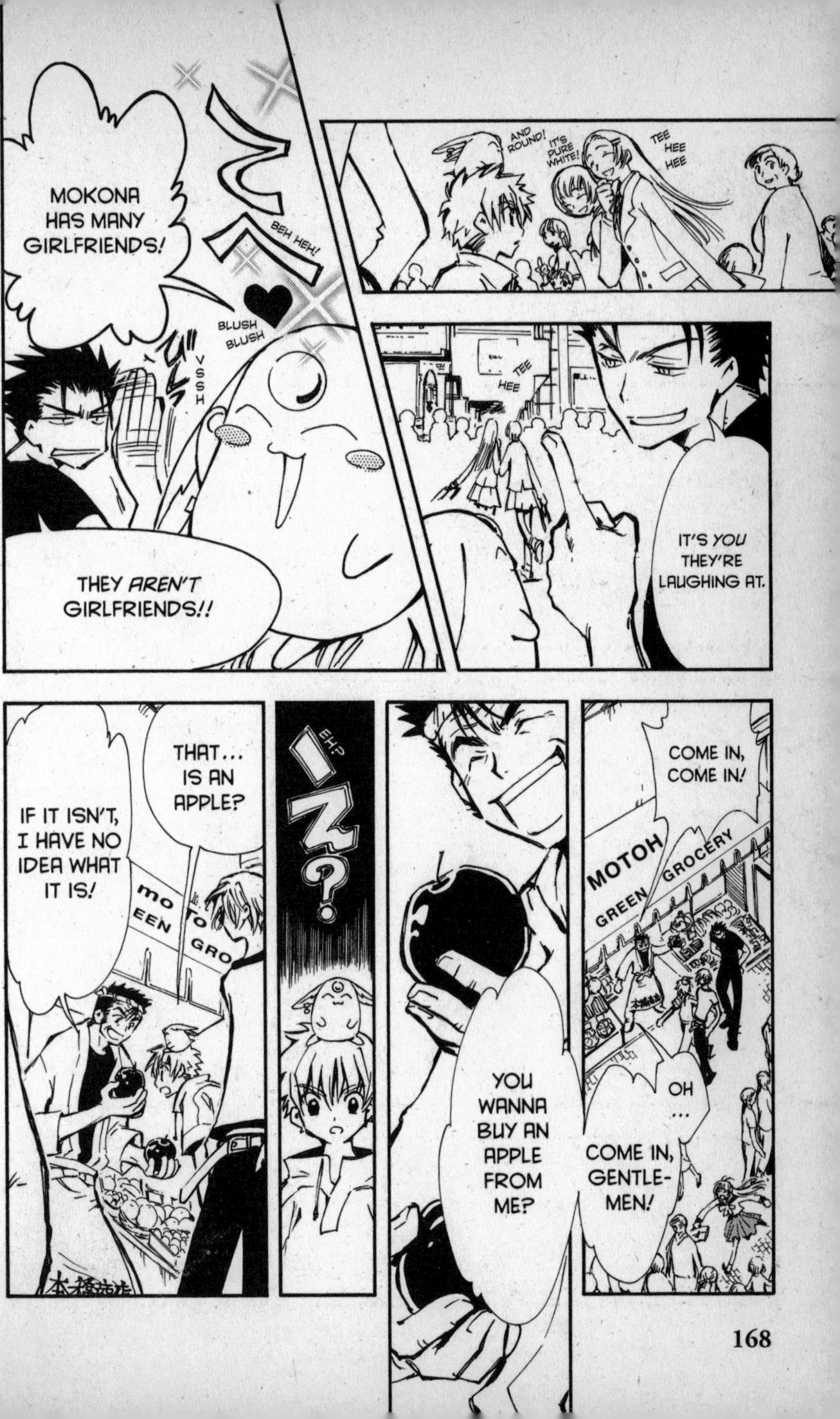
AND ROUND!
IT'S PURE WHITE!
TEE HEE HEE
TEE HEE
IT'S *YOU* THEY'RE LAUGHING AT.
MOKONA HAS MANY GIRLFRIENDS!
BEH HEH!
BLUSH BLUSH
VSSH
THEY *AREN'T* GIRLFRIENDS!!
COME IN, COME IN!
MOTOH GREEN GROCERY
OH ...
COME IN, GENTLEMEN!
YOU WANNA BUY AN APPLE FROM ME?
EH?
?
THAT... IS AN APPLE?
IF IT ISN'T, I HAVE NO IDEA WHAT IT IS!

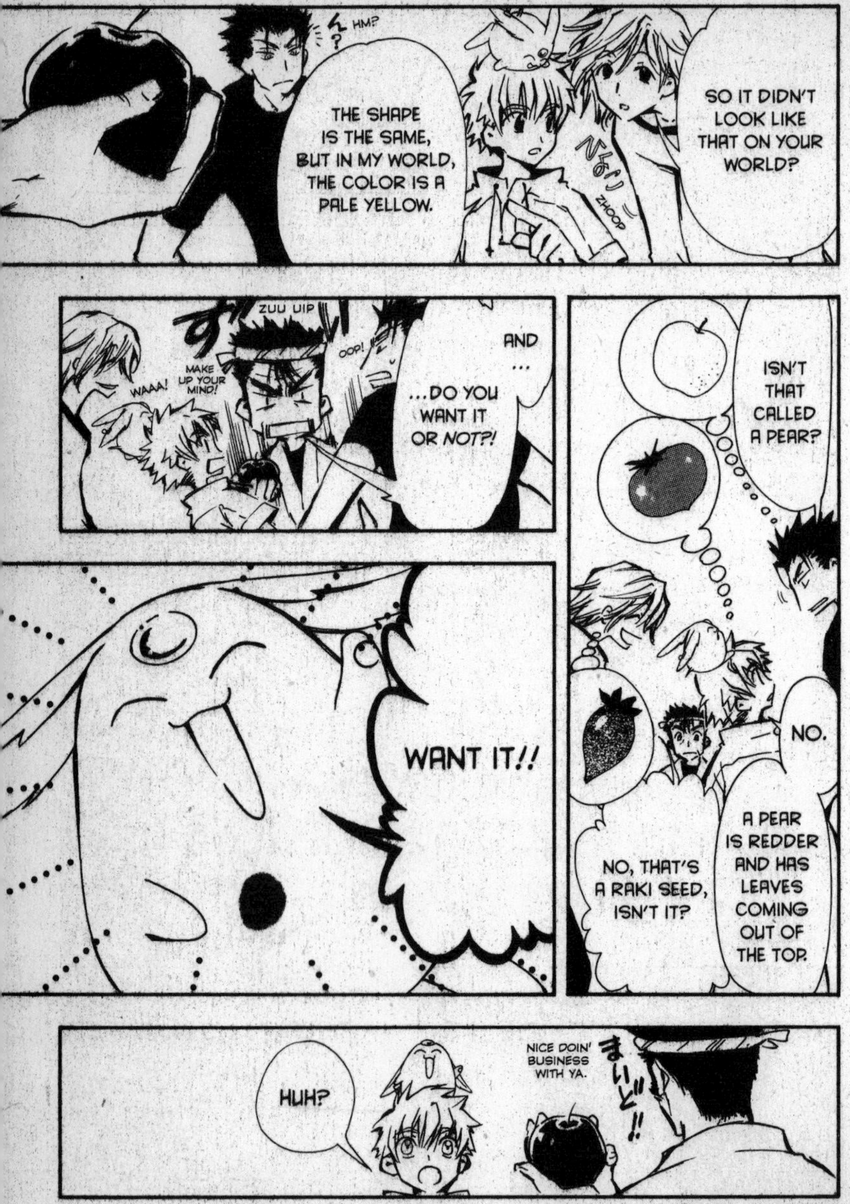
SO IT DIDN'T LOOK LIKE THAT ON YOUR WORLD?
ZHOOP
THE SHAPE IS THE SAME, BUT IN MY WORLD, THE COLOR IS A PALE YELLOW.
HM?
ISN'T THAT CALLED A PEAR?
NO.
A PEAR IS REDDER AND HAS LEAVES COMING OUT OF THE TOP.
NO, THAT'S A RAKI SEED, ISN'T IT?
AND ...
...DO YOU WANT IT OR NOT?!
OOP!
ZUU UIP
MAKE UP YOUR MIND!
WAAA!
WANT IT!!
NICE DOIN' BUSINESS WITH YA.
HUH?

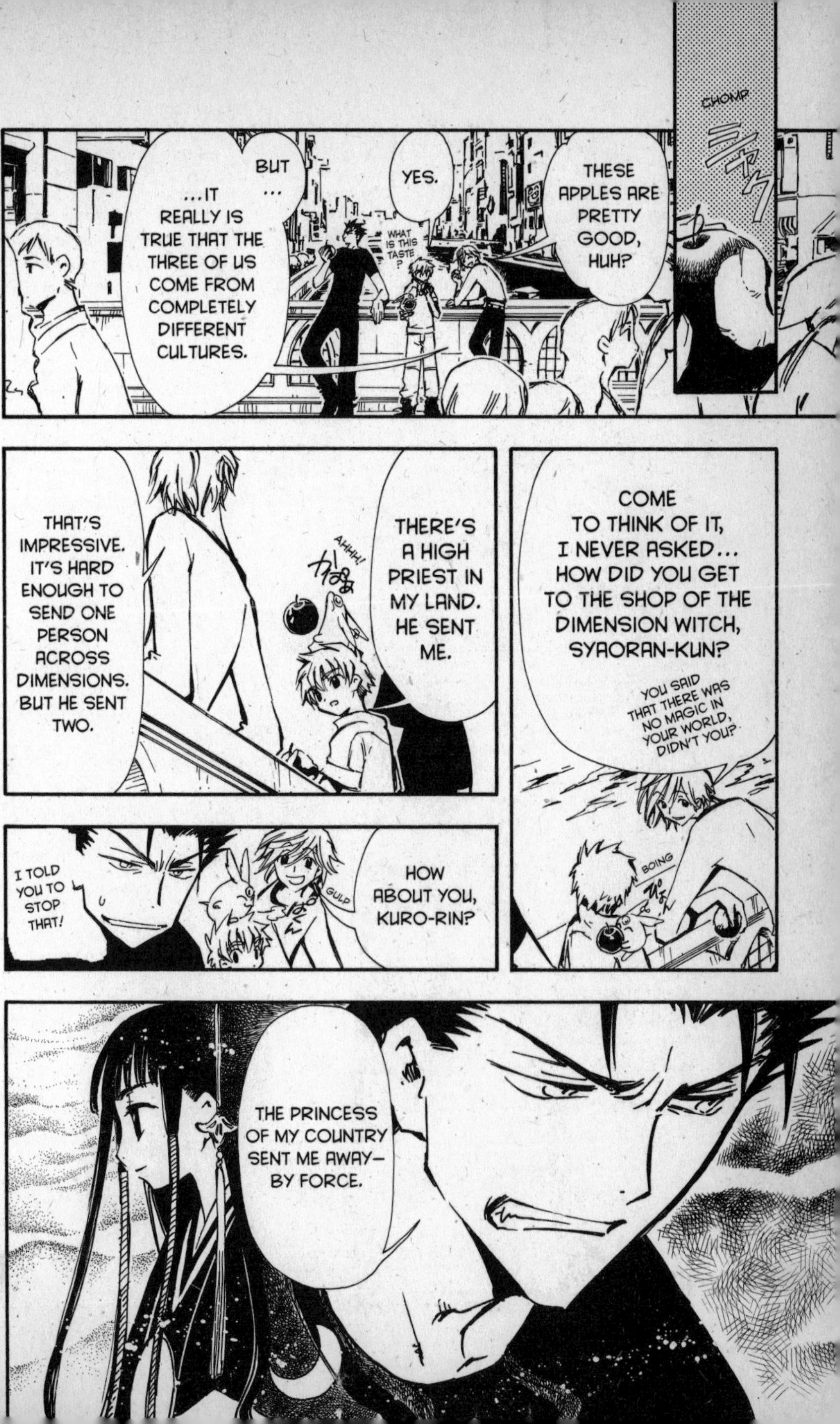
CHOMP
シャク
THESE APPLES ARE PRETTY GOOD, HUH?
YES.
WHAT IS THIS TASTE?
BUT ...
...IT REALLY IS TRUE THAT THE THREE OF US COME FROM COMPLETELY DIFFERENT CULTURES.
COME TO THINK OF IT, I NEVER ASKED... HOW DID YOU GET TO THE SHOP OF THE DIMENSION WITCH, SYAORAN-KUN?
YOU SAID THAT THERE WAS NO MAGIC IN YOUR WORLD, DIDN'T YOU?
BOING
THERE'S A HIGH PRIEST IN MY LAND. HE SENT ME.
AHHH!
THAT'S IMPRESSIVE. IT'S HARD ENOUGH TO SEND ONE PERSON ACROSS DIMENSIONS. BUT HE SENT TWO.
HOW ABOUT YOU, KURO-RIN?
GULP
I TOLD YOU TO STOP THAT!
THE PRINCESS OF MY COUNTRY SENT ME AWAY—BY FORCE.

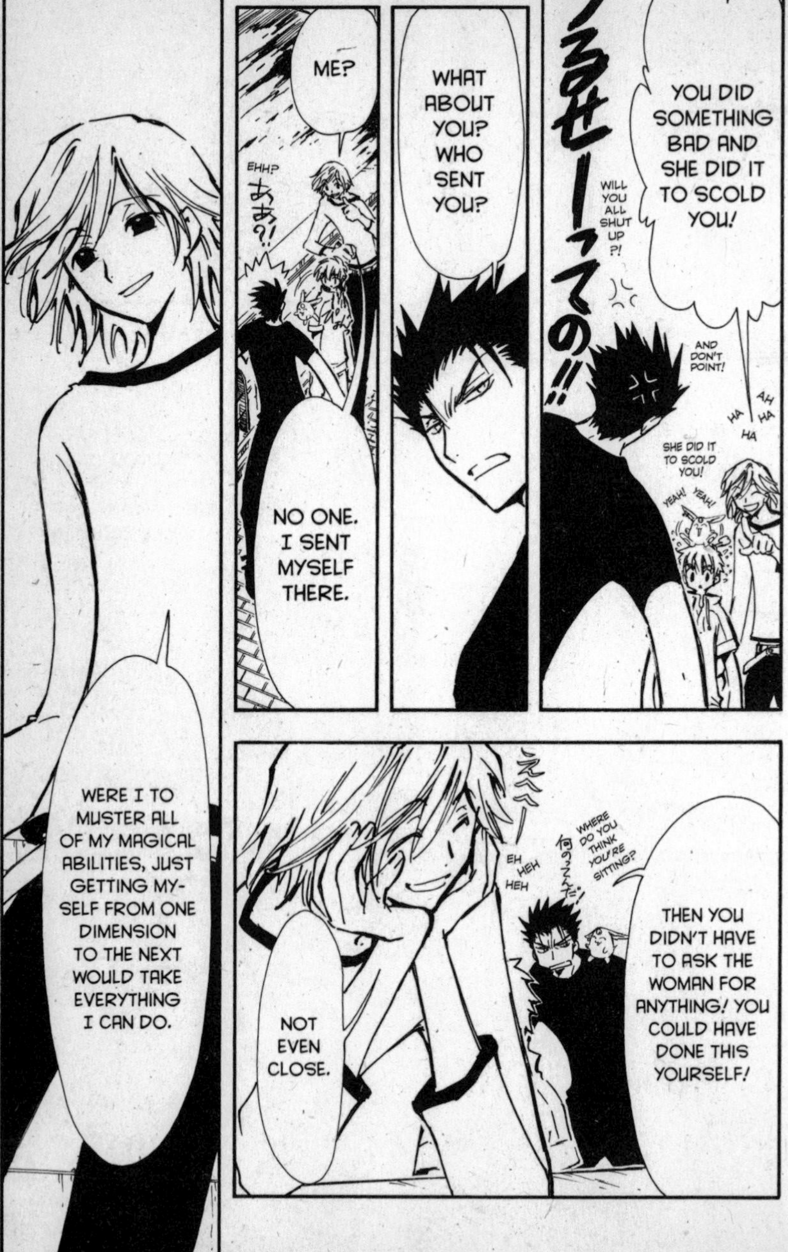
YOU DID SOMETHING BAD AND SHE DID IT TO SCOLD YOU!
うるせーっての!!
WILL YOU ALL SHUT UP ?!
AND DON'T POINT!
AH HA HA HA
SHE DID IT TO SCOLD YOU!
YEAH! YEAH!
WHAT ABOUT YOU? WHO SENT YOU?
ME?
EHH?
ああ?!
NO ONE. I SENT MYSELF THERE.
THEN YOU DIDN'T HAVE TO ASK THE WOMAN FOR ANYTHING! YOU COULD HAVE DONE THIS YOURSELF!
WHERE DO YOU THINK YOU'RE SITTING?
えへへー
EH HEH HEH
NOT EVEN CLOSE.
WERE I TO MUSTER ALL OF MY MAGICAL ABILITIES, JUST GETTING MY-SELF FROM ONE DIMENSION TO THE NEXT WOULD TAKE EVERYTHING I CAN DO.

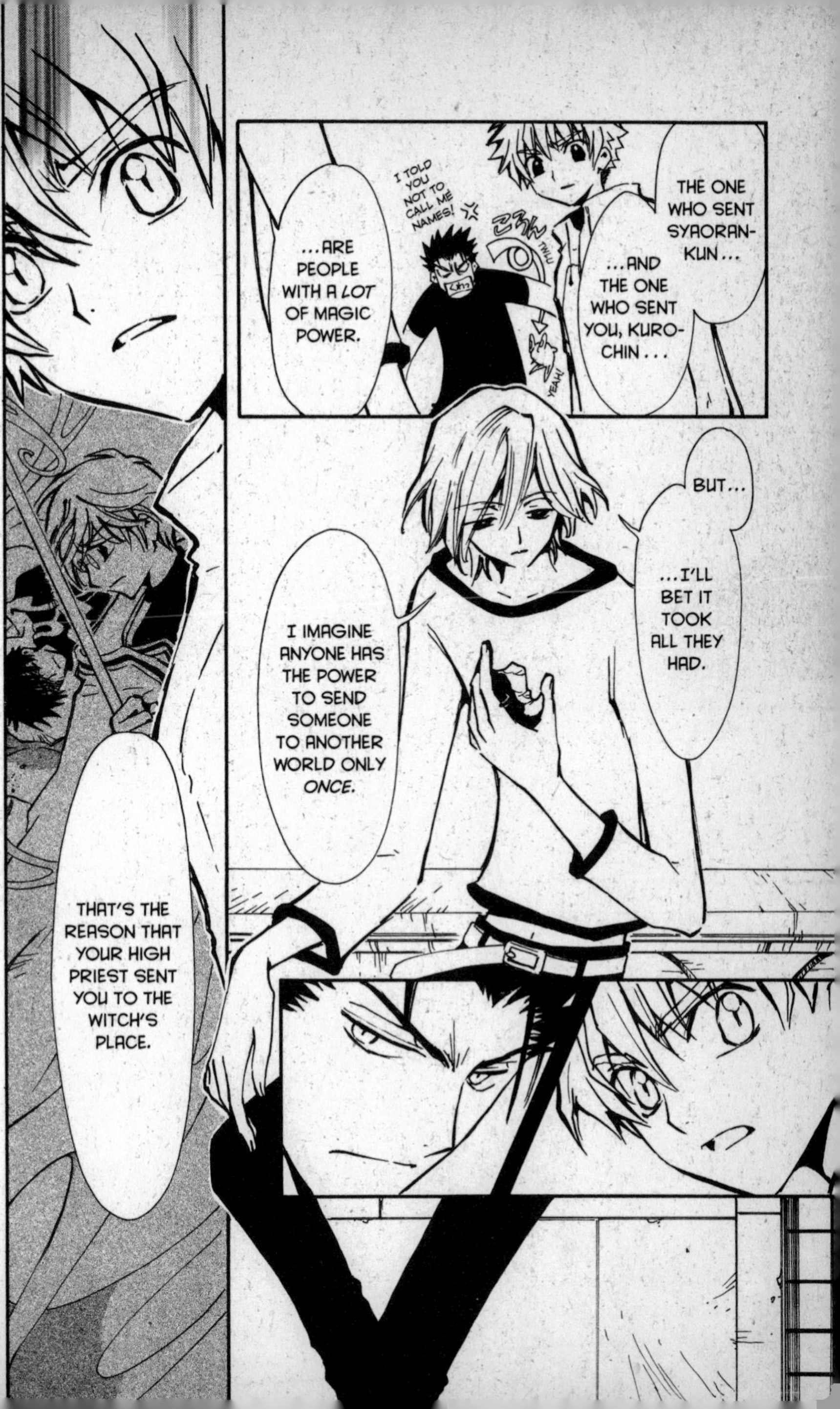
THE ONE WHO SENT SYAORAN-KUN...
...AND THE ONE WHO SENT YOU, KURO-CHIN...
ころん
YEAH!
I TOLD YOU NOT TO CALL ME NAMES!
くわっ
...ARE PEOPLE WITH A *LOT* OF MAGIC POWER.
BUT...
...I'LL BET IT TOOK ALL THEY HAD.
I IMAGINE ANYONE HAS THE POWER TO SEND SOMEONE TO ANOTHER WORLD ONLY *ONCE*.
THAT'S THE REASON THAT YOUR HIGH PRIEST SENT YOU TO THE WITCH'S PLACE.

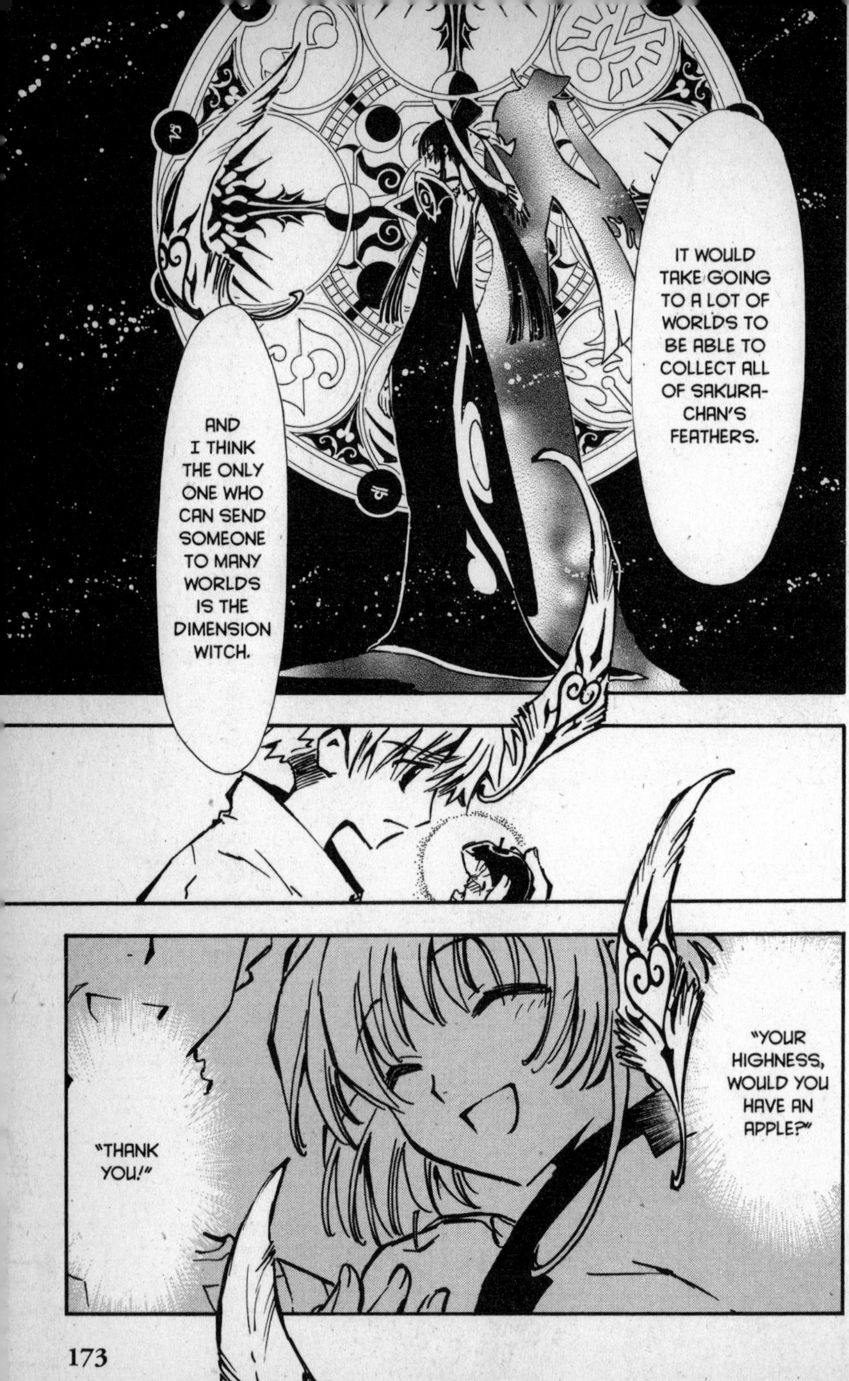
IT WOULD TAKE GOING TO A LOT OF WORLDS TO BE ABLE TO COLLECT ALL OF SAKURA-CHAN'S FEATHERS.
AND I THINK THE ONLY ONE WHO CAN SEND SOMEONE TO MANY WORLDS IS THE DIMENSION WITCH.
"YOUR HIGHNESS, WOULD YOU HAVE AN APPLE?"
"THANK YOU!"

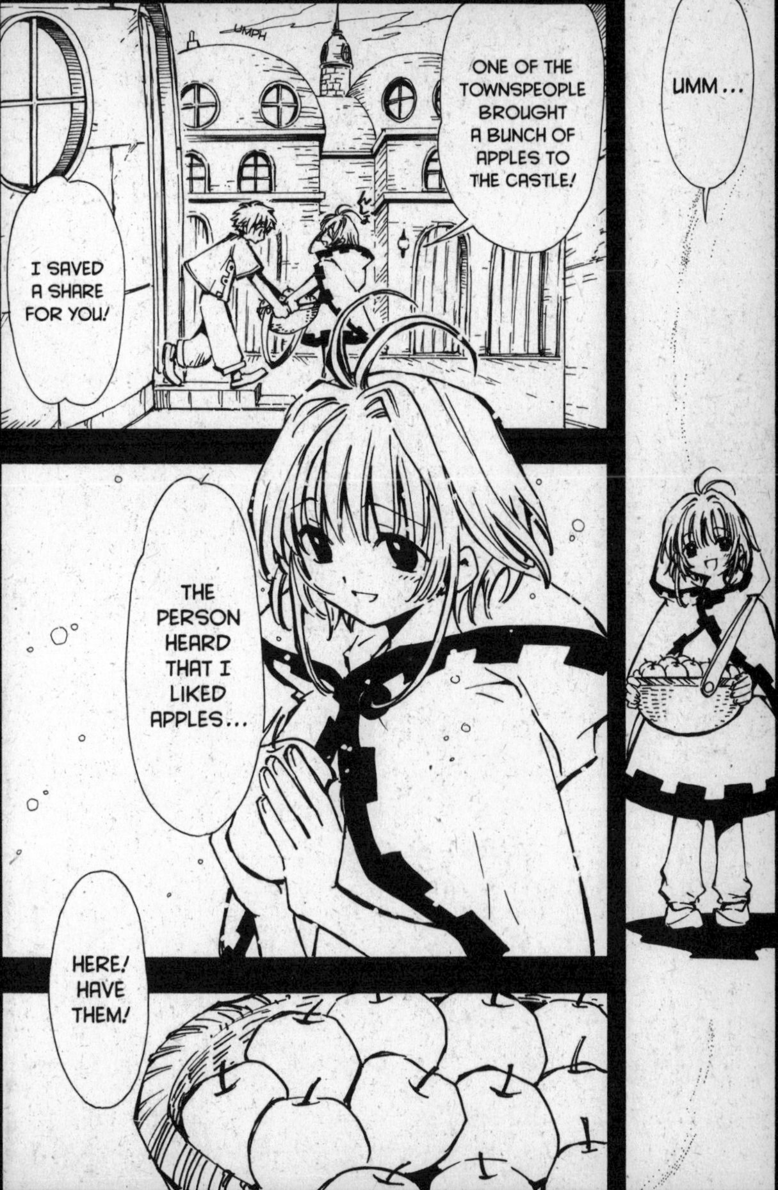
UMM...
ONE OF THE TOWNSPEOPLE BROUGHT A BUNCH OF APPLES TO THE CASTLE!
UMPH
I SAVED A SHARE FOR YOU!
THE PERSON HEARD THAT I LIKED APPLES...
HERE! HAVE THEM!

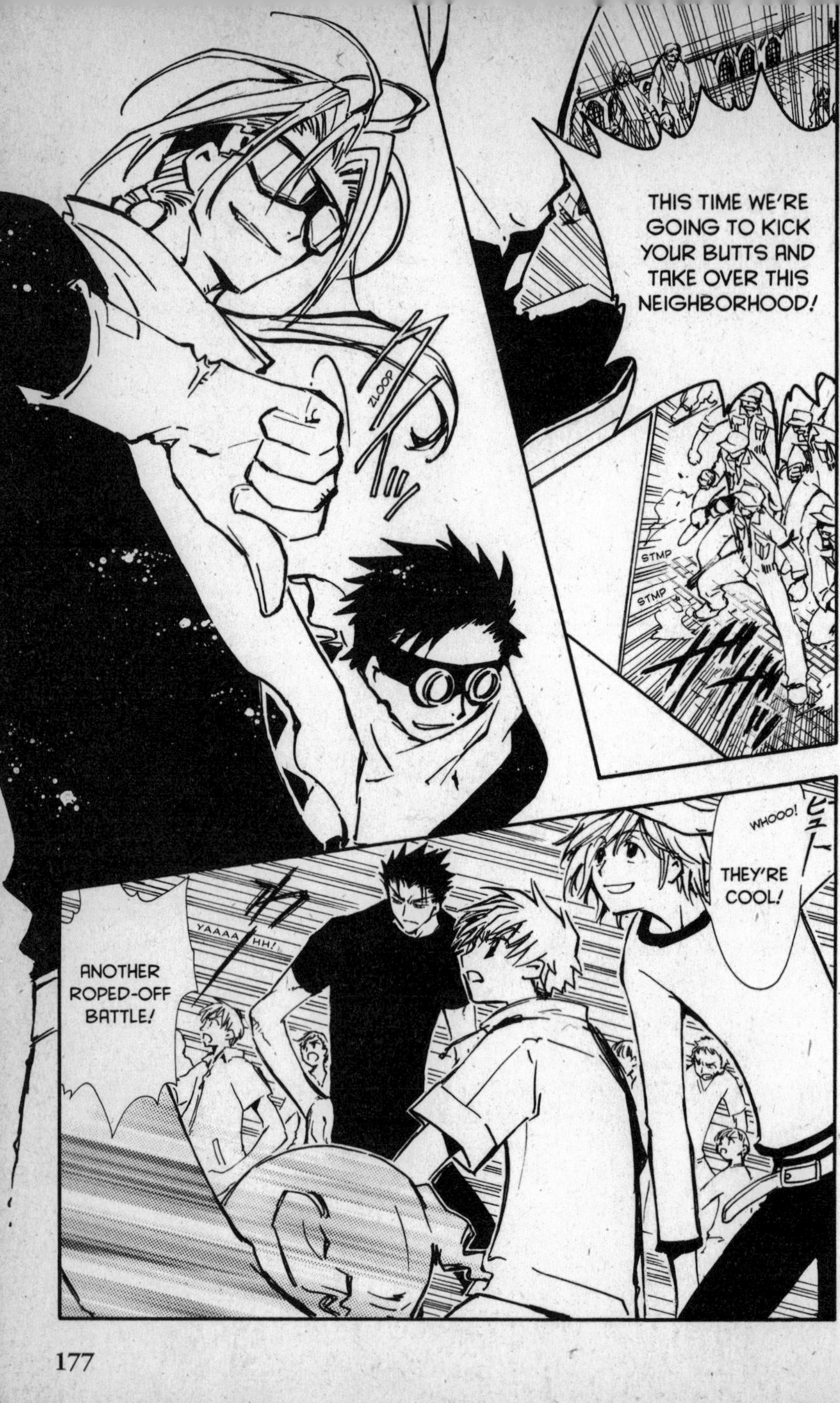
THIS TIME WE'RE GOING TO KICK YOUR BUTTS AND TAKE OVER THIS NEIGHBORHOOD!
STMP
STMP
ZLOOP
WHOOO!
THEY'RE COOL!
YAAAAHH!
ANOTHER ROPED-OFF BATTLE!

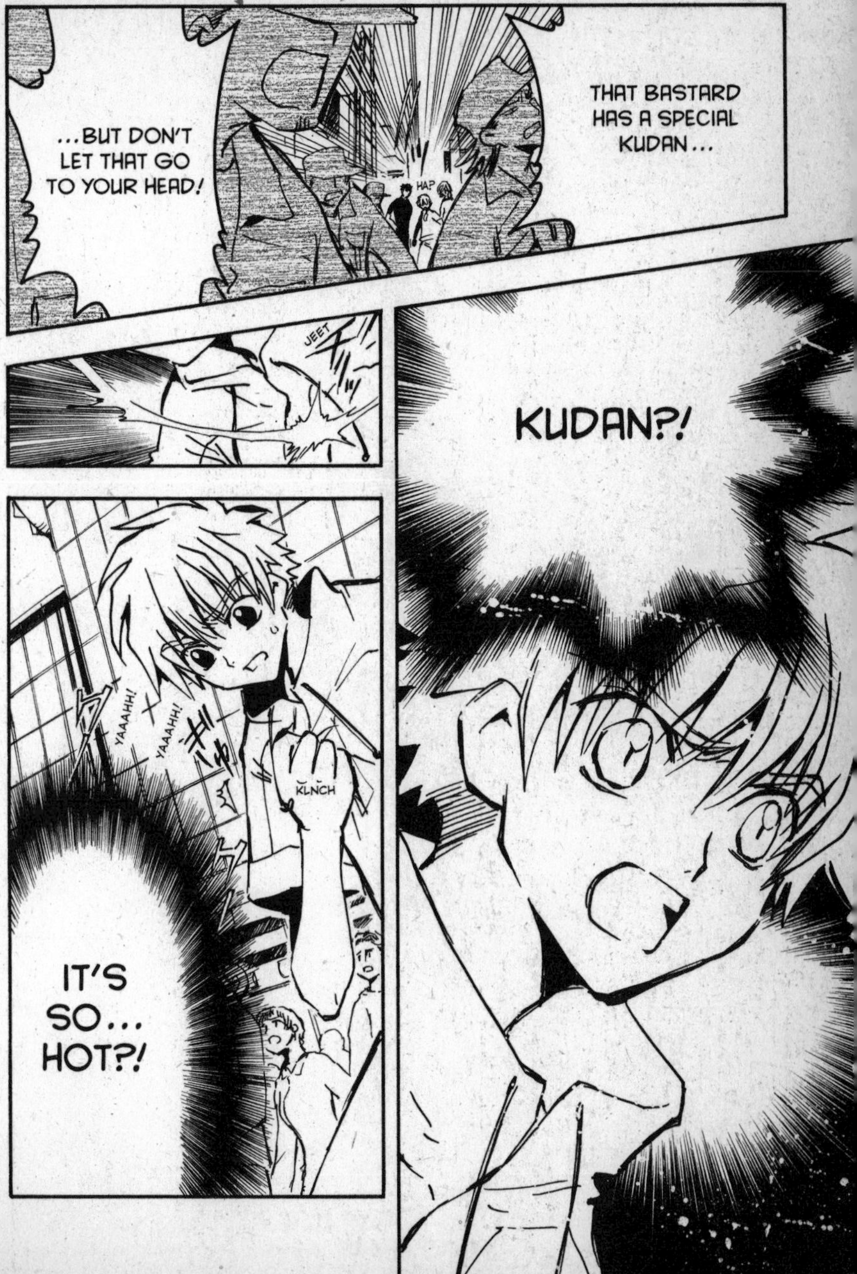
THAT BASTARD HAS A SPECIAL KUDAN...
HAP
...BUT DON'T LET THAT GO TO YOUR HEAD!
KUDAN?!
JEET
YAAAAHH!
YAAAAHH!
KLNCH
IT'S SO... HOT?!

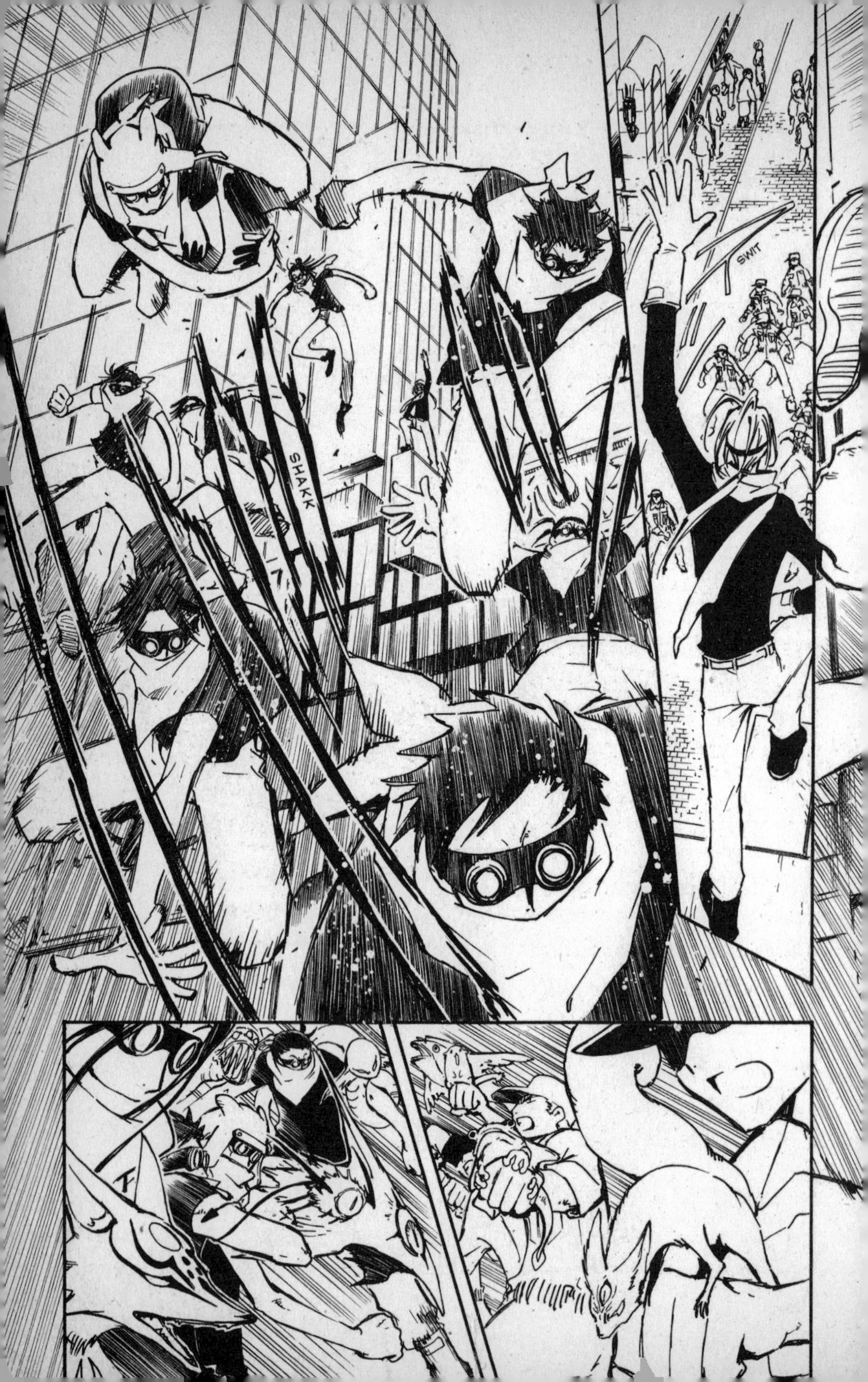
SWIT
SHAKK

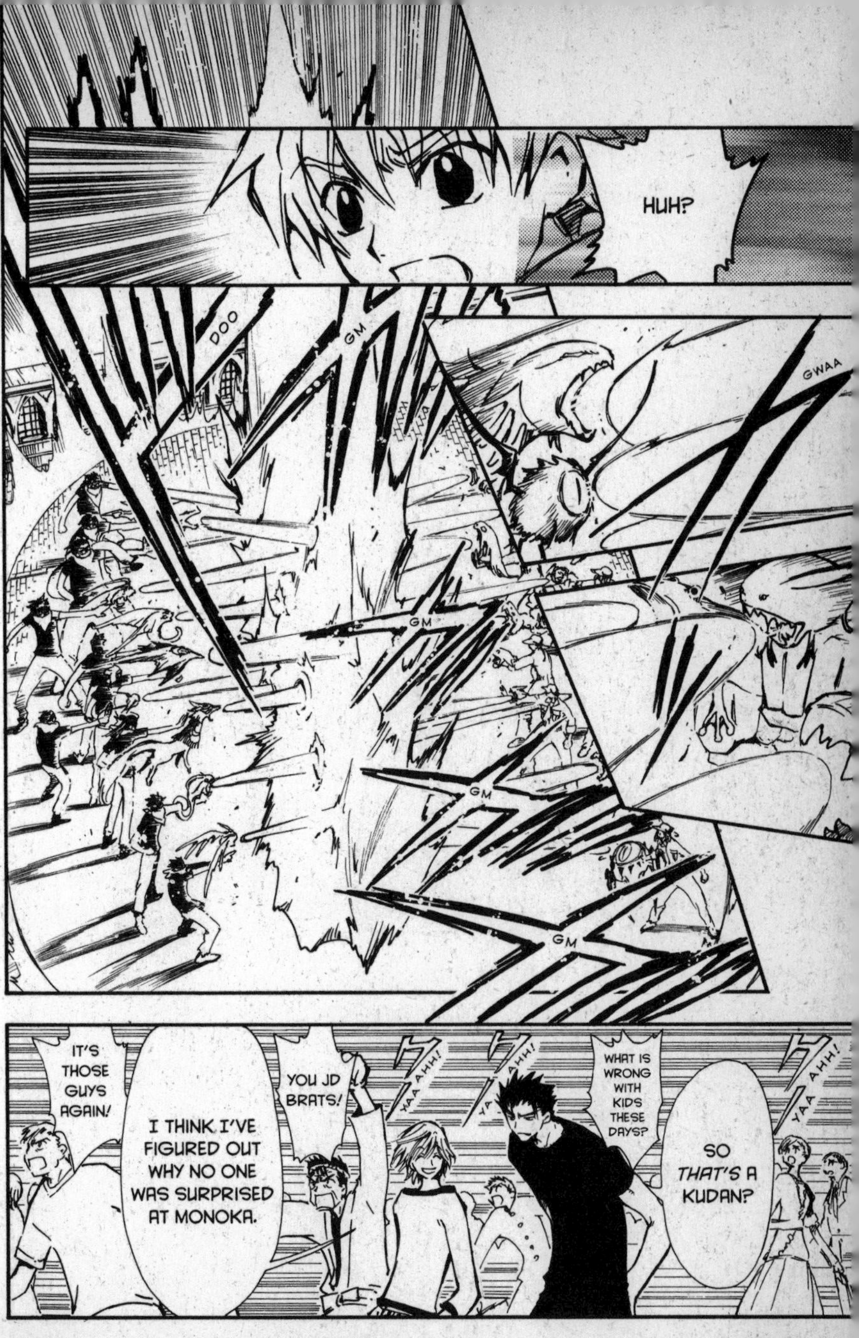
HUH?
GWAA
GM
DOO
GM
GM
GM
YAA AHH!
SO *THAT'S* A KUDAN?
WHAT IS WRONG WITH KIDS THESE DAYS?
YAA AHH!
YAA AHH!
YOU JD BRATS!
I THINK I'VE FIGURED OUT WHY NO ONE WAS SURPRISED AT MONOKA.
IT'S THOSE GUYS AGAIN!

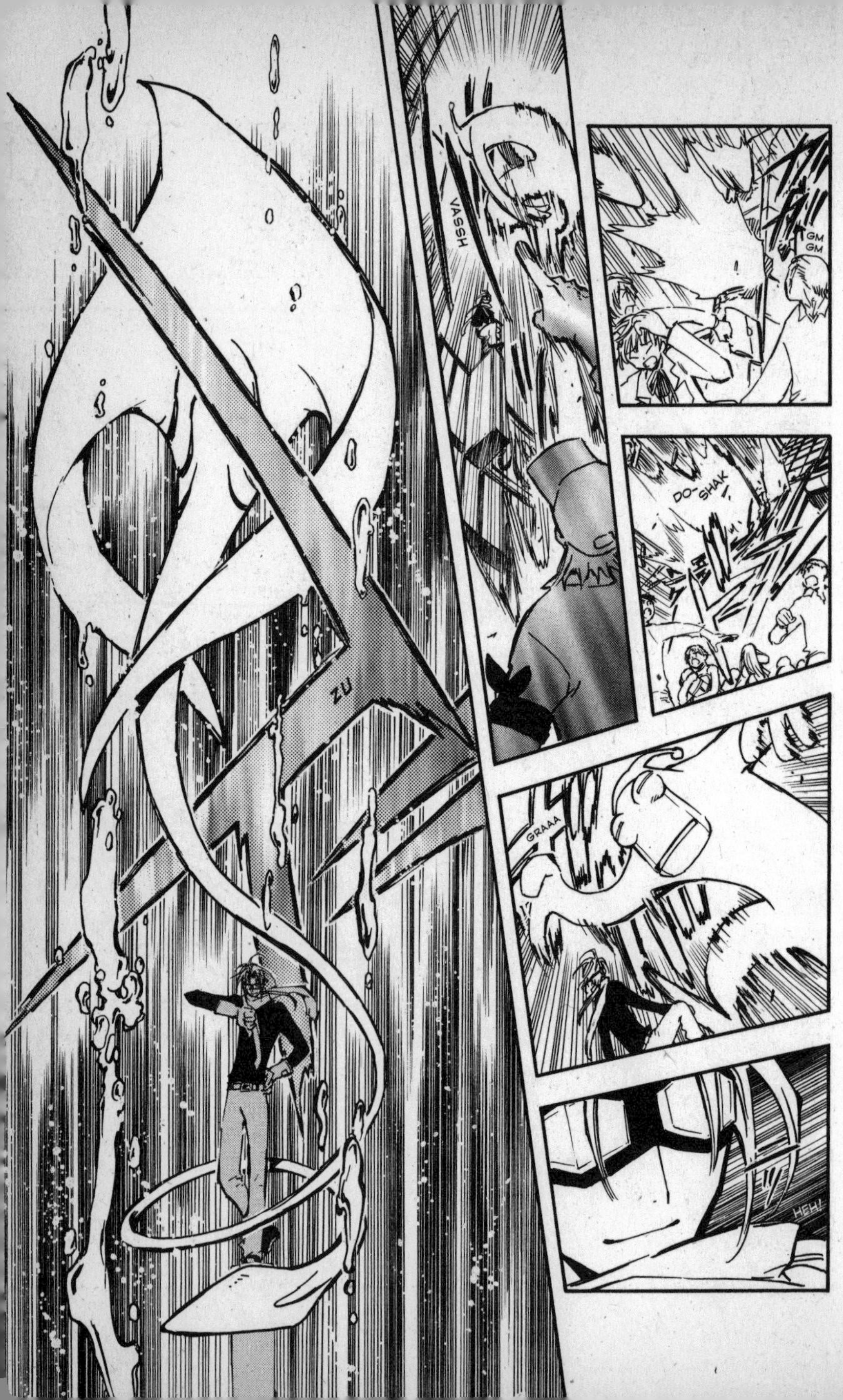
GM GM
DO-SHAK
VASSH
GRAAA
HEH!
ZU

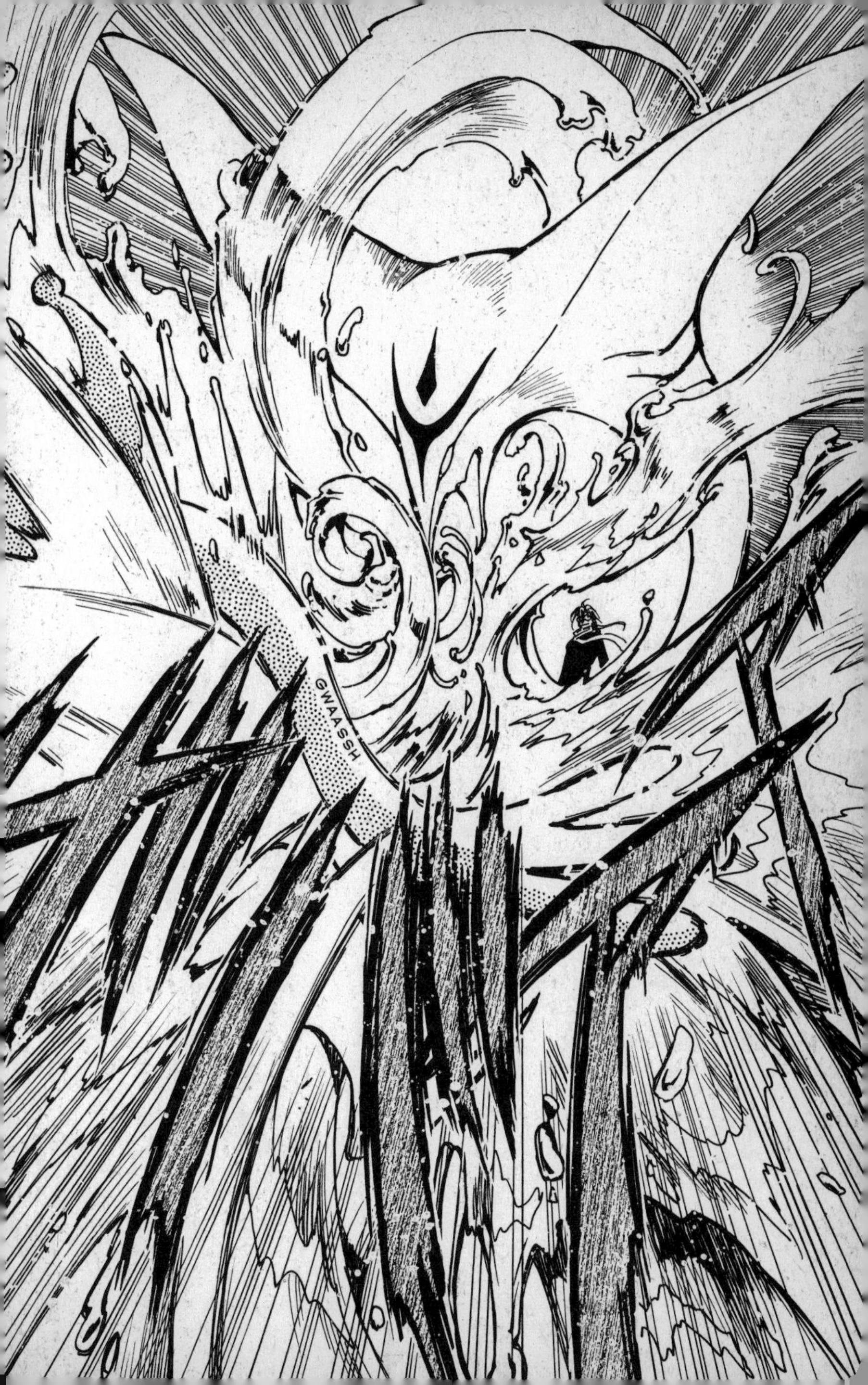
GWAASSH

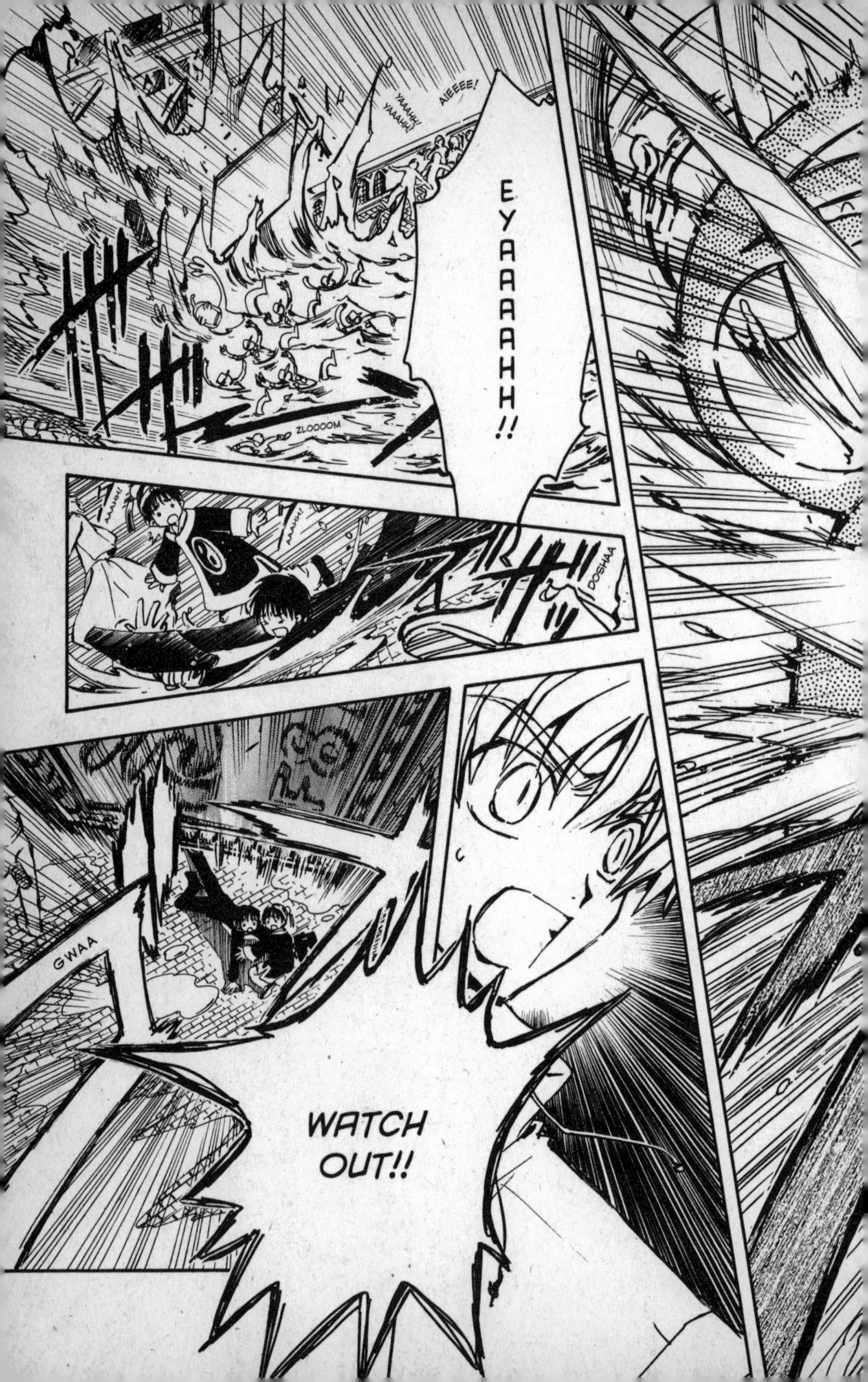
EYAAAAAAHH!!
AIEEEE!
YAAAHH! YAAAHH!
ZLOOOOM
DOSHAA
AAAHH!
AAAHH!
WATCH OUT!!
GWAA

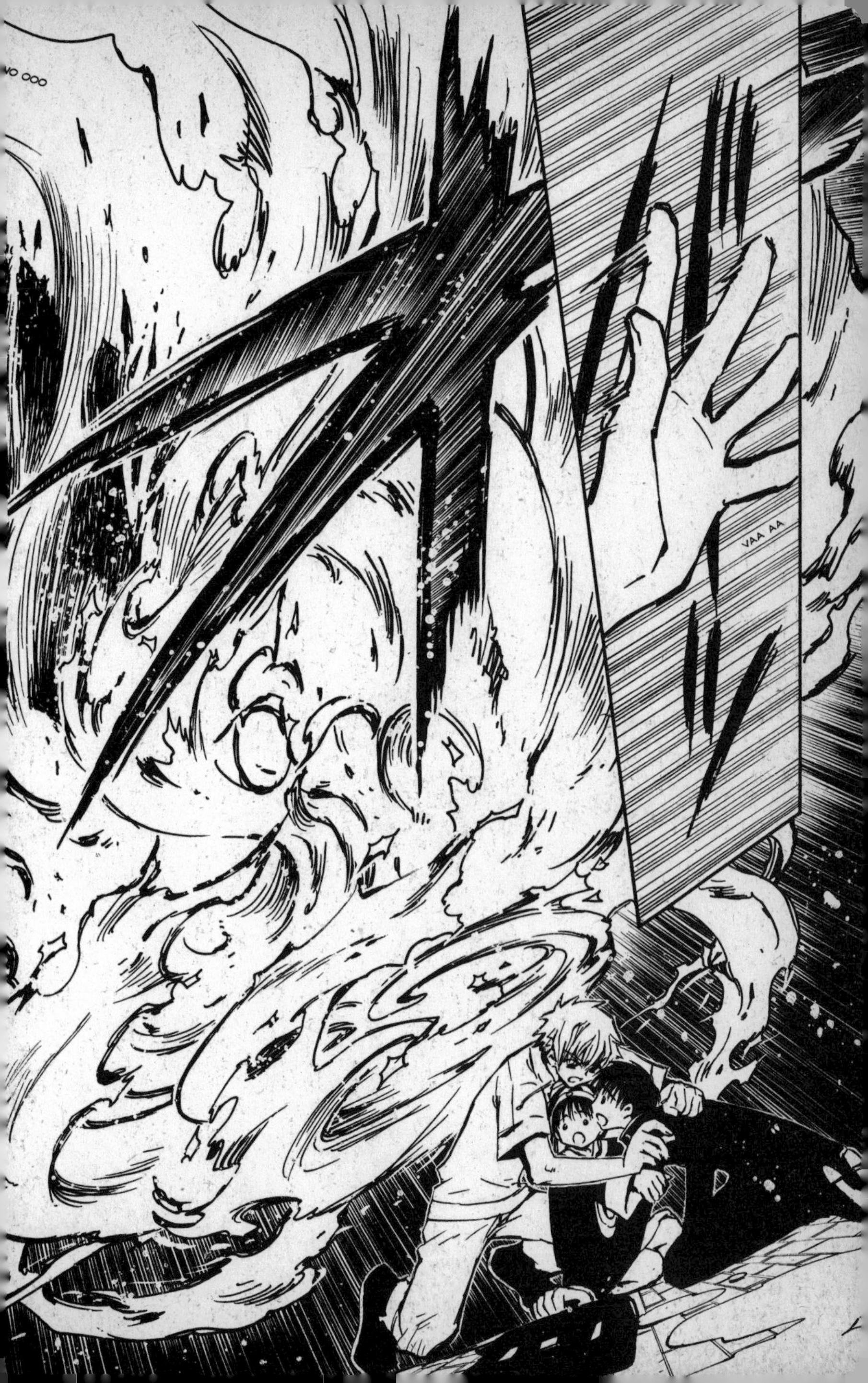
VAA AA

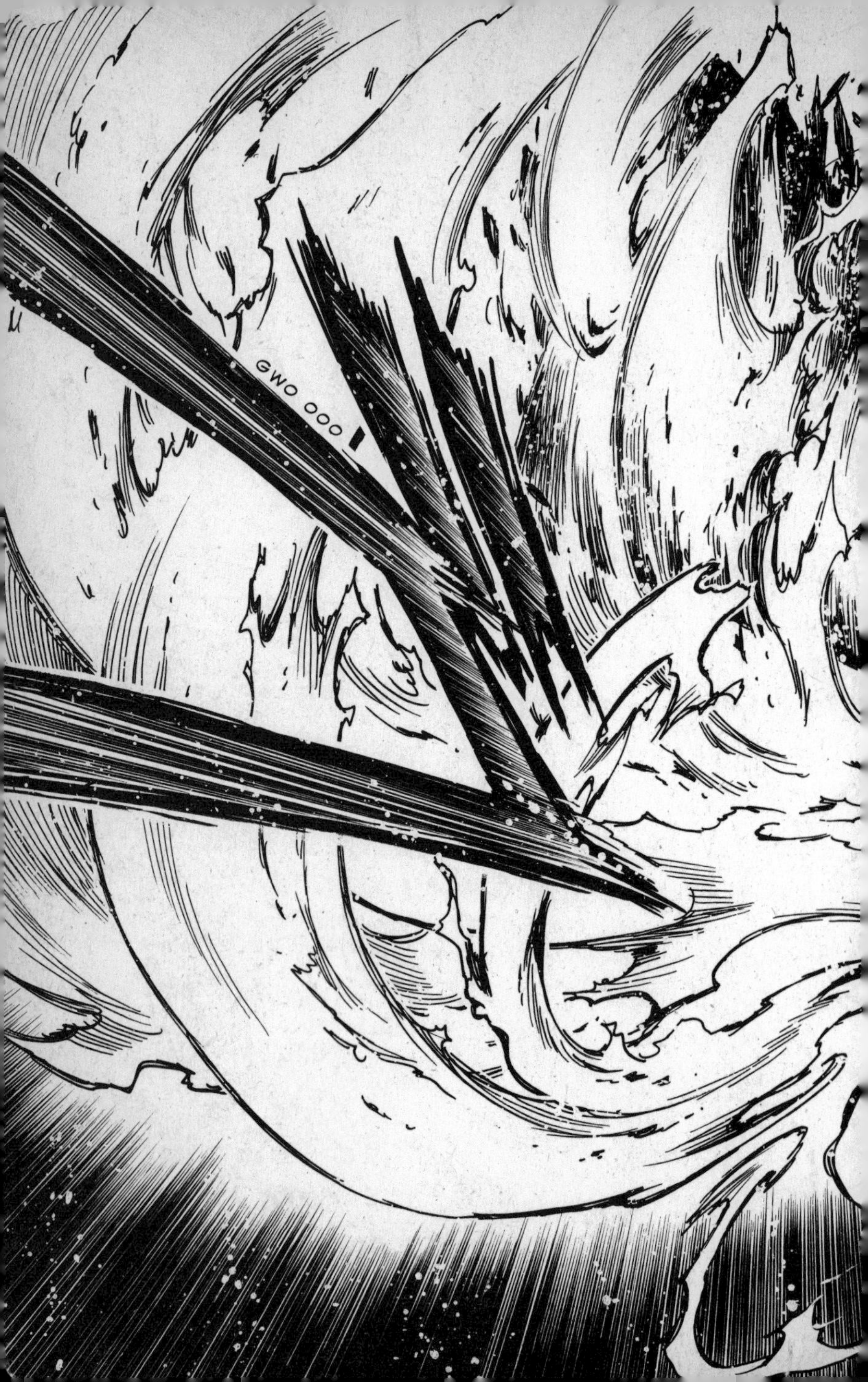
GWO OOO

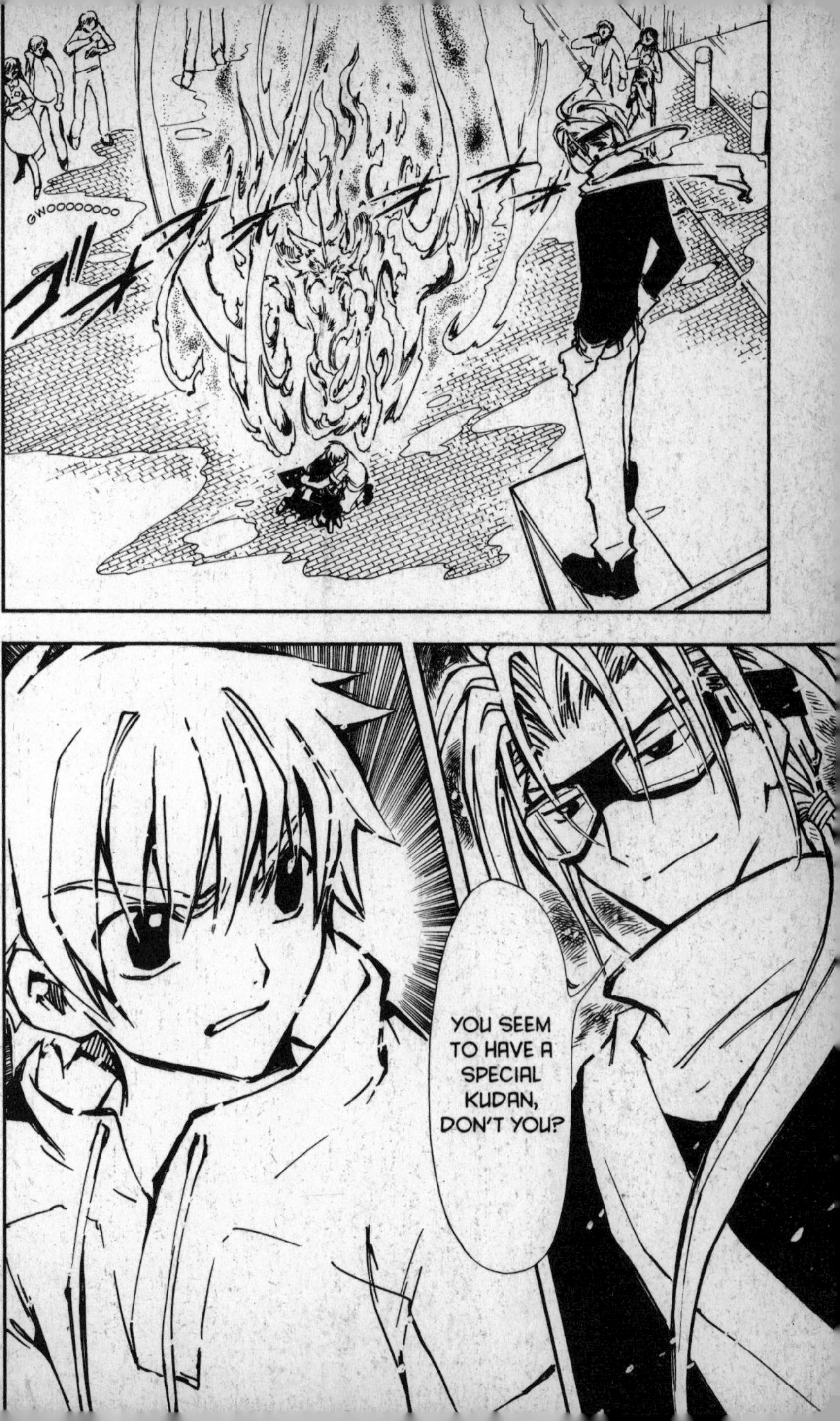
GWOOOOOOOO
YOU SEEM TO HAVE A SPECIAL KUDAN, DON'T YOU?

To Be Continued

About the Creators

CLAMP is a group of four women who have become the most popular manga artists in America—Ageha Ohkawa, Mokona, Satsuki Igarashi, and Tsubaki Nekoi. They started out as doujnishi (fan comics) creators, but their skill and craft brought them to the attention of publishers very quickly. Their first work from a major publisher was *RG Veda*, but their first mass success was with *Magic Knight Rayearth*. From there, they went on to write many series, including *Cardcaptor Sakura* and *Chobits*, two of the most popular manga in the United States. Like many Japanese manga artists, they prefer to avoid the spotlight, and little is known about them personally.

CLAMP is currently publishing three series in Japan: *Tsubasa* and *xxxHOLiC* with Kodansha and *Gohou Drug* with Kadokawa.

Past Works

CLAMP has created many series. Here is a brief overview of one of them.

Cardcaptor Sakura

The first volume of *Cardcaptor Sakura* was released in Japan in 1996, and by the time the series was finished it would number twelve volumes in all. The first six, called simply *Cardcaptor Sakura*, are the story of fourth-grader Sakura, who finds a magic book called *The Clow* in her father's library. The book and its magical guardian, Kero, were responsible for containing the Clow Cards. The Clow Cards, created by sorcerer Clow Reed, have escaped, and Kero needs Sakura's help to find them. Empowered with the key to recapture them, Sakura becomes a Cardcaptor and begins her quest for all of the lost Clow cards.

Over the course of the next six volumes, we are introduced to a wide range of characters, some of whom will be familiar to you after you've read the first volume of *Tsubasa*. Toya is Sakura's brother, and Yukito is his best friend. Li Syaoran is Sakura's erstwhile competitor in capturing the Clow Cards. Still, there are more characters that don't appear in *Tsubasa* than do, such as Kero, the guardian.

If you've read *Cardcaptor Sakura*, even the characters you recognize will seem radically different. The *Tsubasa* versions of Sakura and Syaoran both seem to be teenagers, several years older than their counterparts. Toya is a king, while Yuki is his chief advisor. Toya and Sakura's parents aren't in the picture, while Tomoyo lives in yet another dimension and appears to have no knowledge of Sakura whatsoever!

Cardcaptor Sakura was released in anime form in two versions in the United States. Pioneer released the Japanese version on DVD, while Nelvana released a reworked version on television called simply *Cardcaptors*. *Cardcaptors* was short-lived and incurred the ire of many fans because it was heavily edited and reworked to make it more palatable for an American audience.

In the manga, the main storyline ends in volume six when Sakura successfully captures all of the Clow Cards and is named Master of the Clow. It almost looks like it's time for Sakura to hang up her wand for good, but CLAMP still had a few more stories in mind—and another six volumes to go!

Dramatis Personae

You'd need a scorecard to keep track of all the characters who will be appearing in *Tsubasa* and *xxxHOLiC*, so we've decided to create one for you. Some of these characters will look familiar, but you haven't really met most of them before. Don't read these if you haven't read this volume yet—there's a reason we put them at the end of the book!

Sakura

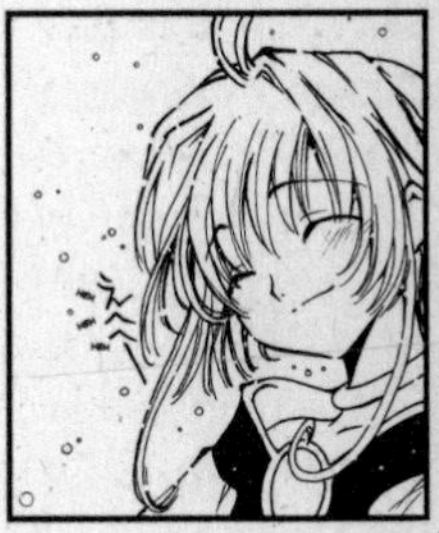

While it's clear that Sakura is older than her counterpart from *Cardcaptor Sakura*, we don't actually know her age yet. She is the princess of Clow, raised by her brother, King Toya. She's a happy princess, well-loved by her people. Sakura possesses the power to change the world, but it will be a while before she—or we—understand what that means.

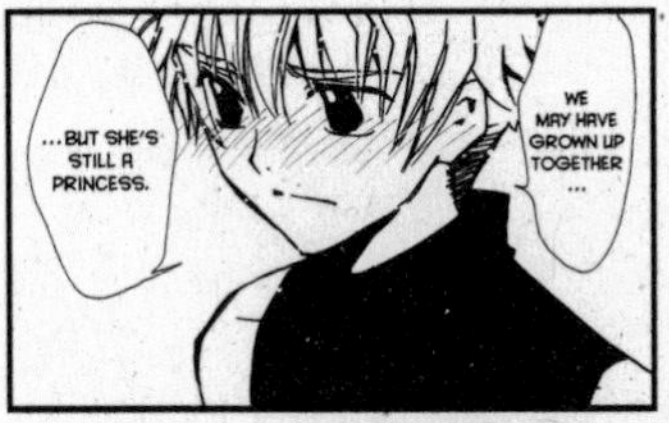
WE MAY HAVE GROWN UP TOGETHER ...
...BUT SHE'S STILL A PRINCESS.

Syaoran

Syaoran's father died in an archaeological dig, leaving him an orphan, but Syaoran felt compelled to continue his father's work. He's closer than ever to uncovering the secrets of the giant wings buried in the sand, but a threat to Sakura's safety sends him on a quest to save her life! The *Tsubasa* version of Syaoran is very different from the character in *Cardcaptor Sakura*. Where the *CS* Syaoran is dour, surly, even rude at times, *Tsubasa*'s version is open, friendly—and clearly in love with Sakura.

Tomoyo

In *CS*, Tomoyo was Sakura's best friend who videotaped her card-capturing exploits. In *Tsubasa*, Tomoyo is the queen of another realm, and like Yukito, she is a powerful sorceress. It remains to be seen if her role in this drama is concluded.

Fai D. Florite

Fai's motivation for visiting Yûko, the space-time witch, isn't entirely clear. Like Tomoyo, he is the ruler of his land of Seresu. He may be fleeing a battle he's lost, or he may desperately need to get away from a battle he's won—we just don't know yet. What we do know is that he is the creator of this world's version of Chi, a character from CLAMP's *Chobits*, and that he is fleeing from Ashura, a variation of the main character of CLAMP's first series, *RG Veda*.

Chi

In *Chobits*, Chi was a persocom, a personal computer found by Hideki Motosuwa. With her memory wiped clean, Chi and Hideki have a lot of work to do to discover her origins. Along the way, each discovers a lot more about themselves and about their feelings for each other. Of course, that's assuming that a machine can even have feelings in the first place. . . .

The *Tsubasa* version of Chi was created by Fai, so she is clearly *not* the same character as in *Chobits*, although her personality appears remarkably similar. As Fai begins his quest, he leaves Chi behind to guard against King Ashura's awakening.

Yûko

Yûko is a witch. She lives in a peculiar house in Tokyo with two peculiar helpers, Maru and Moru. Her work is simple: She helps people . . . for a price. The price is never more than her customer can bear, but the greater the need, the

higher it gets. Yûko is something of an enigma: She comes across as very mysterious and all-knowing, but she also has a playful, sometimes wild side that leads to unfortunate side effects. Like hangovers.

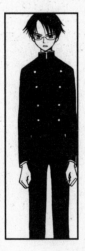

Watanuki

Watanuki Kimihiro will pop up in *Tsubasa* from time to time, but his home is over in *xxxHOLiC*, where he works for Yûko, cleaning, cooking, gardening, and doing whatever other chores Yûko can come up with. It's the price he pays for Yûko to grant his wish—to be rid of the spirit visions that haunt him. Although he's a hard worker, he often finds working for Yûko to be a frustrating experience.

Sorata (Sora) Arisugawa

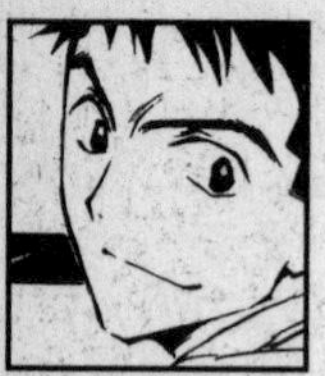

When Sora was three years old, the Buddhist monks of Mt. Koya recognized Sora as a future Dragon of Heaven. Knowing that he would develop powers that could help to save the earth, the monks started training him, and Sora's irrepressible personality turned the monastery upside down. But when the three-year-old Sora was parted from his mother, the tears in her eyes affected him deeply. He determined that he would find the one girl for him, and he would protect her. He would protect her and die for her so that she may never feel hurt the way his mother did. In the story of X (*X/1999*), the girl he found was Arashi Kishu.

Arashi Kishu

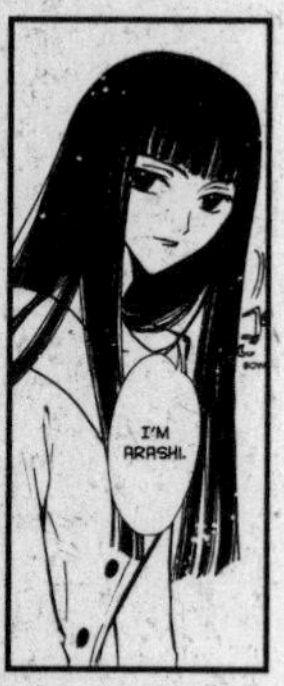
I'M ARASHI.

At age six, Arashi was wandering the streets eating out of garbage cans and wondering if life was really worth it. Her mother had died three months earlier, and although she had asked Arashi to somehow survive, Arashi was beginning to have second thoughts. Being found by her mother's old Shinto teacher and brought into a beautiful shrine still didn't answer Arashi's question of whether to die or go on living. The promise of becoming a Dragon of Heaven, and more importantly, having friends in the future so that she wouldn't be alone, made Arashi decide to give life a try. In the story of X (*X/1999*), she grew into a Shinto "miko" priestess and joined the Seven Seals.

Translation Notes

Japanese is a tricky language for most westerners, and translation is often more art than science. For your edification and reading pleasure, here are notes on some of the places where we could have gone in a different direction in our translation of the work, or where a Japanese cultural reference is used.

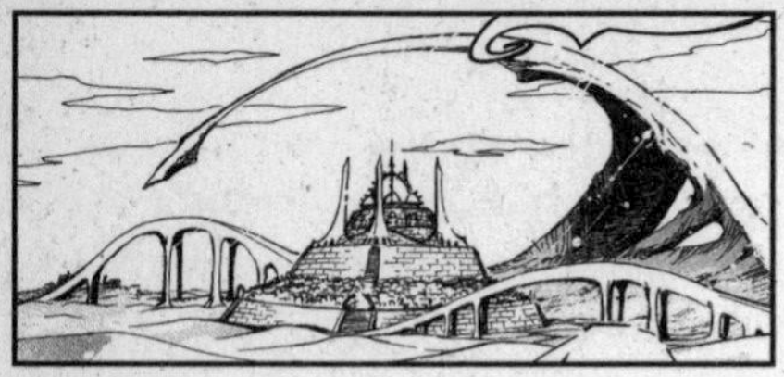

The Kingdom of Clow

Made up of the characters Eternal and Tower, the pronunciation *kurô* sounds suspiciously like Clow.

Intimacy

After Sakura and Syaoran's conversation, you should notice a distinct similarity between that conversation and the later one of Tôya and Yukito. It's all about intimacy. Once two people are close enough friends, they drop the honorifics and titles (see *Honorifics* at the front of the book) and the grammar of polite language, and they become more direct and easygoing.

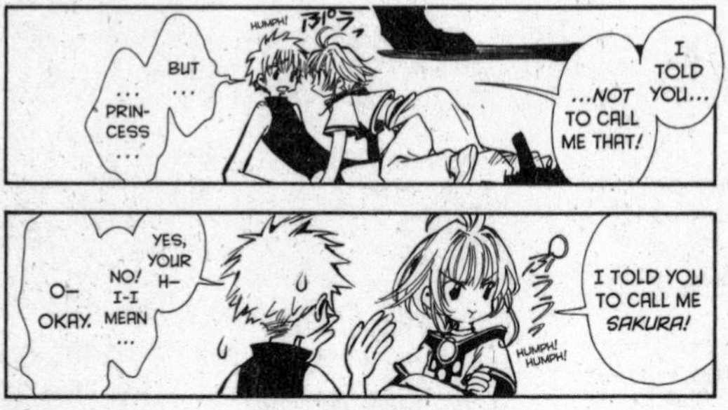

I TOLD YOU...
...NOT TO CALL ME THAT!
HUMPH!
BUT...
...PRINCESS...
I TOLD YOU TO CALL ME SAKURA!
HUMPH! HUMPH!
YES, YOUR H—
NO! I-I MEAN...
O— OKAY.

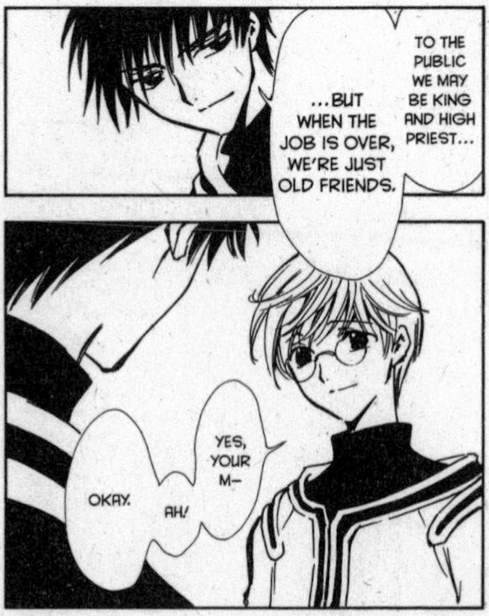

TO THE PUBLIC WE MAY BE KING AND HIGH PRIEST...
...BUT WHEN THE JOB IS OVER, WE'RE JUST OLD FRIENDS.
YES, YOUR M—
AH!
OKAY.

Ginryû

The characters for Ginryû mean "silver dragon," which gives you the reason for the dragon on the hilt.

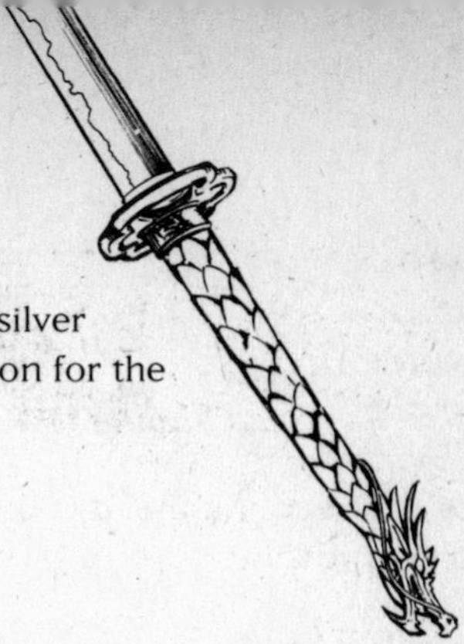

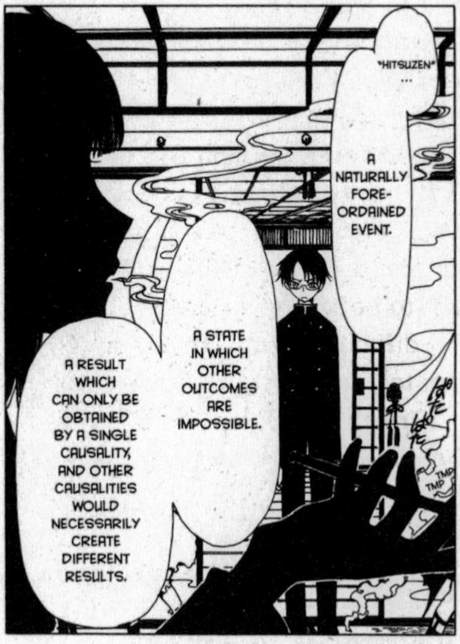
"HITSUZEN" ...
A NATURALLY FORE-ORDAINED EVENT.
A STATE IN WHICH OTHER OUTCOMES ARE IMPOSSIBLE.
A RESULT WHICH CAN ONLY BE OBTAINED BY A SINGLE CAUSALITY, AND OTHER CAUSALITIES WOULD NECESSARILY CREATE DIFFERENT RESULTS.
TMP TMP

Hitsuzen

This is actually defined by Yûko in *xxxHOLiC* Volume 1: "Hitsuzen. A naturally foreordained event. A state in which other outcomes are impossible. A result which can only be obtained by a single causality, and other causalities would necessarily create different results."

Kuro-chan, Kuro-rin . . .

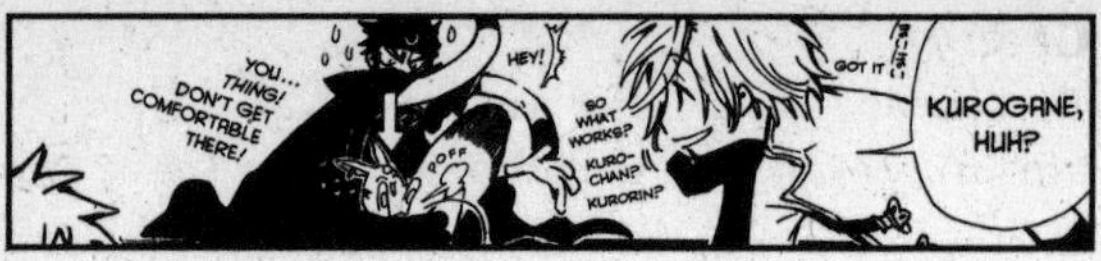
KUROGANE, HUH?
GOT IT
SO WHAT WORKS? KURO-CHAN? KURORIN?
HEY!
POFF
YOU... THING! DON'T GET COMFORTABLE THERE!

All of the names that Fai is trying to give Kurogane are the type of nicknames that one would give cute high-school girls (ko-gals), or that cute high-school girls would give themselves.

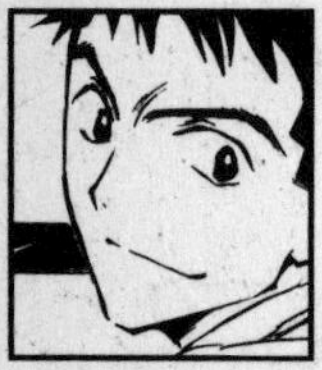

Sora's Accent

Accents in Japanese and English work somewhat differently. In English, an accent is mostly marked by pronunciation—especially of the vowel sounds—and a few differences in vocabulary. So if you take a little time to get used to the differences, you will have no problem understanding even the thickest accent in English. In Japanese, there are some pronunciation differences, but most of the differences are in vocabulary. Since the differences start at the core vocabulary (even the ubiquitous verb "to be"!), and spread throughout, a thick accent is nearly as difficult to understand as a completely different language. Fortunately for most Japanese citizens, the Osaka dialect is very popular in the media, so everyone is used to the different words, even if they didn't grow up in the Osaka area.

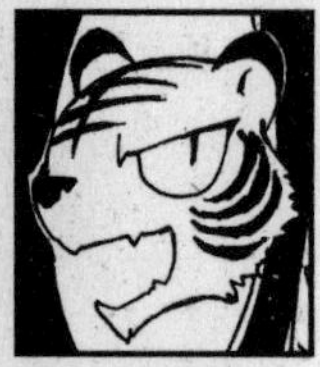

The logo for the Hanshin Tigers

The Hanshin Republic

For those who don't know Japanese baseball, the most popular team in Japan is the Yomiuri Giants. The second most popular team is the Hanshin Tigers, and like other second-mosts, the fans of the Hanshin Tigers are fiercely competitive and fanatical. None more than Sora's character, and so, the Hanshin Republic is the fondest dream of Tigers' fans—an entire nation devoted body and soul to Osaka's favorite baseball club. More on this in Volume 2!

Preview of *Tsubasa* Volume 2

Because we're running about one year behind the release of the
Tsubasa manga in Japan, we have the opportunity to present to you a
preview from Volume 2. This volume will be available in English in
September 2004, but for now you'll have to make do with Japanese!

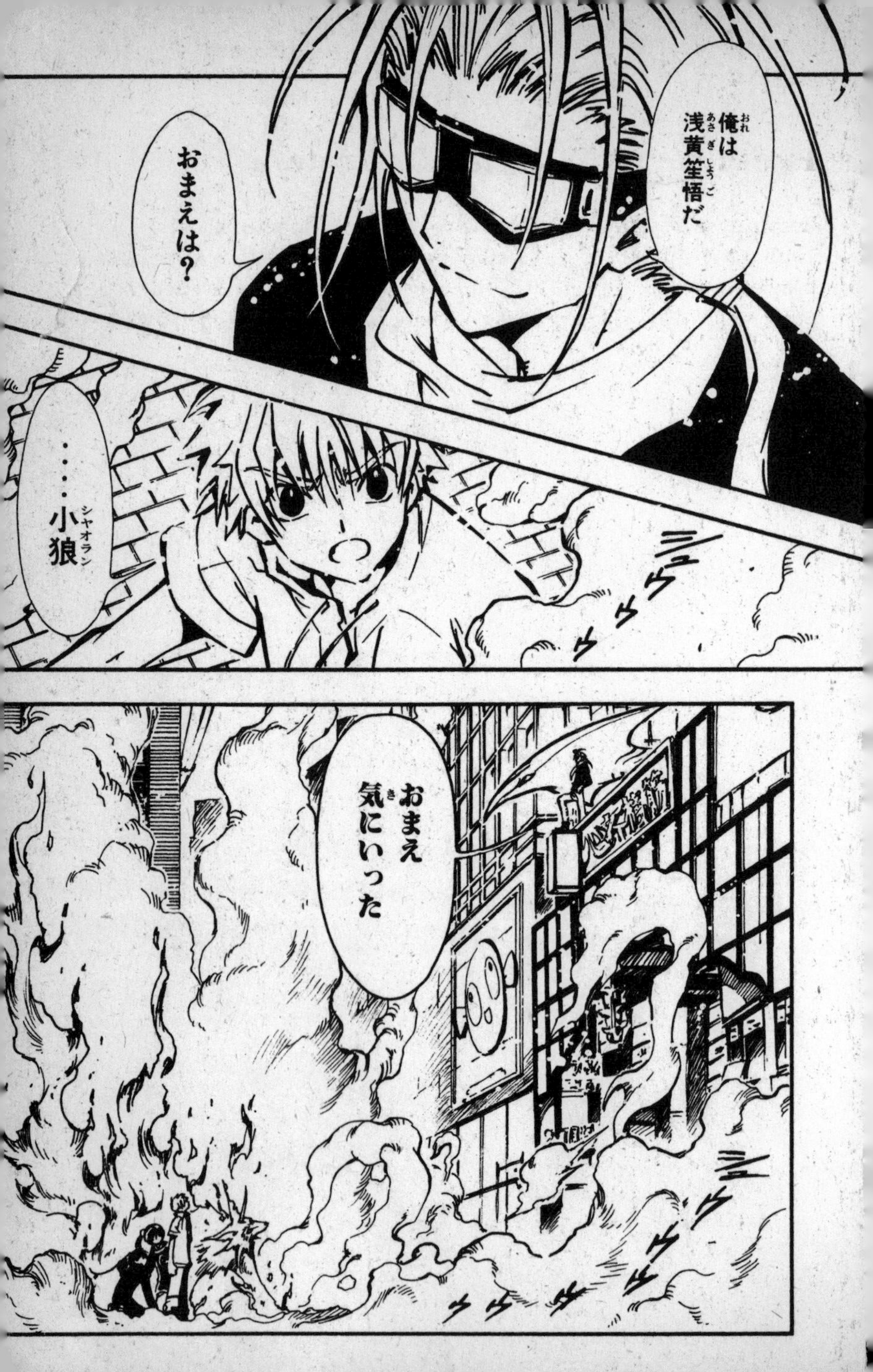
俺は浅黄笙悟だ
おまえは?
……小狼
シュウウウウ
おまえ気にいった
シュウウウウウウ

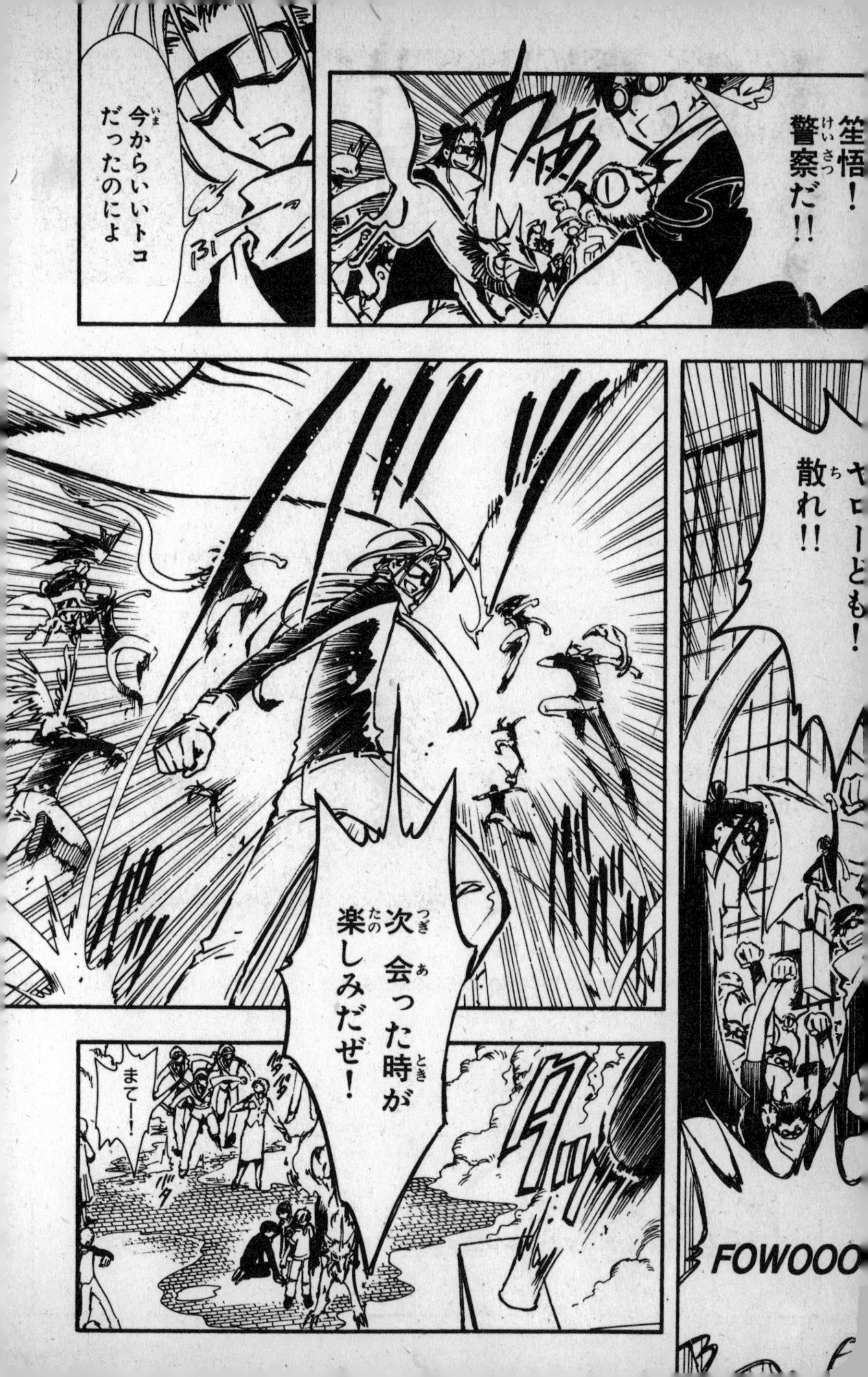
笙悟！警察だ!!
今からいいトコだったのによ
ヤローども！散れ!!
次会った時が楽しみだぜ！
FOWOOO
まてー！

xxxHOLiC

by CLAMP

Creators of *Chobits!*

Watanuki Kimihiro is haunted by visions of ghosts and spirits. Seemingly by chance, he encounters a mysterious witch named Yuko, who claims she can help. In desperation, he accepts, but realizes that he's just been tricked into working for Yuko in order to pay off the cost of her services. Soon he's employed in her little shop—a job which turns out to be nothing like his previous work experience!

Most of Yuko's customers live in Japan, but Yuko and Watanuki are about to have some unusual visitors named Sakura and Syaoran from a land called Clow. . . .

Volume 1: On sale May 2004 • Volume 2: On sale July 2004
Volume 3: On sale November 2004

For more information and to sign up for Del Rey's manga e-newsletter, visit www.delreymanga.com

TOMARE!

[STOP!]

You're going the wrong way!

Manga is a completely different type of reading experience.

To start at the *beginning,* go to the *end!*

That's right! Authentic manga is read the traditional Japanese way—from right to left. Exactly the *opposite* of how American books are read. It's easy to follow: Just go to the other end of the book, and read each page—and each panel—from right side to left side, starting at the top right. Now you're experiencing manga as it was meant to be.